Season of the Runer Book 1: The Trial of Two

Abigail Linhardt

SummerStorm Press

Season of the Runer Book I: The Trial of Two

A SummerStorm Press book

This book is a work of fiction. Names, characters, places, and incidents either are the product of the author's imagination or are used fictitiously. Any resemblance to actual persons, living or dead, events, cultures, or locales is entirely coincidental.

Cover art by Andrei Bat. Edited by Kristen Portillo. Formatted by SummerStormPress.

ACKNOWLEDGMENTS

Special thanks to my beta readers Louise Pierce, Elias L. L., and Kate Seger. What a wild ride that was. Thanks for not holding back on the notes!

For Dad. If you had never taught me how to log head at my problems, this would have never happened. Thanks!

Season of the Runer Book I

The Trial of Two

Abigail Linhardt

SummerStorm Press

CONTENTS

Untitled   xi

1. Thankless Job   1
2. Them   13
3. Dead Rising   27
4. Sybal   37
5. The Betrothed   45
6. Diplomacy   55
7. The Witness   63
8. Inquisition   71
9. The Runing   83
10. A Different Job   93
11. Leaving Home   107
12. Twice Dead   115
13. The Trial of Two   127
14. Training   135
15. Desperate   145
16. Last Hope   157
17. A Job for a Scholar   171
18. Tarkan   179
19. Death to Live   187
20. Porsh   193
21. Runer's Death   207
22. Eye for an Eye   221
23. White Bloods   231
24. Red Bloods   241
25. With the Jongleur   255
26. The Razing of Ala'Nar   267
27. Separate Ways   275
28. Son of the Blasphemer   281
29. Burn the Dead   299

30. The Hunt   309
31. Making of a Necromancer   317
32. Coming Together   327
33. The Sorcerer   333
34. Swap   341
35. Sojourn   351

Appendix   359
About the Author   365

Chapter 1
Thankless Job

THE GRAND NIAZ SAT AT THE HEAD TABLE, DRUMMING HIS ringed fingers hard and fast; his nerves twisted inside as he waited. Word traveled fast when a Runer appeared in the city. Especially if he had tried to hide his presence. That meant he wasn't hunting, and trouble might start. All but the Runer's own crime would send the people into a worried frenzy. Nicolai, the Grand Niaz, tried to put his people at ease, telling them the Runer came on his invitation. They wanted a Runer, didn't they? He checked the letter clutched, wet from sweat, in his palm. Lord Trokovich wrote him almost every day. The livestock would not produce. His children could not sleep. The groundskeeper in the graveyard went mad. Summoning a Runer was the next course of action.

"Yes, it was, of course I'm right," Nicolai breathed under his mustache to steady himself. He had written to Lord Trokovich: everything would be fine. Do not fear. He was Niaz of the hills and would protect his people. There was nothing supernatural afoot. Staring into the middle distance, he told himself one more time that he made the right choice. The pressure from the lesser lord meant others might see something they shouldn't.

Knowing he trapped himself into needing the Runer and a desire to keep up the city's safe façade, he ordered the Runer to meet him in his home rather than the great hall in the city square where everyone would see the rogue enter by the front gate. But Nicolai was no fool and kept armed guards near him as he waited for the Runer to make an entrance.

His eyes flitted from the windows to the servants' entrance and the main doors. Runers were not good men. They could be guilty of many crimes and he, having never dealt personally with one, didn't know if the rogue would sneak in through a crack in the wall and hold a knife to his throat, demand a ransom, or rob him blind. Above him, in her chambers, steady steps of his wife pacing back and forth ticked in his ears. She no longer wept. For weeks she cycled through spells of anger, fear, paranoia, and outbursts of rage. He would have called a witch or warlock to give her a healing tea, but being heavy with child, herbs could not be trusted on a womb. Thinking it would pass, he had her take a bath in salts, breathe in soothing aromas—but the next day, she could hardly stand. Hearing her steps gave him some encouragement.

"Your grace?"

Nicolai looked up, nervously smoothing his beard. A servant boy came in through the smaller door of the grand archway.

"The Runer is here, as summoned."

Cautious, yet optimistic that the evil man desired to come in through the front door, Nicolai stood, straightened his conical crown, and said, "Here? Through the gate? Let him in."

The boy bowed and ducked out the smaller door only to shove open the two great golden doors in the archway that lead into the receiving room. A gaggle of armored guards with round fur hats that made them taller—more imposing— surrounded one single man, pointing their tasseled spears at him. The man stood shorter than even the young servant boy. His jet black hair, swept half up into a high ponytail, was streaked with vivid white strands. His dark, eastern skin showed even darker against his telling, stark white veins underneath. The white bloods some called Runers.

Taken aback by the man's short stature, Nicolai motioned with both his hands for the group to move into the room. Walking, the Runer's tools of his trade clinked and tinkled against his orichalcum blade. He spotted a black leather strip hanging under the Runer's eastern robes and leather armor that held the runes they took their name for. He noticed the full, billowy pants tucked into knee-high boots. The rumor said that Runer's held secret weapons in the folds of their trousers. Unsure what to believe, Nicolai took several precautions, arming himself with a sword and having the guards escort the Runer in.

"Thank you, Miraz," Nicolai said to his head of guard. "Please wait near the door."

The Runer subtly raised a black brow as he watched the glaring guards slowly retreat to the perimeter of the room.

"I don't kill people," the Runer said, slowly turning to face Nicolai. "I'm a little insulted by the greeting."

The Grand Niaz opened his palms and shrugged. "I do apologize, especially since I have invited you here on business. But one can never be too cautious with a Runer." He unabashedly looked the Runer up and down slowly. "So, you are a murderer?"

The Runer frowned.

"You said you cannot kill people," Nicolai supplied. "Was murder your crime?"

The Runer marched to the table, pulled out a chair, and sat down, hands on the surface firmly. "I said I *don't* kill people. What is it that seems to be bothering you?"

Nicolai sat down, his eyes never leaving the Runer's. He knew men from the east had brown eyes. Sometimes golden. But the Runer's were radiated blue like a frozen river in sunlight. The white veins under his brown skin made his own flesh crawl.

"Yes, to business, of course. Tea? Or do you prefer the coffee of your people?"

"Araq," the Runer said, a small smirk twitching the left side of his lips. "In a brass goblet if you have it."

Nicolai looked to the clock on his wall. "It is still morning."

The Runer slowly raised his head.

"But of course!" Nicolai clapped his hands and ordered the servant to bring tea and the white alcohol for the Runer.

They did not speak while the beverages were brought. As the drinks were poured, Nicolai leaned back in his chair as if trying to distance himself as far away from the Runer as possible, his hands pressing hard into the arms of the chair. He did not drink but watched as the Runer took a long swallow from the brass goblet.

"My wife is ill," he began when he saw the Runer would not ask.

"Call a witch or a warlock," the Runer sighed, leaning back a little in the chair. "They can brew her a decoction of herbs. It's what they do as people of science."

"She is with child," he went on. "We cannot have her swallowing herbs. She cannot walk. Almost anyway. She has spells of anger, she sleeps for days sometimes."

The Runer sat up a little now, frowning slightly. "Where does she walk?"

Nicolai frowned too. "I don't know. Outside. She is pregnant, she walks very far some days."

The Runer leaned onto the table, placing his arm on the edge. "I saw a painting of a woman in the hallway. That's not your wife."

Flabbergasted, Nicolai shook his head. "How did you know?"

Pointing to his chest, the Runer said. "The locket on your cravat fell open. That's your wife." He pointed back to the doors he had been escorted through. "That must be her sister. Looks just like her."

Nicolai smiled. "Yes, her sister."

"But she's dead."

Again, blinking in surprise, Nicolai nodded. "Amazing. I have heard the powers of the Runers but never witnessed them. Almost like a sorcerer. Tell me what I am thinking now!"

"That's not how it works." The Runer grimaced at Nicolai's

request; like a stupid child in a class. "This is simple deduction. I am no sorcerer."

Blanching slightly, Nicolai stood up. "Do you want the job or not?"

The Runer nodded. "I'm sorry, I've insulted you. I'll have to investigate first. See what's around here. Examine the route your wife walks. Perhaps question her." He stood up as well. "Do I have your cooperation?"

Realizing he had taken offense at his own ignorance, Nicolai nodded. "I will show you the grounds."

THE SMALL PALACE had extensive grounds for being of small repute. Nicolai took pride in his well-kept gardens, stables, and the vodka distillery he financed on his property. The Runer's eyes took in everything from the worn path to the side of the fence to the one place Nicolai did not take them.

"Where are you going?" the Grand Niaz asked when the Runer finally veered off down a hill.

"This is where your wife walks," he said simply. "To the graveyard."

Nicolai hesitated. "I don't want to...it's not that...Oh, very well." With great reluctance, he followed the Runer down the stone steps towards the sea of mausoleums and headstones.

With great interest, he watched the Runer stop every now and then to examine a seemingly uninteresting piece of stone, a hollow in the earth, or a muddy footprint. Finally, they ended up at a stone bench, once dedicated to a mighty czarina of the realm.

"She sits here," the Runer said casually, kneeling and swiping his hand over and under the stone bench. Squinting into the sun, he reexamined the foreign words on the stone wall of the mausoleum behind the bench.

"You can read our language?" Nicolai asked.

"No," the Runer said gruffly. "Some symbols are universal though."

He stood up and walked to the front where the rusty gate hung at an angle. He ran his icy blue eyes over the hinges and then the ground. Seeing something, he knelt quickly and gently pushed some of the foliage out of the way to get a better look at some grass underneath. The kind that interested him was dead, brown. He stood up and followed the path of dead grass.

"How long has your wife had spells of weakness?" he asked, still following the path.

Nicolai had not noticed weakness exactly. Just her mood swings. He said as much.

"You have not noticed your wife does not eat, that she weeps here every night?"

"How..." Nicolai began but stopped himself. The Runer would say something that would again make him feel ignorant.

"Her tears are corrosive to this delicate stone," he said offhandedly, examining the mausoleum again, this time from a distance. "You have a samca on your hands."

Nicolai's eyes popped and he swallowed hard. "No. My child!"

"Yes," the Runer sighed, taking his curved sword off his belt and removing his black cloak. "If you have seen before what was happening to her, the child might be saved. I don't know if that is possible now."

"But you can save them both!" Nicolai begged. "I will pay you!"

"You will," the Runer replied. "But your denial of what is haunting your wife might have lost you your child. I am not a doctor nor warlock. I cannot save her health. I can rid you of the samca though."

"But that is a specter. How will you kill it?"

The Runer sat down on his cloak, spread on the ground, and took a small book out from his pack. "They can't be killed, even you sever their ghostly head. They are banish. The sword sends them back to where they came. A samca is a woman specter. It's feeding off the energy of your wife, possibly crippling her. Your child might already be dead. She—your wife—came down knowingly, I believe. She knew this samca was here. Which means, it could be her sister."

Nicolai wrung his hands and then grabbed his conical crown in despair. He noticed the Runer's eyes roam aimlessly over the page in the middle of the book he opened. "Why would she do this?"

"Not on purpose. The samca probably fed off her for several nights before she realized what it was. Once strong, it revealed itself to her. She wanted to speak with her sister. But didn't know it was not her any longer. Mutated, rotten. Nothing but a malevolent spirit now. But she kept trying."

"And now you will sit and wait for it to appear?" The Grand Niaz paced ferociously, touching his rings over and over.

"Should come at nightfall, like most ghosts."

"I will leave you to it then?" Nicolai asked, taking some very sure steps towards the stone steps up and away from the dead.

"One hundred rupees," the Runer said stiffly. He locked his icy eyes onto Nicolai's.

"That's an outrageous sum!" the Grand Niaz countered, no longer frightened of the dead. "Fifty."

"What do you need with rupees?" the Runer smiled. "You cannot spend them in your market. One hundred or your wife dies."

"Bastard!" Nicolai hissed under his mustache. "You would hold my wife and child ransom?"

The Runer shrugged. "Are your wife and child worth less than one hundred rupees?"

Pressing his lips together and switching his hands from his hips to clasping in front, Nicolai scoffed. "Fine. One hundred. But I want a guarantee."

"What kind?"

"I want to know that my wife and child will be safe."

"Sure," the Runer said, turning back to his book, his eyes now locked on a single area, not moving. "And Grand Niaz. Keep your wife away. Lock her in her room. Whatever it takes."

THE NIGHTS in this land were far colder than the desert nights he was used to. When the sun went down in his homeland, the heat left the golden sand quickly but turned nowhere near as cold as the nights up in the mountains of Rhostrana. The sliver of moon did not provide enough light. Holding the rune halat in his hand, he waved his arm, slowly drawing the rune invisibly before him. He clenched his fist and a small orb of light appeared above his palm. The rune light showed like a lantern but also brought invisible horrors to light. He took up his curved sword and pressed his back against a tree facing the mausoleum.

The wind blew gently, making him shiver. His breath came out in a thick cloud before his pale eyes. He thought momentarily of the araq he drank earlier and reminded himself to fill his flask before he left again. The road home would be long and he didn't want to freeze in his sleep.

The gate creaked. Instinctively, he held his breath to stop the rising white clouds. Nothing appeared in the mausoleum's small archway. He realized too late, the creak had come from the gate at the top of the stone steps. Cursing, he slowly peeked around the tree. In a sheer nightdress, tears streaking down her face, making the kohl around her eyes run, came Nicolai's wife. He almost reached out to stop her as she passed the tree he pressed himself to, but saw by her vacant eyes that the specter had already hypnotized her. Not wanting to break her from the hypnosis—it sometimes had dire consequences—he snuffed the rune light.

She sat on the bench, almost like she waited for a coach to take her on a holiday. He noticed her face twisted in disguised agony. The samca had a stronger hold on her than he thought. It had gotten inside her head, making her come down to feed it. The end goal: possession.

Taking a different rune into his palm, he drew it before him, closing his fist then opening it again to accent a mark above the rune. A ghostly smoke encircled him. Moving silently, he crept towards the woman. Kneeling slightly, he bent to her eye level. Her green eyes gazed through him, into an unknown only she could see. He'd have to lead her away gently to fight the samca.

He looked up to find the best exit. With a shriek, he drew his sword as he came face to face with the ghostly image of the dead woman from the painting standing right behind Nicolai's wife. The specter blinked, appearing behind him. With a growl like a dragon, it thrust its spindly arm out, sending him rolling over the bench and into the stone mausoleum wall.

Cursing, he realized the protective circle ran out faster than he thought. He hadn't drawn it slow enough. He pulled aside his tunic to see a bruise on his chest in the shape of the samca's hand. He coughed, gasping for air. Being touched by a specter always took his breath away and hitting the stone wall had not helped.

The woman had stood up and began to follow the specter away.

"Come back!" he shouted at her, desperate to save her from the possession. He took up his sword and dashed after the pair.

As he rounded a corner of the stone path, he slipped in something warm. Looking down, he saw a mixture of water, blood, and other fluids he did not recognize. Ahead of him, the woman's white shift began to change to a deep, dark red just below where she clutched her huge belly.

He came too late for the child, just as he thought.

The specter hovered in front of the woman, moving backwards in frightening, jerky movements. Its sunken eyes glowed as it feasted on the last of the woman's essence.

Clutching his sword, he cut his palm with it, smearing his white blood along the blade. He drew another rune. This one gave him a fury he rarely used. With a feral scream, he charged forward, pushing the nearly possessed woman out of the way, entering combat with the samca. The specter tried to block his blade with her forearm but the orichalcum cut deep into her rotting flesh.

With a banshee's wail, the samca seized his free hand, dragging him closer to her gaping mouth. She opened her mouth wide, inhaling. He felt himself grow weak, a white fog almost instantly filling the front of his skull. If not for the fury rune, he might have succumbed. Grunting, he pulled his curved sword from her arm, swung it around, and severed her ghostly head. In an instant, he fell to the ground as her specter form imploded, showering him with a black, sticky essence.

He had drawn the fury rune quickly so the effects wore off faster than the protective circle had vanished. His legs shook with weakness from the specter's feeding on his essence. Looking down at his palm, he saw his white blood trickling out. Runer blood didn't clot. Shaking, he crawled to the unconscious woman's body. He checked her pulse and her breathing: Light and shallow but present.

Sighing, he rolled over onto his back, wiping away some of the black ectoplasm. In the distance, he saw lanterns bobbing his way and heard Nicolai's screams. The Grand Niaz fell to his knees by his wife, screaming as he saw her bloody trail.

"I...I told you to keep her away," the Runer panted, sitting up.

Nicolai faced the wounded Runer. Before the Runer would say anything else, Nicolai slammed his fist into the Runer's face, knocking him unconscious.

꽃

NICOLAI HAD NOT LOOKED FORWARD to the next morning and the Runer could tell. The poor man looked defeated. He sat in the same hall he had first received the Runer in but his mustache lacked the luster and poise it had. He slumped in his high-backed chair. Knowing the man grieved did not stop him from pushing the doors open with all the force he could muster and marching in. He only got a few steps in before the armored guards seized his arms, holding him tightly between the two of them.

"Give me my pay," the Runer grunted.

Nicolai didn't smile, but he enjoyed watching the smaller man struggle against his towering guards. "You lied to me, Runer. My son is gone."

The Runer scowled, straining against his captors. "I said keep her away. I upheld my end of the contract. I got rid of the samca. Pay me and I'll be on my way, and you can grieve."

Nicolai sighed, shaking his head. "I should have known you wouldn't just do the job. I've never worked with a Runer before, you see. I heard you were a lawless bunch. But now I feel like the saint."

Sensing a change in Nicolai's demeanor, the Runer stopped struggling. The Grand Niaz pushed himself up and walked towards the guards without fear. His quivering stopped. "All you had to do was put on a show, let the people see I had their best interest at heart, and weaken poor Bianca enough so she didn't kill Anika when she possessed her. And keep Anika strong enough to not lose the child."

The Runer's mysterious eyes widened in shock.

"You see now, don't you?" Nicolai smiled. "But you failed. All I ever wanted was Bianca, but her father said no and gave me Anika and she was impossible to live with. When Bianca died, I knew I had to have her still."

"You're disgusting," the Runer mumbled with a grimace.

Nicolai raised his brows, smiling, and nodded. "Now I need you to leave my land." He waved his hands to the guards.

"Pay me!" the Runer shouted through gritted teeth. "And I leave. I hate your winters. I've never seen snow and I don't plan to now. Pay me and I will leave."

"And if I want you dead?" Nicolai asked simply.

The Runer rolled his eyes. "I'll never come back here. Your little duchy is shit. I just want to go home."

"Why did you come so far away?" Nicolai asked, mildly interested.

Finally, able to pull his arms out of the guard's hands, the Runer said, "Monsters are few and hard to find. But I found one today."

Smiling, Nicolai began a gentle laugh. "You amuse me, Runer. For that, you may go. With your life intact. I'd hate to think of the specialist I'd have to call in to take care of a Runer haunting."

"Pay me," the Runer snapped again.

"Oh, I will." Nicolai gave his guards a very precise wave of his hands. "You should be grateful I did not hire a Reaver to do away with you."

"As if you'd have the stomach." The Runer stood strong amidst the threat. "You could hardly look me in the eye. You wouldn't even know how to find a Reaver to hunt me down."

Without so much as a warning, the guards seized the Runer again, gagged him, and forcefully removed him from the palace.

Chapter 2
Them

His stomach growled with gale force as he disembarked the tall ship with its many black sails and passed into the boundaries of the red and golden temple kingdom of Bailu on the continent of Bahratt. Traveling from the icy land of Rhostrana to the spicy air of Bahratt, reminded him no matter how far away he traveled for coin, he could always go back to somewhere familiar. Not home. But familiar.

He passed a display of execution on his way to the inner city. Two men and one woman knelt on a makeshift pedestal while a temple magistrate roared their crimes to the watching audience. They spoke in the holy language of the gods and Tzarik could only understand every other word. They must have done something truly terrible to warrant this kind of ancient execution. The woman did not weep, holding her head up high while one of the men beside her cried out for mercy. Somewhere inside, he envied them. Death was the only release. He wouldn't haunt anyone, held no grudges, and would pass on into the darkness of the afterlife. He casually wondered how much they would charge to let him be executed with the others.

As he passed through on his massive horse, some of the city people stopped their tasks to stare. Some spit in his path, others made a sign over their heart as though he were an evil djinn come for their souls. One lady gave him a coy smile from behind a doorway covered in a red veil. She bit the left side of her bottom lip and ran her hands over her shapely hips while holding eye contact. He sighed, watching her as he passed. No good would come from that coupling. Besides, she'd just use the event as bragging rights for her fellow working women. She had spent a night with a Runer. One of *them*.

His horse didn't need him to guide it through the colorful, sandstone city. It knew where he wanted to go. Winding through the covered streets, it slowly made its way—distracted by a fruit merchant only once—to a small, palace-like temple with aureate domes topped with sharp brass. The white walls that surrounded it were impenetrable save by a sewer grate he knew well.

He left his horse in the street, pulling his hood up and covering his face as he slinked through the long leaves of succulents to the unused grate. The temple wardens, dressed in red and gold with hideous gods engraved on their breastplates, took no notice of the small, black shadow weaving between them. Once behind them, he risked moving faster through the tunnel, coming out into a beautiful courtyard. Lotus trees of every color bloomed in the late day sun. Citrus fruits permeated the air with sweet, enticing aromas.

Hiding behind a large fountain depicting a goddess with eight limbs and a furious face, he took a rune from his necklace and very slowly drew it before him. The slow work made his heart race as he heard voices coming his way. Once he finished the rune, vapors shimmered before him, telling him he could not be seen. Two male magi, in flowing purple robes, walked past him holding a small armillary sphere and a star chart. Two more figures walked behind them. One, the maharaja with his crown and gold medallions, the other a female magi in red robes with a golden, six-pointed star in the center of her forehead taking up most of the smooth, dark skin visible under her red veil.

"I am not disagreeing with your father's magi," the woman said softly, lightly touching the maharaja's arm. "I am bringing a fresh

perspective. I have recently come from the schools in the west."
She sighed heavily but still smiled. "Things are so different there,
but I have expanded my knowledge. I do not ask for your blind
faith, I just ask that you allow me to try. I have never led you
wrong, have I?"

The maharaja, young as they always were, smiled nervously
and shook his head. "Thank you, Nefiri. You may go now. I'll have
the magus show me out."

The magi, Nefiri, smiled again as the boy left, but did not
follow the other magi. Instead, she lowered the sheer, red scarf
from her head and turned towards the fountain.

"I can smell you, Tzarik." She arched both her brows, staring
almost directly at him.

Checking to see the other magi were long gone, the Runer
wiped the rune and came into full view, discarding the invisibility.
He did not walk towards her.

"I can't imagine why you're here," she said when he did not
speak.

"I've come for company, cousin," he offered, walking beside
her now.

"I am a magi, we are not cousins by any magic relations," she
snapped quickly. "I cannot help you in *any other* respect," she
added pointedly.

Tzarik scoffed darkly. "Relations. Is that what you call it to
expunge the guilt?"

"It's part of my job." She almost smirked, looking ahead as
their pace quickened. "You were lucky. Any man would have
taken the risk without such trepidation as you showed."

"Except I wasn't a man. You forced your ritual on me." His
steps faltered but he dared not stop walking to face her. She
always held the power when it came to that one dark, terrifying
night. "I told you what would happen, but you drove on with
maddening carelessness."

Now she did stop, glaring down at him. "Always the victim, Tzarik? That's what Azar always said about you."

Tzarik didn't look up at her. Instead, he contented himself with walking ahead of her in the glorious courtyard, turning his attention to the landscape of colorful, rubbery flowers. "You show such compassion to that child. What does he pay you for?"

"To read the stars," she quipped, killing his intent before he got started again. "I couldn't see you, I read that you'd be here, hiding behind a goddess. A goddess, I asked myself. Tzarik follows no gods or goddesses. I thought I was wrong, but I see now the signs were literal."

He inhaled her tangy scent. She smelled like frankincense and cinnamon. "Do you know why I came?"

Nefiri frowned slightly and he sensed her guard fall just enough to answer. "You saw the execution on your way in?"

"I did."

"Those men did not want to die."

"They never do. The fools."

She turned sharply, her jewelry tinkling as she did. She glared down at him with her yellow eyes. "I am tired of this conversation, Tzarik. I tried once, many years ago, to talk you back from this edge. I will not do it any longer."

The desire to leave her almost overtook him but she seized him with her eyes.

"I want to show you something." Her tone went flat, soft, hiding her genuine emotions. "As a sanctuary, we are oath-bound to take in those in need. A man came to us. Pale, bleeding. We thought he'd die before we opened the gates."

Curious—and not wanting to leave her presence yet—he followed her into the temple grounds. No one stopped the Runer who followed a magi of her rank, but a few stopped mid step and stared. His black, dirty clothing could no doubt be smelled and seen from every arched hallway and garden.

Nefiri led him down narrow, sandy steps lined with tiny torches into the underground.

"You put him in the catacombs?" he asked quietly, his voice echoing off every rounded wall.

"His screams were frightening the new acolytes," Nefiri replied just as softly. She stopped and cocked her head, listening. "He is quiet."

Taking her red and gold skirts in one hand, she trotted quickly down the rest of the stairs and into the main room of the dark, sacred catacombs. The walls resembled honeycomb; golden, pocked with open graves. Treasures, gifts, and sacrifices littered the openings of some more revered dead. On a slab surrounded by make-shift tables—covered in bottles of medicines and bandages—a man lay still. Tzarik saw at once why Nefiri wanted to show him the mysterious man.

"Runer," he managed to say around his tightening throat. "But..."

Nefiri nodded. "Rejected by the white oath."

Tzarik examined the man. His veins, only partially white, bulged and throbbed under his pale skin. His beard, neat and trimmed, showed he had been a noble. His black hair stood out against his sweaty flesh. One eye bulged just enough out of his skull to show it would have exploded from its socket had his heart continued beating. The white blood of the Runer ran from his ears, nose, and eyes. Deep scars on his neck showed where he must have clawed at the pain under the surface.

"His eyes are brown," Tzarik mused. "He didn't change. And here," he pointed to puncture marks on his arm and a slash on his neck, "he was drained of his red blood, filled with the sulfates. They killed him."

Nefiri nodded, her hands clasped before her. "Not all survive. The death must have been terrible."

Tzarik also nodded. "They will harden, stop your heart. Suffocate you. Or just poison you. Each man is different."

The magi took two slow steps towards him, her face coming close to his long dirty hair. Her breath rustled a few strands of his hair and he couldn't stop the shiver that ran down his spine. The sound of her inhaling deeply almost froze his own white blood.

"What happened to Azar?" she said so softly he almost couldn't hear her.

He swallowed hard. "I have to go."

"Tzarik!" she shouted, following him out of the catacombs. "I'm trying to help you."

He didn't reply until they were back in the garden with the many-armed goddess. He faced her. "Help me what?"

She angled her face away from him and stared directly at the setting sun. "Find a reason."

He turned to leave. She couldn't give him what he wanted.

"Your runing is more a blessing than you know," she called after him.

He kept walking. All he wanted were words of comfort at the end. She had given them to him once, only after a hideous night he would never forget. But not now. She could be kind to a boy, take pity on a dying man, but could spare no real comfort for him. A man she had a hand in destroying.

"This is no blessing, as I have always said," he growled over his shoulder, hearing her follow.

She held her head high. "You've made it twenty years. Why stop now?"

He held his arms wide. "There are fewer and fewer monsters. Less for me to do. The time and need for Runers is coming to an end. Why go on in a world where every living thing hates you. Where you cannot be touched. Loved?"

Her lips pressed together and she glared to stop the mist in her eyes. "Fine. I have nothing left to say to you. Go. End your life if you cannot find a way to survive."

"And be reincarnated? Don't you believe that a bad death leads to a next life as a bug?" He scoffed.

She shrugged. "Then go to Porsh and die there so the heretics resurrect you before you are born again. And if you do come back as a bug, I will step on you."

He'd had enough. He lifted the grate and slipped down.

"There is a crocatta in a small outlying village of Jarabu to the north troubling a family," she said quickly.

He met her eyes from under his hood. He knew she could see his icy blue stare from the darkness.

Her tone turned practical. "Dispose of that before you kill yourself, will you?"

TZARIK AVOIDED the town square where the lavish, religious executions still went on. Grumbling, he mounted his horse and rode north to the outlying homesteads of Jarabu where Nefiri said the crocatta troubled a family. As he entered the city, he noted its proximity to some small mountains behind it. Crocatta—the hairless, hyena-like monster— had cloven hooves and would be able to scale the terrain easily. By the time he reached the small city, however, the sun had set and he didn't want to investigate anything at night.

He led his horse down a dusty street and found a royal guard near a streetlamp.

"Is there a public house?" he asked simply.

The guard looked him up and down and spat to the side. "You have to pay, criminal. What's your crime?"

The Runer grunted in disappointment and pulled his horse away.

The guard shouted at him in the common Bahratt tongue but Tzarik ignored him. When he didn't stop, the guard took out his short sword and marched toward him shouting, "Stop, rogue! I asked you a question."

Tzarik rounded, taking out a small chakram to threaten the guard with. Being bigger and stronger—like most other men—the guard easily grabbed the Runer's wrist, stopping the attack. Grunting, the Runer struggled to free his wrist and landed a hooked punch with his other hand. The guard seized the hand that punched and head butted Tzarik hard. Despite the darkness, white light burst in front of his eyes. He stumbled, free, and fell backwards.

"Hey!" a voice shouted from down the street.

"This is official business!" the guard shouted back, pointing his sword at the winded Runer.

"I think not." A man in scholar's robes approached the scene, reaching into his wide sleeve. "You want to put the sword away and leave."

Tzarik heard the stranger smiling as he spoke. He blinked, struggling to his feet.

"Why, yes, I need to go," the guard mumbled, stumbling over his words. "Forgive me." His voice warbled as he beat a hasty retreat into the dark street.

"Holy pantheon! Are you all right?" the scholar asked, helping Tzarik to his feet.

Tzarik stood up, his hood falling off his face. He took in the familiar wonder of the scholar's expression: placid eyes change to shock when he saw his white veins under dark skin and pale blue eyes.

"Oh, forgive me," the scholar stammered. "I did not mean to offend, that is to say—"

"It's fine." Tzarik quickly pulled his hood up to hide his telling features. He reached into his satchel and pulled out a silver coin from a foreign land and handed it to the scholar.

"Oh, no, I cannot take your coin!" the scholar said jovially.

"I cannot owe a man," Tzarik said harshly. His face burned in embarrassment and rage. Fed up with backstabbers, men asserting dominance over his short stature, going hungry because the last job didn't pay, and Nefiri's criticism still ringing in his ears all made him irritable.

The scholar smiled and sighed. "Then I'll let you buy me a drink." He motioned back down the street, the way he had come. "But really it's for selfish reasons. I am a learner, you see."

He did. Only scholars wore stupid robes with such wide, impractical sleeves. And the tasseled hat made him look like a court jester.

"I am studying cryptidology at an institute in the west and I would love to speak with you about...monsters?" He ended with the inflection going up, not sure what he should call the things Runer's hunted.

Tzarik stared hard at the man. "I'm a criminal. Don't you want to know my crime?"

The scholar smiled. On the surface, the smile wrote off the fact that all Runers were criminals. But underneath, a kind of knowing hid under the dark brown of his untouched irises.

"Maybe one day we will get to that," he said, leading Tzarik into a public house just steps away.

Inside, an old bard with a long white mustache played a horrid tune on a sitar. Glass pipes filled the air with aromatic smoke and clear cups of tea showed various herbs brewing. The tables were mostly empty as many turned in early to rise with the sun to pray and care for their animals. As he suspected, this city housed more farmers than rich merchants. If a crocatta did lurk here, it most likely harassed sheep and he would not get paid well for it. He decided if they paid him in a hot meal and maybe a bed, he didn't care.

The scholar sat him down at a round table low to the ground surrounded by colorful cushions. He ordered a haunch of lamb, a pipe, several kinds of bread, and a gold pitcher of alcohol.

"I cannot pay for this," Tzarik said gruffly. "My last job did not pay well."

"How so?" the scholar asked, handing him a cup of mint tea.

"A beating and I was run out of town for murdering a Grand Niaz's wife and child."

"Oh, dear." The scholar shook his head. "Introductions! I am Abigor Sharar, but you may call me Sharar. I have studied at several institutes over the last ten years and am a student of humanity and monstrosity. And I consider you a rare and dignified find! What may I call you, Runer?"

"Tzarik is what my mother called me." He didn't mean to sound as rude as he came across, but the scholar was no different than anyone else who saw him as an other. A Them. But getting a large, hot, meal with more than one texture out of it might make it worth it.

Sharar took out a large, leather-bound volume and a bamboo pen with a pot of ink. "Mmhmm, go on."

Tzarik frowned, confused. "What do you want me to say?"

The scholar put some flourishes on the name at the top of the page and then looked up. "Where were you born, Tzarik?"

Discomfort quickly set in. The Runer pulled his hood farther over his forehead as the servant brought out all the food Sharar ordered. He set it down, indiscreetly trying to see under Tzarik's hood. He leaned so far forward that he spilled the cold, clear alcohol all over the floor. He scrambled away, screaming an apology, taking the broken glass pitcher with him.

"This is the kind of life I live," the Runer said through gritted teeth. "I am a sideshow attraction. Or something to hurl cat feces at. An omen of bad luck."

Sharar wrote madly, tearing the paper at one part. "Mmhmm, but you also dispel hauntings, kill monsters, exorcise ghosts."

"Sometimes." Tzarik sighed as the servant brought out another pitcher, this time avoiding eye contact at all costs; he turned his face in the opposite direction, setting the pitcher near the edge. "But monsters are becoming scarce."

The pen stopped. Sharar looked up. "Are they? Would you say the balance of monsters to people is..." he waved his hand as though weighing a costly heirloom, "not right?"

The Runer frowned, unsure how to answer. Unable to wait for the scholar to eat, he tore a large piece of the dark, juicy lamb and bit into it like a wolf.

"Yes, please eat!" Sharar said apologetically. "I forgot. How long has it been since you've had a hot piece of meat?"

Unsure if the scholar was serious, Tzarik looked up from his plate and saw him holding the pen expectantly above the page. Swallowing the meat hanging out of his lips, he said, "Hot food? Months."

"You don't have a home to return to?"

"I was born on Al'Myrah. But I don't have a house."

The scholar smiled. "Me as well! Probably different principalities though. Al'Myrah has so many wonderful, advanced cities. Especially when compared to, say, those of the west." He laughed, thinking they shared a joke. "They don't even have black powder!"

Returning his attention to the food, Tzarik took another bite and washed it down with the cold, clear alcohol. He didn't know what it was, but it followed the sizzling lamb well. He let a small smile break his otherwise down-turned lips.

"Can you tell me about the process of Runing?"

"No," Tzarik snapped quickly.

The scholar's mouth opened a little in surprise and a small hint of hurt flashed over his brows.

"Some things are a Runer's secrets," he said a little more softly.

Sharar shrugged. "Maybe the mystery is why some people treat you so badly?"

"No," Tzarik said again. "It's not that others cannot know. Some people do, like lawyers and judges. It's just not a pleasant outcome to any trial. It's not a way to live your life. Assuming you survive the runing."

Seeing that he had upset the Runer, Sharar licked his lips, put the book away, and took a bite for himself, puffing on the pipe after. "Is there something in the city you have come to see?" he asked coyly.

"Rumor has it a crocatta is harassing a family here."

The scholar sucked on the pipe's tube again, his eyes unfocused. "Hmm, well that will make for some fine fieldwork. But I won't bother you."

"Thank you," Tzarik said honestly. "I work best alone. Don't like worrying about other's safety. Or answering questions while I work. It's better to be alone. In case things don't end well."

Sharar smiled with understanding. "Of course. I'll get you a room. Thank you again, master Runer." He stood up, stretching. "I will no doubt see you again. I may come find you."

The Runer did not miss the glint in the scholar's brown eyes. A look he had seen before, just never in a student. A hunger lingered there. But not just for knowledge; a ravenous, almost mad hunger for secrets. Sharar could be a kind of scholar he had not run into before. Maybe they were all like that? He didn't know; he'd spent little time around properly educated men.

Once the scholar left, Tzarik finished the food, making himself sick. He asked the owner about a room and was led up some sandstone steps to a room with a large window leading out onto a wooden balcony. Inside the room, a looking glass reflected his short, windswept image. He looked at himself as he undressed in front of the glass. Every time he hated his short stature, he hated himself for the self-loathing. A vicious cycle.

He prepared to just sleep when he caught sight of steam rising behind him in the mirror. Turning, he saw a large wooden tub filled with hot water. He reached out an almost shaking hand to feel the warm water, to convince himself it was not a mirage. The heat tingled all the way up his arm. Without waiting, he crawled in, submerging himself in the first hot bath he had taken in a year. Satisfied, alone, fed, and warm he wondered if he would even wake up the next morning. The crocatta might have to wait.

Chapter 3
Dead Rising

Tzarik took his time circling the small farm. The stink of sheep had annoyed him since childhood and it put him in a foul temper now. The family's child, fascinated by him, followed him constantly. The boy called to his shepherd dog to come back as it consistently wandered off as he tailed the Runer. The dog ambled slowly and stumbled often.

"Did you die when you went through the trial by Runing?" the young boy asked. "All your blood just—" He mimicked his belly being slashed open and made whooshing sounds like all his insides came out.

The Runer ignored him. Far away from the sheep and the barn, he could see larger paw prints. "Stop following me," he snapped, "or I'll use you as bait for this crocatta."

The boy didn't leave, but he hung back. Tzarik followed the prints a few yards around the outside of the fence. The sand-like soil had lost most of the traces, but the long grass still leaned where a huge, animalistic body had slowly meandered through it. One of the most dangerous and tell-tale signs of a crocatta was that they did the baiting. Trapping one would not be easy. Scanning the grass and the hills beyond the fence, he couldn't see where one would hide. The forests were sparse here, and these sandy hills did not create caves. He bit his bottom lip, deep in thought. It could be wolves. The tall spires that were the mountain's roots would be no long-term home though. Maybe a lost pack?

"I thought at first the dog lured it here."

Tzarik spun around, angry at being interrupted and angry that the old farmer had been able to sneak up on him.

"The dog?" the Runer asked, scratching his clean-shaven chin. He had not become accustomed to the sensation since the night before and scratched more than usual. "A dog would frighten a monster away. No matter if it were crocatta or wolf."

The farmer stuck his tongue between his teeth where one had gone missing, also scanning the horizon. His skin had been darkened so much by the sun that his white teeth stood out like the moon in the evening. Tzarik noticed his canine teeth were missing.

"Normally, yes," the farmer went on, "but our dog, our shepherd Milsaq, ate some bad carcass in the hills over a week ago. She didn't make it..."

A dark unease began to churn in Tzarik's belly. "The dog that your boy has with him right now?" he asked.

"The very same." The farmer's fingers quickly tapped against each other in a nervous rhythm.

The Runer checked his surroundings for traps, hidden assassins. "Why are you telling me this. What do you want me to do?"

"I don't know!" the farmer cried. "This is your trade. There was a man, not three days ago, who came throughout the village and he...brought Milsaq back. Pulled her from the earth like a root vegetable! We didn't tell anyone for fear they'd think we'd made a deal with a djinn."

"Did you?" Tzarik snapped, ready to run and save his own skin should demons come into play.

"No!" The farmer raised his hands, showing he did not carry the demon deal like a deed to his land in his hand. "The man looked like you...in a fashion. Runes on his skin. He was kind to us. We gave him a room for the night and he gave us our Milsaq."

"She was dead when he brought her back?" Tzarik asked.

The farmer nodded. "So I thought this...undead dog might be bringing bad karma to us." The farmer looked more sincere and frightened than any man Tzarik had seen in months. "Can you help us, white blood?"

The Runer scoffed, shaking his head. "Of course I can. But dead dogs won't draw in a crocatta. It won't draw anything if you don't believe in any god. But this man you mentioned concerns me. He sounds like a Porshain."

"Oh!" The farmer raised his hands to his mouth and muttered a rapid prayer. "The dead city? The city of heretics?"

"I know very little about it," Tzarik confessed with a heavy sigh. "They are necromancers and according to many, that is heretical. I've never seen the work of one."

At that moment, the boy and his dog jogged up, stepping high over the long grass. Now that he knew what ailed the dog, Tzarik saw it. He chided himself again for not realizing sooner that something was very wrong with the animal. The dog lumbered, no doubt suffering from partially decayed legs. It's eyes milky white, expressionless, and its tail didn't wag. The dog looked up at him, seemingly sensing his stare. Looking into its eyes sent a shiver down his spine. It was like looking into a stuffed hunting trophy with an exceptionally crafted frame. It made him uneasy.

"He didn't seem as evil as they say necromancers are," the farmer tried to justify when he saw how much the news affected the Runer.

"I can't tell you," Tzarik said gruffly. The dog's gaze made his white blood tingle. "The history of Porsh is shrouded in darkness and taboo. Some say a djinn cursed the island. Others think they were taught from a young age to use this unnatural magic. They follow a lich king."

The farmer glanced sideways at the Runer. Tzarik felt words erupting in the farmer's mouth as he stopped his tongue. Wasn't he unnatural? Wasn't he an evil man, punished by dark magic? Didn't he do evil things and hunting was his punishment? Not even monsters had white blood. They shared the red, innocent blood of man. Even the immortal animal people, the Masakh'-cepholus, had red blood.

"But let us work with the problem at hand, white blood," the farmer said forcefully. "What do we need to do?"

Tzarik tapped into his reserve of patience, his jaw tightening. "I have to wait for tonight. I'll stay here, see if it shows up."

"Won't you come back to the house?" the farmer asked. "I am not the cook my dearly departed wife is, but my bread is the talk of the village. And a traveling scholar has stopped by for room and board. Paid in red gems!" He whispered this last part, knowing the rareness of the red gem in question.

"Then I will most certainly not be coming in for dinner," Tzarik sighed. The dead dog stared at him and Sharar wringing him for answers like a wench at a washing well. He'd rather swallow the ashes of his grandmother.

⁓

"You didn't come in the house to eat," Sharar said merrily, bringing out a clay pot of stew and a round, flatbread.

The Runer grunted, inhaling deeply to arouse his mind from the trance he had been in. Opening his eyes he saw the dark outline of the scholar and his absurd, wide sleeves.

"This is no place for you," Tzarik murmured half-heartedly. By now he knew that stupid people loved to put themselves in danger if it meant watching something odd like a Runer in action. Sometimes even educated people like Sharar acted stupid.

"Just giving you the stew," he smiled. He placed it on a smooth sandstone near Tzarik and backed away. "What do you hope to find?"

"A crocatta," he said simply. "A simple family like this does not deserve to be plagued by such a monster."

"Is that the one they call the wolf of the voice?" Sharar asked interested.

"Yes."

"Why do they call it that?"

"Leave." Tzarik didn't mean to growl as much as he did, but the scholar took the hint. The man would spout his knowledge all day and still not know that a crocatta spoke with the voices of loved ones to lure victims out.

He sat again in silence, keeping his eyes on the passage they told him the crocatta used. His icy eyes could see just well enough in the darkness. One of those unnatural powers he had. Nothing came. A large kind of rodent with sharp front teeth and a bushy tail wandered down but scampered when it heard a howl.

He hummed to himself. "Wolves. How unfortunate."

He stayed out into the morning and all the next day, tracking fresh prints. They were not the same as the large paw prints he had seen but thought that it must have been a different pack. Besides, crocatta had cloven hooves.

"I suggest you track and hunt the wolves yourself," he told the farmer as the day's sun began to set. "I looked all over the hillside and up into the beginnings of the mountain. Nothing. Teach your boy how to hunt. Skin the wolves and sell the pelts. They should fetch a good price for a merchant from Rhostrana."

"Are you sure?" the farmer asked, wringing his hands.

When Tzarik assured him he had nothing to worry about, the farmer offered to put him up for the night, indoors this time, and pay him a few coins for his time. Tzarik accepted grudgingly, mildly angry that no monsters appeared to slay, earning him a far heavier pay. Part of the job meant wishing bad luck on innocent people; hoping a ghost, monster, or hex had been placed so he could get paid.

THE RUNER LAY in the straw bed, staring up at the arched, sandy ceiling, thinking of the hot bath he had at the public house, when the soft pat of bare feet alerted him to the young boy running down the stairs. Glancing out the window, little more than a hole in the wall, he saw the moon still high among the stars. Curious, and not able to sleep, he left his room and followed the little boy down the wooden steps. He stopped when the child halted by the front door to slip his lambskin shoes on.

"Mama, I'm coming," the child whispered. "I'm sorry, I was sleeping. I didn't hear you."

Tzarik perked his ears. Had the child heard his mother's voice? Had he been wrong in assuming a wolf stalked the family's farm? There were no prints. No sign the night before. How could he be wrong?

"Almud!" a sweet, ghostly, far off female voice called. "I am by the fence. Come see me, my son!"

"I'm coming!" the boy whispered.

Panic buzzed in Tzarik's skull. Many called crocatta the wolf of the voice for this very reason. The monsters lured victims out of safety by mimicking the voice of someone dear to them. Preferably someone departed so the urge to follow came strong and irrationally.

The Runer ran back up the stairs to seize his sword. For just one split second he could not remember where he laid this scimitar and had to look just a second too long. The damn thing had disappeared underneath his leather armor. Angry at his sloppiness, he charged down the stairs. Once outside, he had to look for the little boy. The boy stood so short that his small black head almost vanished in the long grass.

Cursing the agility, stamina, and speed of children, Tzarik

caught sight of his trail in the grass. The child headed to exactly where he thought the crocatta might bed down. He dashed after the boy but knew already he was too late. Leaping over the fence, he sped into the sandstone piers. There in the shadows lay the boy's body. Bloody hoof prints smeared the sand where the crocatta no doubt slipped in its hurry to get away.

Cursing, Tzarik scanned the alcoves, outcroppings, seeing if the damn beast waited to pounce on him. But the beast knew better. He didn't waste time tracking it. Picking up the boy's body, Tzarik went back to the farmhouse, preparing to tell the father the same thing he told so many others.

"Wolves!" the farmer shrieked. "You monster, you told me it was wolves!"

The farmer threw the Runer's pack out, his face soaked in tears and mucus from the unbearable sorrow he had just bore.

"I was wrong," Tzarik said mechanically. The words lost all meaning years ago. He had seen grown men, war-hardened warriors, and emotionless magi break down into earth shattering sobs when a beast—of not natural means—took away a loved one. Somehow, death by monster made the sorrow much worse. "I am sorry. But now the crocatta will move on. They hunt mostly women and children."

"What a comfort!" the farmer cried. "I have nothing. No wife, my only son dead. Leave my land at once!"

Tzarik didn't fight. People in grief were never rational. Part of him wanted to offer to help the farmer end his life, but he knew he couldn't kill a sentient being. Maybe that's what stopped him from ending his own life? Now was not the time to philosophize on his own mortality.

He picked up his things from the sand and took his horse's reins. He'd leave the land, but he wanted to find that beast. Revenge had never been his flavor of tea, but this thing had cost him a second payment. Sharar left before he could swindle another meal and room out of him.

Angry and hot, Tzarik went back to the site where the crocatta had quickly ripped the boy's throat out. Not a print nor disturbed rock showed that the thing had returned.

"It didn't come back for its prey?" he mused.

Not all monsters save their kill for later but crocatta were base beasts. It needed food, it hunted, it stalked, and rarely ever left anything to waste.

"Somethings not right," he whispered, beginning to follow its tracks. Striking hoof marks showed the hasty retreat it made when it knew he came right behind the boy. This showed that the monster had every intention of coming back to get its prey, but hadn't even come back to investigate.

Tzarik grunted, climbing up the sandy rocks. He pulled himself up a particularly steep ledge and rolled onto the ground once he cleared the edge. He blew his hair out of his face and froze. Staring right at him, all four cloven hooves on the ground, stood the crocatta. It's short fur patchy in places from scars and its long main down its neck matted with sandy mud. He solidified every muscle, willing his nerves to not so much as pulse with his rapid heartbeat.

The crocatta didn't blink as beasts often would not do when stalking prey, but this one did not crouch, its ears didn't perk up, and its eyes stayed wide, not narrowed and focused. It almost looked like a stuffed animal in a hunter's lodge.

Raising his head just enough from the ground, Tzarik checked the monster's ribs. Yes, they were rising and falling slowly with breath. Very slowly. As if it slept where it stood. Cautiously, he pushed himself up onto his knees. It didn't react. He stood up, even dusted himself off. The crocatta remained still as a petrified tree.

Trying his luck, Tzarik took one slow step towards the beast. Its nose didn't twitch, sniffing for him; its eyes stayed focused on whatever magical scene only it could see. Holding his breath, he reached his hand out to it. It stayed frozen.

He took a step back now, realizing some kind of magic bound the creature. He had seen people under the influence of psychic control and this beast had similar signs. It waited to be told what to do, all of its natural instincts on hold while someone else held its mind still. With humans, and even the immortal Masakh people, the control was usually gentle, easily broken. Harmless. This seemed stronger. And Tzarik did not know how one would hypnotize a monster like a crocatta.

Unwilling to wait and see what would happen, he unsheathed his scimitar and easily cut its hypnotized head clean from its beastly shoulders. Picking up the head, he returned to his horse and took the road back to the farmer's front door. With a grunt of spite and anger, he lobbed the head towards the front door where it crunched against the wood and smacked wetly onto the sandy front step. He waited a moment to see if the farmer would come out. The door swung open gently, jostled by the blow of the slight breeze. Nothing inside the small house moved or came to see the gruesome trophy.

"So you got it?"

Tzarik turned to see Sharar on a horse he had not had the night before. His packs tied to it and the many scrolls he bore were rolled up and stowed on his back.

"Yes, it's my job."

"Funny wasn't it?" Sharar asked, smiling. "How it didn't seem to move? I watched the whole thing. From last night with the voice to your epic decapitation. Splendid work, Runer. I may have use of you yet."

"What?" Tzarik wheeled his horse around to look the scholar directly in the eyes. "If you saw it last night, why did you let it kill the child?"

The scholar smiled and clicked his tongue, turning away. "Research, Runer. All for research."

Chapter 4

Sybal

"I do not want to go down to the mines, but if you will not make these men work then I have no choice," Sybal snapped at her brother.

She had been enjoying the Al'Myrah midday sun and a cool mint tea on her balcony while the many silken veils hung over her windows danced lithely in the breeze when her brother rudely interrupted. She pruned the misbehaving branches of one of her favorite plants: a potted bush with glossy, rubbery leaves and enormous, multi petaled flowers. They bloomed in various shades of blue. The liquid that oozed from the pruned parts was poisonous. She loved it because of the care it took to grow one in a pot and because if she did not wash her hands carefully after pruning and plucking, she ran the risk of putting herself into a deep, potentially fatal, sleep.

"We agreed to run the plantation together," her younger brother, Abdul, reminded her. He wiped the sweat from his face with the kufiya on his head. "You are stronger willed than I and the eldest. I don't know what else to do. Father's ship is to set sail in the morning and we have not begun to load the gems."

Sybal took a deep breath, held it, then released it as she looked out over the acres of mining land her family owned. They were not lords, but her father had been blessed with land that sat on top of some of the most diverse and rare gems to ever be discovered in the earth. She reminded herself that her father, a self-made man with an immigrant for a wife, depended on her strong will to see to it that these mines turned a profit.

"We have to maintain our sales and income to maintain our staff," Abdul said, almost begging. "We have no title. We must keep the mines open and the workers happy."

Pushing herself up off the golden lounge, Sybal went to the rail of the balcony and looked towards the mines. A few carts moved here and there and some workers milled about among the glowing sand. In her room behind them, a large pool in the marble ground waited for her, filled with petals and surrounded by incense. "I thought my marriage to lord spicy breath was supposed to take care of that." She winced, thinking about his imminent visit.

"That's rather rude to all of Bahratt," Abdul said in his most judgmental tone. "And you said last time he wasn't that bad and even found him attractive."

She nodded, raising her brows in surprise. "He wasn't dull. He laughed at my bad attitude, as mother put it." She grinned. "And he was cute as a puppy. I do like him, but that was five years ago. And..." She touched her yellow hair. "They told me my mother's hair would darken with age. It hasn't. I'm a genetic monster: father's dark skin and eyes and mother's pale hair. I should wear a kufiya like you instead of these veil-like adornments. So he can't see."

She touched the mint green veil on her head and the golden circlet that held it in place. She was grateful a prince had spied her in her elegant trappings and chose her for his bride that one summer his family toured Al'Myrah while signing peace treaties with the sultana; but she felt so unworthy. Couldn't she just stay here, manage the diamond mine until she grew older still and hunched over? Maybe lose an eye in a mine raid and be known for her biting scimitar?

"He's doing me a favor," she sighed. "An older woman. I'm

twenty-five, Abdul. He'd be better off marrying our sultana in Hatal."

Adbul came to his sister's side and nudged her gently with his shoulder. "He won't mind. Besides, it reminds other suitors of the Al'Myrah gold we mine."

Sybal blushed and tried to suppress her smile. "Who says that?"

He shrugged. "Men about town, I suppose."

Smacking Abdul playfully on the face, she smoothed her full pants and straightened her veil. "I suppose I must go tell those workers who pays their wages."

"Protect what is yours." Abdul quoted their family mantra in relief, handing her a curved scimitar.

⁂

WHILE OTHERS PREFERRED the speed and smoother ride of horses, Sybal loved her camel. The giant beast had been a gift from her intended two years ago and had arrived with an escort from his kingdom bearing delicious fruits and colorful flowers from his land. Her favorite had been the lotuses he sent. She sketched them often and even decorated her camel's blankets and saddle with them. She secretly hoped that when he came to visit he brought more. They had similar flowers in Al'Myrah but they were far away in the more damp areas of the continent.

Strapping her own bejeweled scimitar to her hips over her feminine garments, she made sure her veils and full pants did not hide the hilt or the sharp blade. She clicked her tongue to make her camel, also named Lotus, trot as she drew closer to the main building where the miners and their officers often congregated. She trotted past the gate and in through the front door on her beast. The men yelled as the monster made its unique cry while she pulled the reins, turning this way and that. Lotus kicked her legs gently, warning the men not to get close.

"What is the meaning of this rude entrance, sabi?" the head officer shouted over the camel's protests. He quickly stowed the ledger he had just been writing in.

Too late, though. She saw sums crossed out, new numbers etched in over the old.

"Dorsa, I have heard that you and your men are thinking of refusing to work unless we meet some demands," she said sternly. She knew, robed in glittering black and gold with her visible scimitar on her hips, that she cut a threatening picture. Her mother often chided her for conducting herself in this way. "My family has done well by you, have we not? We have given you doctors when you need them, time off when requested, family leave, holy days off. We provide good tools and safe conditions, yes?"

The officer, Dorsa, stood his ground. "The mines in Alika have guilds now!" He started in right away with his argument. "Not even a private family can hire them without heeding the guild's rules and the workers' demands."

Sybal pulled Lotus's reins so she stopped fidgeting. She glared down at the officer. "Do you know the cost of being part of a guild? The miners in Bagdula formed a guild and they all lost their jobs because not every man who owns the land a mine is found on can support the outrageous claims a guild can implement. Assuming you can afford to pay guild dues and are organized enough to make demands, that is nothing compared to the cost of paying to be before a jury and a Grand Qadi if we chose to fight your demands, which, mark my words, we will. We have been fair with you. We have treated you well. You work for my family and my mines at will; if you choose to leave you may." She leaned towards the man off her saddle and narrowed her eyes. "With our wages, prosperous mines, and connections, there a million men willing to take your place. Is this really something you want to pursue?"

She saw Dorsa swallow hard. She felt the other men watching him, waiting, judging. They had to know it would be a fool's choice to join a guild and leave the benefits brought on by working for her father. She knew in her heart that the miners were treated well. This guild nonsense came from the west where work was cheap and land-rich lords treated those in their employ like slaves. She blamed it on their lack of sun and the cold winters. She hated snow even though she had never seen it but knew anyone in their right mind should not work in it.

"Well?" she snapped when the officer did not reply. She did not let her eyes falter. She knew they saw her as lesser than her brother. Most people did. After turning twenty, she spent the next five years showing just how hard she could be. She had trained herself to see beyond emotional choices. Abdul was too soft. She had to make the difficult decisions. Over time, she made herself good at it.

"Yes, sabi," he murmured, turning his face down.

She leaned back into the saddle, resting her hands on the front bar. She sighed. "I would like to know," she checked her tone and softened it, "do you have a complaint? How can I make this job better for you to avoid discussions like this in the future? We want to keep you around."

Dorsa shook his head. "You and your family are just and fair." He still had a note of resentment in his voice that she did not like.

"Fine," she said simply.

She clicked her tongue and turned Lotus back towards the door where Abdul sat on his tall, black stallion. He smiled.

"Oh, and Dorsa," she said over her shoulder, "make sure you don't take the coin from the family's vault like you are planning."

"Ill founded accusation!" the officer grunted, planting his hands on his hips.

Sybal, screaming like a banshee, whirled around, unsheathing her scimitar. She leapt down and dashed towards the ledger she saw him writing in before she'd interrupted. Dorsa made a dash for it. With a high-pitched grunt, she slammed the sword down onto the table, cutting off the officer's grab towards the ledger.

"Don't think I won't have you punished for embezzling," she hissed, her grip not lightening on the sword hilt. "I've personally flogged over forty men myself."

Letting go of the sword, she flipped over the scroll. "Mmm, a rounding error perhaps?" she asked, pointing to the scratches and unbalanced numbers.

Dorsa swallowed hard again. "What will you do with me, sabi?" His voice quaked.

Sybal jerked her sword out from the table. "My father is not merciful with the workers who rob us. I believe in mercy. Helping those who need it. Or who show a need." She met his eyes steadily. "Do you think now would be a good time to exercise tempering justice with mercy?"

"Yes, of course!" the man stammered. "Give me a second chance, sabi. You are right. And just! I will atone for the things I would have done."

"True," Sybal said sternly, thinking. "You did not actually commit a crime. You were going to." She sighed. Times like these tested her character. She wanted to punish the man, teach him and others after him a lesson. "Why?" she asked instead.

"Sabi?" Dorsa asked, confused.

"Why do this? You have worked for us since I was a child. As far as I know, you have not once tried to cheat my father. You have always been treated well. I am confused and, I hate to admit it, hurt by your actions, Dorsa. I've grown up knowing you. Please do not take advantage of my kindness."

The officer blinked rapidly. He stammered a few times and finally wrapped his tongue around what he wanted to say. "I don't know, sabi. I suppose I see what I have and wanted more?"

She nodded, frowning, trying to understand. Mercy came to

her as easily as any instinct. "If this season passes with the profits we expect, we can discuss a promotion and higher pay. I want to do right by you, but you have to help me. Does that sound fair?"

Dorsa beamed, almost laughing in relief, and puffed out his chest. "Oh, yes, sabi, it does!"

Smiling, she offered her hand and he shook it energetically. "I expect you to work harder, then. Bring in more profits and see about expanding our trade. Is that understood?"

"Yes, sabi!"

Her sword back in its sheath, the storm quelled, she took the reins and clopped out of the offices on her camel to Abdul who waited outside.

"Saw the whole thing!" he smiled, slapping her on the back. "This is why you are better at these things. I wish I could ride a camel into the office, slam a sword onto the desk, and shout at a man the way you did."

"Being as tall as they are helps." She sighed. "I hate towering over all my friends, but when it comes to these workers, being six feet tall helps. And being an unmarried woman in her twenty-fifth year keeps them guessing what I will do next. Since I am almost expired, you know."

Abdul smiled again before sighing.

"I know that sigh," she said, glancing sideways at him as they walked to the distillery next. "What's wrong. We just had a great victory!"

"Remember that diplomat from that mountain country. The one above Oceanya?"

Sybal's stomach churned and the elation she had just achieved vanished like a sandstorm. "Whoang Xiaoh?" she moaned. "The man who loves his white monkey a little too much?"

Her brother tried to smile. "The one who recently devastated an entire kingdom, eviscerated the people in their own homes, and placed his own man on the throne, yes."

"Gods," Sybal breathed. "What about him?"

"While you were ensuring father's mines keep honestly operating, a messenger came from Rahul saying Whoang Xiaoh is crusading in our direction."

"Rahul?" she exclaimed. "A messenger...is he here?"

"Yes," her brother laughed. "On his way, anyway. But he says Whoang Xiaoh is not coming to fight. He only has a small entourage with him. Perhaps he comes for a diplomatic crusade."

"Why us?" Sybal gasped, unable to control the fear and anticipation at seeing her betrothed at the same time. "Why not ride to see the sultana instead?"

"Diplomacy," Abdul said again. "We are very influential. We are at court all the time. He knows that."

Sybal nodded. "Get the people, get the monarchy," she mused. "I can't worry if he's not charging on us in a raid." She couldn't stop the smile. "Rahul is coming!"

Chapter 5
The Betrothed

TOSSING HER SCIMITAR ASIDE, SYBAL RAN INTO HER INNER chamber, crying for her mother and a maid. She made such a ruckus that an older lady in waiting, Mila, came flying through the veils covering her doorway, clutching her stuttering heart.

"My child, are you hurt? I saw the sword!"

Sybal stripped herself quickly and ran into the pool in the center of her bathing room, splashing fragrant, colorful water all over the marble floor. She grabbed handfuls of the petals in the baskets surrounding her and crushed them, rubbing them on her body and discarding them into the water after.

"You wild monster!" Mila scolded, not a hint of love or hidden admiration in her wrinkled face. "I thought you were hurt. Why must you do this to my poor, aching heart!" she sobbed.

"Dear, sweet, Mila," Sybal cooed, swimming up to the pool's edge like a seductive mermaid. "Please, take my hand and let me kiss your palms. I am sorry."

"No!" the old woman stamped her foot. "You will pull me in again. You laugh, Sybal, but I am over ninety years old." She sighed, looking at the woman she helped raise. "You have grown so tall. Taller than your brother. Rahul may not like a woman who towers above him."

"Or one with yellow hair." She stopped scrubbing herself and pouted. "I have been too frightened to dye it. A girl in the northern mountains once did, my mother said. It never went back to her color and she cried and shaved it off." Sybal shivered, protectively holding her long, yellow locks in her hands against her chest.

She clambered out of the pool, grabbing a towel, and ordered Mila to find something nice for her to wear when Rahul arrived.

"Just put the black one back on," Mila grunted, going to the wardrobe. "It's still clean. Smells of camel, but what of yours doesn't?"

Sybal considered the black and gold garments on the floor. They were stunning, authoritative, and one of her favorites to wear. She wore something similar the first time she met Rahul because she wanted to threaten him, make him change his mind about choosing her. But then he helped her plan pranks on the royal family, took her fishing, showed her how to tie dozens of knots, and bought her that scimitar. He also did not care that she was older than most brides. He understood her.

She sighed heavily, smiling into the looking glass. She imagined him riding up on one of those white horses they bred in Bahratt. He'd wear red and gold as most royals did in that country, and a turban of silk with jewels and coins dripping from its folds. She once saw his wrist poking out of the wide sleeves and loved the contours of his bones and muscles. She sneaked a better peak while he and her father spent time together preparing a fishing boat. His much darker skin covered chiseled, dancing muscles on his forearms as he guided his steed. She didn't realize it till Mila clucked her tongue at her, but she had clasped her hands on her chest and tilted her head—daydreaming about Rahul.

"How can you threaten a man's life one moment and dream in gold and gems the next?" Mila sighed, shaking her head. "Wear this one if you want to swoon so much."

She handed Sybal a pink, low-cut coat with gold and turquoise trim. The brocade glinted with varying shades of both, depicting camels and peacocks among trees. The full, luscious pink pants gathered at the ankles to show off her golden shoes, which were larger than the average woman's.

"He will see my big feet in that," Sybal protested. "Can't I just cover my entire body and walk on my knees. Tell him I caught the plague and had to have my legs amputated."

"So self-conscious," Mila murmured. "Put it on and I will braid your hair."

ABDUL TRIED to tell her that Rahul would not arrive until the next day or even the day after that, but she knew otherwise. She felt in her bones and in her heart that pumped her eager red blood that he would come before the sun set. She waited near the front of the house with her mother and father.

"This is quite a turn," her father, Sheikh Riyadh, mused as he moved a piece on the board of a game he played with his wife. "I have not seen you wear that color in some time."

His wife, Sheikhah Freja, clicked her tongue disapprovingly. A tall, pale beauty, she had once been able to wield a warhammer as well as any man since the women of the northern west were shieldmaidens, often riding into war. Now her limbs were lithe and elegant. Often wearing the laced dresses of her people, everyone in the city of Ala'Nar knew Freja by sight. Tall and blond, she stood above a crowd.

She studied the game board before her, pressing her lips to one side. "Don't insult your daughter, my love. You should be rejoicing that such a man as Rahul chose her and even more joyous that she does not hate him. I told you how my sister poisoned her husband."

Sheikh Riyadh scoffed in disgust. "Of course, he was her uncle. But that is beside the point, yes?"

Sheikhah Freja froze and glared up at her husband through

her pale, yellow lashes. Gently, she adjusted a leather headband encircling her head. "I cannot vouch for my people and their backwards ways. I must praise the gods that a wild barbarian from the east liberated me."

Riyadh smiled pompously, moved a piece to take out two of Freja's, then bowed his head respectfully towards her. "If only I hated my wife, I could use my venomous tongue against her as she does me."

"If only I hated my husband and could kill him in his sleep," Freja joined in, leaning over the game board so her ample breasts were exposed more. She gently touched her exposed skin and smiled coyly at her husband.

"Please stop!" Sybal rolled her eyes and went to sit in the open window. "Oh, yes, I see. You have such love and I better make the best of it or else. As you said, I don't hate Rahul. I'm sure we will be fine."

"And bear me a grandson!" Riyadh called out as Freja took three of his pieces.

Sybal smiled politely. "I want children. Rahul says we should wait five years before that though." She picked at a flower that grew up the side of the house near the window. "I suppose I understand. Get the affairs in order, right? But..." She stopped, feeling her parents look at her. "I don't mean to be a weeping maid, crying for children. I just know that I wouldn't mind having Rahul's children."

Freja pulled a face Sybal could not see clearly as she forced herself to keep her eyes on the road outside, but it made both her parents snicker and laugh as though sharing a dirty secret.

"It's just what I want," she went on. "It's not for every woman. The princess is next in line to the throne; she does not need to have children to show her worth. I don't either."

"My sweet," Freja said softly, "no one wants to force you to have children."

"No, you misunderstand," Sybal sighed. "I am happy with who I am, running the estate, but I also want children. It's not fashionable right now, though."

"Oh, yes," Riyadh mocked, "women having children? What an unpopular opinion. It will be out of fashion in a few seasons, just you wait."

"Stop!" Sybal laughed again. "I'm serious. I want to have children. The cousins made fun of me for it though. But they mock me for not being married either. What am I to do?"

Freja smiled lovingly over at her conflicted daughter. "Do as you wish, my love."

"She will without your encouragement, you snowy barbarian," her father muttered.

Sybal ignored her parents' jibes. She had just spotted something glitzing on the hill coming towards their estate. Golden banners, red flags, a lotus crest.

"He's here!" she cried, pinching her cheeks for color.

"How DID YOU KNOW?" Abdul asked, smiling as they all stood outside with a welcoming party as Prince Rahul and his entourage rode through their gates. "Are you a magi? Did you divine from the stars that your love would be coming today?"

Sybal jabbed him hard in the ribs. "He is not my love. I just don't hate him."

Then she saw him. Rahul was tall for a man from his country, but still shorter than her. While astride his white stallion however, he struck a strong, manly image. He'd trimmed and oiled his beard to shine in the setting sun. His chiseled jawline framed his smile perfectly. Sybal waved, unabashedly at him. When he saw her, doused in pink and glowing to see him, his smile broadened to show even, white teeth. He threw one leg over his decorative saddle and leapt down before the animal even stopped. He walked quickly to Sheikh Riyadh and bowed.

"Mighty sheikh," he sang in his deep voice. He rose and kissed the signet ring on his finger before turning to Freja. "Oh, Sheikhah Freja, how happy I am that one such as you deigned to come down from the mountains of the north and live amongst us desert rats." He kissed her palm as was their custom.

"Save your pretty words for the ears who care, prince," Freja said, raising her elegant brow. "Someone has not stepped away from the window since hearing of your arrival."

Turning to Sybal, beaming, Rahul came to her, both his arms held wide. Smiling like a girl presented with a pony, Sybal strode to meet him, embracing him around his shoulders. She became keenly aware of how his face came close to her chest. Curse her height.

Making light of it, she pulled away and let Rahul look her up and down. When he smiled, she spun to show off the shimmer and gleam of the fabric and the gold that decorated it. As she met his face again, he held up a lotus flower.

"You remembered!" she gasped, taking the giant bloom in both hands gently, smelling it.

"Well," Rahul kicked a pebble, looking down at the path, "Abdul told me you embroidered it on your saddle. I thought you must have liked it. And..." He pulled a purple velvet draw-string pouch off his ornamental belt. She watched him gently pry it open with his long fingers. After dipping into the bag, he pulled out a solid gold ring. "To make it official."

Her smile came so quickly and strong that her eyes nearly squinted shut from joy. She held her hand out, biting her lip hard, and let him slip it onto her finger.

She sighed deeply, satisfactorily, looking into his eternal brown eyes. Then she remembered. "It's not all lotuses and lokum, I am afraid." She lowered her voice. "Your messenger arrived only hours before you. Only Abdul and I know of Whoang Xiaoh. We have no news other than hearing of the awful things he did in that city. I don't know what he wants."

Rahul leaned closer to her so she could hear him over the ruckus of his entourage unloading their gifts and moving inside. "I know very little as well. But I heard he was traveling this way and knew I had to come. I had to see you. To know that you were safe. I don't doubt that you can protect your family. But I had to know."

She smiled. "I understand. I am glad you are here. I need your help in finding a diplomatic solution. I have ideas, but I'd like the aid."

Rahul smiled, taking her hand. "What else are we betrothed for?"

<hr />

"Take me to your favorite place," Rahul whispered as they pulled away from her family and the caravan that accompanied him.

"Alone? Together?" Sybal gasped in reply.

Rahul wiggled his dark brows mischievously, grinning. "I know you won't let me do anything inappropriate, my love. I hear you like to sever limbs in anger."

Sybal clicked her tongue and rolled her eyes. "Abdul talks nonsense. I came to a diplomatic solution with Dorsa."

The prince's eyes didn't waver from her face, almost like he feared to lose her if he looked away for even one second. "Take me to your favorite place. The sun is setting. The sky is orange. The night is cooling."

Desperate to hide her joy, she tried to pinch her lips to hide her smile. "I have a place. Follow me."

He took her hand as she led him around the borders of her

walls. Once they were out of sight from her family and the entourage, she giggled and sprinted away down a mossy hill.

"Where did this moss come from?" Rahul asked, leaping over a gray rock to keep up with her.

"My favorite place!"

Ahead, a white structure, made of pure glass and ivory appeared from behind a large oasis. Sybal stopped to let Rahul take in the sight.

"Oh, my Kashish," he breathed. "A greenhouse!"

She took his hand and led him behind the short white spires that surrounded the expansive yard. A gray pebble path led around the grounds to fruit trees, fountains, and small shrines to the gods of Al'Myrah.

"This is the best part," she whispered so as not to interrupt the colorful birds that nested in the leathery leaves of the trees.

Around a bend, a small pond gurgled and spit water down a manicured, rocky waterfall. The water flowed blue, contrasting with the bright green leaves and yellow flowers around the edges.

"I'm going to plant lotus," she smiled. "They don't grow here so the conditions had to be made."

Rahul slid his fingers into her hand. "It's like a small part of Bahratt right here." He faced her, looking up slightly. "You make this place look beautiful."

Her heart ticked against her ribs, not quite a thud. Trepidation at being alone kept the heat inside. "I want to say something to you but I'm afraid it will ruin what we have."

The dying sun made all the gold surrounding the prince's face turn to fire. His black eyes smoldered when he smiled. "Sybal, nothing you can say will stop me from marrying you. I signed a contract between my kingdom and your father's estate, so I'd go to prison if I broke off our betrothal." He chuckled boyishly.

Sybal playfully smacked his chest. "You are horrible." She took a deep breath. "I don't want you to get a big head after what I say.

Your turbans would look ridiculous then. And I can't have a ridiculous husband."

Rahul smiled so hard, his dark eyes almost disappeared into his sharp cheeks. He guided her to a stone bench behind the splashing, blue waterfall and sat her down. When she settled, he knelt before her. "Sybal, I loved you from when I first met you as a child. When we met in Hatal at the sultana's coronation."

The memory painted vivid images in her mind. She treasured that memory. They were thirteen. Almost twelve years ago. She flirted with him, despondent at realizing she was the only one of her friends unengaged. They dared her to toy with the prince's emotions and get him to fall in love with her.

"I told you what they put me up to," she recounted. "And you said, 'Let's make fools of them all'." Allowing herself the gesture, she slowly reached out and touched his forelock. It slipped like fine sand between her fingers. She loved him and it hurt not to touch him.

"And we did," he grinned. His hand hovered over her knee.

"You can touch me." Her voice almost blew away on the evening breeze, it came so quietly from her throat.

His hot palm rested on her knee. Taking her fingers in his, he opened her hands upward and placed his face down into her lap, kissing her palms.

She bent over, kissing the top of his head. The fragrance from his tresses warmed her inside as she drank deeply of his scent. "I thought I'd have to tell you no. To wait until marriage. But you've never forced me to do anything. But it's me who's had to force feelings away. When I saw you today, I thought I'd take you right then."

Rahul stood up, swinging one leg over the bench and turning her to face him the same way. "I wish you would have. Then your father would have no doubt about our union."

Without waiting, he pushed himself forward, kissing her so

quickly she felt her lips bruise. He gripped her head, holding her to him while she reciprocated. Emotion rising, she panted and quickly wondered if he could smell the coffee on her breath from earlier. When he didn't stop, she scooted her hips closer to his, entangling her fingers in his soft hair. She moved one hand down his neck, feeling the contours of his veins and muscles. His flesh slid under her fingers like silk. When her hand went to the sensitive spot below his collarbone, his kisses slowed.

She froze. Her eyes opened and panic, not passion, made her heart pound. Did she go too far?

Rahul pulled back and licked his lips, frowning. "Did you drink chocolate coffee earlier today?"

Falling into a giggling fit of relief, she covered her face with her hands, her cheeks flushing. She sighed. She'd almost gone too far. He politely stopped her. Unable to show her face, she kept it covered and drew her knees up, embarrassment eating away the fire.

"Sybal." The prince peeled her fingers away from her red face.

She loved her name in his voice.

"I'm so sorry," she sighed, looking away. "I let my passion get the better of me."

"But you stopped. You knew my feelings and you stopped." He planted a quick kiss on her forehead. "You don't have to be embarrassed at knowing that I wanted to stop."

She bit her lip, wanting to touch his hair again. "Can you just say it next time? I'd feel less of an ass."

His dark eyes ignited again with a devilish smile. "Next time, I won't have to tell you to stop."

Chapter 6
Diplomacy

"Ah, Sheikhah Freja, I praise every god and goddess from every continent that you deigned to return home with this ugly sheikh," Rahul crowed as they all sat down to a meal.

"Sybal is half me as well, you know," Sheikh Riyadh laughed, pouring the wine himself. "Perhaps your children will be as ugly as me."

"Father, stop." Sybal smiled, covering her mouth. "Rahul's blood will stamp out any hint of your hairline, have no fear of that."

Raising their glasses, they all shared a smile and a laugh. Servants brought out piles of fruit, gelatins, and savory lamb and fowl. They dined in silence for a few minutes out of respect for the famished travelers. Sybal ate but her stomach clenched, making it hard to digest. Somewhere, maybe just beyond the walls of her father's estate, a hungry warlord lurked. She caught Rahul's eyes on a few occasions, his brows furrowed. He clenched and released his fingers when the conversation lulled.

"I wish this was all there was," Sybal whispered to her betrothed softly when the others applauded for a bard who came in to entertain over coffee. "My family loves you. And you are not bothered by our cavalier ways."

Rahul gently placed his finger between her brows and traced down the bridge of her nose. "There is no need to fear a battle if we can find a way to placate Whoang Xiaoh. It might be a steep price, but anything is worth stemming the flow of blood."

"We can make a trade perhaps?" she suggested. "A percentage of our mines for peace."

Rahul pressed his lips together, scratching the back of his head. "And what if he demands more and more? Or if we are accused of off-continent accounts?"

She shrugged. "Then we become paupers. Safe, alive paupers." She narrowed her eyes. "Unless you do not want to marry a poor, land-rich heiress?"

"It's true," Rahul sighed, nodding. "I only want you for your diamond mine."

She giggled and kissed him.

"My lord!" A servant, covered in sand dust, dashed into the dining hall. "Horses and elephants! Whoang Xiaoh is practically at our gates! He has men with him!"

The sheikh rose, checked out the window, and then looked back at the servant. "Are you certain?"

"Wait!" Rahul interrupted, catching the war-seasoned sheikh before he reacted rashly. "He is not coming to fight. I saw him before I arrived and sent a messenger ahead with the news. Abdul and Sybal know. He is coming to bargain with you. I am sure of it. His entourage is small, two elephants at most. Maybe twelve men."

Riyadh paced back and forth a few steps, touching his beard. "Yes, we are too close to the royal family. He would not risk attacking us. What does he want? My land?"

"We are going to find out," Sybal said quickly. "We are going to act diplomatically and not start a war with Wu-Tang. No matter how much he provokes us, we will not succumb to violence. We can't."

"And if he takes our home?" Freja asked, clutching her husband's arm, stopping him in his pacing.

"Then we lose our home," Sybal said. "Better to be homeless and poor than dead. Don't you think?"

Riyadh sighed, covering his face with his hands.

Freja, her face twisted in agony, nodded to Sybal. "I trust you," she whispered.

᠅

"I WILL NOT LET you meet him alone!" Riyadh roared as they stood in Sybal's study an hour later.

She made sure her maps were clearly visible on the table, the armillary spheres spun impressively, and the books on arcana were first on the bookshelf.

"I am not alone," she snapped back, clasping her belt and scimitar to her waist. "Rahul will be just outside the window, ready to leap in at any moment. And you will be in your study just around the corner. Keep his men outside the walls. If anything goes awry, sound the alarm, get mother and Abdul out through the back tunnels, and see to it Rahul leaves with you."

Her father's face turned purple as his eyes bulged. "This is madness!"

Outside her study, she heard the clamor of armor and the strong, staccato language of Whoang Xiaoh.

"Go!" she hissed, pushing her father out the back door. Turning to the ground-level window, she asked Rahul, hidden in the garden, "Do you see his army?"

"It's not much of an army, like I said," he replied. She found him atop the wall, looking through a glass. "Maybe twelve men. They look tired. Armor is worn. Beards are long. Most are sleeping under the trees." He leapt down then turned to face her. "Be careful. I'm going to be a ways off so he doesn't get suspicious. Tell me everything he says. If you need help, call for me. He knows I'm here."

"I love you," Sybal mouthed as he disappeared into the colorful foliage.

She took a deep breath and it caught in her throat when the servant knocked, announcing the warlord. She tried to make her face as passive as she could, but she didn't know what that felt like. So instead, she frowned gently, clasping her hands before her.

Both doors opened and Whoang Xiaoh entered. He stood tall, but not as tall as she, and strode with easy, sure steps. His high cheekbones and narrow brows reminded her of the dragons his people hunted. He had black hair, brushed to a shine, long down his back. She noted that he wore the embroidered silks of royalty and not armor. He carried two, single edged swords on his hips, however. A myth said that some warriors of Wu-Tang could summon the elements to fight for them. She thought that story foolish until seeing the menacing gleam in his dark eyes that snapped with lightning. She watched his hands, knowing those fingers had eviscerated children in their own home.

"Whoang Xiaoh," she said more stiffly than she meant to, "I hope you don't mind me being forward and asking what you are doing in Al'Myrah, but it is far from your home."

The warlord bowed at the waist, smiling. His teeth were pointed like fangs behind his thin lips. "Lady Sybal, this is why I admire you and your family. You never let one become at ease, settle in." He reached down for the brass container and helped himself to her wine. He raised the small glass towards her. "Let's get started then. What can you offer me?"

Her brows twitched up and she let her eyes droop. "I am not amused or threatened by your cavalier attitude, Whoang Xiaoh."

"Please, Sybal."

His smile made her flesh crawl. Her name in his mouth, on his tongue, churned her stomach.

"We are both commanders in our own right. Call me Xiaoh as we are equals."

She swallowed. "How goes this crusade of yours, Xiaoh? We have heard of your...victories. Why not take this city? Our ruling government is several days ride away. It would take a week for word to reach the sultana."

Xiaoh poured more wine and moved to the spinning, brass, astrological tools, lightly tapping one to make it spin. "You know, Sybal. I want to negotiate. I know you are in the sultana's pocket. She is strong. Her sons are masters of discipline. Your military is astounding." He came back and tapped his home on the map. "My people...they do not like as much. So I left. Traveling elsewhere to find a piece of this world to rule as my own. If I can take a city here and there, leaving in place my own government and leaders, soon my people will regret exiling me."

She listened carefully. She didn't know Xiaoh had been in exile. His country could not be held accountable for his evil actions. He was a rebel. She placated her face to hide her interest.

"A civil war, Sybal," he went on. "That's what my people need. And they will get one. Civil war brings a nation together. We have seen it in the past. Makes us stronger." He clenched his fist close to her face.

"Yes, killing off one's own people and dividing them on an agenda is the correct course to take," she sneered. She regretted her tone immediately. Her mind raced to come up with a plan while staring into his evil eyes.

"Don't be that way," Xiaoh whispered, resting his empty hand on the hilt of one of his swords. "We are getting along well; don't ruin it."

"Go on then." She cleared her throat to steady her nerves. "If it's war you want, I assume you want our resources. Oil, gems, the steel in the mines."

Xiaoh smiled. "Clever girl."

His sweet, condescending tone almost broke her resolve and

she physically bit her lip to stop herself from speaking. She wanted to kill him.

"Yes, among other things." He lifted his leg and half sat on her desk, leaning closer to her. "I need absolution though. I need to know that my resources will be coming in. Your family is small compared to the sheikh on the west side of this city, yes? He has other resources—food, herbal medicine, leather, and such—and will also be useful. He also has many sons from many wives. Your dear father does not do the same?"

She began to wonder what he was trying to get at. The other family had never been their close friend, but they had no animosity for each other.

"I confess, I don't understand," she said steadily. A twinge at the base of her skull alerted her to her instincts.

Xiaoh sighed, shaking his head. "I am going to remove your entire family, Sybal. Your father, mother, and dear little brother. After precious prince Rahul takes his leave. After you convince them all that everything is fine and he can leave. Then you stay, as my seventh wife, and run this place so none of your desert rat citizens have anything to fear."

She couldn't stop her breath from quickening or her eyes from widening at the horror she heard. Her hand went to her scimitar hilt.

Xiaoh reached over and touched her hand with his. "And if you say no, one of the other family might be murdered in the night and see someone wearing your brother's clothes making a hasty retreat over their wall." He shrugged. "A family feud will erupt. The people caught in the middle. A man from Wu-Tang settles the affair, saving an entire city. It sounds easier than it will be, but I am used to a challenge."

"The sultana will never let you hurt us," she whispered, her voice trembling. "Rahul will—"

Xiaoh leapt up from the table, landing on the same side as her.

"Do you want his family—his country! —involved in this as well?" he hissed through his bared fangs. "A world war, Sybal. That's what you are suggesting. All because of you. Millions dead, civilizations toppled! Thousands of war orphans, widows, broken homes. Destroyed continents." He raised his brows. "Think about it."

His face hovered only an inch from her trembling lips. He hissed every word he spoke, as though he knew they were being spied on. He proved more alert than she gave him credit for. She had been foolish, ill-prepared. Overconfident.

"You want children, correct?" he said, smiling again. "You will have dozens."

A wave of illness swept over her, imagining bearing his children, seeing him touch her intimately. Those hands...

He leaned away from her and took a deep breath, closing his eyes. "Citrus?" he asked simply, raising his voice more than he had the entire conversation. "I do love citrus trees. Add those to the deal." He motioned to a quill on her desk.

Too petrified to defy him, she picked it up and began to write. She willed her hand not to shake so he could hear her fear as the pen scratched. She would not allow this to be the end. She'd find a way out.

"We will start with thirty percent of your mine?"

She stopped writing and looked up. He returned her gaze, a coy smile on his face. She couldn't argue. Not now. Another time. Her mind hardly paid attention to the other demands he rattled off. Her hand went steady as she thought of ways to be victorious over this exiled warlord. She could rally the people. No. No one need perish for her. There had to be another way. A more secret way.

Reminding herself to not overestimate his cunning and intimidation again, she decided to plot an escape that could spare her family. She had to decide what was worth risking.

Chapter 7
The Witness

XIAOH LEFT SOMEWHERE BETWEEN HER OUTWARDLY submitting to his demands and Rahul calling her name from the window. His voice rang through her head like the loud gong of a brass bell. She gasped and turned to face him. Her heart pulsed in her throat and her eyes dried from how wide she held them.

"What happened?" he whispered, leaping through the ground window. "I couldn't hear. I tried to get closer but didn't want to ruin your negotiation."

Sybal blinked and ran her finger under her eyes to wipe away any kohl that might have succumbed to the sweat on her face. "Everything is perfect. Just as I intended."

"Sybal!" Her father burst through her doors, his face pale and steps heavy. "I should have spoken to the man first. I just had the most mysterious exchange of words in my life. What did you tell Xiaoh?"

Freja and Abdul hovered in the doorway like frightened ghosts, waiting to hear their fate.

She took a deep breath, but it shuddered. She exhaled strongly, firmly placing her hands on the table. Her eyes caught the map of her city. Over 32,000 citizens lived within a day's walk of her family.

"I promised him ten percent of our income." She kept her

voice deep and slow to hide her fear. "In the form of the mine's produce and currency."

"Ten?" Freja breathed, clasping her son's arm. "So little? How did you convince him?"

Sybal froze mid swallow. Rahul's eyes bored into the side of her head and she dared not look his direction.

"I doubt it will remain ten for long," she said. This sounded like a convincing lie. And Rahul mentioned that Xiaoh would ask for more as time went by. "We must double our growth, look for more land to work, and ensure our worth rises. To keep up with his demands and keep our workers."

Riyadh stroked his salt and pepper beard, his hand shaking. "It is better than I would have done. I would have struck him down here and now."

Sybal's heart stopped now too. "What about his army?"

"Twelve men?" Abdul asked, scoffing and smiling now that he assumed they were safe. "They'd probably disband. They may choose to cause havoc on their way out, but his followers bear no love for him."

"Then why are we cowering so?" Sybal asked, choking. She had to leave her family's fights. She wanted to get away where they could not see her. She had to fix this. They didn't know the danger they were in.

"A soldier's loyalty is not so simple," Rahul answered. A warning made his voice soft but sharp. "These matters must be dealt with softly. With care and planning."

She smiled. "Of course."

⁙

THE NIGHT PASSED WITH HER, Rahul, and her father writing up sums, planning the land, examining the tunnels, and preparing for a trade she knew would never come. She learned from Rahul that

Xiaoh and his men procured ground for their camp in the fields near an orchard about a mile from their walls.

After the lamp oil had long burned away, her father went to bed, exhausted and still terrified. Rahul kissed her on the mouth and promised to come to her chambers at first light. She watched him ascend the stairs into the wing they'd given him and his entourage for his stay. She listened to the pat of his soft shoes on the marble floor. Watched the sway of his hips. Committed his sigh to memory.

Back in her room, she lit one candle and paced madly, stamping her foot every now and then when only a half formed idea came into her mind. Xiaoh's smile loomed before her in the darkness. The memory of how he made her blood boil and her skin turn clammy all at once came back in a wave of nausea. She wished he'd die. Vanish.

Suddenly, she stopped, holding her breath in case the sound of her breathing drove the idea from her head. She could do it. She'd fought looters and bandits off before. But the fighting style of Wu-Tang was foreign to her. She could never overpower or duel him. Her eyes drifted to the single flame next to her favorite flowering succulent. Its poisonous petals almost glowed in the moonlight.

She grinned.

She blew out the candle. Without ceremony, she donned black clothes made of cotton so nothing shined or tinkled when she walked. She wrapped her face in a black veil and covered her bright yellow hair. It would be easily seen on this full moon night. The sands turned white at night in Al'Myrah and the full moon reflected brightly off it. She wouldn't need a torch but she could be spotted if she wasn't careful.

With gloves on, she pruned a branch from her potted poison and bound it in a kerchief she'd have to burn after.

"I love you, Rahul," she whispered, looking up into his

bedroom window. The solid gold ring he had given her glowed in the dim lamplight.

She slipped out of the house and beyond the walls. Taking a horse, she knew the orchard Rahul mentioned lay somewhere in the southeast. She took the main roads and found it near a small oasis she used to play in as a child. She forgot it existed.

The camp stuck out in the space around it, dying fires smoldering in the utter blackness and their tents shimmered bright red against the white sands. She left the horse and slipped closer like a shadow over the dunes. Xiaoh's tent stood taller and more pointed than the others. Not a light could be seen inside. The sand muffled every step and she only had to keep to the shadows to not be seen by the few men who paced the perimeter.

She made her way around Xiaoh's tent, intending to enter from the back. She had to muffle a cry as she rounded the corner and spotted him. He stood with his pants unlaced, relieving himself on a tree. Immediately taking the opportunity, she went back to the front and ducked into his tent. Just as she had hoped, a sea glass bottle of the clear alcohol made from rice from his country rested on the table. Still corked, a small glass waited next to it.

"Protect what is yours," she sighed, focusing.

Listening for his stream, she unscrewed the top, dropped in her sprig, and began to screw the top back on. She heard him sigh. Holding her breath, she slipped out and made her way back to her horse where she watched his tent, waiting for him to fall asleep. A deep sleep. Hopefully one he wouldn't wake up from and would allow her to strangle him.

To her surprise, after she dosed off for what she thought was just a few minutes, Xiaoh hobbled out of his tent. Gasping in shock, she scrambled to her feet, blinking to clear her eyes. He shambled away from the camp, the bottle in his hand, and began to roam towards the orchard homes.

"No!" she hissed, racing after him, trying not to slip on the sand.

The warlord stumbled but had a decent head start. He seemed delusional rather than sleepy. Maybe the poison didn't affect him the way she thought it would? She remembered a witch telling her once that not everyone reacted to the same herbs the same way. She figured poison was poison and would drop him like it did everyone else.

She chased him down towards a well in the middle of a few homesteads. He leaned up against it and vomited. Knowing that would clear his system in a matter of minutes, she dashed towards him. He saw her but didn't seem to recognize her. He mumbled in his native language and dropped the bottle. He already leaned backward over the well so when she reached him, she tossed aside a dagger he had, and then seized his throat.

Xiaoh coughed and weakly tried to push her off. When he struggled, his face came into the moonlight and she saw his eyes were red and blood dribbled from his mouth. She didn't care.

"You will not threaten me, my family, or my city," she hissed, close to his ear. "Do you hear me, warlord? Do you understand!" She pressed down hard on his throat and felt something collapse under her fingers.

Xiaoh croaked and gasped, gurgling in the blood and straining against her hands. A few moments later, he ceased fighting.

Sybal looked into his eyes. She saw his life leave. One second, he clung to his last breath and the next, his eyes turned to ghostly, ominous glass.

Gasping, she leapt away, her arms outstretched as though trying to get away from the thing that had just snuffed out the life of a man.

"Oh, Hadad!" a withered, terrified voice softly swore on a god.

Spinning around, she saw an old woman drop a pail, clutching her heart. She wore a shabby nightdress and a threadbare shawl. Her long, gray hair came down to her hips in front of her.

"No, please," Sybal called to her through her face covering. "Don't go. It's not what you think."

But the old woman cried and began a desperate dash back the way she had come. She could hardly walk and her run looked pathetic, hobbling from one sore foot to the next.

"Guard!" the woman feebly called towards the inner city.

"Stop!" Sybal leapt at the old woman, tackling her hard to the cobblestones. "Please, just listen." She turned the woman over. Her mouth went dry.

The old woman looked up at her from dim eyes now. Her mouth disfigured in a scream or gasp of fright. A perfect death mask. Bright red blood trickled down from the woman's white tresses. She'd hit her head on the cobbles sticking out of the sand.

"Oh, gods!" Sybal gasped, tears drowning her eyes. She couldn't stop herself now. She wailed, clutching her heart as her chest burst in fear and agony.

Her cries alerted a dog who began to bark. Adrenaline and horror fueling her, she ran back to Xiaoh's body and heaved him up onto the well wall. No other place to hide the bodies presented itself and any moment, someone would come to investigate the screams and wailing. With a guttural roar, she lifted Xiaoh's body up and flipped him into the well. She heard his head and flailing hands slap the stoned sides before splashing beneath the water.

Not daring to wait another minute, she dashed back to the woman's body as well. No one needed to know she had been here. Xiaoh's men might just leave. If not, the city guards would see to it they did now that their leader had gone. Everything would be fine.

Sybal grunted, lifting the old woman from under her arms. She walked backwards when she heard them. A bell near the city borders rang. Men shouted. Lamps inside the homes flickered on. She froze. She couldn't think! Run?

With a scream, she dropped the woman and began to retreat. She cut between two small homes and leapt over a small creek. She landed hard and her mind spun until she stumbled backwards. Taking a few breaths, she rose up again.

Standing before her were five armed city guards, holding back a terrified mother, father, and five children.

SYBAL DIDN'T FIGHT the guards. She went with them with no struggle to the barracks where she'd wait while they investigated. She thought they'd find the woman and Xiaoh's body in the well, ask her a few questions, then release her when they found out she took care of the reviled warlord. She waited until her back ached from the adrenaline rush and in the silence of the cell, her breathing slowed. Soon, she grew tired.

Sighing, she laid down flat on the stone floor and stared up at the damp ceiling. This kind of rock often absorbed water and then at night it dripped out. Closing her eyes, she waited.

Chapter 8
Inquisition

Tzarik came to with a jolt as he began to slip off his horse sideways. It nickered and stopped when he made the sudden movement. He rubbed the sleep out of his eyes and the more he woke up the more he realized his body ached. His thighs could not feel the saddle clutched between his legs, his feet were so bloated they strained against the leather of his boots, and his lower back screamed in agony.

"How long have we been on the road?" he asked his mount. He looked around but the sky loomed pitch black and the full moon hung low. Ahead, a city glowed in the night. Thanking no god in particular, he weakly kicked his horse and entered the city.

The people had long since gone to bed, the day's happenings over, and the only ones milling about were the ones who came out at night to see to shady business and pay for love. One such establishment caught his sight ahead as the only one with a lit lamp outside its door. Smoke wafted out of the windows and the scent of sweat and cheap love reached out to where he sat on his rank horse.

"Great. Just like home," he mumbled, kicking his horse towards the door of the sultry establishment.

Sliding off his horse, he limped to the doorway where a young man in once-fine gold-trimmed silks stood. The man wore his hair in his face, and tilted his head in what he must have thought would be an attractive angle.

"Twenty rupees for a cover charge to go in," he said, pushing off from the wall, holding out his hand.

Tzarik hated the young man instantly. His stylish hair, smirk, and the way he rubbed his fingers together in anticipation of the gold he didn't have. "Your clothes are new," he started, "but they appear to be covered in pig shit and mud. You have no coin belt, and your teeth are abnormally straight and white. You know what that means?"

The man's eyes flicked up and down the street quickly. He suddenly sobbed. "I was robbed! You're right, I don't work here. I just need a few coins to help me home. I am the son of a very powerful sheikh and I was kidnapped. For ransom!"

He added the last part so quickly, Tzarik couldn't stop his left brow from flicking up in disbelief as a smirk slowly appeared. "And they let you go because you asked so kindly?"

The man touched his once beautiful collar delicately. "I am an educated man, sira. A man of refinement. I have a silver tongue and convinced them to let me go for the coin in my pocket."

"And they took your ring?"

The man quickly put his left hand behind his back.

Tzarik said, "I can see where the ring should be because the sun has not touched it. Funny you still have the finger it should be on. Isn't that a traditional ransom threat? Sending the ring still attached to your finger to your weeping mother?" Perhaps his exhaustion made him engage in conversation. He grew tired suddenly.

The man's face contorted into a worried grimace. Finally, he exhaled, his arms going limp at his sides. "You are obviously a mindreader of some kind."

"Just observant," Tzarik mumbled. "That's how I know you are not completely lying. You are right: you have a good tongue to mix truth with lies. And you are a lord's son. No one else is as stupid as that cast and thinks they can lie to a Runer."

"Oh." The young man smiled politely. "Have any luck recently, Runer? Fight any monsters?"

"Met a few."

"Wonderful!" The man clasped Tzarik around his shoulders and ushered him into the front door. "My name is Vicdan and it is my utter great fortune to meet you. Buy me a drink?"

"No," Tzarik said quickly. "I only have enough coin for me and the horse."

Vicdan smiled modestly. "My dear, Runer, this place is full of plebeians ready to lose coin. Buy me one libation and I will win you back sevenfold what you spend on me."

The Runer sighed. "No reason not to, I suppose. I don't care. Do what you want. But only one drink."

A few moments later, the two sat at a table drinking. Tzarik took it slow, watching the man's hands and noticed they often strayed to where his purse should have been. He was used to feeling for his coin to ensure it stayed with him. He wondered what it might be like to constantly have a bag of gold weighing down his belt.

After a few more minutes of silence and Vicdan ordering another drink, he faced the Runer square on. "I may have lied to you, but I am quite good at looking as well. Tell me, Runer, why do you want to die?"

Tzarik hid his face behind his tankard to mask the surprise at the young man's studious observation. He never met someone who matched his ability to observe.

Vicdan put his cup down and clasped his hands on the table. "I have seen the look. Many times. In the mirror. You don't care about anything and it's horrifying. You'd sooner stab me than save yourself. You want to die. Why?"

"I can't hide what I want," Tzarik confessed. "Never have

been able to. Yes, I don't care for my life anymore. Haven't for some years. Thing is, my lord," he didn't mean to sound as mocking as he did but he ignored it even though he caught Vicdan's smile, "that as far as I know, I am the oldest in my profession. Besides the few who have left it behind and become monks or keep bees in the prairies of the west. Runers are not meant to live as long as I have. I've been hunting since I was fifteen. It's no life for anyone. I wouldn't wish it on my worst enemy and I would never encourage anyone to take up the runes. I'm tired of it and there is only one way out."

Vicdan's brows knitted together, a mixture of concern and curiosity in his eyes. "How tragic. Why not just off yourself?"

"You know the laws of runing?"

The man shook his head. "That cannot apply to one's self? You cannot commit the crime for which you are runed. If that was murder, then you cannot kill another being. Including yourself? But doesn't the magic work that if you break your Runer's judgment you die? So commit your crime. And die."

Tzarik sat back, biting into a fruit. "I'm more complicated than that."

Vicdan smiled mockingly. "Of course you are. Now." He looked around. "Allow me a few hours and I will have scammed fifty men of their family jewels."

The Runer didn't watch the man's work. Lying, scams—these things were beneath him. He needed to concentrate on getting paid back what he spent on filling the youth with alcohol. Especially after he somehow swindled him into speaking so much. The boy had a gift, true. Ten years ago, he'd stab him later in his sleep for knowing too much. Now he didn't care—he'd be gone soon.

He retired to the room they rented. He had to wave away so many women looking to fill his loneliness that eventually, he barred the door with a small settee inside the room. Lying down, he closed his eyes only able to tuck his orichalcum sword between him and the wall before sleep drowned him.

His sleep took him so deep that it seemed only minutes later when an angry maid prodded him awake with a broom. He had not slept so deep in some time. So much that he thought about lopping off the head of the maid just to get a few more minutes of sleep.

Sitting up, he saw his pack and the small bag of rupees he earned were gone. Everything he owned but his monster-slaying sword and the runes around his neck taken by that slimy, disinherited lord child. Now he had to find another monster. Another beast, specter, or apparition to dispel.

"Shit," he moaned.

※

"IT IS A CLEAR CUT CASE," the Qadi said sadly from his throne above the witnesses in the house of judgment. His shoulders sagged under the weight of his traditional black robes of arbitration.

Sybal had been standing in a metal cage in front of a myriad of onlookers for hours. She thought after her testimony of how Whoang Xiaoh blackmailed her and that she killed him to save the city, they would see sense. But things had not gone her way at all.

"My family loves this city!" she said, clasping the bars desperate to escape them. "I made the choices I did to save you all."

Behind her, her mother, father, and Rahul listened to her horrifying story. She glanced back at her betrothed whose face twisted in betrayal and sadness.

"Rahul, I wanted to tell you," she whispered. The room had been built to amplify all spoken words however, so her secrets words echoed off every vault and archway. "I wanted to do it on my own. The fewer people knew, the faster I could resolve the issue—"

"Your first instinct was to kill," the Qadi cut her off. "And dumping the bodies in the well would have poisoned that entire community. Forgive me if I hold little sympathy, sabi. The woman you killed—to cover up your initial crime!—is grandmother to over fifty citizens. You murdered a man and no matter your intentions, murder is punishable by death. And then to make sure no one knew of your bloodlust, you killed an innocent woman."

Sybal was trapped by more than just the bars and chains. If the older woman indeed mothered so many of the village, even a jury might condemn her out of spite. She clenched her fists onto the metal harder, trying to stop her shaking.

"I can leave. Exiled. To my betrothed's kingdom," she said quickly.

"Why would you move your sin to his home?" Sheikh Riyadh roared.

"I can take her," Rahul put in desperately. "I love her, I don't care what she's done."

The Qadi tented his fingers, eyeing the young prince critically. "Our laws do not permit exile in the face of an unforgivable crime. The tension that could create between our king and yours...I suggest you think on it, young prince."

A lump formed in Sybal's throat. "I love you, too," she gasped, her sobs unable to be hidden anymore. "I shouldn't have said that. I can't take my crimes to your home."

The Qadi stood up. "Then it is up to these people who have heard your testimony to decide on your fate."

In a matter of seconds, half the room—no doubt the fifty descendants of the old woman—roared for her execution. The Qadi's eyes slowly swept the onlookers and finally, sadly, rested on Sybal.

"That is an overwhelming majority, sabi. I am sorry."

"No!" Freja screamed. She made to leap over the wall that separated the people from the lawmen but Rahul and Riyadh held her back.

"Prepare a pyre," the judge mumbled to the city guards standing by.

As a child, Sybal joked about being burned on a pyre. She meant to do so after leading a holy rebellion, saving a ship of slaves in a foreign land, or for some other righteous reason. Not because she actually murdered a man. She never wanted to be burned as a criminal. Her heart raced as the doors to the house of judgment were thrown open. Already, a pile of brush and kindling began to stack up. Instead of saving her family, she would cause them grief. Her mother would never recover from watching her daughter burned alive for a crime she did commit.

There had to be a way out. A way to spare her family.

The Qadi's face contorted in conflict as their eyes met over the iron bars that separated them. He leaned back, stroking his waxed beard, consulting his own mind. The others on the bench leaned out to look over at him in the sudden silence.

"There may be a way to spare your life, sabi," the Qadi said sternly at last. "It is not a worry of mine." He stopped and raised his brows, showing the opposite. "There is an old law that details how one who commits an unforgivable crime—one of those being murder—the individual may request trial by runing in which they willingly take on the process of having their blood drained and replaced by the sulfates of the Runes. The magic holds you to your oath. It is an ancient and, dare I say, barbaric punishment."

"I'll do it," Sybal screamed so loudly, her voice reverberated twenty times, making all present cover their ears.

"Gods!" Riyadh breathed.

"What do you mean?" Rahul cried.

Encouraged by how everyone stopped and stared, she repeated herself with conviction, "I will do it."

"You'll die, anyway," Freja gasped, tears streaking her cheeks, bringing her kohl with them. "Who survives a runing?"

"The ones who survive," Sybal said, her voice quaking in fear. "But I have a chance. I need not die, mother. I need not cause you the pain."

Freja pressed her hand to her chest. "This is ten times worse!"

"I will not allow you to do this," Rahul said firmly.

"Would you rather I die in the city square, children spitting on my charred corpse?"

No one spoke for a time, eyes darting from the stunned Qadi to the mortified family, back to the murderous prisoner.

To Freja and Riyadh the Qadi suddenly stammered, "I may have spoken too soon. We don't know how to contact a Runer. I would hate to bring this further shame onto your family, sheikh."

"Give us a week to find one," Freja pleaded, ignoring her husband's dignified nod. "They have to exist somewhere."

Rahul leapt over the railing that divided the onlookers from the aisles leading out of the hall and to one of his servants. Gripping the boy hard on the shoulder, he leaned close to his ear, whispering madly, his free hand waving in frantic chaos. Frowning bravely, nodding so his hair bounced, the messenger ran out of the house of judgment.

TZARIK LEANED back against the soft purple cushion, holding the sweet smoke from the pipe in his lungs. In just a few more swallows of the clear alcohol and maybe one more puff of the pipe, he'd be in the spinning haze that took his mind of life for a few hours. If he timed it just right, he'd pass out and wake up at sunrise—an entire evening of consciousness avoided.

Somewhere to his left, the doors and curtains to the entrance flew open, the other patrons gasped as a messenger flew through,

clutching his stomach and panting. The boy ran to the keeper of
the kegs, his hands frantically flicking through the air as fast as his
mouth moved. Then the keeper pointed over to Tzarik.

The smoke suddenly made him sick and his head became too
heavy to hold up. He let it fall back, groaning as the sound of the
boy's sandals approached him.

"Are you the Runer, sira?" the boy asked shyly while also
hopping from one foot to the other like a racehorse.

"I'm a corpse," he replied. He waved his hand over his torso.
"Can't you see I'm lying here dead?"

"I come on a mission of love!" the boy squeaked, gripping his
own fingers tightly. "Won't even the dead rise for love?"

Tzarik snapped his head up, grimacing at the boy through the
haze in the distance. So close. Now this child ruined it. "Does it
pay?" he asked, sitting up fully.

"Does a corpse need coin?" the boy asked, ready to play his
games now that he had the Runer's attention.

Tzarik closed his eyes and reached for the small, gold-rimmed
glass on the round table before him.

"We need a Runer," the boy cut in, taking the glass out of
Tzarik's reach. "In the courts, a woman whom my master loves, is
about to be sentenced to death. She has requested trial by
runing."

The shock almost sobered Tzarik right away. He rubbed his
eyes then met the boy's, frowning. "Trial by runing? A woman?"

"Yes, please, sira! Will you come?" The boy went back to
hopping from one foot to the other again.

Long lost, dark memories bubbled up to the front of his mind's
eye. He absently rubbed his course chin as he mulled over what
this could mean. He'd be taking on a responsibility that these
people clearly didn't understand. A Runer could not change a
sentient being like that and just leave them. There were usually—
supposed to be—consequences for that. But if he stayed and took

her on as her mentor, he'd have something else to occupy his mind. A challenge. A reason, Nefiri called it.

But a woman?

"Take me to the courts," he said cautiously.

THE QADI LOOKED on the woman with sympathy. "There are no women Runers. Even if I found a Runer willing to risk his life to take yours, it cannot be done to a woman."

Sybal shook her head. "We don't know that. We are all living beings. A Masakh can become a Runer and they are not human. I am sure a woman can."

"And you think we will find a Runer willing to do this..." He swallowed hard, breaking under Sheikh Riyadh's fiery glare. "Willing to do that to a woman? It is a risk to them as well. If you die and murder is also their crime, they will pay with their lives. This is why there are no Runers left in the east."

"Because there is too much crime?" Sybal chided. "I want to pay for my crime. But let me do it in a way in which I can give back tenfold. Find a Runer and give me a chance."

"Burn her!" a woman from the angry fifty cried out into the sudden silence. "Why give someone so evil a chance to arm themselves with runes. With magic! She killed my grandmother. Why give her this chance, these tools?"

Sybal rolled her eyes. "So I can banish her vengeful ghost ass when she comes back to haunt you."

A roaring gasp went up at this and Sybal instantly regretted her words, shrinking in her cage.

"Burn her!" the woman shouted again.

The Qadi held up his hands to silence the steadily growing murmuring of outrage. "As a citizen of your city, this is her right! We will not renounce our laws because of outrage." He met

Sybal's eyes and glared at her now. "Consider this a mercy, sabi. I do not condemn you to a life of hunting monsters and specters. You are choosing this life. We have all heard the stories of Runers. They are not good men. Not even the trial by runing can erase what some of these men have done or what they might do to you. It is not a world I would wish on anyone. They are evil men: rapists, murderers, they have tortured people for delight. I dare not imagine the world you, young lady, are entering."

Freja breathed in to steady her nerves, her imagination already running wild thinking what kind of life her daughter would have to lead now.

Afraid her mother would no longer support the idea, Sybal shouted, "I know what I ask. I understand the life I am seeking out."

The Qadi tented his fingers and leaned forward, narrowing his eyes—not in anger—but concern. "I am not sure you do. Ala'Nar is a blessed city, empty of such foul men and the creatures they hunt. For now, anyway. Lady Sybal," he used her Northica title, "you are known in this city. You will not be welcomed as a hero or a folk legend simply because you take up the runes. As the witness has stated, magic is a sin against the temple. Trial by runing is trading one sin for another in the hopes the people will not rise up against you. I tell you now, if you do this, you cannot stay in Ala'Nar."

He weakly waved his withered hand towards Rahul. "And as a man of the law, I cannot advise you hide in your betrothed's city either. As the heir to Jarabu, appearing at this trial alone, not publicly breaking an engagement to a murderer, will harm his right to rule. Do you understand how you wound those in your life now, sabi?"

The words of judgment stabbed deep into Sybal. Reminding herself to hold her head high, she stiffened. For once, she had no words to defend herself. She'd look petty and selfish to the entire house of judgment if she begged Rahul to let her leave with him.

Word would spread. His father would hear and perhaps exile her or disinherit him.

"I don't know what I'll do," she whispered, choking.

"Invoke the trial of two, should you survive the runing," the Qadi advised.

"We have found a Runer!"

Both the double doors to the hall burst open, slamming against the walls from the force. Rahul's messenger flew back into the hall panting, clutching his chest. The Qadi stood up in shock, his face twisted in the horror at the thought of what they might have to do if a Runer had actually been found. And so soon.

"A Runer stayed the night near the border," the messenger gasped. "I bargained. He said he'd do it for a fee."

Freja murmured a curse and began to weep anew.

"Bring him," the judge commanded. "What do they call him?"

The messenger stopped to answer before running out the door again. "He is called Tzarik."

Chapter 9
The Runing

TZARIK'S STEPS HALTED JUST OUTSIDE THE HOUSE OF JUSTICE. The last time he entered one, he had been completely human. Clean, runeless, full of living blood. This one looked just like the place where he lost his life.

The messenger had been insistent that money would not hinder his negotiation, so he asked for an immeasurable fee. When the messenger agreed, his skepticism began to take over. His senses went on high alert and every move anyone made, he took note of.

One of the representatives came out to greet him when he did not enter. The man's eyes roved over Tzarik's body to the point of discomfort. The Runer knew he took in his white veins, the bright white strands of his hair mingled with the black, and finally his icy, foreign blue eyes.

"Come in through the back will you?" the representative asked, eyeing the orichalcum sword now.

The pair went around to the back and through the doors where only the judges and other lawmen entered. This brought them through a dark hallway up onto the elevated loft where the Qadi sat, looking down at the people and the accused. When he came to the bar, he felt hundreds of eyes touch his strange flesh as a soft gasp of awe went up. Suddenly, his own skin seemed to fit wrong and he couldn't stop fidgeting. He wanted to cross his arms to hide his partly exposed chest, to meld into the shadows away from their curious glances.

This was why he hated people and their prying eyes.

"State your name for the scribe, if you please," the Qadi instructed.

"Tzarik," he mumbled.

"Of...?" the judge prompted.

"Nowhere. We give up origins once we take up the Runes."

"Ah." The Qadi waved his hand towards the mass and the small iron cage before them. "The accused, Sybal El'Freja, daughter of Sheikh Riyadh."

Tzarik bit his tongue when he heard the word daughter. He finally looked hard at the accused. A tall woman with the skin of her people and the hair of her northern mother. Her face rested in determination, a small glittering tear of fear in the corner of her left eye. Her mouth, though hard, held a mocking smile that only he could see. Looking on her and seeing her bravery in the face of torture and perhaps death, he admired her.

THE RUNER, Tzarik—bathed in sunlight, his white veins vivid against his tan skin, looking her straight in the eyes with his glowing blue ones, sword at his side—looked like an angel come to save her. He stood almost at attention and seemed unfazed at all by the eyes judging him. She heard them whisper words like freak, monster, and horrible. She noticed he would be shorter than her if they stood side by side, but she didn't care. Right now, he towered, impassive, strong. He would take her blood, maybe her life, but she trusted him in that moment. He would be her savior.

"Is THERE a law about women and Runing?" the Qadi asked.

The Runer weighed his answer, watching the bar of judges before he spoke. "What was her crime?"

"Murder," the judge replied. "She killed a foreign warlord and then a witness. An old woman of this very city whose family you see before you."

Taken a little aback at the idea that a lordly woman would murder, he scanned her again. She stood tall, far taller than him. Her yellow hair against her dark skin made it look like fire. Her fear dissipated the more he looked on her. Yes, he could see her killing a man.

"I have never met a woman Runer," Tzarik began. "But that doesn't mean it can't be done. It is your law that a citizen charged with an unforgivable crime has the right to request trial by runing. You must uphold your own laws."

An angry onlooker, probably one of the old woman's relations, shouted, "Shall we obey every law someone makes a plea to? Let us read the law and see what it says."

At this, the panel of Qadis began to nod, stroking their black beards. He couldn't hear the murmuring, but the way they began to lean in to one another told him they were cooking up a scheme. Then he thought of it: if they wanted to dig up the law scrolls and examine them, that would give the angry people time to amend the law, maybe petition to even change it, taking trial by runing out completely.

"I am afraid we don't have time for that," he cut in to the sudden plan making. "I see what you want to do," he glared down at the woman who mentioned the idea. "But part of the Runer's oath is that once I have seen and heard in a court of law that a citizen has asked for trial by runing, the Runer must see it through."

"Fine, fine," the Qadi sighed when the angry woman stood up in rage. "As judge and protector of the city and keeper of the peace, I sentence you, Sybal El'Freja, to trial by runing at the hands of Tzarik the Runer. As of now, your fate is out of my hands and the jurisdiction of the people." He picked up a crystal glass and smashed it over the bar, symbolizing that his word was final and the trial was over.

⚜

SYBAL WAITED in the prison while her Runer found a place to commit the runing and gather supplies for the cursed substance that would give her the powers all Runers had and most people feared. The only thing they didn't envy was the runing itself. She didn't know how he prepared, what went through his mind as he gathered the instruments and ingredients for the vile sulfates.

The night the guards came for her, she found she could no longer contain her fear. She waited all those days for Rahul, her mother, or Abdul to visit, but no one came. The guard didn't prove any comfort as he marched her at the tip of his spear to a slaughterhouse.

"What are we doing here?" she gasped through tears.

"Best place to let blood," the Runer grunted from the doorway. "Everyone has left. You'll...want privacy."

Her heart pounded so hard she felt her ribs pulse with it. She couldn't seem to draw a breath into her tense lungs. They went inside. Meat hooks, chains, cleavers, and other instruments of death hung from every beam and on every wall. To the side, a table with shackles and empty buckets stood waiting. On a smaller table next to that one rested beakers, several vials of mysterious liquid, solid, and even gaseous materials.

"Lady's choice," the Runer said in a deep monotone. He pointed to shackles hanging from the beam. "Upside down, the blood drains faster and the sulfates move in quicker." He pointed to the table with shackles. "Lying down you are more comfortable for a time. Takes longer."

She couldn't even spout the profanities desperate to ejaculate from her horrified mouth. As she glanced back and forth, the Runer took a string of runes out from under his tunic and began to draw them around both places.

"Do you want to die?" the guard asked, a sneer on his face.

Tzarik and Sybal both looked at him.

"I will not die," Sybal said in a quaking voice.

"You deserve it," the guard muttered back.

"Out," Tzarik snapped. To Sybal he said, "Take your clothes off. It's easier that way, trust me."

Sybal didn't know she could become more horrified. She clutched the front of her skirt with her bound hands, frightened at the thought of exposing herself to a man for the first time. And it wouldn't be Rahul or followed by lovemaking.

"Now." The Runer met her eyes this time. She saw something in his face she didn't expect: worry.

"Have you done this before?" she stammered, not moving to remove any of her clothing with the guard leering in the doorway.

"Yes."

"Have they lived?"

"Yes."

Then what did he have to be worried about?

"Will you go already?" she hissed at the guard.

"What do you have to be shy about?" the guard laughed.

A loud, screaming hiss of magical steel being drawn like lightning cut the air. Tzarik unsheathed his orichalcum blade and marched without fear towards the guard.

"I've got duty, anyway," the guard stammered, tripping over his own feet as he practically fled, slamming the door behind him.

"Thank you—" Sybal began.

"Move it," the Runer interrupted, tossing the blade aside and beginning to mix the mysterious ingredients into the beaker.

Sybal began to unlace her top. When the cold wind kissed her chest, her mind collapsed in on itself in fear, going dark. The slither of her clothes falling to the ground tickled her arms. She couldn't see or feel anything as the panic numbed every sense she possessed. She remembered glancing to the door to make sure the stupid guard didn't come back.

When the Runer faced her, he halted before taking her forearm and guiding her to the table. Not sure how she came to lay on it, the cold shackles bit her skin and that's when she realized she held her breath. Then the sobbing came. The Runer cut her deep, the sting taking almost the last of her consciousness. She heard him speaking and saw glowing runes around his neck hanging on his chest. She begged him to stop when what burned like fire in her veins crept down her arm and up the opposite leg. The closer the fire got to her heart, the clearer demons, shadow people, monsters from the deep darkness she could never dream of came into view. They watched her with hollow, white eyes. Slowly —without visibly walking—they crept closer to her, looking down at her, curious about the naked, bleeding, bound woman before them.

"Get away from me!" she screamed so shrilly, she didn't doubt someone—anyone—would come to her rescue. Pulling desperately against the restraints, she tried to escape. Her body out of her own control, she thrashed in pain. No one came to save her. Something touched her chest, her inner thigh. Gasping in total agony and fear, the world finally went black

TZARIK PULLED his hand away when the woman screamed. Her cry cut right through his stone heart. He looked up at the pallet and thatched ceiling, avoiding watching her thrash. If she was anything like him, she'd remember this eventually.

Her cries lessened in a matter of seconds and he finally

allowed himself to look at her. *She's so thin,* he thought. Tall and thin. Her soft fingers showed no signs of use. Gently, he pressed her hand open with his leather-bound fingers. He'd never seen—let alone heard of—a woman Runer. The few Runers he encountered in his life were men. They never spoke of women Runers. Was she the first? A rare find. A diamond in the rough.

She would be a challenge. An opportunity for him to give what had been denied him.

If she lived.

No, he growled to himself. *I won't give myself that opportunity.* What was the point in opening himself up to loss? Failure? She might live, she might not. She might get killed after he chose to bind himself to her. If he left now, the runes might take him for breaking his oath to her.

What would that matter?

***

WAKING up felt like she had slept wrong. Her arms tingled with no feeling, her head ached from lack of oxygen reaching her brain, and her legs were too heavy to lift. She lay on the floor. Her eyes burned as though she had looked into smoke for hours. She blinked, trying to clear the fog but nothing helped. When she pushed herself up, her stomach churned and cramped like never before. Clutching her stomach, she stood up.

The Runer had packed his things and just finished tying his saddlebags closed when he turned to look at her.

"There was nowhere to lie you down. Sorry." He picked up the last of his things. "Well done, you made it through."

"I feel like shit," she gasped, her throat stung when she spoke. Everything stung. Touching the ground hurt. She gently ran her finger down her forearm and the tingle caused pain to shoot through her entire body. "What's happening?" she gasped. She held her hand up. The back crisscrossed with white veins that she could actually see pulsing.

"The runing is just finishing," he explained. His voice turned deep, quiet. "You will be fine in a few days. Make sure you eat something. Make your runes. If you don't, your body might reject the sulfates. You could die."

He picked up her full, black pants—the only piece of clothing she missed—and tossed them to her. He lifted his belts and sheath and made for the door.

"No, wait!" she croaked, stumbling towards him, throwing the pants aside. Every step was agony, sending lightning strikes of pain up her legs. "I...I invoke the trial of two. You took my blood, it's an oath!"

Tzarik turned to glare at her. "You know a lot about Runers."

She gasped, her lungs searing. "You have to take me with you. Show me the way." She collapsed onto her knees, her lower belly cramping in extreme pain. "Help me!"

The Runer weighed her with his icy eyes. She watched him gauge his response. She knew before he said it what it would be.

"No."

Desperate, she tried again, "I've said it, it's an oath. You cannot break the pact, by law as well, you are required to teach me." She stopped. Her stomach moved inside her. A pain like none she ever experienced before ripped through her lower guts and down her thighs. When she took a moment to breathe, Tzarik replied to her plea.

He sighed despondently. "There are more monsters on Bahratt. Do not go to Jarabu. They told me who lives there. Start in Bailu. The villages surrounding it are haunted all the time. That's all the help I can give."

"That's...all?" The desire to vomit bubbled up her belly and into her throat. Still unable to see or comprehend the space around her, she leaned against the bloody table. Touching anything to her skin seared with a million pins and needles. "You have to help me. Don't leave me. I don't know what's happening to me."

When he opened the door, the sun blinded her. She could almost feel the sunlight penetrate her new eyes, slamming into the back of her skull. She cried out and fell over from the pain.

Wanting to chase after him, she tried to find her clothes only to see that he had dressed her. With a desperate grunt, she pushed herself up and ran stumbling out the door. A ways down the path she spotted her family and the black smudge of Tzarik walking quickly away from them.

"Wait!" she screamed, reaching towards his dark shape. The too bright sun blinded her. "Help me, please!"

With one final twist in her stomach, a hot gush of blood and other fluids poured from down her legs. It came as some relief because the unbearable cramping lessened to a dull ache. Looking down, her heart stopped. She stepped back to see what lay on the street.

Between her feet, dripping, shriveled, and black something twitched she had only ever seen in books written by scholars. A mutilated sack with tubes and membrane covering it. Suddenly, she knew why her stomach no longer cramped. She gasped to get air to her head as she stared in horror at her shriveled womb.

Her family ran to her but she could not hear them. Her ovaries splattered on the cobbled, dusty street, slowly leaking down the way. She couldn't move. She heard her mother's screams and cries as if from down a long well. Her father had stormed away minutes ago. A blur that was Rahul moved before her but she could not hear him.

She didn't know how long she stood in the street, half clutching her now empty, useless belly. Her tongue stuck to her dry mouth. When she blinked, she realized she could see the city and the streets. People passed her by, shouting insults, screaming, cursing her. She could hardly blame them; a woman with her womb drying between her feet, standing hunched in the street with her clothing half flapping in the wind was something worth cursing at.

Shaking her leg, she stumbled down the street, away from the walls of her home.

Chapter 10
A Different Job

THE AFTERNOON WORE ON, THE SUN SETTING AND TZARIK felt he didn't deserve its warm, comforting rays. Glancing at his hand that clutched the reins of his horse too tightly, he noticed her blood still caked under his fingernails. She lived. Why did he care so much about abandoning her? Should he go back?

"I didn't abandon her," he mumbled to himself. "She's not my job. She'll be dead soon. And maybe I will be too."

But he did need a job. After watching the naked woman scream in horror, fight him, and after he left her to die hoping her death would break his oath with the runes, he couldn't take what the Qadi offered him. When he reached for the bag of gold, it made him sick.

"Figures I'd get a conscience right at the end," he mumbled to his horse. His gaze returned to his hand, flexing his fingers. He didn't feel different. Did the woman not perish? She lived still. He pulled on the reins to stop his horse. Should he go back? Take her under his wing and train her as a Runer. A lady Runer. Shaking his head to rid it of her, he continued down the streets. He'd spent years perfecting his desire to end it all and the woman interfered. He needed something to distract him.

He scanned some lampposts, announcement boards outside public houses, and even the sides of manure carts for any postings about jobs. A lot of families had lost cats, parrots, wanted their cheating spouse taken care of, or someone thought they were being haunted by an evil djinn. Nothing of substance and most were too petty to bring in even a copper piece. He needed something big that would land him a few weeks of food, drink, and somewhere with at least one wall and a roof.

The city of Hatal had one domed palace within its borders. The golden globes of the palace towers shined against the sandy mountains behind it, protecting it from any attacks from the sea. The palace wasn't just home to the sultana and her family. Nobles from all over the world often lived there for years at a time to see Hatal and the other wonders of Al'Myrah. They would have deep pockets. Some might think they had been cursed and need saving. Others might be haunted by a specter they betrayed in life. Perfect targets. There was one place world travelers with coin would go when visiting a foreign land: the tailor.

Tzarik only had to ask a few citizens to find the most expensive tailor who often ministered to the worldly lords and ladies. To his interest, the tailor didn't blanch at being asked questions by a Runer.

"You are in time for traveling royalty," the tailor mumbled through a mouth full of pins as he worked on an elaborate golden gown covered in delicate details and beading. "It is the sultana's birthday and she is throwing a three day long gala. Art, acrobats, troubadours, and a lot of rich people. Some from Caerwren in the far west. Not much call for Runers out here, but you could offer other services."

Tzarik winced, dropping the hat he had been absentmindedly admiring. "Other...services?"

"Bodyguard." The tailor sighed, flaring the hem of the robe out on his floor to check the line. He looked up at Tzarik over his round glasses. "What did you think I meant?"

"Bodyguard?" he asked instead, crossing his arms and pushing out his chest.

"Hatal is an advanced kingdom, Runer. Not all see our ways as civilized; some see it as a mad grab for power. There is an entire

world out there, you know. Our sultana has survived three assassination attempts already. The assassins have never been caught."

Tzarik grunted, thinking. "Then why throw a party? Doesn't
that open her up to more attacks? Wouldn't she have her own
trained guard?"

"She does," the tailor nodded. "Can one ever have too many
swords? Or trained eyes watching?" Now he looked up at Tzarik.
He didn't flinch when the Runer's unnatural eyes met his.

"Thank you. I don't have any coin to give you for your
information."

The tailor shrugged and went back to the hem. "No matter,
Runer. We are patriots. Watch out for our sultana."

THE ONLY BENEFIT of being a Runer was that Tzarik rarely had
to introduce himself, explain his presence, or barter for an audience. When he told the guard at the door to the palace that he
wanted to offer his trained observations and sword for the safety of
the sultana, they let him inside and brought him to the sultana's
First Man, Kalil. He expected the favorite bedfellow of a powerful
sultana to be sullen, tall, and chiseled. Kalil hardly stood taller
than Tzarik, had a boyish smile, and energy to last for days as he
practically skipped down the ornamented halls to greet him.

"Runer!" He grinned broadly, showing some of the whitest
teeth Tzarik had ever seen. "I told my habibi, 'you know what we
need? A Runer! Their eyes can see things ours cannot' and here
you are!"

Tzarik stiffened as the youth wrapped his arms around his
shoulders and embraced him. "We don't have magical eyes. I just
observe what's already there."

Kalil wagged his finger in the Runer's face. "No, no! Look at
those icy gems. Fantastic! Now, please, follow me. No offense, but

you stink to the gods and back. Let's get you washed and clothed, yes?"

Before Tzarik could even think of the words to argue with, the gilded young man guided him down more open hallways with colorful scarves and banners waving in the hot wind. Guests already covered the man-made green lawns, smelled the flowers, and some even took their boots and sandals off to walk in the fountains and pools underneath waterfalls.

"I've never seen a grander palace," Tzarik mused to the kind youth.

"Our sultana has done much to make it the jewel of the east. And Hatal is the biggest, most advanced city on Al'Myrah. Here." He ushered the Runer inside his own chambers. The round room opened wide onto a balcony doused in potted flowers and colorful lounges. A bed the size of which Tzarik had never seen waited in the corner, covered in silk. A vanity with a poof stool and a large mirror showed him his haggard face and the clothes the cursed Vicdan had left him.

Kalil's face poked over his shoulder as he glared at his reflection. "Not used to seeing yourself, I imagine?"

"I hate mirrors," Tzarik confirmed.

Tzarik waited for the First Man to pull open a privacy screen and allow the Runer to undress and bathe in the golden tub without an audience. He didn't even hear the man vanish and reappear, tossing a pile of silken garments to him from the other side.

"Some of my finer wear," he said and Tzarik could hear his smile.

"Tell me about tonight," Tzarik asked as he cleaned and dressed himself. "I only know rumors, but I am guessing by your willingness to allow me in there is a scandal afoot."

"You come during dangerous times," Kalil admitted from behind the screen. Tzarik heard him combing his hair. "The politics are outrageous and our sultana hopes to quell some smoldering fires before they erupt into wildfire."

"I've never cared for politics."

"But we have coin, of course."

The Runer pulled the light blue silk over his head and thought about his price. Watch the sultana. How hard could it be?

"Three days?" he asked.

"This is day three," Kalil offered. "We have been fortunate the last two nights. But I..." he sighed heavily. "I think she is too cavalier. We have been lucky is all. The assassin has to have been here the last two nights, just never had his chance to strike. He will tonight."

"Hmm," Tzarik mumbled. "You love her, don't you?"

"Of course. I was her first. We were thirteen, you know. Too young, my parents thought. But when the sultana of Hatal asks for you to be one of her harem you hardly say no, do you?"

"I don't know," Tzarik confessed. "Like I said, I don't understand politicians. And male harems even less."

Kalil shrugged, planting the Runer before the vanity now and brushing his long hair. "Can I ask a question?"

Tzarik met the young man's eyes in the mirror.

Taking that as permission, he asked, "What is a foot long and slippery?"

Confused, Tzarik frowned and shook his head.

"A slipper!" Kalil crowed, victorious in his joke over the Runer. "Don't be offended, I didn't mean to laugh at your expense."

The Runer's left brow flicked up and down quickly, and he nodded. "I get it."

Kalil beamed, tying the Runer's hair up into a high ponytail. "I was wondering if you could laugh. I'll take the brow as laughter. I heard that Runer's lose all emotion when they lose their red blood."

"Lies," Tzarik said, standing up. "Helps those who kill us rest their conscience, I assume." Inspecting his reflection, he couldn't help but touch the soft fabric. "I smell like incense."

"It's called clean." Kalil smiled again. "Let me show you the grounds."

They left the sleeping wing of the palace and Kalil excitedly showed him the kitchens, the servants' quarters, the gardens, and the entryway for the last ball where the lord steward would stand during the evening, calling the names of the dignitaries and their escorts. Tzarik made note of anything that caught his eyes: the banners that ran the entire palace above them just for decoration. They were not thick but a well-trained acrobat or fighter could perch on them. Especially someone of smaller stature like himself.

"I'd like to see the sultana's library," he said when he caught sight of a guest with a book. He had not seen a single bookshelf yet.

Kalil winced, bouncing down the hallway unbothered by the odd request. "It is her personal collection. I'd rather introduce you to a few of the guests." He raised his brows, biting his lower lip with expectancy.

Tzarik understood. "I'd love to speak with them."

THE COOL DESERT night air gently rippled through the halls. Tzarik faced the wind to calm the white poison in his veins that rushed to his face, turning him pale as the moon. Beside him stood Kalil, the sultana in all her finery, a dignitary from Bahratt with lotus flowers embroidered on his coat, and a pale, yellow-haired man from the continent of Caerwren. He stood with the most attention, eyes bulging in fear as he tried to comprehend the rapid foreign language he knew little of. He laughed on cue but the sweat beading on his upper lip told Tzarik he hardly understood.

He had not interacted with people of this caste often so he kept his mouth shut, observing rather than expending the energy to interact. No one seemed to mind at first, but he felt the onslaught of questions coming later.

Sultana Amira pulled herself away from the lord from Bahratt and smiled at Tzarik from behind her face veil. Jewels encrusted her face, making her dark eyes sparkle. "Kalil has explained my special situation to you?" she whispered in a melodious, sensual tone. "I expect you to blend in as well. No butchering brutality if you please."

The Runer tried to keep his face passive but felt his eyes narrow in annoyance. "I will do my best."

She smiled gratefully. "Then escort Kalil, will you? I have appearances to keep up."

Tzarik stepped away from the entering royals and lined up outside the door with Kalil. The young man also bedazzled his face to match his sultana's and a colorful kufiya hung down his back. They gave their names to the man at the door. Something unfamiliar overtook Tzarik amidst the finery and pomp of the palace and he gave a false name to the man.

Kalil walked out into the light with Tzarik at his side and the man announced, "Kalil Al'Amira and Ice Ucksmel Eebals!" loudly to the watching crowd. It had the desired effect and several of the guests look up confused and some laughing.

Kalil's eyes went wide and he spit from laughing so hard. "Really, Runer?" he guffawed. "I had no idea you had such a humorous side."

"I owed you a good joke for the slippers from before," he replied, his left brow flicking up and down quickly.

"It was divine." Kalil beamed. "But here is where I leave you. Please, watch the guests. We cannot stand a royal assassination right now."

The crowd milled in waves out into the gardens and back into the dance hall. He passed a woman who boasted about how she bought all new clothes in Hatal. Her hair was mercilessly tied into a veil with dozens of golden clasps. She continuously fidgeted with a ring no longer on her finger. She traveled to Hatal just to gala-vant with a particular merchant and leave no trace.

He wondered if the woman—Sybal her name was—had been this kind of woman. He watched the unfaithful woman, trying to imagine her in Runer leather, wielding the blade and a string of runes. He couldn't quite make it happen and imagined Sybal instead. Suddenly, he lost his appetite. Something made him feel ill. Maybe this job was a mistake...

The yellow-haired man from Caerwren found him first, cornering him in a hallway with little light across from the glowing gardens. He braced himself for whatever questions the foreigner might have.

"You are a Runer?" the man asked agonizingly slowly in Tzarik's own tongue. "Do you speak Caerwren at all?"

"No, sorry," Tzarik said quickly, his eyes roving over the man to spot any danger before he made a move. "But your Al'Myrah is fine." He wanted to say he talked like a child but reminded himself to not insult the royalty.

"We have Runers, too, of Caerwren," he smiled nervously. "A guild. They are in a guild. But with your coloring, you stand out."

Trying not to be insulted by the man's ignorance and comments on the color of his flesh, Tzarik steered the conversation another way. "How does your government like Hatal and its leader?"

"Amira?" the man asked quickly. "Love her! Trade so good in Caerwren."

He tried to remember that just because a man could not speak his language, did not make him ignorant. Or stupid. "She is power-ful. It would be a shame if someone from another continent wished her harm."

"Aye, it would!" His hands didn't flinch, his face open and sincere. "Should Hatal ever need aid, we have ships on the sea!"

Nodding, Tzarik began to walk away. This man was harmless. He ignored the hollered-out questions and moved on. He spoke to the man from Bahratt next. Surrounded by a gaggle of fawning women and even a few men, he boasted about his own wealth.

"For a woman with such an advanced civilization, she really should have a public library," the princeling said, holding his chin high. "In my city of Bailu, we have the grandest library open to the public."

"She likes to keep her library private," Tzarik mused cautiously.

"She doesn't have a library," the man from Bailu said pompously. "I would have found it by now with my thirst for knowledge, trust me!"

"You are so wise," one of the girls gasped, reaching out desperately to touch the man's arm.

Curious, the Runer pried himself from the group and retraced his steps to where Kalil first mentioned the library. It had been down a narrow hall, smaller than the grand openings of the other walkways. He kept his icy eyes sharp, watching the people watching him. A woman from the snowy mountains of Rhostrana eyed him as he passed. The royalty in Volograd kept Masakh slaves. Beside this woman stood a Masakh with feathered skin, bird-like legs which ended in the clawed, bare feet of a falcon. They had human faces and often human hands mixed with the features of their immortal animal-kind. The Masakh slave watched him with sad, yellow eyes. Part of him wanted to tell the Masakh to leave the woman; in Al'Myrah, Masakh were free, revered people. He would never understand how an entire continent enslaved such powerful beings.

"Have something to say, white blood?" the Rhostrana woman barked when she saw him look too long.

Against his better judgment, he ignored her, knowing she would go and gossip to her fellows about the rude Runer. But he had bigger things on his mind: like the giant purse of gold he would acquire if he made sure the sultana lived through the night.

He stuck to the shadows, turning his face away to hide the glow of his blue eyes whenever a guest passed. Taking in the structure of the palace he deduced where the library might be and eventually found himself in an empty part of the royal wing. Recalling some tall, glassed windows from the outside, he followed the hall to a statue in a dead end. The bust showed a powerful woman clutching the world in her hand and a scimitar in the other.

"This has to be the way in," he mumbled. But no door presented itself. He examined the statue but found no part of it moved or lowered to open a secret door.

He took up an oil lamp and used his own flint and steel to light it. He let it burn for just a few moments then blew it out, watching where the light smoke went. Repeating this all around the statue, he watched as the smoke drifted towards it, then passed behind it like something sucked it back.

So it did open.

Stepping back, he examined the statue. He couldn't force it open, it would be too heavy and he might knock it over, breaking it and alerting anyone nearby. Judging from the dress and posture of the statue, it was the likeness of a past sultana. She held the world in her hands. This woman wanted to be worshiped.

Checking to see no one else stood behind him, Tzarik knelt and moved to kiss the statue's feet. When he put pressure near its sandaled feet, a whirring from behind softly started and the statue began to rotate. When it did, it moved so fast that he didn't think before leaping through the tiny opening it created. Landing softly, he crouched behind a large desk. This was one of the rare times where he appreciated being short.

Voices from a few yards away stopped when they heard the soft sounds. He reached into his tunic and held the buhkar rune in his hand, slowly drawing it before him. Finished, he stowed the rune and stood up, invisible for a few moments, allowing him to see the ones conversing.

Surprised, he saw Amira herself and her own guards, scribe, and advisor Aziz. The sultana's face shown red in the moonlight and Aziz's brow furrowed in aggravation.

"This is the last night," Amira hissed. "Get it done, Aziz. I want Kalil's body on the wall in five minutes or it will be yours! And you," she turned to the captain of her guard. "How hard is it to kill a few low level dignitaries before supper?"

Buhkar wore off. He had not drawn slow enough to make the rune last longer. He didn't move.

"You are planning to kill yourself?" he asked.

The group before him jumped, drawing weapons. Amira covered her face quickly, pulling her veil up.

"How did you get in here, Runer?" Amira spat. She shook her head. "Do I have to kill you, too? Shame. Runers are becoming so rare."

"I wouldn't," Tzarik began. "Others know I am here."

Amira's body shifted as she searched for a solution.

"Creating international hostility is stupid," he went on. "I should have known that you were designing the assassination yourself. I can't stop you, but you need to think beyond the market you want to create with war." He easily kept the surprise off his stoic face. "I am surprised though. You control an entire continent. Do you know the damage you could do? You are our ruler, sabi."

The sultana scoffed, arching her back in a laugh. "I didn't think you cared. I thought a Runer would be perfect. But now you have to go and put your boar in the fight."

"Kalil worships you, sabi." He chose to speak politely. "Your city is thriving. Al'Myrah is one of the most advanced continents on the map. We colonized Bahratt and parts of Alika over hundreds of years. Why do this?"

Aziz stepped forward, blocking Amira from sight. "The dead rise, Runer. This is the end of times. Tribes from Porsh move across the desert sands, their black wagons are mass graves. Dead things—creatures—do not stay dead. Do you know how long it has been since Porsh made a wave in civilized society?"

He didn't reply right away. He saw the farmer's dead dog watching him. Slowly, he replied, "I have seen what you speak of. Once. Perhaps. I'm not sure."

Amira slumped, leaning against a bookshelf. "I am sure. You will see for yourself soon enough, I think."

Now Tzarik understood. The sultana and her advisors thought the world was coming to end and wanted to take down their entire kingdom with it. They were far more frightened then they needed to be.

"Killing monsters is my trade." Tzarik tried to sound comforting. "Don't hurt your people just because you are scared of what *might* happen. Wait. Just a few months."

"I said we should stay strong," Aziz put in, visibly relaxing. He sighed loudly. "I am glad you are here, Runer."

"But what am I to do?" Amira asked, her voice breaking slightly. "All those closest to me know what I planned."

"Do whatever you did before you swallowed the fear," Tzarik advised. "Leave this to those whose job it is to kill monsters and don't become one out of fear."

ONCE THE SUN ROSE, Tzarik left the palace faster than he had ever vanished before. Even faster than the one time an entire village of inbred maniacs wanted to cook him with potatoes.

"This is why I hate royalty," he told his horse as he saddled it up outside the palace walls. "Something small happens, they panic, and have the power to destroy an entire continent with their foolishness. One man, or woman, should not have that much power."

Part of him wanted to spend all the gold in his pouch. Amira paid him to keep quiet rather than to save her life from her own assassination and to report back to her if he learned anything about the Porshains or the rising dead. He wouldn't get paid to investigate but the draw of the mystery pulled at him.

"Maybe this is the kind of monster I need," he mused, leaving Hatal. "Something dead to take me with it."

His horse nickered lightly.

"Mmhmm." He nodded, having no idea what his steed wanted to communicate. "She might have made a fine Runer."

The horse gnashed the bit between its teeth.

Tzarik sighed. He had told Sybal to head to Bahratt. Maybe she had taken his advice. Maybe she was there now hunting a ghoul or were-creature. She probably needed help.

"Fine," he sighed. "Back to Bahratt then."

Chapter 11
Leaving Home

THE OUTSKIRTS OF ALA'NAR ALWAYS LOOKED LIKE A DARK moat surrounding the city. A place Sybal never thought she'd be. The gutters smelled of excrement, the people ran barefoot, and smoke drifted out of most windows. A woman claiming to be a magi sold her card readings for a dozen coins next to a shop that sold substances she thought had been outlawed inside the city. An old shop with wooden instruments of string and wind stuck out as the brightest front in the whole place for a mile with its vibrant yellow façade and green door.

As the sun set behind the golden walls, taking its heat and light with it, she had to find someplace warm. Her skin sent cold shivers down her spine when she touched it. Rubbing her arms for warmth felt like touching a marble statue in the moonlight. She could not stop staring at the veins under her dark skin on her wrist. Where once a blue, life-giving river had flowed now a hard, almost stagnant white poison slowly slithered through her veins. Without the warmth, she could not stop shaking and breathing came in gasps as she tried to get oxygen to her brain.

Close to the city gates, a public house called The Last Chance loomed over the streets like a vulture. She could not leave the city in the dead of night. Scared she might be stabbed for her jewelry, she waited and watched the patrons go in and out, wondering if one might be decent enough to help her. She didn't know how to talk to these kinds of people.

A young man in worn, but wealthy clothes, swaggered up to

the door. The man at the door stopped him, shaking his head, and flexed threateningly as he grunted a warning. This was her chance. The man appeared to either be a lord or a son of a lord. Her kind of people. She quickly walked up behind him and tapped him on the shoulder.

"Are you traveling?" she asked quickly, pulling her garments over her exposed shoulder.

The man turned to face her, his forelock attractively falling in front of his dark brown eyes. He smiled crookedly and yet charmingly.

"I am desperate to leave this sordid city and return to real finery like Hatal," he grumbled. "But I have not the coin for transport."

She saw his eyes flick to her necklace and back to her face so quickly, she almost gasped in surprised when she caught it. She noticed how the soles of his elegant boots were worn thin. He kept one hand behind his back. His hair had polish in it from probably a week ago. Not understanding how she observed everything so quickly, she also shocked herself by putting together all the pieces and realized that this man had most likely been kicked out of his estate and disinherited. She also saw the tips of his fingers had shiny calluses.

Taking his bedazzled arm in her shaking hand, she pulled him aside and whispered. "Do you play an instrument?"

The young man frowned at her, shocked. "Yes, the wheel fiddle. How did you know? My father forced me to. Stupid instrument, crying and droning like a cat in heat."

Personally, Sybal loved the wheel fiddle. The clicking of the keys and buzzing of the wheel always made her want to twirl and move her hips like the vagabond street dancers.

"Look, you have no money and your family is obviously not going to help you."

"How—?" he started again but she kept going.

"My name is Sybal. I need to get out of Ala'Nar as well. Far away to Bahratt. I know how desperate you are so if I get you a wheel fiddle, will you play in that public house and get us a room?"

Intrigued and hungrily looking her up and down again, the man smiled. "Vicdan is the name. Gambling is my game." He shook her hand enthusiastically. "How do you plan on getting your hands on a fiddle?"

She almost smiled. "Theft was not my crime."

STEALING a wheel fiddle from the bright, cheery shop proved easier than she thought. The guilt set in before they even left the store. Vicdan distracted the merchant by asking him about a few long horns that reached from his mouth all the way to the floor he had imported from Oceanya while she found a small, ornate wheel fiddle decorated in greens, blues, and yellows. She easily slid it under her dress, holding it in place like a woman cradling her preg- nant stomach. She swallowed hard to not allow the emotion or the memory of her life-creating insides spilling from her like waste cloud her actions.

She wandered out of the store then called for Vicdan like a nagging wife and together they ran back down the blocks to the dilapidated inn.

"You are a natural," Vicdan beamed, taking the instrument and giving the handle a few turns making the strings sing. "What is your profession?"

Sybal looked him in the eyes. Could he not see her blue eyes? The white veins under her skin? "Disinherited heiress," she smiled, shrugging, trying to make light of their sorrows.

A different man stood guard at the door this time and let them in when they made themselves out to be traveling jongleurs. He pointed them to the owner, instructing them to speak to her. The innkeeper, an older woman with jet-black hair, red lips, and a glare that would frighten an army general, stared unamused as they bargained for food and shelter. After Vicdan played a few notes for her to prove he wasn't a charlatan, she told him to sit near the back to play.

"I bet you thought I couldn't play," Vicdan smiled as he cranked the handle.

Sybal frowned. "It was my idea. I knew you could. Now sing something good." She drained a mug of weak mead and set the cup out for coin as he played.

Collapsing onto a seat next to him, she dropped her face into her hands. The mead only slightly warmed her. She waited until there were a few silver coins before going back to the innkeeper to rent a room. Desperate to get a moment alone, she told Vicdan to keep playing and went up alone to take stock of her new self.

She shut the door and locked it from the inside. Two beds with a washstand between them set her heart at rest. She slowly walked to the mirror on the stand and prepared to behold her new appearance. Confused, her eyes did not glow back at her in the dim light. She leaned forward, wiping some of the grime off the mirror. Her veins were hardly white. Her eyes were still brown. A trickle of fear ran down her spine. Had the runing not taken to her? Would her body reject the sulfates? Gripping the side of the washstand, her heart skipping a beat, she knew she had to find the Runer who had changed her. Only he would know.

"And that is how it's done!" Vicdan announced, barging in with a second key. He took her hand in his and gave her a portion of the coin. "Enough left for a ride on the next caravan out of Ala'Nar."

Grateful, she pocketed the coin and rolled onto her bed. She gasped when Vicdan rolled next to her, sliding his arm shamelessly around her waist.

"What are you doing?" she cried, pushing him hard. He hardly budged.

He smiled through his draped forelock again. "Congratulating you."

"No." She turned away.

With a sigh of defeat, Vicdan rolled off and she heard him kick his boots off, mumbling about hot water and women. She didn't try to listen, didn't care. She needed to find the Runer before it was too late. He mentioned Bahratt. Would he be there?

Forcing her eyes closed, she hurried herself under the blankets, desperate for warmth. If her heart had been able to, it would have pounded in fear.

SHE WOKE EARLY the next morning, desperate to get on a caravan to take her across the straight to Bahratt to track down the Runer. She lay awake for just a few moments, contemplating stopping in the colorful kingdom. Rahul might have already returned home. He might still be in Ala'Nar, wondering what to do now that his betrothed not only transformed into a monster but committed a monstrous crime.

No, she thought, taking a deep breath. *I will not go to Jarabu.* It would put him and his entire kingdom in danger. She'd bypass Jarabu and go to Bailu like the Runer said. Gods willing, the haunted villages would be a decent training ground. Maybe a knowledgeable witch or warlock could tell her what to do with this new life.

When she started to rise. Every part of her from her limbs to the roots of her hair screamed in agony with such buzzing pain that she let out a cry. Every little movement pulsed agony, like her whole body had lost blood flow for hours. Slowly, she moved her fingers, trying to get the sulfates flowing again. It hurt. She moved her right leg and the white pain exploded up to her chest. The will to get up had never been so dire. She knew the caravans left early and this was her only chance.

Screaming, she sat up and dropped her feet over the side of the bed. Her head spun and an instant headache split her skull. Out of habit, she reached to straighten her necklace. Her fingers delicately touched only her flesh. Looking around, no sign of Vicdan could be found. Her bracelets, earrings, necklace, and the pile of coin he had given her were gone. Bellowing a curse like she never had before, she stood up. She needed clothes and a ride. Things that were not easy to come by.

Stealing the blanket from her bed, she climbed out the window so the angry innkeeper would not see her leaving with it. If nothing else, she would not be cold at night. Dashing through the early risers, farmers, and merchants she made her way to the gate where the caravans were already beginning to move. She made a quick scan for Vicdan but did not see him. She wanted to hate him, but the scandalous side of her admired the thieving rogue.

A fish merchant with a large covered wagon caught her eye. Running to him, she cried out, "Where are you headed, sira?"

The man looked down at her from his wagon in disgust. "What you want, vagabond? I have no more fish on me. Go beg somewhere else."

Calling on her patience, she said, "I don't want food." Her stomach had not even mentioned being hungry since the runing, and she hoped it stayed that way for some time. "I want to ride with you. I'm desperate. Please."

Pressing his lips to one side to look like a fish in thought, the man's eyes slowly roved up and down her midsection. "What can you pay with?"

Her heart sank. Of course he'd want to be paid to let her sit in the back of his wagon.

"I had money," she said, lowering her head. "I could have paid you. But I can't right now. I can later."

The fish man laughed, his hairy, fat belly rippling. "Always later with you folk. Never now. You know when later is, sabi? Never!" He spat and tucked his kufiya around his neck. He clicked his tongue and his mules began to clop towards the sands.

"Wait!" Sybal shouted, running after him, pulling on the reins. "What can I do to come with you?"

A sneer the likes of which Sybal had never seen before spread his scabbing lips wide over yellowing teeth. "There are a few things a girl like you could do. If you're really desperate."

"Wait!"

Sybal spun around, somehow having already committed the young singer's voice to memory. "You!" she shrieked.

"Don't call the guard on me," Vicdan pleaded with a grin, holding his hands up.

With a cry like the wild women of the north, Sybal cocked her elbow back and cracked her fist into Vicdan's alabaster nose. Blood soaked her fingers as she gripped the front of his tunic and readied another blow.

"I said wait!" the young man coughed, spitting blood and saliva onto her face. He reached into the little satchel on his belt and pulled out a cloth wrapped around a dozen tiny objects.

Furious, Sybal took the package and pushed him away. He stumbled and fell backwards, still reeling from the impact of her punch. She opened it to find her jewelry and a few coins inside. The anger sizzling in her still-nauseated belly dissipated and her shoulders dropped.

"I'm sorry to have hit you, but you disappeared. With my things!" she shouted, brandishing them.

Vicdan nodded, staying down and holding up one hand to ward her off just in case. "I know. I'm sorry, it's a force of habit now brought on by my desire to survive. I..."

He stopped and wiped the tears from his eyes. He grinned broadly despite the pain that must be have been ringing through his skull.

"Then why bring them back?" she asked, forcing herself to speak gently.

Sensing it was safe, Vicdan pushed himself back up onto his feet and dusted off his backside. "I'm not a monster, Lady Sybal. I have a conscience. Sometimes. It doesn't help when one is starving though."

Looking the pathetic man up and down, she understood. With a heavy sigh, she handed him back all but the coins. "I need the motivation. Take it. And make better life decisions."

Vicdan's brown eyes grew large with gratitude and he kissed her hand, taking the proffered items. "You're kind, Lady Sybal."

She nodded, wiping his blood onto her silks. "Sometimes."

Turning back to the ugly man, she held the coins up to him. "For passage into Bahratt."

Chapter 12

◆

Twice Dead

"I'M LOOKING FOR DEAD THINGS," TZARIK REPEATED TO THE old man. He stood in a small, thatched town hall with sandy walls. The old man before him sat on a throne made of wood and quartz with a wide turban on his head that he continuously had to set straight as the weight kept tilting it to one side with every movement.

He had traveled a few days and ran into a small village south of the grand metropolis of Hatal. It would be days to Bahratt and he needed a job along the way. He couldn't come to Sybal with empty pockets.

A fence made of woven branches surrounded the place. Meant to keep out strangers, the archaic weave hung so loose and shallow in the earth that it flapped in the wind, only able to keep out disoriented drunks. The rocky ground made for a solid foundation, but the homes were so small, add-ons made them look like mutating monsters. The one-room-town hall had a firepit in the center and the elected officials tried their best to put on airs for the visitor. When Tzarik mentioned he was a Runer, the little man almost shot his turban off in excitement.

"We could use your talents," the village chief said hopefully. "We have an abu al salasel, you see."

"Really?" Tzarik didn't mean to sound condescending but his face could not hide his casual disbelief. "That's a pretty mean spirit. Are you sure?"

The chief shook his head. "No, but it hasn't always been here. A man came to our village with a companion of ill repute. I believe he was a sorcerer."

Tzarik rolled his eyes and turned to leave.

"Don't go yet!"

He snapped back around. "Sorcerers are rare. The power it takes to trap a djinn is unfathomable. There have been two in recorded history. I doubt one is going to show up at your doorstep and cast spells in the streets of your pathetic rock village."

Obviously hurt, the chief sank into his quartz throne, nervously wringing his fingers. "There was a man in black. With eyes like yours."

Now, this interested him more. "Go on."

"Black robes. Hooded. So pale. His flesh was like alabaster. But the scriptures upon his skin were...terrifying."

Tzarik knew of only one sect of magic users that wrote scriptures on their skin. "Written in black? Like a tattoo?"

The man nodded. "On his face and hands. The rest of him covered by his horrible black robes."

Necromancer. He dared not speak the word out loud to the frightened chief. The students of death from Porsh hardly ever traveled alone. They were a tribal people.

"You spoke to them?" he asked.

"Not to the man in black, no!" He shivered. "The other man was...normal. Said they were headed back to Bahratt."

"Thank you." Tzarik picked up his cloak and strode away.

"What about the abu al salasel?" the old man called after him.

"Just listen for clanking chains. If you hear them, run."

He wanted the coin. He wanted to fight and an abu al salasel would be a worthy opponent. Maybe even finally end his life. But too many preached on the afterlife. He saw firsthand what happened when a restless, angry spirit turned vengeful. The arts of the Porshains were forbidden, dark, evil magics but if anything could stop his spirit from returning to this world after death they would know. He had to put aside all the horror stories he had heard about necromancers and reminded himself that if this man in black killed him, that was, after all, what he wanted.

Taking a small ship across the Black Sea, he landed on the shores of Bahratt once again and somehow knew exactly where to go. Drawn by instincts, he cut across the continent with a caravan and returned to Bailu. Something in the runes told him that's where he needed to be.

THE TANG of blood stung his nose and the roar of thousands of screams split the air before Tzarik saw the growing central city of Bailu in the sand and dust the wind had kicked up. Rushing up a tall dune, he looked down at the city nestled near the roots of the mountain. Terror twisted his guts. Screams flew towards him. He had not felt a wind the entire journey and once Bailu came into view, the hot force ripped his hair back behind him. The gale torrent seemed to appear out of nowhere.

About half a kilometer away, a caravan of merchants, families, and travelers began to scatter. Some ran towards Bailu while others fled for the hills. Knowing they would run into monsters, he dashed towards the city, shouting for them to stay outside and away from the mountains.

"Hide in the hills!" a man screamed as his flock dashed away.

"Don't be stupid," Tzarik cried over the wind. "Get away from the city. Can't you see it's under siege?"

As he ran closer, gasping for air in the sand-sodden winds, he heard the fighting. Clashing of swords, the bang of a black powder bomb, screams. The tangy scent of iron stopped his breath.

"What happened?" he shouted at a young shepherd fleeing the city.

"Black magic!" the boy screamed as he ran like a madman.

Tzarik covered his face with part of his head covering and drew his orichalcum blade. Gripping the halat rune tightly in his palm, he drew the protective circle around himself. He drew as slowly as he dared but got interrupted when a pack of fleeing warriors rounded a corner. One was wounded so badly he couldn't walk, two others holding him up. Behind them, he saw a battle.

One group comprised of the citizens, warriors, and what military Bailu had at the moment—mostly temple guards. The others were a ragged, thin, jerky fleet of mismatched fighters with spears, bows, and swords. Some didn't even have weapons, charging citizens with their bare hands. The city had once felt empty to him, when he had come looking for work, finding the crocatta, and failing. But now, the streets were glutted to immobility with terrified people.

Taking his sword, he vaulted off the wall and stabbed an incoming enemy directly through the face. The man fell backwards, tongue lolling out of a gray, shriveled face. He didn't have time to look on in horror at the corpselike man before another attack came from behind. A swarm flooded around a corner.

Tzarik leapt up a stack of empty barrels, vaulted off another wall, and landed on top of a building, looking down. Observing, he tried to see where the flood came from but he couldn't find a specific point of entrance.

Clamoring alerted him to an attack from behind. The staggering steps and swish of garments told him the assailant had lunged sloppily towards him. Leaping up, he flipped backwards over the attacker to stab him in the back. The attacker growled a deep groan but didn't stop. Flailing its sword, it reached around, nicking his neck.

Confused and shaken, Tzarik pulled his sword out and stepped farther back. The enemy turned with stilted steps, head lolling to the side, and began to advance on him again. Taking only a second to look him over, Tzarik saw the possessed man donned a coat of arms from Rhostrana and still wore the thick fur cloak of his people. The gray flesh hung off the warrior's body around his chin, exposing dried up muscle and sun-bleached bones. Looking over the edge of the building he perched on, he noticed many wore Rhostrana garb from various czars' armies. Some were over a hundred years old. Others in the attacking mob wore Bahratt uniforms and some looked like people from Ze'oul, in the far east, with wingless dragons coiling around their armor. A few staggered with only bones for legs and others' bodies still had flesh covering most of their insides.

Not being a religious man, he couldn't think of a god to swear by as he tried to wrap his head around these monstrosities.

He watched too long. The Rhostrana fighter lunged onto him, pushing him back over the edge. With a cry, Tzarik somersaulted over the fighter and landed hard on his back. When he hit the ground, five others swarmed to him, stabbing at him with various sharp weapons.

One small spear pierced his side. Grunting, sweat beading on his scalp, he quickly drew the halat rune with one hand and the jiun with the other. The first pushed the attackers back just inches and the other ignited the fury flowing through his veins. The jiun rune allowed him to push past his inhibitions, making him faster and stronger. With a scream like a wild beast, Tzarik flipped up onto his feet and parried the attacks, dismembering the small swarm with quick, deft, terrifying attacks. In a matter of seconds, he made an opening of retreat for himself.

Clutching his side, he ran through the crowd, drawing artiah over his wound. He moved quickly, making the rune weak but enough to staunch the bleeding. His body would not replace the sulfates, he had to hold on to as much as he could. He fought off a few more enemies as he made his way to the farmer's home.

Before he reached it, however, someone cried out to him.

"Runer!" a woman with wild, blonde hair whipping about in the wind screamed. She appeared in front of him, blocking his path a few yards away. Her eyes bulged in surprise at seeing him.

He recognized her as the woman he had put through the trials little more than a fortnight ago. She did as he said and came to Bahratt. Seeing her brought back the memory of her thrashing.

Azar abandoning him...His own fear. These memories always brought him back to the frightened boy he had been.

He couldn't do it. Not now as she looked him in the face. Tzarik dodged down a side street and ran, pushing past corpses and fleeing people.

"Don't run from me!" she shouted. Somehow, she appeared right behind him, galloping down the streets like a wild mare.

He had to admire her tenacity. Trying to be cleverer than her, he stalled so she almost caught up, ran up the wall—flipping over her head—and tried to dash away. But Sybal was too fast. Like lightning, she seized his hood and slammed his entire frame onto the dusty ground. Tzarik cursed his small stature as the wind was knocked out of him, banging against the sandy stone.

Sybal screamed before addressing him as one of the invading army staggered at her, swinging wildly with its sword. Flipping his legs while using his arms to leap up, Tzarik managed to kick it in the face. They both gazed in horror as its partially decayed head left its body like a ball kicked into the air.

"You could have gotten killed!" Tzarik roared at her, pushing his long hair out of his eyes.

"Because you wouldn't stop," she spit back, unafraid of his malice.

Grabbing her arm, he pulled her aside as a fresh mob of both citizens of Bailu and the rotting soldiers clogged the street.

Reaching down, he pulled a sword from a dead woman and handed it to her. "We have to get out of here first."

Together, they slinked through the streets, cleaving any who got too close. He observed how sloppily she handled the sword. She swung at a diving attacker and almost took his head off with its head.

He stopped, slowly drawing halat before him.

"What are you doing?" she panted, holding the sword between her legs as she tied up her hair.

"Protecting myself from you," he grunted.

"This is why I need you," she pleaded in the midst of the onslaught. "You have to show me what to do."

"Move!" he shouted, pushing her as a rain of arrows cascaded down from a handful of enemies armed with bows.

They fought their way towards the center of town where Tzarik was sure they could see the flow of soldiers. Scanning quickly, he saw a few in ranks as if just entering the battle. But he couldn't see far as most everyone in the town towered over him.

"Woman," he barked, "can you see where those marching troops are coming from?"

"My name is Sybal." She craned her neck. "Yes. The north gate." Quickly, she scanned the square and pointed. "To the water tower. Come on."

Not arguing, Tzarik followed her and together they scrambled up the ladder.

"What am I looking for?" she wondered out loud.

Tzarik squinted. "The wind didn't reach me until I crossed over the dune. Look towards the mountains."

Only a second passed before Sybal cried, "There!" She pointed north. "On the outcropping of that cliff. A man."

Glaring through the sand storm, Tzarik spotted a figure in a black robe. The man stood still as a statue, his hands in front of his chest, inches apart. Taking up his glass, he commanded Sybal to take care of the enemy that began to ascend the ladder behind them. He heard her grunt, gasp, and scream. Looking through the glass, he could just make out the man's chilling blue eyes under his deep hood.

"Necromancer," he mused. "Sybal, come back. Over the wall."

They climbed to the top of the tower and leapt to the adjacent wall. Sprinting low to the ground, they ran to the north gate. Tzarik tied a rope from his belt to one of the spires and they descended quickly. He saw the remains of the footprints of a hundred undead soldiers washed away in the swirling wind. Clever.

"What is that?" Sybal coughed. "Can we fight it?"

"We might not have to," Tzarik replied. Drawing halat again, he cut a path through the sand, pushing his hands wide so the man in black would see them coming.

They marched towards the robed figure undaunted. Tzarik was surprised how long it took for the necromancer to realize they advanced on him. Either that or he did not fear them and stood his ground. They were close enough now to see the details of his garments and the black scripture tattooed on his forearms, hands, and face.

"His eyes!" Sybal gasped when she noticed them. "Is he a Runer?"

Tzarik didn't reply. He unsheathed his sword with force, gaining on the necromancer. Seeing him unafraid, the necromancer dropped his hands. Instantly, the wind began to die down and cries of relief went up from behind them in the city. The black robes furled menacingly as the necromancer turned and fled into the hills. Tzarik heard the galloping hoof falls of a mighty horse. Cresting over a dune, the necromancer raced away on a living horse towing a black wagon behind it. He was gone.

Taking a huge, clean breath now that the sandy winds had died down, Tzarik sheathed his sword and turned back to the city.

"What was that?" Sybal asked, easily over-striding him to get in the lead.

"I don't want to say yet," he mumbled.

He led her to the farmer's house he stayed at last time. He stopped at the gate. All around them lay the corpses of the undead army. Mismatched uniforms, clothing, and weapons said this lot had been gathered from several continents. Tzarik inspected a few outside the farmer's fence.

"What are you looking for?" Sybal asked, exhausted, her skin bleeding white from the sharp sand.

"Anything," Tzarik replied. "Just observing. See how they all have various crests? This one is Alika. So is this one, but from under a different king." He pointed to another rotting corpse. "Rhostrana, under Czar Demetrium. You can tell from the lion crest. This one, also Rhostrana but under Czarina Amali."

"So?"

"Tsarina Amali ruled Rhostrana over a hundred years ago. This soldier has been dug up from his grave."

"I don't—"

Tzarik cut her off with a hiss, raising his hand. His eyes trained on the door hanging to the farmer's home. It hung from one hinge, slightly rocking. Sand drifted into the doorway, weeds overran the once meticulously curated gardens. The place looked like it had been empty, abandoned for weeks. Slowly, he drew his sword and opened the gate. He thanked any god who would listen that Sybal did not ask another question as he stealthily made his way to the door.

He had almost reached it when a gurgling roar accompanied a huge, fleshy monster with four legs. The thing launched itself from the darkness inside, tackling Tzarik. His sword arched from his hand, landing back by Sybal. With a shout, Tzarik once again landed flat on his back, the monster snapping its foul teeth close to his face. Using both arms, he pushed it a few inches away, but the creature's strength overpowered him. Panting, he saw now with bald flesh and cloven hooves that it was a crocatta. Grunting, he shoved at the monster again and tried to roll away.

He dislodged it partly but when he tried to flip up onto his feet, it retaliated by clamping its black jaws down onto his shoulder. Screaming in pain, he gouged at its eyes with one hand while prying at its maw with the other. As they struggled, he saw something horrifying around its neck. Crawling across the crocatta's flesh, encircling its entire neck were neat, precise stitches. On the side of its fleshy head, a script had been recently scrawled in black ink. Swallowing hard, he realized this was the one he had killed just weeks ago. Back again from the dead.

The undead monster shook its head back and forth, tearing his flesh and muscles underneath. Screaming as his white blood spattered the ground beneath him and his own face, he saw Sybal dashing towards him with his sword held in her hands. She clasped it with both hands, the blade pointing down. Understanding what she was about to do, he yelled, "No, stop!"

Sybal plunged the sword down through the crocatta and Tzarik felt his own blade slice his side. Gasping in pain from being cut by the magic metal, he gripped the blade and kicked Sybal away. He pulled the sword out and, holding it by the blade, stabbed the crocatta sideways through its neck. It hardly fazed the monster but it gave him leverage to tip it over onto its side so he could get up. Once back on his feet, gripping the sword like a leash on the monster, he pulled upward, slicing the thing's head off once again. With the black script severed from its body, the crocatta stopped moving.

Overcome, exhausted, angry, and bleeding from three wounds, Tzarik dropped the sword and fell to his knees. He didn't care that the woman saw him in this weak state. He just wanted to rest.

Sybal ran to his side and clutched his shoulders. He wanted to throw her off but lacked the strength, weakly pushing on her. Instead, he pointed to his sword.

"That is orichalcum. It kills monsters. Do you understand?"

"I saved you," she fought back, a little affronted.

"You almost killed me!" he screamed back. He stopped and took a breath when his entire body quaked from weakness. "We are monsters, woman. Orichalcum kills us. The sulfates in our veins are not natural. Or body does not replace them like red blood."

Sybal scoffed. "A sword through the ribs would kill most people."

He glared at her through his matted hair and dripping sweat. "You don't know anything about fighting, Runers, monsters. Idiot."

Shoving him hard so he toppled over, Sybal jumped to her feet. "I wanted to help you. Of course I don't know anything about all that. You left me! I'm a wealthy lady; that wasn't my life. And just so you know, I know a little. I've dueled before for my honor. And..."

He noticed tears well up in her brown eyes. She went pale and wrapped her arms tightly around herself.

Her voice shaking, she said, "Do you know what I went through to get here? To find you?" A sob wracked her and she almost doubled over. "You are a horrible person. I hate you, but I need you."

She held up her hand, showing her white veins. "I'm not changing. And I ache every morning. I feel..."

"Like you're dying?" he asked weakly. His vision turned gray and a slight panic overtook him, stopping him from chiding her again. He tried to push himself up but his arm shook.

"Are you all right?" she asked suddenly, her own grievances seemingly forgotten. "Runer?"

He heard her voice from far away, muffled and clouded.

"Take me to the house," he mumbled. "I'll..." He coughed, his lungs throbbing. "I'll tell you what to do. Hurry."

Chapter 13
The Trial of Two

HER HANDS SHOOK AS SHE LIFTED HIM AND DASHED TO THE abandoned farmhouse. She expected to find a family inside, but when she entered, she realized her first impression of it being abandoned was right. She dodged past the door leaning to the side on one hinge, dodging past something heavy hanging from the ceiling, and laid him out on the wooden table in front of a mud-made hearth. Glancing up subconsciously, she screamed, covering her mouth quickly as the rotting corpse of a farmer wearing a wool vest swung gently from the rafter. Her first instinct was to cut him down but the struggling, rasping breath of the Runer drew her back to the present.

"What do I do?" she asked. She made up her mind in that moment, despite his arrogance and poisonous words, she'd help him. She had no choice. He was her future.

"Horse cargo," he sighed through gasps of air.

Carefully moving around the swinging farmer, she skittered out the door to his massive horse. The black steed eyed her suspiciously as she charged towards it and even took a few cautious steps back. It must have sensed her need because eventually it stilled itself and let her remove the entire set of saddlebags. She groaned as they fell to the ground and she had to lift them. She had not suspected there would be heavy materials in a wanderer such as Tzarik's life.

She slowed down again, squeezing past the farmer to get to the table. Once by the Runer's side, she dropped the bags onto the ground.

"If you are going to let a human corpse bother you that much," Tzarik grunted, "then I don't know what to tell you about supernatural monster corpses."

She flipped open the bags and began to pull things out, ignoring his jibes. Although she had no idea what she looked at in all the jars, bottles, and leather satchels, she had an instinct about which ones would draw out the poison. In a larger leather bag, wrapped in thick cotton, he had a mortar and pestle.

"Wait," he rasped. His hand weakly reached up to stop her coming closer. It shook.

"What?" she gasped, unsure whether to weep or panic, every muscle so tense her bones ached.

He met her eyes, his dancing back and forth between hers. He squinted and his brows pinched with worry. Confused, she laid her hand against the side of his damp face. Did he want comfort? Why did he stop her? She licked her lips about to ask, but he dropped his hand, no longer able to hold it up.

"I...can't," he managed weakly. He turned his face away in what she thought might be shame.

"Yes, you can!" she spat, turning back to the strange medical items.

Tzarik swallowed. "Knife first."

His veins bulged from his skin, black as night. Where the white veins had looked simply foreign, the black ones seemed to carry an omen of death. She grabbed the knife, unsure what he wanted her to do.

Shakily, he indicated the bite wound on his neck that had festered closed already. "Cut...the vein..." he gasped.

"What?" she cried.

"Let out the eldritch poison...faster."

She couldn't argue. His face went pale and the black veins

showed up darker, creeping near his temple up his jawline and hollow cheeks.

"Don't go to sleep!" she cried, pressing the large knife against his vein. "I'm so sorry." Her hand vibrated as she quickly slashed his vein. The black poison spurted out onto her face and she screamed as it dripped down her chin.

"Black...case," he gasped, letting the poisoned sulfates flow freely.

Opening the second bag, she found a small black chest with a key lock on it. The chest was not made of wood or leather but something in between. She grimaced at the hard, fleshy feel in her grip.

About to cry that it was locked, she looked up to see his quaking hand offering her a leather cord with several keys on it.

"Black one," he sighed. Just after he spoke, his hand went limp and his eyes rolled back into his sockets. His lids did not close and his body stilled.

"Gods!" she cried, prying the lock open with the little key slipping between her sweaty fingers. Flinging the horrendous lid open, inside she found two, flat, corked and waxed-closed vials of white sulfates, mixed and somehow pulsating. Also, a long, flexible tube made of what looked like the lining of an animal's stomach with a thin, silver needle at each end.

Understanding, she reached up with the blackened knife she used to open his throat and cut the farmer's corpse down. It tumbled stiffly half onto the table where she kicked it off with one foot. Turning one of the flat vials cork-side down, she shoved the needle into the cork, feeling it pass through the other end. She tied it with the rope hanging from the rafter and then jabbed the other end of the tube into his bare arm.

The veins in his body slowly cleared of the black sulfates, now splashed all over her bare feet and the dirt floor under his prone, still figure. Looking up at his neck, his veins receded and were hardly visible. Gently, she unlaced his tunic and opened it, exposing his chest. She stopped, frozen by the atlas of scars, burns, and a few utterly mysterious marks that made a canvas of his torso. She wanted to examine them all as she knew each one held a legendary story, but the Runer's life drifted in and out with every second. Inspecting his chest and arms, she found that none of his veins throbbed black anymore. Looking at where she had jammed the needle into his arm, she saw the comforting white sulfates begin to spread.

Satisfied, she covered him with a blanket and went to work on the large cut she made on his neck. Sorry she shook so bad, she stitched the jagged wound and cleaned it with a couple small bottles of ointment and—to her surprise—soap she found in his bag.

Scared, but satisfied, she made a fire in the hearth, closed the window shutters, and screwed the door back on with tools she found in the barn. When he still did not wake up, she set about pulling the vegetables from the farmer's overgrown garden and boiled them all with a plethora of random herbs she also found.

She had drunk a cup of tea and eaten three bowls of the vegetable soup when she finally heard him stirring. Eager, she ran to his side.

"I thought you might have died," she whispered, putting her arm behind his head and helping him up.

"I see you were torn up about it," he groaned, looking at the fire and hungrily eyeing the pot on the hearth.

"In case you woke up." She took a second bowl and scooped the soup right into the bowl. "I have read that those who go through transfusion are famished after." She looked away. "I wasn't, but I had good reason."

Tzarik gulped loudly, devouring the concoction. Dropping the empty bowl, he asked, "What happened after I left? Just curious."

Sybal glared at him in the firelight. His curiosity didn't seem reason enough to express exactly the pain, torment, and lifelong sorrow and shame she would now bear. Instead of wallowing in her sorrow, knowing full well this man would never empathize, she asked, "Is it reversible at all? Most of your blood came out just there. What if I was drained again and given proper blood?"

Shaking his head and trying to slide off the table to get more soup, he said, "It's a magic covenant. An oath between you and the runes."

"Is it like witchcraft where they get magical knowledge from the earth? Or magi who can read the future in the stars with divination?"

Again, he shook his head. "I don't believe in any of those gods. How can I when the magi here know one god and the magi on Bahratt have dozens of gods with dozens of arms and heads, I might add."

Sybal wracked her brain for other magic users. Magic was no longer something to be feared like it used to be just a hundred years ago but not common either. "The Masakh'cepholus use magic," she said out loud, handing him a full bowl again.

"They are born to it. Most with known powers—if you can call them that. Not like a sorcerer."

"Oh?" She lifted herself onto the table and sat next to his feet. "I learned about that great sorcerer from ancient Al'Myrah. The one who conquered the world using the power of the djinn. He was called Malik Jaakoba and he is said to have used his last wish to flee to the west, discovering the new world."

Tzarik looked at her over the rim of his bowl. "I don't know. Never had much opportunity for formal learning. But we are not like that."

She noticed his hand go to his neck to feel the stitches. His eyes unfocused as he ran his finger up and down. A slight frown brought his brows together as he calculated in his mind.

A few moments of silence passed and she let them go without

interruption. The quiet wrapped around her like a blanket and she liked it. He struggled to get up and she helped him in silence. She stood by as he went through an outside clasp on his saddlebags and tossed her a cloak of black, smooth material.

"I don't have anything for you. Not for a woman, let alone a monster the size of you."

This hurt but she forced herself to bury the anger. "Thank you."

"We'll leave at first light," he went on, packing up his things but taking out a small bedroll.

She had spied a bed in the loft above them and decided she would pass the sleepless night there since she had no bedroll. But too much burned on her mind to let her sleep and she had to have at least some answers now.

"I still hold to my invocation of the trial of two." She didn't whisper but she kept weakness—unassuredness—out of her tone. She dropped her hands to stop fidgeting and look steadier. "I don't feel the sulfates binding to me. I'm not changing. And I'm dying. You need to train me."

Tzarik swallowed hard; she saw his throat constrict and he stopped moving, his hand still inside the pouch. He didn't look at her as he said, "I do not love, I do not care, about anything or anyone and that applies to you, do you understand?"

"Yes."

"Do you?" Now his icy, cold, glowing eyes pierced her soul.

She shivered. She understood what he meant. He would not save her if it meant going out of his way. He would not put out effort to help if she needed it outside teaching her the ways of runing. She would have a companion, but she would be alone. Forever. Being alone she could do, but being alone with someone was the actual trial.

"Yes."

He lifted his bags. "Good, then we'll head north. You need runes, an orichalcum blade, and clothes."

He tossed her the bedroll and went for the stairs.

"I thought," she began.

"Your sulfates are not taking," he mumbled ascending the stairs to the loft and the bed. "You should not sleep in a dead man's bed."

Chapter 14
Training

TZARIK LAY AWAKE THE WHOLE NIGHT, MAD WITH wondering what he was supposed to do with this woman who refused to leave him alone. She followed his instructions and came to Bahratt. He went against his better judgment and runed her as his duty as a witness at the trial demanded. They offered him pay. Payment always erased his concerns but not this time.

Looking over the edge, he watched her sleep without complaint on the dirty floor. She lay on her back, her bright hair spread out over the ground. He had a moment where he thought about stopping her from saving him that afternoon. Did the loss of blood make him give in to her ministrations? It could have all been over in that instant. But her eyes—large, concerned, determined—staring down at him had stopped him. The trial of two used to be preached as a sacred oath between Runers and their apprentices but had not been upheld in his lifetime. He hadn't been able to invoke it successfully when he had been runed...

Pushing the dark, juvenile memories out of his head, he drank heavily, forcing himself to sleep. He dreamed in black and white images of Sybal. Her naked body, hanging upside down, her red blood draining out and spreading across the floor. In the dream, she died. Unwilling to leave her behind, he wrapped her corpse in a gray sack and lashed her to his horse, traveling the world with her. When he finally opened the sack, her eyes bulged open and she screamed for help.

Shouting in rage, he woke up, slapping his face. Alcohol always gave him dark dreams. The drink mixed fine with the living, red blood of humans. But the white sulfates seemed to turn demonic when paired with the spirits.

Outside, the sky turned that cold, pink before the sun came up. He quickly packed and woke the woman up. He had no clear idea where to go or what to look for. The best option would be to find a job to get coin for her needs. She would have to fight, even though she had no idea what to do.

*

"Do you not have a home?" Sybal asked him as he finally gave in to a horse seller who would not part with a stunning steed for anything less than what it was worth.

Tzarik knew she would ask these kinds of questions. "No. I sleep where I can. I am on the road all the time. You should have thought about that before you asked for the trial."

He noted how she took offense to his tone and answer. He bargained hard for the tall, slender horse he now handed over to Sybal. They had very little coin and she needed a great deal. The farming village would not have anything beyond basic needs so they had to leave and travel and the thought of sharing his horse with her made him uneasy.

"Thank you," she mumbled, taking the reins.

Sensing her about to ask, he leapt up onto his tall mount and said, "We ride. Bigger cities will have more jobs. Somewhere northwest where they have greener pastures and brighter gems."

Sybal suddenly lit up. "My family has a mine."

They headed towards the village's exit as he mulled this over.

"If you think they would give you valuables, then they might let you stay. Why did you leave?"

Through his peripheral vision, he watched her, noting her mannerisms as she came up with an answer. She licked her lips, looked away from him, then back down at her hands. She hadn't even made contact after. Or she had but didn't speak. Something happened that stopped her. He didn't press her.

"We'll make it on our own," he offered. "But it will be slow going to get started. And hard. You need to train. You are weak."

"Maybe physically, but I am strong in other ways. Your words hurt but I won't lash back at you."

"That is what I mean," he shot back, kicking his horse ahead. "Don't tell me those things. Keep it to yourself. Bear it."

Clicking her tongue, she shot ahead of him and shouted back, "You need to learn a thing or two yourself."

OVER THE NEXT several days as they crossed over the straight and headed towards Bagdula, because Tzarik insisted only large cities on Al'Myrah had good enough pay and the resources they needed, he forced her to train. He knew she wanted to learn about the runes, the special blade, but didn't want to put such dangerous weapons into the hands of a wealthy lady who had no sense of danger.

They rode most of the day and set up camp just before sunset. As he gathered fuel for the fire and prepared the preserved jars of food, he gave her a list of exercises to do.

"Chest all the way to the ground," he shouted with his back to her as he dumped a cacophony of mystery jars into the little pot over the fire.

"How do you know I'm not?" she grunted, finishing a pushup.

"I can tell by your breathing."

Groaning, he heard her cough as she inhaled sand from going all the way down. "I can't do another."

"Too bad," he sighed. "Because you have ten more to go."

Another exercise she hated was where he made her squat all the way down, jump, and land in a pushup. Once he learned she hated these above all else, he made her do them for a minute at a time.

"Keep going!" he shouted when she stood up from a jump.

"My arms are on fire and my ass is killing," she argued. She reached for the flask of water and took a long, gulping drink.

Reaching up, he snatched away the flask, making her spill water all down her thin front.

"What?" she coughed. "Am I drinking water wrong now?"

"Small sips," Tzarik said, motioning her to start again. "If you drown like that, you will weigh yourself down and make yourself sick."

He knew she would only take a few days of this abuse but was surprised when she didn't complain. She wanted to; he saw it in her eyes. Admiring her constitution, he pushed her harder and harder. They road all day and exhaustion took her at night but she bore his physical training.

They were just hours outside a city when she finally asked, "When will you teach me about runes?"

"When you have runes," he answered shortly. "This—training at night, seeking out higher paying jobs—is exactly what I wanted to avoid."

"What would you have done otherwise?" she asked. "I stink. I have never had this much sweat in my hair in my life. I haven't bathed in over a week. I have done every stupid exercise and pose you have asked me to do. When does the real training start? Where can we rest?"

"You rested last night."

She glared ahead at the approaching city with its golden roofs and sprawling towns. "So this truly is it. No home, no place to call your own."

Tzarik felt her animosity rising. "That is not even half of it. Blood, monsters, the hate from those you save."

"For a price," she reminded him. "You do a job for coin, they don't have to like you."

Now she annoyed him. Of course she was right. He grew used to the regular insults and being spit on. She had not experienced it. She needed to know. To understand.

"Sacred Bahl!" she exclaimed, calling on one of the gods of the continent. "We're home. This is Ala'Nar. Why did you bring me back here?"

"There is nothing romantic about being the other," he grunted, pulling his long black scarf around his neck and over his face.

He showed his runes to the town guard at the border and steeled himself for whatever lay inside the city.

"Covering yourself like that just makes you more of a threat," she sighed, arrogantly rolling her eyes.

"Explain," Tzarik ordered.

Sybal's excitement at being back in her own city was palpable. This opportunity to teach her a valuable lesson about being a Runer could not be passed up. He faced her, his icy blue eyes boring into hers as they wound their way through the darker outlines of the city.

She relented under his gaze. "Hiding who you are, your face. Makes people uneasy. It encourages the stigma you seem to hate so much."

"It protects me," he answered in a more scholarly tone than he meant to have. "No one can know my face, track me. I'm just another Runer."

TZARIK FOUND A SMALL JOB, something just for her. He wanted to watch, to test her, knowing full well she most likely would fail. A ghoul had begun lurking in a graveyard near an older temple in town. No one had yet been taken or killed, but witnesses had seen the monster skulking about near a triangular mausoleum.

Using the last of their coin, he had Sybal rent them a room in a public house and gave her the patents with the details on it.

"What can I do?" she asked impetuously, flinging her arms up, empty of all weapons and runes. "I have no way of killing this thing."

"Ghouls are more physical than most monsters," Tzarik answered, lounging on the bed in the room, eyes closed. "You should be able to kill it with your scimitar. Wait till night and head out to the graveyard."

He watched her fight her inner voice. She wanted to argue, to contradict him but she didn't. Happy with her victory over herself, he advised her, "Cover your face as you go out. People here know you. They will not be glad you have returned."

SYBAL TOOK the missive and went to the temple-keeper's rectory near the temple and the fenced-in graveyard. The sandy city made for terrible traditional graveyards and had instead buried their dead in small pyramids across several acres. Larger family mausoleums dotted the vast graveyard.

She tried to keep her mind on the task at hand as she knocked on the door, gently touching the holy mihal as she crossed the threshold. It had been too long since entering a house that kept the temple scriptures above their door. Her father insisted on it. The little scroll reminded her of home.

Wrapping Tzarik's too-short cloak tighter around her tattered dress, she reminded herself that completing this job, no matter how difficult, would buy her clothes, make her feel like a person again.

The grave-keeper was an older man with leathery, tanned skin and one good eye. The other, milky white, warbled in its socket as he spoke, pointing to where he had seen the ghoul. Sybal didn't know what questions to ask, what strategy needed to be implemented, so she held herself tall to cover for her insecurities. The grave-keeper stopped as he described the gait of the ghoul.

"Are you...?" his one good eye scanned her up and down. "The woman. The murderer." His voice trailed off as he took a step back.

"Does it matter?" she asked, placing a hand on her hip but found her voice quivering slightly.

"You killed Madam Tallery," the grave-keeper gasped. He stepped into his tiny house and closed the door till just his good eye glared out at her. "What do you want?"

Scoffing, Sybal raised the patents to the slit in the door. "To kill the ghoul. Half now, the rest on delivery of the corpse," she said as strongly as she could. "You wrote this patents, didn't you?" She glared at it in the bright sun. "Half now."

The grave-keeper nodded slowly. "I thought you left town. That's what the rumors were."

"Give me half and I'll leave now." Deciding there was no use in guarding her tone, she growled. "Like it or not, I can help you."

To her surprise, she realized she could almost tell what the old man thought as she reacted. She saw his body weight shift, his eye flick to the graves behind her. He planned something.

"Very well." He tossed a small leather bag out that clinked with the unmistakable sound of coin when it hit the sandstone step. "Come back after sunset."

Without another word, Sybal scooped up the coin and went back into town to find a smithy and a tailor. She knew where all the fashionable tailors worked but this was not the time for them.

She had to ask a few people where to find a leatherworker and was greeted with glares, spits, and choice insults. One woman used so many curses that Sybal laid her hand on the hilt of her sword to silence the woman.

"I need leather armor," she said, tossing the purse to a craftsman when she finally found one. "Runer armor," she added.

The craftsman looked her up and down, doubt and a smirk twisting his worn face. "A woman?" he snickered.

She reached to take the pouch back.

"I can do that," he said quickly, taking the coin. "I've only got black."

"That will do."

FINALLY OUTFITTED in the cheap garments that didn't hang from her shoulders properly and exposed her when the wind picked up, Sybal walked more confidently than she ever had. Black leggings, boots up to her knees for protection, and fitted leather across her chest filled her with a kind of pride she knew she had not earned. No expert, she could still tell from the thin material that this armor would not last. It was not the kind Tzarik wore. And the blade did not glint with rainbow colors. Still, these cheap imitations would work for now. She kept Tzarik's cloak even though it hung just to her knees. She smiled lightly thinking about how she could always see over his head. She imagined taking him down in combat and how easy it would be with her height advantage.

She waited outside the graveyard wall as she remembered the scars on his torso. She thought of one that went from his collar bone all the way down his side and disappeared underneath his belt. Biting her lip, she thought about his chiseled arms, defined chest, and hard stomach. Raising her own arms, she thought about the pain he forced her to go through with the exercises. Maybe he was right to make her stronger...

Not sure when ghouls came out, she waited by a few tombs away from where they said the ghoul emerged. She crouched, hood pulled up to meld with the shadows. Thinking the monster would not show till late when the moon and stars were at their brightest, she gasped softly when the creature appeared at the base of one of the pyramids. Seeming to partly form out of shadows and crawl out from beneath a hidden gateway, the ghoul's eyes glowed green in the dimming light.

It looked just like the ghouls in fairytales she read as a child: skinny, long legs like a frogs, hair on its scalp that ran down its back, dragging and hissing along the sand. Its fingers were long and muscular for strangling and she could see how its wide mouth could unhinge to devour a whole child.

Quickly putting aside her childhood excitement, she lifted her sword, as quietly as she could, following the shadows behind it. Noting it's thin state, this ghoul had not fed yet. The grave-keeper had spotted it early on before it had taken any victims, which was a good thing.

Unsure what to do, Sybal picked up a handful of sand. Using her best girlish voice, she pretended to weep and called, "Mother, where are you?"

Working just as she hoped, the ghoul froze, one of its eyes spinning backwards towards her voice, thinking it had happened upon a lost child. As the ghoul slowly turned, no part of its body moving, she tossed the sand into its face and hacked like a madman with her scimitar. A smatter of black, physical blood splashed up onto her face and her blade clanged loudly as she cut clean through the ghoul, hitting the mausoleum it hid beside.

Opening her eyes, she groaned. The ghoul lay in two beneath her wild strike but she had not calibrated, swinging stupidly. She hit the pyramid so hard, her scimitar blade broke. She picked up the corpse, stowing it in a waterproof bag Tzarik supplied her with, and the pieces of her scimitar.

Frustrated with herself, she hammered on the grave-keeper's door. When he didn't open it right away, she banged harder, screaming for him to come to the door and face her.

"Stop!" the old man shouted from inside the door. "I hear you. I saw through the window that you have the ghoul. Please, how can I stop more from returning?"

Frustrated, tired, sore, and hungry, Sybal mocked the man. "Hang a talisman made from seagulls dung and woven with the hair of a virgin at the gate's entrance."

"Payment is in the pot," he mumbled, fear in his voice.

Looking down, she saw an empty flowerpot with a larger bag in it. She picked it up and weighed it in her hand. Not a lot, but a start. She dropped the ghoul's corpse on his doorstep, smeared her bloody hand across his post and lintel, and headed back towards the inn where Tzarik no doubt slept the night away.

Her stomach grumbled even louder when the smell of smoke reached her. Thinking someone must have been curing meats, she looked up to follow the smell.

Her heart froze. Off in the east, a pillar of black, thick smoke rose to obscure the moon. A few other city folk pointed and even less ran to help, buckets in hand. The smoke came from where her father's home stood.

Chapter 15
Desperate

Her cheap boots tore a little at the ankle as she sprinted over the crest of the hill that brought her family's estate into view. She ran with such demonic fury, that her lungs burned and she coughed before the smoke reached her. Clutching her chest, her watery eyes beheld the inferno before her. The walls surrounding her home crumbled as the fire spread from the center where she knew her father and mother rested their heads. Even the mine houses behind smoldered in a fire long since lit.

"Help!" she screamed as she dashed to the gate that lay open, smashed and destroyed. "Get water! There is a well in the courtyard."

A few frightened workers who she recognized, formed a line, dousing the flames as they reached out towards the city. She ran to one and asked, "Where is Sheikh Riyadh and Freja?"

The man stopped so quickly, recognizing her face, that he spilled the water from his bucket. "Sabi Sybal!" he gasped. "They told us you were dead. But then this!" Tear tracks cut through the ash and dirt on his face.

Now she understood. Tzarik's words of warning came back. Someone spotted her in the city, many had but she had paid them no mind besides cursing them in her head. Then they came here. To her family.

"Abdul!" she screamed. As she scanned her burning home, she

spotted a man's outline in her brother's window appear then vanish. "This is my fault," she cried out. "Keep hauling water!"

"Sabi, no!" the man shouted.

She dodged away from his saving grip and dashed into the house. She wished more than ever now that Tzarik had taught her to use the runes. One created a protective circle from physical harm and would have been terribly useful at this point. Thinking of him made her wonder if he had noticed that she had not returned yet this evening. She wondered if the fire consumed her, would he just leave town, assuming the ghoul killed her? Then a worse thought entered her mind: what if he had her track and fight the ghoul to keep her distracted all night as he slipped away, leaving her behind again? Did she care or just angry she was weaker than she should have been?

Leaping over fallen beams, dodging dripping fire, she made her way to the stairs that led to the family's quarters.

"Abdul!" she shrieked up the stairs. "Father! Mother!"

The floor beneath her gave away. Screaming, she fell a few feet before grasping the banister, stopping her fall to the cellars below. Gasping, she watched as fire fell onto the alcohol below in wooden barrels and glass bottles. Remembering how the drink spread fire, she screamed with the effort of hauling herself up. Once back on more stable ground, she ascended the stairs only to find the bedrooms empty.

"Abdul!" she screamed again, sobs taking her breath, choking on the smoky air.

"Sybal!"

A deep, angry, man's voice called her name. She turned but the ceiling collapsed, shooting hot ash into her face as the doorway to her brother's room was cut off in a fiery barrier. Having leapt out of the way, she looked up from where she fell to the ground and saw the roof above her begin to crack.

"I'm in here!" she cried. "But the ceiling is blocking the door."

Peering through a small open space in the slats, she saw the short, black-clad figure of Tzarik on the other side.

"Get a cloth and dampen it," he shouted over the roaring fire. "Then put it over your face to breathe."

A hiss and small explosion told them the alcohol cellar had been breached by the ravenous flames.

Not hesitating, she grabbed the washrag from the basin on the vanity and did as he instructed. To her surprise, the smoke didn't make it through the damp rag and made it easier to breathe.

"Why are you here?" she shouted angrily. "This is my doing. I caused this."

"Shut up and find something to cut the timbers with," Tzarik ordered her. "Now!" he shouted when she didn't move.

Not knowing how he knew she hadn't moved, she ran to her brother's wardrobe where he kept a few swords. They were ornamental and probably would not survive the hacking, but they were all she had. Tying the wet rag around her head, she lifted a halberd from Wu-Tang and began to hack through the wreckage.

"I thought you'd left me," she grunted. After a few strokes, she could see him on the other side. Somehow, her heart lifted and she had never been so happy to see him.

"Give it to me," he snapped, gingerly reaching for it. "I can finish this in two strokes."

"Don't patronize me," she quipped back. Grunting, she hacked at the fiery barrier again. For the first time, she saw Tzarik's face twitch in anxiety, his browsing knitting in worry. But he didn't fight her.

Finally, the crashed ruble gave away just as the halberd snapped in two. "This way," she called heading to the stairs.

"Servant's stairs are less charred," Tzarik said, hurrying in the opposite direction.

"I have to find my family!" she screamed at him, tired of his orders and contradictions.

He also appeared to be tired of fighting her. Running to take her hand and force her to follow, he lunged at her. She saw him coming and lifted her long leg, kicking out at him. She would not leave without her family. She had more strength in her legs than she remembered, and they were long enough that she hit him square in the face before he reached her. She heard him grunt and watched him fall backwards.

The weight of his fall was all it took. He hit the charred floor and fell through with a startled cry.

Immediately regretting her rash actions, she ran and fell to her knees at the edge of the crumbled floor. He grasped the burning floor before falling into the cellar below.

"I'm so sorry!" she cried, reaching down to him.

Without berating her, Tzarik yelled in an effort to hoist himself up far enough to grab her hand. Relief flooded her when she grasped his sweaty hand. Both moaning, she pulled him back up, and together they ran down the servant's stairs and out into the front. When they emerged, Sybal saw her family—father, mother, brother—outside, safe.

"How?" she gasped, ripping the wet mask from her face. She turned to the short, gasping man behind her. "You?" The disbelief did not offend him.

"I knew it was your home when I saw the smoke," he coughed. "I told you: they will not love you. You can't come back here. You put them in danger."

Sybal turned and looked at the flames, reflecting in her eyes. "They did this to them...because of me? How could people be so cruel?"

Finally getting a hold on his shuddering breath, Tzarik sighed. "I cannot begin to explain why people are this way. If I could, I'd be a philosopher. A rich one."

She swallowed. "I want to speak to them."

He didn't reply. Didn't take her arm to stop her. But she

couldn't make herself. She couldn't walk to them, show herself. She had done enough. More than that, she almost killed one of the only people left in her life who didn't spit on her as she passed, didn't call her a monster.

"We have to leave," she whispered.

"A CARAVAN IS LEAVING for Bahratt in an hour," Tzarik said two mornings later.

They spent the last two days buying better armor and shoes for Sybal to which she was eternally grateful. Tzarik somehow came across more threatening to the wily smith and procured better quality of goods. They found a few blank rune stones but could only afford two with the money they had left.

"Why must we go back to Bahratt," she sighed, working on carving the last of the two runes. Tzarik insisted she had to carve them herself but taking knife to stone had cramped her hand beyond function in the first day.

"Why not?" he asked. He sat in the window of the inn, maintaining his orichalcum blade.

"All we do is go back and forth. Travel. Run down caravans. Don't you ever stay in one place and just live there?" She looked up from her carving. "We just came from there. I'm exhausted of all the travel. We are never not traveling."

The Runer ignored her.

Hopelessly, she went back to the rune. "Rahul, my betrothed, is prince of Jarabu."

"That is unfortunate," Tzarik replied. "Al'Myrah used to deal in orichalcum merchants. I haven't had to purchase such a blade in fifteen years. The market has changed and I didn't know. Jarabu is the closest city I know of that has a man who deals orichalcum. The smaller cities don't tend to carry such useless metal."

"Useless?" she grunted, digging the blade into the stone as hard as she could. "I thought it was the best for monster hunters."

"There are not a lot of Runers left," he sighed. "As far as I know...I'm the oldest. That's why we travel so much."

She looked up, taken in by his honesty. He had never opened up about anything before. Not so much as his favorite food. She watched in the last two days, trying to figure out what he liked, didn't like, what he drank. But no patterns emerged.

"I suppose people in this profession don't live that long?" she asked. "And not many choose this life. I guess that makes selling orichalcum a bad financial decision."

"Also makes it so you can charge the best price. Makes up for dealing with the likes of us."

Sybal bit her lip, stopping her work. Taking a chance, she asked, "What was your crime?"

She expected him to be silent, maybe glare at her. Say his crime did not concern her. But he didn't even flinch or miss a beat in the oiling of his blade.

"To know a Runer's crime gives one power over him," he said simply. He quickly tapped the bruise that took up the whole right side of his face. "You have taught me to not give you power over me."

"But you know mine! That's not fair."

He met her eyes, his face placid, expressionless. "I didn't choose to. I needed coin. And we need coin." He stood up, slinging his sword onto his back. "We will take the riverboat caravan with the water gypsies," he said quickly. "That way we come up from the backside of Jarabu. We can avoid your lover's walls."

They had to leave right away as the straight was a good walk from the walls of Ala'Nar. The sun rose bright, orange, and hot as they paid their very last coin to the chief of the caravan. The last time they crossed the straight had been uneventful and only a few straggling cattle boats. This time, colored riverboats of various sizes and shapes lined the shores, waiting to journey together. Most of the boats were owned by a single person, renting them out, taking the journey together. But with what little money they had, Tzarik and Sybal boarded a larger boat with about a dozen other creatures. The owner of this boat was a tall, bird-like Masakh. Sybal had never seen one up close and couldn't believe the being before her.

Long, feathery ears topped his head like a cat, but pale, flesh like a man from the west covered his exposed torso. His long hair interspersed with colorful feathers growing right from his scalp. He stood well over six feet tall with legs like a bird's, proportioned to his man-like body. But more than his mixed appearance, she was shocked by how attracted she found herself to him. He smiled, winking at her as he took their payment and made jokes in a voice that reminded her of a court jester. His attire glittered bright, patched, and worn.

"Then the barkeep says, 'Hello, beautiful,' and I lean over the counter, take a drink from someone else's goblet and reply, 'Hello to you, too,' and he throws me out!" the Masakh cawed, laughing through his own story to a gaggle of dreamily enraptured girls. "He was talking to my partner of course, but how should I know? I'm so damn good-looking!"

The girls giggled, covering their mouths as they all blushed.

"I thought Masakh were immortal beings," Sybal whispered to Tzarik as they boarded, claiming a corner of the riverboat.

"They are," he replied, confused.

"This one seems so...normal," she went on. "I expected them to be stern, stoic. More like the legends."

"Those stories you read are about an oppressed people in slavery," he whispered as their host trotted past, his talons clicking on the wooden boat. "That slavery still exists in some parts of this world."

Sybal shook her head. "How does a magical, immortal race become enslaved?"

The Runer slung his pack down, moving his sword from his back to his hip, tightening the belt. "The human race is capable of great wickedness," he mused.

"Could we go to their land someday?" she asked, curiosity and wonder driving her decorum away.

"Alika?" he provided. "That continent does not have cities like we do. Or rather, Mysir is the only one that resembles the civilization we have here. Most of Alika is tribal, run by chiefs and warlords. But the city of the Masakh has completely different customs. It is old."

Moments after securing their spot on the top deck, the line of colorful floating homes began to move, unleashed from the docking posts. The river ran swiftly this time of year, despite the blazing sun, and gave travelers willing to risk the water a quicker way to reach the neighboring continent even if the small part of the ocean they had to cross was dangerous.

A few nomads leapt on board as they passed river communities but for most of the day, the ride was silent. Sybal kept her wits about her and decided against making conversation with Tzarik. He didn't say so, but she felt his animosity towards her every time his hand went to the bruise on his face, his finger gently jabbing at the painful spot then tracing down to his healing bite wound. He used the healing rune on his bite but decided against removing the bruise as quickly.

The sun painted the sky purple as it set in the west and the river caravan hit the quickest waters before heading out into the ocean track. Ropes and long wooden poles marked the current for the riverboat but that didn't stop the ocean crossing from being taken seriously by the chiefs. Soon, they would insist all passengers head below decks while they crossed the salty water. Pirates and dangers in the fathoms below would not be taken lightly by the river dwellers no matter the ignorance of their land-locked clientele.

Sybal leaned against the railing, looking out over the darkening water when a man slid up beside her. "Fancy getting cozy under the deck, sabi?"

Gasping softly, she saw Vicdan, his hair outlined in the sun as it fell elegantly over one eye. He grinned at her start.

"What are you doing here?" she hissed, her hand instinctively going to her empty money pouch.

"Traveling!" He thumped the wheel fiddle slung across his back. "Thanks to you, this is my life now."

She glared at him, standing up straight. "I did not hand you this lot in life."

"No, no," he smiled, facing her, leaning back against the railing now. "It's better. Good. I play and people pay me." He leaned in close to her and whispered, "Sometimes I have to take a fee though."

Scoffing, she shook her head. "You are unbelievable."

"I know." He pushed himself up, still smiling, and gently pushed her hair behind one ear. He ran his finger down her temple. "The veins are starting to show."

She hadn't even looked in a mirror in a while. She touched the spot on her temple where his finger lingered. "How's it look?"

His heavy-lidded eyes slowly roved her new garments, lighting back onto her face. "Fierce."

If she had had blood in her veins, it would have run hot at those words. As it were, the sulfates boiled under her skin at the flattering words and gentle caresses.

"I do other things for money too, you know," he whispered, taking her chin in his hand. "Things my rich father would scold me for."

Sybal swallowed hard. Her eyes adjusted in the darkening sky so she saw his large, brown eyes locked onto hers. "You stole everything," she hissed but still did not pull away. "And we're on our way to see my betrothed."

"We?" Vicdan asked softly. He moved so close now, she could see each individual, thick, black eyelash.

"We."

They both jumped and turned to see Tzarik glaring at them, arms crossed, and his legs firmly planted apart.

"Runer!" Vicdan crowed in mock pleasure, throwing his arms wide and spreading his fingers far purposefully. "Never thought I'd see you again."

"I figured," Tzarik said shortly. "If you value your hands now at all—which it sounds like you do—keep them off her."

The dishonored lord pouted and nodded, moving away towards the Masakh captain. "Understood. See you around, Sybal." He winked.

Tzarik took a threatening step forward and Vicdan turned, dashing into the dark of the deck. The Runer's lip almost twitched into a smirk with satisfaction but it turned to a grimace.

"Why?" Sybal snapped.

"What?"

She fought to find the words, opening her mouth and raising and dropping her arms. "I deserve happiness."

The Runer grimaced. "You were not thinking of going with him...to..."

"I don't get to love a man," she hissed, marching up to him and looming over him. "Would it have hurt my training to let that one... touch me? Hug me? Anything to alleviate this crushing loneliness! We're going to see Rahul, there is no way to avoid that. He loves me and I can't touch him. Feel his hand on me again. Run my fingers through his beautiful hair. But I suppose a hardened fighter like you doesn't care."

"Sybal, he's an idiot!" Tzarik said, using her name for the first time while she could see him. "He's a thief. Gutter trash."

She shook her head. "We're from the same caste. He'd understand me if we had a moment to talk. I don't expect a dirty, homeless, feelingless monster like you to understand."

Sybal left him in the dark at the back of the boat. She knew she
hit her mark from his quiet retreat. She made him see just how
other he was. He had no say over what she did with her body or
how she dealt with the gaping loneliness inside her. She looked
but only fleetingly for Vicdan again. He must have already found
another pretty girl to prey on.

She contented herself at the prow of the boat, looking out,
knowing they would have to head below deck soon. He said her
name. Closing her eyes, she heard it again. Hearing someone she
loved say her name always made her giggle, warmed her. Curious,
she found when Tzarik said her name, it had the same effect.

Smiling, she imagined her name in his voice again.

Chapter 16
Last Hope

"WE CANNOT DISEMBARK!" THE AVIARY MASAKH SHOUTED AS screams erupted over the entirety of the river caravan. His words did not stop panicked travelers from leaping over the side, running down the line of boats, or turning to mutiny.

Tzarik saw it before the others. Standing at the prow of the boat, he smelled the brimstone and fire before the shores were properly in sight. He gathered Sybal and went to the Masakh.

"Let us off. We can deal with this."

"I don't care," the bird-like man replied quickly. "I need these people to stop ruining my boat!"

"Stop!" Sybal screeched over the ruckus. A few of the travelers stuttered in their scramble to flee. She saw Vicdan, his white undershirt unlaced, his bronze chest glimmering in the sun. His hair hung messy in his eyes and she noted he clung to a bundle of bags and tunics in his arms, preparing to abandon ship.

Tzarik saw her gain courage as they gazed at each other over the deck.

"We are Runers from Ala'Nar," she shouted. "We will dispatch the threat in Jarabu; you have nothing to fear. If you take or destroy property that is not yours in this panic, you will have the law of the land to answer to. Stay on the boats. Do not go into the city. It's miles away, you are safe here."

He may have chided her the night before, but how she wrangled the mob impressed him. "Well spoken," he whispered to her as they ran down the gangplank.

"I cannot stand uncivilized mobs," she replied.

Enough praise had been lavished on her. He turned his eyes to the horizon where the blue city swept across the yellow sands. Colorful tiles covered the city's homes, the palaces, temples, and other larger structures swept up and down with curved archways, tall turrets, and round domes—all splashed in multiple, vibrant colors. The city rose up a hill so the majority of it could be seen from the river. Throughout, rooftops and balconies were dotted with golden statues of the many-armed gods with their pointed crowns and red tongues. Far behind it sprawled the beginnings of the Bahratt jungle. When the wind came through the jungle just right, one could smell the waterfalls and mysterious creatures that lived inside its green webs.

The two Runers galloped on their horses towards the city. Tzarik scanned the jungle and saw the black, leathery serpent diving in and out of the foliage.

"That's not right," he panted, pulling his horse to a near stop.

"We have to hurry!" Sybal screamed, reeling her horse around, slipping in the hot sand. "What are you doing?"

Tzarik ignored her angry tone. She worried for her betrothed, he knew that. But they could not rush in. Not when this dragon did not belong here. Taking out his long, brass glass, he tried to follow the quick movements of the dragon. He grunted in annoyance when he could not lock onto it.

"Dragons are rare, Sybal," he said darkly, squinting into the sun, tracking the beast. "Despite what the stories tell you, they do not rise up every morning and come to a city looking for a virgin sacrifice." He glanced over at her, a brow cocked.

She glared at him, panting and gnashing her teeth as she ignored his look, focusing ahead.

"Dragons in the east tend to be red or yellow, lots of scales and sometimes have manes like lions. And they don't fly with wings like that one."

He sensed her calming down and listening. She knew a lesson when she heard one. That was good.

"This one is black. Leathery. No scales. And has a pair of horns. Four legs." He raised the glass to his eye again and finally caught it.

The black beast arched its long neck and undulated from its head to the end of its rat-like tail. Taking a deep breath, it coughed a wave of powerful kinetic energy down onto the city. The walls cracked and one of the turrets on a temple exploded from the impact.

"We have to go!" Sybal screamed again, tugging hard on the reins of her steed making it turn tight circles with a drawn out whinny.

"We have to plan!" he snapped back, reaching over and grabbing the reins from her hand. "This is a black dragon."

Still angry, she asked, "What cities lie in the Black Sea?" She breathed, actually thinking.

Tzarik's face fell and his blue eyes dimmed. "Porsh."

"The City of the Dead?" Sybal's voice went soft as if speaking a deadly curse.

With this new angle to factor in, Tzarik let go of her horse. "We have to get inside the city and find the orichalcum smith. We are going to need some mighty big spears."

EVEN RUNNING, it took them more than five minutes to reach the city walls. Inside, the people already looted in a panic. Recognized by their garb and Tzarik's eyes and pulsating white veins, many clung to their cloaks, begging the Runers to defeat the monster. Quickly, they were pointed to the smith who dealt in orichalcum.

"What about the dragon?" Sybal asked, her voice trembling.

"It doesn't have scales and will burn in this sun. With any luck, it will crawl back to wherever its hiding and wait out the sun. It must have flown during the night."

"And we'll attack it then?"

"Oh, yes." Tzarik could not keep the sarcasm out of his voice. "We'll roll a whole ballista with about five orichalcum spears up into the thick jungle, up the mountainsides, over the rivers, and shoot it while it sleeps."

"Bastard," Sybal hissed, glaring down at him.

He saw in her eyes and the way her body went stiff that she wanted to kick him again in the face. He liked the fight in her but could not take her ignorance. She needed to learn...but to learn, she had to be trained.

"Hey!" Tzarik called, hammering on the door with a tongs and anvil sign above it.

"Go away!" a high, male voice inside shouted. "Or can't you see the giant black demon in the blue sky?"

"We're Runers," he shouted, glancing over his shoulder to keep one eye on the beast. As he suspected, it flinched and roared a high-pitched scream to the sun.

"It's retreating," Sybal whispered, shading her eyes and watching it dip towards the jungle. "Don't they have sun in Porsh?"

"They do, but it's not as harsh," Tzarik mused. He hadn't been positive the thing would hide, but relief filled him when he realized he'd have time to prepare. He turned to the smith's door and raised his hand to slam his fist down again when it opened.

A boy about Sybal's age with the black skin of Alika and their trademark dreaded hair bedazzled with gems and metals opened the door. He sighed, placing one hand on his hip, looking them up and down.

"So you are," he said in a thick accent that rolled his Rs and enunciated his guttural tone. "You have coin?"

"No," Sybal sighed, hanging her head.

"Quiet," Tzarik growled at her. He noted her flinch. To the smith, he said, "We will dispatch the dragon."

The boy smirked, rubbing his fingers together. "The absence of dragons does not fill my belly or keep my sister off the street, Runer. Just like it won't buy you orichalcum."

Sybal put her hand on Tzarik's shoulder and squeezed, pulling him back a step. "I am close friends with Prince Rahul," she said. "I am Sybal of Ala'Nar, his betrothed. I can promise you payment once the dragon is dealt with."

The smith looked her up and down. Her veins were not pronounced yet and her eyes had not turned enough to be suspicious. "You don't look like a Runer. No runes, no special blade."

"I hired the Runer," she said quickly, jumping on the opportunity to sell Tzarik as the sole fighter. "Rahul will pay you. You have my word."

The scream of the dragon echoed down the blue streets. The smith pressed his lips to one side, looking past them at the damage the beast did with one shout from its terrible maw.

"Fine," he snapped. He stepped back into his shop and led them out the back to his workstation.

The inside of the shop had been lined with elegant and elaborate swords, halberds, spears, and other weapons Sybal hadn't seen before. Most looked ridiculous and unfit for a real fight. Outside, the fires and bellows heaved with work in progress.

"Oh!" Sybal gasped when the liquid metal greeted her eyes. It swirled and glinted like an oil covered rainbow, glittering all the way through, not just on the surface.

"I was working with your special metal already," the smith said, wiping his hands on his leather apron before grunting and pulling on the bellows. The fire erupted, snapping and hissing. "What did you have in mind?"

"Ballista," Tzarik said simply, picking up a small orichalcum blade. It wasn't curved. It pointed out straight and the pommel resembled a short sword from the far west where the pale men lived. Tiny gems dotted the hilt.

"That's pretty immobile," the smith said, cocking a confused brow as he nonetheless poured the molten metal into a cast.

"Just need one shot," Tzarik said simply.

"Have you hunted a dragon before?" Sybal asked, genuinely intrigued.

Tzarik waited before answering. A memory came back, stopping his words and his breath. A dragon, a wound, fire. The horror that only comes from being abandoned and bleeding out.

"No." His voice strained past his tense throat. "But the knowledge of other hunts can influence something you've never done before. Past experience can help in almost any situation if you can deduce how to adapt."

Not wanting to wait, Tzarik instructed the smith to tell him when the spears were finished. Not beckoning Sybal, he left to wait in a shady part of the city and meditate on his plan.

Taking a large drink from a glass bottle, the burn of the alcohol warmed his cold veins. Hoping the drink would wash away the risen memories, he downed half the bottle in a matter of minutes. He casually leaned against the golden walls of a high-end pub, listening to a jongleur inside trill about a pirate and a kidnapped wench. The sweet smoke from the pipes and the mindless chatter always helped him focus. The way people immediately forced normalcy after an upset always surprised him. Across the road, his huge black horse began to grind its teeth on the hitch post.

Sybal left the smith and he watched her look for him. She even called his name but he stayed hidden among a crowd— a technique he taught himself in the throngs of Wu-Tang on the continent Xia. He wanted to keep an eye on her, knowing full well she might rush to the palace and try to get an audience with Rahul if she thought she was alone.

"I didn't touch her!" a young man shouted as a huge, wild-eyed woman in glittering, moth-eaten clothes tossed the jongleur out of the pub into the street. "Don't!" he cried as his broken, wailing wheel fiddle followed him out with a mighty crash.

What little interest Tzarik showed in the disruption vanished when his cool eyes rested on Vicdan's distressed body lying in the street. Unable to help himself, he smirked.

"Did you try hiding in her pocket?" he asked in a deep, gravelly voice. "I'm sure you emptied it before."

Vicdan pushed himself up, sniffling and collecting the pieces of his stolen instrument. "This is what you get when you try things the right way, Runer. When you play by their rules, they hate you just the same."

"Huh," he grunted, not completely disagreeing. Remembering how Sybal took to the youth even though he picked her pocket clean as well, he got an idea. "Come with me. There's coin in it for you."

WITH VICDAN'S HELP, Tzarik rolled a ballista—secured from the royal guard—to a good point outside the city. Up a few sandy dunes and some rocky slopes, he began to position the war machine.

"Push when I pull," he grunted, sweat stinging his eyes. "Wait." Unable to help himself, he removed his cloak, weapons, runes, and tunic. He tossed them aside.

"Gods," Vicdan exhaled when he saw the scars and web of marks across his body.

Tzarik noted his tone and the immediate respect as the jongleur immediately did as instructed.

"Where is Sybal?" the young man asked as Tzarik brought out pegs and rope to anchor the ballista.

"I don't know."

"Don't know or care?"

"You're mouthy for a lord. Most can read social cues and know when to keep their lips shut." With a shout, he hammered the first stake into the hard ground, checking the aim to make sure it hadn't moved too much. "She might be at the palace," he added quietly.

"I knew it!" Vicdan smiled. "She's a lady for sure. No doubt engaged to a wealthy lord."

"Prince," Tzarik said, not caring if he gave away Sybal's secrets.

The young man's mouth went comically wide, gasping in theatrical glee. "Prince Rahul is engaged to our Sybal?"

"She's not *ours*," Tzarik snapped. Realizing what he said, he roared again, driving the last stake into the ground. "Not yours."

"There you are!"

Both men turned to find Sybal fighting her way up the last stretch of the stone hill, leading a sad looking mule with the ballista shots on its back. Tzarik quickly ordered Vicdan to help unload the shots. He placed one on the ballista and ran his bare hand up and down the shaft slowly. The smith knew his work; his fingers didn't hit a single notch, deformity, or crack in the precious metal.

"We only need one shot," he began to lecture. "Aiming is the hard part. You can't fire when the target is in the center of the crosshairs here." He pointed to the metal ring with an X in the center. "It will travel too slowly, fall, lose height, and momentum. So you want to—"

Vicdan screamed and tore back down the path they had just trudged up. Tzarik spun around. A flock of terrified birds erupted from the jungle and the roars of frightened tigers rumbled across the horizon. The huge, black wings of the dragon rose into visibility over the trees, leaving its shady hiding place. Not wasting time, the great black monster twisted midair and launched towards the city.

"I thought you said it would only come out at night?" Sybal gasped, running to the ballista.

"It should." Tzarik was so struck by the sudden reappearance that fear hadn't even touched his tone yet. "Move, let me aim."

Pushing Sybal aside, he gripped the huge mechanism. Glaring through the crosshairs, he began to track the monster. Frustration quickly clouded his mind as the dragon whipped back and forth, making it impossible for him to guess its movements. It dove, with a cracking roar like thunder, a blast emanated from its maw, plowing through the palace walls.

"Shoot it!" Sybal screamed, gripping her hair in agony. "He'll kill someone!"

Anger quickly overcame the frustration. Why did the dragon fly so erratically? Almost like it bucked, trying to throw a rider from its neck.

Wiping the sweat from his brow, he took a calming breath before trying to plot the dragon's flight patterns again. The drink in his gut reached for his brain, blurring the world and pitching the solid ground he stood on. Why did he care where she went? She could stay with her lover if that's what she wanted. It didn't matter.

Gasping, he locked on to the dragon, finally seeing an opportunity. It just needed to dip once more...

With a savage scream, Sybal threw her entire body against him. Her being a foot taller than him, the drink sloshing around his brain, and the heat from the sun all added together sent him sprawling. With a grunt, he landed on the orichalcum spears. He gasped again as he felt the monster-killing metal slice his lower hip just above his belt. The magic metal did its work immediately, boiling his white blood.

"Don't!" he shouted, fighting to get to his feet. But too late.

Sybal fired the shot, missing the dragon drastically. The metal spear flew towards the city, clattering somewhere behind the walls.

Despite the pain in his every limb, Tzarik lifted another shot and ran to the ballista. "Bitch, move!" he grunted, kicking her hard in the side of her knee. She tumbled down with a scream of pain.

He slipped, hurrying back to the machine.

"Wait. I see him!" She struggled to stand on her one good leg.

Tzarik cursed her sharp eyes. He spotted Rahul before, standing out on a ledge, giving orders to his men. The prince didn't cower inside his palace or leave the fight to another: he faced it himself. With the delay from their tussle, the dragon vomited one last blast against the golden palace. Half the structure gave way under the attack, clouds of sandy dust obscuring the place Rahul stood. It would be minutes before the dust cleared, but he'd seen structures destroyed before. He knew, without a doubt, that the ledge was gone. As would be anyone who stood on it.

"No!" Sybal shrieked with a throat-tearing cry, her eyes locked onto the place. "He's fine, he'll make, he'll..." Her voice devolved into gasps and hopeful sobs. "Tzarik?" she pleaded.

This time he didn't aim. He didn't wait. The pain in his veins slowed down. A feeling of doom replaced the burning inside him. He couldn't see into the palace, didn't hear any cries. He just knew. The melancholy that welled up inside, cooling him off, wasn't for himself.

Sybal would be torn. Maybe destroyed. He just knew.

Holding his breath, he fired the ballista. The shot flew to its mark, downing the giant beast as it circled back wide towards the jungle.

OUTSIDE THE PALACE, Sybal paced back and forth with Vicdan for company while Tzarik went in to retrieve their payment.

"You should have let me go in," Sybal moaned outside the palace gate when Tzarik emerged, sacks of coins and gems weighing down his stallion's saddlebags. "Please, I want to see him."

He gripped her upper arm, glaring into the distance, and pulled her away. "No," he said sharply.

Sybal's face went pale, her brown eyes going wide. Somehow, it hurt Tzarik's heart to see her face turn to utter despair.

"Is he...?" Her eyes snapped back to the demolished palace and she made a run for it, screaming his name.

"Don't!" He threw himself onto her, tackling her hard to the ground. To his surprise, she was exceptionally strong in this moment and almost threw him off. "Sybal, stop!"

"Rahul!" she screamed, tears tearing a clean track down her cheeks. "He was all I had! He loved me! He *wanted* me!"

Vicdan joined Tzarik in supporting Sybal's long body as she collapsed in on herself, still fighting to go inside the remains of the palace. Around them, women and children cried for their dead prince, flowers and other offerings already piling up around the parameter of the palace.

"Let go of her," Vicdan chided Tzarik as he tried to haul her to her feet. Once the Runer disentangled himself from them, Vicdan wrapped his arms around Sybal, stroking her long blond hair as they sat in the street.

"We need to get out of sight," Tzarik hissed as passersby began to point and whisper. "Things will get dangerous. These people are already angry."

These two didn't understand, their rosy lives coloring the city people. Too often he dispatched a monster and then had been driven out of town out of fear for his own life because not every citizen could be saved. The people would turn on a Runer faster than the ocean during a monsoon. Yes, he saved them, but if not every person came out the other side alive, it was his fault. And he had to pay.

"Let her weep, for Krishvu's sake," Vicdan snapped back.

Tzarik waited, but a few palace guards stopped their pacing to stare at them. A few citizens began to close in.

"Vicdan, we have to go," he whispered.

Sybal's weeping had not quieted at all, drawing more viewers.

"Heartless," Vicdan murmured.

Having enough, Tzarik shoved the young lord away from his apprentice, hauled her up onto his horse, and threw his own leg over. Just as he moved, so did the angry mob, drawing all kinds of weapons and screaming as they moved in on the Runers who had caused the death of the prince. He understood. When a farmer died or a peasant, the people were angry for only so long. This time the ruler of the land had perished.

"Go!" Vicdan shouted, cartwheeling up behind Tzarik on his huge steed.

Clutching Sybal in front of him with Vicdan's arms wrapped tightly around his middle, he gripped the saddle hard with his legs as they spun around, fleeing the city in a cloud of dust to tumultuous roars of anger.

He wove through the streets out the back end, towards the jungle. While unfriendly, the jungle would offer protection and more than a million places to hide. Not to mention water and hunting. As he came out the back, the corpse of the dragon lay in stark contrast to the golden sands.

"What's that?" Vicdan asked, pointing to the dead beast.

Tzarik saw them too. All along the dragon's wing muscles and on its face, tiny white runes stood out, painted on its black skin.

"Necrotic runes," he said, anxiety boiling up in his gut. He'd hoped to be in and out of the city quickly, just here for wares for Sybal. Instead, they'd found the necromancer.

Vicdan, despite his ignorance on the subject, knew this was not a good sign. "Necromancy?" he breathed in horror.

New theories began to cobble together in the Runer's mind. This dragon in Jarabu couldn't be a coincidence. The scriptures inked into its soft flesh were a sign. Did the necromancer know where they would travel? Did he follow them? A different kind of burden settled on his back as he wondered if he was now being hunted.

Chapter 17
A Job for a Scholar

"BUT IT WAS ALIVE," VICDAN PANTED WHEN TZARIK FINALLY slowed the horse in the dense, rubbery underbrush of the jungle. "Why necrotic runes? I don't understand."

"Shut up," Tzarik barked, slowing his own breathing, eyes darting around the varying horizon, rocky outcroppings, and tall trees.

"Why did they come at us?"

"Quiet!" he snapped in a hoarse rage. He raised his hand to backhand the young man and he suddenly went quiet. "These jungles are full of predators. Most of which you cannot see."

"Most are terribly poisonous."

The voice came from the left, so strong and fearless, that Tzarik's blade screamed as he drew it, turning to face the hidden man. Crouched among brightly colored flowers in a mottled rainbow robe hid Sharar. A leather pack on his back, a quill and parchment in his hand, and spectacles sliding down his sweaty nose, he rose and smiled.

"Our paths are starting to cross a little too much, Runer," he said jovially. "What a wonderful circumstance that we both came to Jarabu to study oddities."

Seeing that Tzarik knew the man, Vicdan slid off the horse,

helping Sybal down. The two of them made their way to the other side of the big steed, towards a small patch of clearing. The bubbling sound of a spring convinced him here was a good place to rest. Instructing Sybal to find the water, he turned back to the scholar. She didn't argue, eyes glassy, and slid off the horse, slowly walking into the underbrush with the jongleur.

"I agree. Are you following me?"

Sharar sucked his lips in, trying to hide his smile. "You are too perceptive, Runer."

Tzarik grimaced and turned to his saddlebags to take a few supplies out. "It doesn't take your organized learning to know you are following me. I have never run into a single person so often. I just can't understand why."

"You're an interesting specimen, Runer." Taking his glasses off, Sharar rolled up his notes and stowed them in his satchel. "It would give me great pleasure to open you up one day and pin you under glass and a lamp."

Not easily rattled by violent threats, this one turned Tzarik's stomach. As a boy, he once saw a naturalist at work. He had a wide board of insects, small animals, and other creatures pinned with their limbs splayed wide. Their chests open for observation. Sometimes, they removed the insides of the animals and placed them in neat little, labeled jars.

"You don't have a lot of friends, do you?" the Runer asked after this last comment.

"I have money," the scholar said meaningfully. He locked his eyes on the Runer.

Now it became clear. Tzarik sighed, taking his bedroll and water bag off his horse. "What do you want me to kill? A rival bookworm? I don't do humans or Masakh."

Sharar tapped his lip, smiling. "Was that your crime?"

"How much you paying me?" he asked.

"Something you've never heard of: a steady income." He

tented his fingers and began to pace. "Monthly payments that you can draw from most any bank in a large city. An account of your own."

Intrigued, Tzarik finally met the scholar's eyes.

"Yes, you've never had something like that before, have you?" Sharar's smile widened, his eyes darkening. "It will cost you though."

His guard went up, but curious, he replied, "What do you want from me?" He motioned to his horse and his person where his runes and sword hung. "I don't have much."

"Just two things. Nothing to a man such as yourself." The scholar pretended to pick at his fingernails nonchalantly. "First, tell me your crime?"

Knowing a Runer's crime gave one power over him. Not control, but knowing what a Runer could not do often proved to be more powerful than knowing what he could do. Runers were hard to deceive so not many had fallen into the trap of being tricked into going against their runing oath. But Tzarik knew a few who had. One in particular stood out to him.

Licking his parched lips and choking on a dry swallow, he mumbled, "Everything."

"Excuse me?" Sharar's brow went up and his arms tensed, unamused. "How does a man commit every crime in existence?"

Shrugging, Tzarik said, "As you said: I am an interesting specimen." The rise in color in Sharar's face told him the scholar thought he taunted him. He also had a habit of bouncing on his heels when conversation did not please him. "What's the second thing?"

"You're body."

"What?" the Runer exclaimed, unable to hide his own discomfiture. A million scenarios began to run through his head of what the scholar would do to him. What he would want with his body. What it meant when he said that.

"When you die," Sharar added, smiling darkly at the perplexity that flashed over the Runer's face. "I'd like to take your corpse for science."

A small trickle of relief dripped down Tzarik's back. "Fine. I won't need it then anyway. Now cut this shit out and tell me what you want me to kill."

Sharar appeared at his side, holding out his hand. "Shake on it. We are gentlemen, after all."

Wanting him to leave, Tzarik took the proffered hand without hesitation and shook it. He had the soft hands of a man who had never done a day of work in his life.

He needed to find Sybal and get out of the stifling jungle.

"I want you to track a Porshain for me."

Tzarik flexed his brain into action. The story went that the Porshains were necromancers. The city had a history he didn't know everything about, but he learned most of the legend as a child like most on Al'Myrah. The crocatta came to mind. The runes on the dragon.

Morbidly curious, he cocked his head, examining everything about Sharar visible to his naked eyes. His skin glowed dark and tan with sweat. Necromancers were said to be pale; bloodless. They had blue eyes like Runers and their skin had to be tattooed over with the Necrotic Scriptures. Sharar had none of those qualities.

Sharar smiled, understanding Tzarik's suddenly intense gaze. "No, not I, unfortunately. His name is Tarkan. He is a lone necromancer."

"Porshains are a tribal people," the Runer cut in. "Have been since the fall of the city. Generations. He won't be alone."

"This one is," Sharar assured him. "I can't say why, and I'd like to know."

Something inside Tzarik stopped him from mentioning the battle of the risen they ran into in Bailu. It had to be the very necromancer he hunted. Sharar must know about the attack, but he didn't mention it. Tzarik decided to keep it to himself as well.

"He specializes in bestial necromancy," the scholar said when he brought himself back to the present.

"Bringing back animals rather than sentient beings?" Tzarik asked. Sharar was right: a necromancer actively roamed the sands. Had he been sure this one traveled alone, he might have pursued him harder.

"They don't. You are beginning to see the reason for my interest in this one."

"The dragon!" Tzarik turned to peer through the thicket. The dragon corpse had already vanished. So the Porshain was close.

"Yes," Sharar nodded, tapping his chin with his finger. "Somewhere out there, an undead dragon is preparing to unleash necrotic fury on a poor unsuspecting people. Oh, dear what should you do?"

The Runer didn't need to try to hear the ulterior motives in the scholar's words and tone; he spoke them like a sermon. He didn't know exactly what they were, but they lurked just under the surface of his glittering offer.

"You have an apprentice now," the scholar went on to convince him. "You have monetary needs. I am not an unreasonable man. Find him. Bring me reports."

He didn't like the man but that didn't give him reason to not take his money. A few obstacles halted him. Necromancers were closely related to Runers in their magic. He had never hunted one like himself before. It would be dangerous and Sybal was still new to the entire lifestyle, adjusting slowly.

She saved his life once, back on Bailu in the dead farmer's home. He owed her a little respect. When she requested trial by runing, she threw herself into his care without knowing him. She did it out of hope, for a chance to live. Her will to live put his to shame. Being close to her—in her mere presence—put his dark desire out of mind. He didn't even realize it went missing. For a time, with her, he lived. She needed to be taken care of, trained, given shelter. He could do that for her after what she gave up. After all she lost.

"I'll do it," he said finally. "How do I get word to you?"

Sharar smiled, rubbing his palms together greedily. "Excellent! Just leave word at whatever bank you withdraw from. The message will find me. I don't need updates every month, but I'd like to know whenever you find something or...kill something."

VICDAN DID WELL, no doubt out of fear of Tzarik's rage. He pitched the tent on a soft patch of moss near the river and started a small fire. The clearing stretched wide enough that should a predator wander into their camp, they had room to fight or flee. All around them, monkeys and other creatures in the branches above screamed and chattered at the setting sun.

Sybal sat near the water's edge, her feet dangling in the river, arms limp at her sides. Her long yellow hair fell to the ground behind her and her brown eyes gazed at images from long ago. Tzarik came up behind her.

"We have a job," he began.

"I've never touched a man," Sybal interrupted softly.

"Really?" Vicdan asked from behind them.

Tzarik turned and glared him into submission. To Sybal he said, "We have to prepare. I don't know where to start but the only lead we have is the dragon. We can track it after we get you outfitted."

"He was the first boy I liked," she went on, her voice ghostly and quiet. "I knew my family would hate me after everything just...fell out in the street. I wanted children, you know. His children. I dreamed so many times of our boy and girl. He'd look like me. Dark skin, yellow hair. And our girl would look like Rahul. Blackest eyes. A lotus in her hair. I've seen them so many times. I wanted to be a good queen."

"Are you listening to me?" Tzarik sighed.

"Can you let her weep?" Vicdan cut in.

"She's been crying for an hour!" the Runer snapped back. "We have to keep moving. But not you." He pointed hard at Vicdan. "You will stay in the city. I'll take you back first thing in the morning when I go and purchase the rest of what she needs to fight."

The jongleur went rigid, nodding stoically. "Fine."

EARLY MORNING HAD most citizens still abed, making it easier for Tzarik to go into town, get the garments and orichalcum blade for Sybal, and get out without having to spend the energy in avoiding the ignorant normals.

"Got paid anyway?" the smith's tone dripped with disdain.

Tzarik didn't deign to reply. Instead, he fixed the smith with a quizzical eye as he heaved the wrapped Runer tools and leather armor up onto his counter.

"The dragon got away," the smith said, unfazed. "After you shot it and let it devastate our city, it went down outside the walls. Then flew off an hour later."

Tzarik heaved the massive bundle up, grunting. "Didn't notice. Was too busy trying to flee for my life from you ignorant animals."

The smith firmly placed his palms onto the counter that divided them. "Our prince is dead. Our land is vulnerable. Or don't you care?"

Tzarik's brow flicked quickly. "I don't care."

Chapter 18
Tarkan

SURPRISE ALMOST HALTED HIS STEP WHEN HE ARRIVED BACK at the jungle camp and found Sybal rolling up the last of the items and tethering them to his tall mount. A quick glance around told him Vicdan had gone as well. He studied her quickly, noting her gait, face, breathing, and how she handled the items. Her steps were weak, not stomping or determined. She fastened her bedroll but when it slipped to the side, she aggressively yanked on the leather strap to tighten it and turned quickly to pick up another item. Her face remained placid, her lids a hard line. From this, he deduced she was still raw but ready.

"For you." He handed her the things he'd hauled back from the city. "I should have known a smith would swindle you out of good quality since you can't tell the difference."

She stopped, surprised at his gentle tone. "Thank you."

He watched her gently run her fingers over the curve of the shiny blade. He noticed her eyes flick to his orichalcum scimitar on his back and back to hers. Hers reached longer, curved more thinly as she stood nearly half a foot taller than him. He mentally prepared himself for the jokes she'd make about it later.

"Put on the armor," he instructed, taking her gear from her and turning to his horse. "I'll finish packing."

"What are we doing now?" she asked, moving behind a large patch of ferns to change out of the cheap armor.

"We have to track that dragon. I hope it leads us back to whoever raised it." He glanced over his shoulder.

Her tall, elegant frame rose above the ferns and his eyes caught the sun glancing off her broad, dark shoulders. She already had the slightest amount of new muscle showing. The line of her spine curved gently down to her lower back.

Picking up her belt where her satchel hung, he opened it and saw she had only carved two runes. She finished halat, the protective rune, most thoroughly. "You need to finish your runes. I'll teach you how to use them as we go. Drawing runes is a work of patience."

She stepped out and reached for her belt. He caught himself before he smiled and looked her up and down critically. The black leather armor gracefully hugged her hips. Where the tunic came off her gently curving shoulders, it left a gap. She'd have to protect her back.

They mounted up and he led them back to where the dead beast had taken flight. He trotted around the large prints in the sand, examining them from every angle.

"Look," he said, instructing her, "see how it took three or four long strides before flapping its wings." He pointed to deep ruts framed by lines in the sand where the wings would have pushed against it. "Four strides, three flaps before it took off."

He squinted to the west, pulling his black hood further over his forehead to block out the sun. "I don't know what's over there."

Sybal turned her white steed around and glared into the sun as well. "Small towns. Maybe one or two have an alderman. They don't have names this far out."

Tzarik weighed the information. The dragon could have gone that way without heading back to whoever brought it back. But it was the only lead they had.

The horses were used to traveling over the sand and they made good time. The jungle reached out farther the more west they rode. Several hours out, and ready to take a break from the glaring sun, they came upon harder earth and a small road leading into a jungle village. The trees and plant life spread far and wide, surrounding a village of huts. Some were built on the ground and others rose up from the earth into larger trees where rope bridges and platforms connected them. Colorful flowers flecked the green branches alone with vibrant fruits. The sun cut through the overhead thicket in bright yellow beams, reflecting off a blue river that ran right through the middle of the village, powering a mill.

A mix of human creatures and Masakh flowed through the village lanes, and some resembling the monkeys chittering in the trees crouched on the higher branches picking fruit.

"It's beautiful," Sybal sighed, a shy smile relieving the stress and melancholy on her face.

No sooner had she spoken the words of awe and the sand surrounding the village began to shift. Taking even Tzarik by surprise, he hissed and clicked at his black mount when fear took over its senses. The horse whinnied and began to buck, tossing its head. Seeing its fellow beast in terror, Sybal's white mount began to react as well.

"What is that?" she gasped.

The wind overtook them, ripping at their cloaks and kicking the sand up. From nowhere, an instant sandstorm erupted like a geyser, creating little whirling tornados.

"Look!" Tzarik pointed and Sybal followed his gaze.

From beneath the sand, hands, arms and legs fought like burrowing creatures to escape the shifting earth. An army of armored soldiers rose up from the ground and ran towards the beautiful village.

"We have to help!" Sybal kicked her horse, crying out as she thundered towards the village.

Tzarik knew calling out to stop her would be useless. All he could do was chase her down and try to make sure she didn't die fighting off an army of risen soldiers. Unsheathing his own blade, he rode after her, hoping she wouldn't hurt herself with her noble intentions. He did not believe in any deity, but if he prayed for one thing, it would be for her to not charge into an unknown fight ever again.

The monkey-type Masakh in the trees leapt down, staves in hand and began to beat the risen soldiers mercilessly. A few bird-types leapt into the air, slashing with their talons. The Masakh were a beautiful and old race but fierce in battle. A few brave human villagers took up pitchforks and other farming instruments to defend themselves.

Wanting to stay astride his horse as long as he could, Tzarik took out his recurve bow and fired a few shots into the attackers. The village already swarmed with them. Whirling his horse around, he saw a few rising up from the soft ground near the river —dozens came up inside the village.

"Runer, watch out!" a Masakh shouted, leaping up into a tree and hanging from his feet, using his tail for balance.

Tzarik turned and fired a thick black bolt right into a soldier's eye socket. He expected it to fall backwards but instead, the head jerked back, hanging by a few tendrils of its neck, and the creature continued to advance, grabbing his leg.

With a cry of disgust and terror, Tzarik kicked out at it, completely removing the head from the rotting shoulders. He heard its jaw crack and a few teeth flew out from the impact. He couldn't relax though. The headless, undead soldier regained its balance and walked towards him again, slashing mercilessly with its rusted sword.

"They won't die!" the Masakh in the tree cried out.

Tzarik soon ran out of breath staving off the attackers. No matter how he cut them, the risen soldiers would not stay down. One he hacked into five pieces; each limb severed. Only then did it slow down, the arms crawling with fingers digging into the earth.

"Tzarik!" Sybal screamed from the other side of the river. "Come to me!"

Continuously wheeling his horse around to keep the attacks at bay, he craned his neck to find the woman. He spotted her cowering against a tall wall of gray rock. Her hands stretched out before her with her halat rune clutched in them. He saw a weak protective circle faintly warbling around her as undead closed in.

With a savage cry, he cantered towards her and up the tiny earthen mound behind the bolder. From here, he had a clear sight-line to the rocky hills behind the jungle village. Something black caught his eye. He couldn't look yet. Leaping from the safety of his horse, he reached his hand down to Sybal. With a high-pitched grunt, she leapt up and took his hand. He groaned from the weight of the tall girl but managed to pull her up.

"Did you see?" she asked, pointing over his shoulder.

He turned to look now and saw it. Like in many paintings and tapestries that told the stories of the cursed city of Porsh, a lone black-clad figure stood far off near a large black crate.

"That's him!" Tzarik grabbed the reins, clawing his horse. "Sybal, take your horse and ride at him from the north, I'll come from the south. Make sure he sees you."

"Bait?" she cried, going more pale than normal.

"Do as I say for once, damn it!" he barked, kicking his horse.

"I can't leave the people," she protested.

Tzarik wheeled around, his blue eyes sparking like lightning in his dark hood. "Do this or so help me I will leave you to die here," he growled.

Fear lit Sybal's eyes and she quickly obeyed, mounting her horse and galloping out the northern side of the village.

He took off in the opposite direction, making a wide circle so the necromancer might not detect him amongst the fleeing villagers. Bodies stretched across the earth, blood reddening the river. He ignored it, eyes locked onto his pray.

Sybal's horse kicked up a cloud of dust in a straight line that the necromancer noticed almost right away. As Tzarik had hoped, he turned and began to stride towards him. As he rode, Tzarik slowly drew buhkar, the vapor rune. His form wavered and vanished even from his own sight. He abandoned his horse and dashed towards the accursed man. The necromancer marched towards a large sand dune where the black crate rested, his black robes billowing in the wind.

Tzarik took out his bow, the rune wearing off, and took aim. He didn't know what powers a necromancer would have but he couldn't kill him. The scholar wanted him alive. Taking a deep breath and holding it, he fired.

The wind caught the arrow and it wobbled on its way, missing its mark. The bolt shot through the ample length of the necromancer's undulating robes. The man turned, shock freezing his frame.

The necromancer was not unlike himself in appearance. His icy blue eyes glared out from under his black hood from a face so pale, Tzarik thought he wore a mask. The bit of his arms and hands that the Runer could see were covered in a black script, metal rings encircling each long, white finger. The man's face, while strange, did not show age. Tzarik almost felt as though he looked into a mirror.

"Why, Runer?" the necromancer called over the roaring wind that began to dissipate.

Behind him, a joyous cry rose from the village.

"There is a bounty out on you, necromancer," he offered simply.

"Tarkan," the necromancer supplied for his name. "Have things gotten so bad that a Runer is reduced to a bounty hunter? I have only just begun, Runer—found my freedom. I am sorry, but I will not be stopped."

"Don't move!" Sybal shouted, her chest heaving from the effort of running up the hill. She aimed her own bow at Tarkan.

The necromancer's face fell when she came into view through the whirling sand. "The trial of two?" he called to Tzarik. "How blessed you are. But how foolish of you to interfere with me. You have put yourself in the crosshairs, Runer. And now her."

Tzarik saw Tarkan telegraph his next move. He was going to run. "Stop!" he shouted, raising the small bow to take aim again. This time he had to calculate. The wind hadn't slowed anymore and it would affect his shot again.

"Don't get in my way, Runer!" Tarkan shouted back.

The necromancer turned, and behind him, the sand dune exploded into the sky with a deafening, earth shaking roar. The black dragon burst out of the sand, having been buried there, and a shot erupted from its gaping maw. Sybal screamed as it tore her side and the force of it knocked Tzarik off his feet.

He sat up just enough, coughing from the sand blowing into his nose and lungs, to see Tarkan mount the dead dragon and urge it into flight. The beast gripped the black crate in its long claws.

"You didn't have to cross me, Runer," he shouted. "I give you this one chance to leave. If you pursue me again, I will not take mercy on you."

Tzarik wanted to gallop after him, but Sybal lay screaming on the hot sand, a blast of white blood stroking through the sand under her. She clutched her ripped side, legs kicking in agony.

Bundling her into his arms, he hurried back to the village. The necromancer, Tarkan, threatened him and therefore her. He had angered his prey. Sybal was weak, untrained—guided by her need to save—a liability. He had no choice but to swallow his pride and fear and train her. The world—and Sybal—were not ready to deal with a renegade necromancer. He had to accept the trial of two.

Chapter 19
Death to Live

"KEEP HER SAFE," TZARIK ORDERED, PANTING AS HE DUMPED Sybal onto the doorstep of a scared, confused Masakh woman with feline attributes.

"I don't know Runers!" she protested. "I am a nursemaid! Pups, babies, kittens!"

He didn't stop to listen to her excuses. Driven by an urge he had not felt in years, he rushed to dispose of the burdensome woman and give chase to the undead dragon and his necrotic rider. He lost precious time tending to her needs and putting her in a safe place. He hadn't strode five steps before guilt made him toss the poor Masakh a cask of the sulfates with a rubber hose and needle. That was all he could do. Shouting for his horse, he gave chase to the black dot in the vast blue distance.

He didn't gain on his prey, but he got close enough to see the dragon clutched the large black container in its four claws. A story from the small fishing village of Moshav told how necromancers, who devastated the city thirteen years ago, traveled with wagons full of corpses. A mobile army. An army that could not be killed. What reason a necromancer would have to come out of hiding, forsaking his tribe, mystified Tzarik. He spurred his horse on as white froth gathered on its shoulders and flanks.

Why attack small, seemingly useless villages?

The continent of Bahratt lay in the southern west of the map if he remembered correctly. He knew how to get from one continent to the other but had not looked at a map in years. Al'Myrah hovered above it. The necromancer had been to both. Cursing his ignorance, he grew hot trying to think where the other continents lay in conjunction with his position. Oceanya scattered over the south-east...Xia ruled the northern east and the surrounding seas?

With a scream, he kicked his horse in anger, making it grunt with guttural protest. He felt its back hoof catch as it dragged through the sand. Looking up, his eyes flashed in rage: he lost sight of the airborne prey. With a roaring whinny, he pulled on the reins, turning his head this way and that. The glare off the desert sands burned his blood and his eyes.

"Don't follow me, Runer!"

Tzarik's bow creaked as he drew it quickly, whirling around to aim behind him. Several yards away near a rising hill that opened into a dark cave stood Tarkan, surrounded by his undead soldiers— a dozen at least. Behind him, crouched and dead, white eyes trained on him, waited the black dragon. To the side, open like a gaping maw, the black crate he saw clutched in the dragon's claws lay open.

Catching his breath, Tzarik swung his leg off his horse, unsheathed his orichalcum scimitar, and marched toward the necromancer.

"You cannot fight me, Runer," the necromancer called from behind his wall of undead. "Our magics are similar but mine are more powerful. Mine doesn't die. No blood, no life. A heart but no beat."

"You killed innocent people."

Tarkan laughed, rolling his head and smiling. The gesture looked odd, out of place. Like a joke at a funeral. "You are not a hero, Runer. Innocence doesn't matter to you. Nor I. We have more in common than you think."

"I am alive." Tzarik rushed the first two risen soldiers and cleaved their heads off with the curve of his sword. The corpses toppled down but stood right back up.

Tarkan took a step back, raising his hands to shoulder height. The wind picked up as the soldiers began to advance. When commanding the soldiers, Tzarik saw black veins crawl underneath Tarkan's flesh and the necrotic scriptures wavered. The veins pulsed even on his face, his blue eyes glinting like lightning.

Remembering how the soldiers fell, collapsing after he broke from such a stance before, Tzarik realized that Tarkan had to set himself apart from his army, concentrating his magic.

Taking down one more corpse and kicking the first two he had decapitated away, he grunted, "I just have to get to you."

"You should thank me, Runer." Tarkan moved a few steps further back, closer to the dragon. "Monsters are few and far between. I raise them back from the dead. You killed that crocatta twice. Without me, you will be out of a job sooner. People are no longer afraid of monsters like they used to be. They are rare now. And you are becoming useless. I give you purpose."

As he pushed closer to the necromancer, the risen soldiers closed in, forcing him to back away or become encircled and trapped. Tarkan's words rang true. A darkness inside him rose up over the years as monsters became harder to find, forcing him to travel into the farther reaches of the world to find darker more dangerous specters and creatures to eradicate.

Gasping, he quickly clutched the halat rune and quickly drew a circle that followed him as he fled to a higher, rockier ground that led up to the lip of the cave. One soldier lunged at him, breaking on the magical barrier. With the few seconds of safety he had, he drew jiun as slow as he dared. From the jiun rune clutched in his sweaty palm, he felt its fury penetrate his veins.

Jiun, the fury rune, allowed him to push past his inhibitions and any pain in his physical body. His wounds ached and his brain had gone groggy. With jiun pulsating in his sulfates, he pushed past and mercilessly hacked at the soldiers. The adrenaline moved him faster and stronger, allowing him to fell several risen soldiers to the point they could only crawl. Jiun often came as a last result as Runers could injure themselves in the fury and not know. But Tzarik thought this situation warranted a little fury.

In the rage of the jiun rune, Tarkan's words came more clearly to him. A purpose. Yes, he had been looking for a reason to live. But he couldn't take his own life...Something else needed to do it for him. Nothing mattered to him anymore. Life had lost its reason years ago. But now even death seemed impermanent. So what would be the point of dying? What was the point of anything?

"Even when you want to die, you want to live," the necromancer said. A few soldiers shuddered where they stood as he lost his focus for a split second, dodging away from Tzarik and his newfound high ground. "You are desperate for a reason to survive. *I* want to survive! Why can't you leave me be? Stop following me!"

A roar from the dragon almost stopped Tzarik from spinning towards Tarkan, taking several heads with him, but the rune pushed him on, the protective circle vanishing. Instinct took over and made him dodge the dragon's pulsing shot but the move threw him into the rusty spear of a nearby risen.

"It's my job to rid the world of monsters," Tzarik smirked, unconcerned with the fresh wound. Drawing artiah near his side, the wound began to lightly mend itself just enough to stop the bleeding and silence the pain. Jiun's effect began to wear off and the aftereffects began. His vision turned gray and misty.

"I'm a monster, Runer?" Tarkan taunted from somewhere in his peripheral vision now blocked out by the rune. "We're not that different, you know. We work for pay. We both...are hated. You are but one man and cannot fight back against that hate because those who hate you pay you coin. Surrounding yourself with dead is the best defense."

I'm a monster, he thought. Gulping for air now that jiun wore off, he parried a few blows and dodged away from the blur that was the dragon. He needed to keep away just a few more seconds and the aftereffects would dissipate.

"And you are bound by your oaths," Tarkan went on, now several paces to the left of his dragon.

Drawing buhkar quickly, Tzarik vanished into black mist, slipping between the risen to get closer to Tarkan. As he neared the necromancer, the silver rings stood out on his long pale fingers in the sun. One gleamed with blackish red veins.

Before he came close enough to strike, Tarkan either sensed his presence or saw him. Dropping his hands, he dashed away towards his undead dragon.

"Face me, coward!" Tzarik roared, reaching for his bow on his back.

"You really do mean to kill me!" Tarkan laughed as he and his dragon rose into the air. "You didn't have to come after me, Runer. Let me take the cities, let me raise my army. I will keep you in business. Give you a reason to live."

Glaring into the sun, he fired a bolt. With a satisfying thud and a scream of pain from Tarkan, he confirmed that the necromancer was made of living flesh and not like his risen entourage. Preparing another bolt, he leapt over the fallen soldiers and climbed up onto the black crate the corpses had been transported in to get a better shot. Tarkan stood on the dragon's back, cloak billowing.

"You're involved now, Runer. You didn't have to be. I'd have killed you happily, but you just tried too hard. I can see you won't stop. What about that woman of yours? A tall, strong, lithe and supple child, Runer. Probably never been touched by a man... unless you?"

He heard the smirk in the necromancer's voice more than saw it. Furiously, he let the bolt fly but it missed drastically.

"A risen Runer," he shouted as he finally straddled the dragon, taking control. "What a fine addition to my army!"

Tarkan fled once again on his dragon, not back to the village as he had threatened, but towards the silver mountains in the north that lined the ocean. Rage boiling his white blood, Tzarik cast about for his horse but didn't see the creature anywhere. Cursing its yellow belly, he leapt from the crate, sheathing his sword. It would be a long walk back to the village. The necromancer's words rang in his rage-fueled mind.

Feeling the chase, the desire, the hunt had given him hope for just a day. Coupled with the notion of training Sybal, he forgot about ending his life for a few blessed hours. Seeing a future, not desiring death, confused him.

Sybal confused him.

She charged in to save others, even him, without any thought to herself. Courageous but foolish. If she could be trained, she'd be a different kind of Runer: a Runer with a moral center.

"Different will kill you," he reminded himself. Maybe keeping her around, training her, would be the death of him. Would that be so bad?

He was involved now; Tarkan spoke truth. This man, this necrotic monster, would harm others unflinchingly and spread fear. Some larger force, more than he had ever cared to think about, began to move. Did he have to take action against it?

"Damn you, Sybal," he grunted, planning where to begin.

Chapter 20

Porsh

SYBAL PRIED OPEN HER EYES BUT THE FEVERISH NIGHTMARES
played in front of her over the visible reality. The ceiling made of
thatch and the soft coos and pets from the feline Masakh were the
only tangible things she held onto in the time she spent semi-
conscious, trying to bring her head out of the nightmares. She tried
to sit up but her body ignored her, paralyzing her to the canvas-
stretched bed. Sweat trickled down to her backside, making her
jump, thinking something was crawling down her spine.

The images she saw while pulling herself from the sleep paralysis terrified her. She tried to breathe but something wrapped tight
around her ribs, suffocating her. She wanted to cry out for her
mother and father but knew they wouldn't come. And Rahul...he
could not save her anymore. She wanted to go home.

"Mother!" she finally screeched when she got a deep enough
breath. Her side tore in agony and fresh, white blood spilled over
her hands.

"Stop!" Tzarik shouted angrily from behind the red nightmare
fog. "You're ripping your stitches. I don't have enough sulfates
made. Sybal!"

Tzarik cared? He came to her? She knew he wouldn't mind if
she dropped down an abandoned mine but he was all she had.

"Help me!" she cried, reaching up and feeling his shoulders as
his hands gripped hers, pinning her down.

Finally, the paralysis released her. The red vision vanished and she bolted up, wrapping her arms around her mentor's neck. To her surprise, his arms embraced her waist and one of his hands stroked her hair. Gasping, she smelled his hair in her face. For once he smelled clean, like frankincense and sandalwood. She breathed deeply and steadily like he taught her to do and soon the world stopped spinning. The bright feathers and the worried eyes of the bird-like and feline Masakh greeted her as she clutched him in fright.

Tzarik pushed her back into the bed and opened her chemise to inspect the damage she had done. She tried to cover herself but saw he had already done so with his cloak.

"It's not as bad as I thought," he said flatly.

His fingers traced a hot, tender spot on her side. She gasped but smiled at the tickling touch. "Sorry," she quickly added when he glared at her. "I've never been hit by a dragon before."

"Anyone who has is long dead," the Runer mused, lacing her top back up and preparing her armor. "Runers are a tough folk. You do the name justice."

She fought hard, stopping her breath and willing her face to light up when he complimented her. This new found fondness for him intrigued her. With no one else left in the world who cared about whether she lived or died, he'd be the one she'd pick if she had to. But he all but told her he had no will, no reason, to go on living. Looking up into his blue eyes, his white veins glinting in the sunlight, she wanted to be his reason. She could save him. She'd ask questions, force him to see that he had to stay for her. If this kept him alive, she'd consider all she'd gone through a success. He'd be annoyed, maybe even chide her—it would hurt—but she'd have to be strong.

"Where are we going?" she asked, swinging her legs over the side, forcing a grunt and groan to stay behind her lips.

Tzarik didn't answer outright, quickly—without anyone else

but her seeing—flicking his head towards the onlookers. "Back to Al'Myrah. We have a job to investigate."

He handed her a small vial sealed with red wax, a clear-grey liquid inside.

"For the pain," he instructed her to drink it with a flick of his hand. "On the way, we finish your runes."

The warm light inside her that began with his embrace, erupted like the mountains of the island nations, warming her as she quickly shot the vial's contents. The taste hit her after and made her shiver. But it quickly melted in the fire of excitement.

"HALAT," she whispered as she gouged the river stone with all her strength. Her hand slipped, palm dripping with sweat, and a small cut opened on the side of her thumb. Cursing with a few names of gods, she dropped the stone and the tools.

"Your blood will strengthen them," Tzarik said softly from across the fire where he lounged, flipping through a book with beautiful illuminations. "Don't worry about it."

Desiring nothing more than to throw the runes and her mentor into the small fire, she instead took a long draft from a sack of mead the Masakh gave them before they left.

"I have buhkar, artiah, and atan done." She smiled, spreading them out inside the ring of light cast by the campfire. Admiring her handy work, she opened her satchel and began to mix paints to add to the runes. She felt Tzarik judging her over the fire. "If I have to wear them, I want them to look nice," she said defensively.

"I forgot you were of noble birth." The Runer flipped the pages until he found another illumination and began to study it.

"My brother used to only look at the pictures too." She smiled. "Before he learned to read." She started to laugh.

Tzarik didn't give her a look, but she caught a change. She had never been very observant, but the recent training and the instincts from the Runer's blood heightened her observational skills. Tzarik still saw more than her and could deduce anything from a person's age to whether or not they were going to temple that evening and what sin they would be confessing.

She saw him tense. He started with his toes. Hidden from any regular observer in boots, they wouldn't see the anxiety begin. It traveled up his short, lean legs to where he ever so slightly repositioned his hips on the sand. Then his fingernails paled as he tightened his grip on the book. His face did not change, which made her doubt her deduction for a moment.

Guilt slackened her smile and she set her hands on her knees. "I'm sorry," she said softly. "I didn't know."

"I didn't tell you. I suppose it's too late to warn you that I know very little about very much."

"I suppose I took my education for granted," she said softly.

Carefully using just her eyes, she looked up at the book he gripped in his hands. *History of the Runic Codex.*

Daring to question a no doubt sensitive topic of the man she had just forced to feel inferior, she asked, "Why do you have them if you can't read?"

Tzarik leaned closer to the illustration. "They were my mentor's. I kept them out of spite."

She heard the lie in his flat tone. Looking him over and replaying his reply, she tried to ascertain the truth. Nothing came up. She'd have to observe him more, learn his ticks. She didn't want to waste another apology. It would have no effect on Tzarik. There was one thing she could do.

"What are you trying to find in there?" she asked, going back to her work.

"Anything about our mark."

Frowning, she stood up and walked around the fire to sit next to him. "This is a history of runes."

This time, Tzarik's tepid anxiety turned to frustration. "The necromancer had runes on his skin. I saw them on his face and hands. I assume they were all over his body." He pointed to an illumination near the back of the book. "See this one."

A naked man and woman stood together, one palm facing out, their bodies entirely covered in black runes. Sybal's eyes immediately bored into the image: below the woman lay a shriveled, black mass. Looking again, she saw the illustrator had drawn a tear on the woman's face, but she held the hand of the man next to her.

"Are they like us?" she whispered, afraid speaking loudly might frighten away the image or anger Tzarik.

He took a shallow, quick breath. "They might be."

"Why does that scare you?"

He slammed the book shut and threw it at her, making her jump. He shoved her out of his way and stood up, going to the horses to retrieve another blanket. The desert night would turn cold.

"Is it that he knows more about death than you?" she snapped, clutching the book, ready to throw it back at him. "That you want to die but now know someone could bring you back, an eternal life of servitude, trapped in your rotting corpse? That's what death is anyway, Runer! It's loneliness. Isolation. Black nothing, unable to find love or joy."

His blue eyes glowed at her from the darkness. She became aware of her entire body, illuminated by the firelight while he hid in the darkness. She saw him blink, take a blanket, and walk farther into the dark desert. The moon hung in a waxing crescent not providing much light.

Annoyed, she opened the book and lay on his bed, which he had already made. She read until her eyes hurt and fell asleep with the book propped open on her chest.

THE JOURNEY DAYS went on longer when Tzarik made her walk, telling her she needed the exercise. The nights came no less relaxing; she carved her runes or he forced her to do weight training. Exhaustion crept up on her without a restful day after they crossed the river back onto Al'Myrah. The only rest she got came when she insisted they stop in Hatal and rent a room in a public house. Tzarik bypassed Ala'Nar and she didn't mention it. In Hatal, she spent her share of the prize on a room and a hot bath, saving the coin from her own job for later.

She made Tzarik wait in the common hall while she bathed. Catching sight of her long, now thinning body in the tall mirror stopped her as she climbed into the copper tub. She pulled her blond hair over one shoulder and admired her healing scar at her side. The dragon blast hurt but she smiled: her first trophy scar. She lay in the tub for almost an hour, dozing off. She expected Tzarik to burst in and demand a turn but he didn't appear. She scrubbed her feet and washed her hair to her satisfaction, dressed, and returned to the common hall. As he passed her to use the room, he whispered, "Watch your coin," and left.

While she waited to sleep, she ordered hot food. Neither of them were any good at hunting. They almost exclusively ate dried meat, lentils from a preserved jar, and dried fruit for days. The lamb and dark alcohol put her into a daze. Never again would she take for granted hot water, warm food, and a bed off the sand. She scanned the room, practicing her observation skills. She spotted a female jackal Masakh on her way out the door and saw a man, with a wife on his arm, quickly let his eyes flick to the Masakh as she left. Looking harder, she spotted a few gray hairs from the Masakh woman on the man's wife's trousers. Scoffing, smiling in awe at the infidelity, she took a long drink. She guessed they both had lain with the jackal female and neither of them told the other.

"Why would you jeopardize the love and relationship you already have?" Her judgment made the words crack in her throat.

Wondering if any other Runer frequented these kinds of public houses, she removed her hood and let her barely-visible white veins show. Her eyes had begun to pale from brown to an odd purple, but she still did not have the Runer's eyes. Using her distinct features as a beacon, she hoped another Runer might spot her and join her at the table. Instead, all she got were second glances and a wide birth from passersby.

Her loneliness grew with this reaction. Runers did work for every man, why did they hate her so? Yes, they were criminals, but they had paid for it with their lives. How many damned souls lived beyond the runing? And how many of those lucky ones lived past their first hunt? Tzarik mentioned once that as far as he knew, he was the oldest Runer. She guessed he might be thirty-five.

Were the necromancers just as lonely? Were they guilty like Runers? Did they kill and then raise the dead?

She contemplated the book from the night before while she waited for bed. After an hour when Tzarik did not return, she went up to the room. He had left the lamp on in the center of a small table near the tub. Squinting in the darkness, she saw him sleeping in his bed. Carefully, she tiptoed over to get a glimpse of him in the most vulnerable state. He slept on his left side, one hand on his sword next to him, his head resting in the crook of his other arm. She smiled and curled up on her own bed, glad to have something soft and not full of sand fleas to sleep on.

The rest of the journey around the south of Al'Myrah, she dreamed of that bed and that hot bath. They passed a few villages, a small town holding a fleece fair where she picked up a patent for a monster in Hatal, and finally arrived at the place near the channel that cut off Porsh from the rest of the continent. The ground turned from sand to hard, black glass. The waves of the Black Sea lapped at the cursed, brittle earth making high, clinking chirps as it hit the contours.

"Lightning sand?" she asked, kicking it with the toe of her boot.

"Looks like it," Tzarik replied, adjusting on his horse. "Or some kind of affliction, blight, or corruption."

Looking more closely, the sand seemed to have withered, forming a sharp, uneven wave. Like the wind picked it up, forming dunes, and it just froze there.

Beyond the channel, nothing could be seen. A thick, gray mist or smoke hid the city beyond. It muffled any sound coming at it from beyond the channel. A gull squawked but it didn't echo past the channel, like the bird had screamed into a wool blanket.

"If it's cursed," Sybal asked, hoping her ignorance didn't annoy him, "will we be affected by walking into it?"

"Leave the horses. We walk." Tzarik slung his sword across his back, strapped his crossbow to his thigh, and slung the recurve bow and quiver over his shoulder.

They wrapped their cloaks around them, covering their faces as well. Together, they walked closer to the channel. When they were practically in its depths, Sybal spotted a bridge once made of stone, now glassed over like the rest of the earth. Cautiously, Tzarik began to cross. Once they made it halfway over the withered bridge and into the gray smoke, all sound stopped.

"Whoa," Sybal gasped when her ears popped. Her voice, stopped by her face cover, hardly reached farther in the mist. "Can you hear me?"

"Barely," Tzarik replied. "Listen well, I can't see far."

Once beyond the bridge, the city of Porsh loomed into view. At first, Sybal thought the structures must have been huge, reaching up to the sky. The sun perpetually shone into the gray mist at a setting angle, blinding them as they proceeded in. Turrets and temple minarets stabbed through the light and fog.

"Gods..." Tzarik whispered once they were near enough to the city.

"I can't see as well as you," Sybal whined. But she stopped her words when the Runer blood adjusted her eyes.

The castles and other evil edifices looked so tall because the earth on which they sat, loomed elevated yards above the withered earth. The rocky formations hung suspended in the air like some great being tossed them up and they stuck in the gray mist. Not all the buildings floated on levitating earth. Some still latched to the ground like immense structures should.

Carefully, they entered the city, not a soul to be heard or a rodent seen. Every inch of the city preserved in the strange glass or turned to the substance. The deeper into the city they went, the more a feeling of doom closed in. Tzarik shivered.

"You feel it?" Sybal asked, unable to stop herself from quaking. Not from cold or fear, but from something she could not describe. The more she tried not to shake, the greater the vibration.

"Necrotic ether." Tzarik didn't sound sure. "Look for a home with this symbol." He handed her a parchment where he had traced a family sigil. "Tarkan had this on a ring that looked like a family crest."

"The book said necromancers were tribal, so this is a good start," she agreed and began to scan the city's homes.

The days and nights did not come and go. They walked for hours until finally, Sybal swayed on her feet from exhaustion. They drew a map of the city as they investigated, marking where they had been. Realizing the sun would not set or rise inside the cursed city, they slept with only their instincts to guide how long they rested. Tzarik found the entrance to a great palace that neither of them wanted to go in. The gates were sharp, black, and wicked looking. Evil, edged runes covered almost every stone of the palace, painting it black.

"The book mentioned a place of apostles," Sybal informed him as they walked the parameter. "Just here and there in that chapter." She squinted into the never ending sun, scanning the sprawling building. "Necromancer school," she joked.

Tzarik did not laugh and his brow deepened into furrowed thought. "You might be right. The legend is that Porsh found a forbidden book."

"Mahit'onomicon," she said, understanding dawning.

Tzarik looked over at her, surprised for the first time, raising his brows. "You read that, too?"

Afraid to answer, she looked away. As she did, her eyes landed on the sigil she had come to hate in the days they spent walking the city.

"That's it!" she screamed joyfully. Pointing, she galloped one block down from the apostle's palace and skidded to a stop on the glassy surface before a mansion half raised like the floating masses around them. Sand blew in over the years, not yet cursed, making the ground slippery.

Overcoming their fear of being spotted two sleeps ago, they pushed past the decaying doors of the mansion. The inside boasted all the trappings of a once rich family with dark secrets. Hidden passages lay open behind bookcases, a trapdoor leading down stone steps yawned open, and once-golden pillars gilded the foyer. Marble stairs led up in two directions to silk-covered doorways.

"We go down," Tzarik said suddenly.

"Why?" Sybal asked, following him anyway.

"A guess," the Runer grunted, lowering himself into the dark passage. "We know the necrotic people are similar to us. Maybe they change the same way. Their business is the dead. They want to keep their secrets close. So, a hidden crypt underneath the family residence."

Sybal couldn't argue with his deduction. Not all of Porsh had to be fine with the cursed events, so some might join the dark cult and keep it hidden. Carefully, she followed her mentor down the spiral staircase into a cold, dark underground.

Tzarik slowly drew atan, telling Sybal to do the same. As they did, the rune glowed bright white, splashing light from wall to wall. Sybal's mouth dropped as her eyes beheld the crypt.

The walls reminded her of a salt mine, almost entirely white and sparkling. This had been a rich mine, indeed. Thin black shelves lined the walls covered in vials, bones, and skins from animals, humans, and Masakh alike. Maps of the world and creature anatomy hung above tables with evil straps and suspicious dark stains.

"Look," she whispered. Holding her light up, a family tapestry came into view.

Black writing on a white canvas. It detailed a long, old family line. Most near the top were faded out, deteriorated by the salt in the air. Near the bottom, the name Ishmael was stitched in, joined to the woman's name, Isis. Below that, two lines came out. One read Tarkan and the other had been burned out so badly, it burnt through the tapestry and a black mark marred the wall behind it. Below Tarkan, however, the name Zeva had been penned in with charcoal by hand.

Confused, curious, and worried all at once, Sybal remembered the image of the woman in the book. Had she misinterpreted it?

"Does he have a child? A daughter?" She gaped at the name, touching it lightly.

Tzarik's jaw clenched and he swallowed hard. "I doubt it. And if he did, it would not be a human with intelligent thought."

She had to look at him as he said this with such anger, malice, and spite in his voice that she realized he had experienced the thing he spoke about.

"A monster," he whispered finally.

This time, she knew not to ask. A cold trickle ran down her throat as she imagined what he could mean. Her own experience had been horrible. Did something similar happen to him? She shook her head, banishing the thoughts.

"Sybal!" he cried after walking a fair distance away.

She caught up to him, redrawing her rune to give more light. On the other side of the crypt, that they now saw spanned the length of the house, lay several marble coffins.

"They raise the dead." She rubbed her temple, trying to put clues together like Tzarik had done. "Would they do it to their family too?"

"I thought necromancers might be immortal," Tzarik mused, approaching the coffins. "Maybe not?"

Remembering he couldn't read, she came to his side and cocked her head to read the names. "His wife," she said, touching one. "Isis."

Before she could move, Tzarik roared and shoved the top slab with all his might. He may be shorter than her, but he was strong as a dragon. The slab moved until it slid more easily and tumbled to the side.

Sybal gasped, covering her mouth. The woman inside lay like a sleeping maiden. Her healthy, dark skin was not pale like Tarkan's, and her black hair shined glossy and smooth in the rune light. Sybal almost expected her eyes to flutter open and see her breathe. She wore a white gown and her arms were covered in gold. A gold headdress donned her black tresses with strange blue and turquoise jewels.

"She's beautiful," she sighed once she caught her breath.

"This one?" Tzarik asked her, pointing to another name on the next coffin.

A little taken off guard by him asking, she leaned over to read the name. She felt him tense up as she did. "Ishmael. Tarkan's father. And this one," the next, "must be his brother. The name is blasted out. The coffin is covered in old blood."

She pushed the lid off with the blasted name and inside lay what should be in a coffin: a skeleton with no flesh or eyes. No gleaming hair. A dead man.

"Burn them."

"What?" Sybal gasped, turning to see Tzarik grab a glass of the clear fluid from a nearby table.

"They are not innocents, Sybal. We need to find this necromancer. Let's see how he likes his family being destroyed."

Tzarik dumped the clear liquid onto Isis and the remains of the unnamed son. He ordered her to get the flint and steel while he pushed the lid off the coffin of Ishmael. When she had the tools in her hand, she watched him dump the liquid onto Tarkan's father. He too lay preserved perfectly, a neat beard on his chin, thick, serious brows furrowed even in death. But his flesh was pale, covered in the black runes like Tarkan. This stopped Tzarik mid pour.

"Is he alive?" she asked, whispering again. "Or is he a lich?"

Sighing this time, Tzarik looked up into her eyes in the rune light.

"Yes, I read it in the book. A lich is like an ascended necromancer. I had to look it up because it kept getting mentioned. They don't need living necessities to live. Tarkan probably eats, sleeps...feels." She drifted off, seeing the necromancer couple in the book holding hands.

"He's evil," Tzarik said, interrupting her thoughts. "And we need to find him and stop him from whatever it is he's planning."

"But a lich doesn't need that," she went on. "They are somewhere between life and death. He could have been sleeping for years. Necromancers don't age as they are masters of death. Tarkan could be..." she shook her head, "hundreds of years old."

Tzarik poured the rest of the liquid fuel onto Ishmael and took the flint and steel from her. He smacked the tools together a few times before the flame took to the torch he pulled off the wall. He took up another, handing it to her and lighting it with his.

"Burn her," he ordered callously, pointing to Isis.

"But my crime!" she said suddenly, holding the torch above the woman.

"She's dead, burn her!"

Praying they were already dead, knowing Tzarik would not endanger her, she dropped the torch onto the woman. Her body immediately erupted in fire. Her hair evaporated into smoke, the stink filling the crypt. She didn't move.

A deep, bellowing scream shook the salt walls. Tzarik shouted in surprise. Spinning around, Sybal saw Ishmael flail in his coffin.

"Help me!" Tzarik shouted, pushing up on the massive lid after tossing the torch inside.

Not even thinking about a man burning alive, she rushed to her mentor's side and heaved the slab up. Ishmael fought, his fiery limbs pushing his undead body up, but they replaced the slab before his flaming corpse could escape. His screams came muffled from inside the stone bed and slowly died away.

"He's not dead if liches are somewhere between life and death," Tzarik mused, stepping away. "But he's not alive either."

***

SYBAL DIDN'T ASK WHY. There were a lot of things about Runers, their jobs, and the world she didn't know or understand. She sensed this to be a victory for them. She wondered if Tarkan, bound as these tribes seemed to be, would know that someone had defiled his home, burned his mother and father where they lay. She also wondered how Ishmael had fathered two sons.

With so many questions, she could not wait to make camp and read another chapter. Learning about the mark seemed like the Runer thing to do.

Chapter 21
Runer's Death

CROUCHING BEHIND DEW-SOAKED FERNS, SYBAL SHOOK HER hands out for what felt like the millionth time that morning. Tzarik called her name twice but she couldn't move. Her legs locked up where she had squatted to hide the convulsion taking over her body. They began happening after they left Porsh but her instincts told her visiting the withered city and her fits were not connected.

They started after a long ride one day and a hard workout when they made camp. The tingling started in her hands just like now. Like a wave in the ocean, it trailed up her left arm and made her chest cramp. Then it crawled up her spine like a frightened spider. When it reached the base of her neck, if she had not found a safe place to fall, collapse and convulse, she would have hurt herself on nearby objects. The first time this happened, Tzarik had been away from the camp and she fell, hitting her head on a rock. She thought the feeling vibrating up her spine had actually been something touching her and tried to swat it away. Then she fell. She remembered her vision going gray and white and not being able to stop her tumbling body.

Now a new sensation came before the tingling. Her hands and feet would go numb, heavy as lead. Her head then lolled to the sides, as she became unable to hold it up any longer.

"Sybal!" Tzarik shouted now, anger growling in his throat.

She tried to call back but her jaw locked and her throat constricted so hard she thought invisible hands gripped her. Then it came. She shook, her spine bent, and she knew she just had to wait out the terror.

"What are you doing?"

Tzarik stood over her. He held the reins of both their horses in one hand and her pack in the other. Sitting up, she dusted the sand off her black garb.

"I tripped?" she said, courage faltering.

His blue eyes didn't waver, and she jerked away. He had a way of reading her like she had not mastered yet. Pulling her hood over her head, she knew he already guessed something was wrong.

"There's a, uh, job near Hatal." She spoke as genially as she could, pulling out the patents of bounty.

"We are not going to Hatal," Tzarik countered, frowning gently, watching her every move.

She hated when he looked at her like this, not quite concerned, just curious. Like she was an exotic animal about to do a trick or expose a frightening new disease.

"Before we entered Porsh, someone at the fleece fair said..." She shifted her feet and looked away from him. Why was it so hard to speak? "Someone said a Runer left it at the tavern there. Said he left for the capitol city." She begged him to just understand. How could she tell him that he had wasted his time on a weak, ill female? She had to be as strong as him.

Her mentor wrinkled his nose and turned his face towards the rising sun. "To Hatal then."

⁂

A SIDE JOB wouldn't hurt exactly. One of the biggest banks in Al'Myrah resided in Hatal, the capitol city. The sultana lived there in her great golden palace. Compared to even Jarabu on Bahratt, Hatal was a booming metropolis of stone and iron. The city sprawled out from the main center for miles, almost reaching the ocean. Tzarik didn't mind the side work since he had to leave word for the scholar anyway. And pick up his first payment.

He watched Sybal carefully as they made their way to the city. He noticed every time he wore her down with training, she disappeared either that night or early the next morning, rumpled and shaken.

When they neared the city, to his surprise, a convoy came to greet them. The men sat astride the great white and black horses Hatal famously bred, their red capes flourishing in the hot desert wind. Spears rested in the crooks of their arms.

"Halt and declare your business," the captain of the guard shouted, lowering his spear like a javelin.

"I have a shibboleth," Tzarik offered instead, reaching into his saddlebag. As he leaned over, he caught Sybal's eyes.

She swayed slightly on her horse and her eyes were blood red with spidery veins. He froze, his hand in his bag. Looking closer, he saw no ghostly white veins lurking under her dark skin. She panted but no sweat dripped down from her scalp.

He quickly shoved the shibboleth scroll at the guard and the moment the convoy let them pass, he trotted into town to find a room for her to rest in. Their room, though cheap by Hatal standards, was the nicest they had ever had, fully furnished and with a hearth glowing on one wall.

"We should find the bounty master," Sybal offered once they paid, had washed in cool water, and eaten warm bread with butter.

"Can you fight?" Tzarik shot across the table to her.

She sat straighter in her chair, tossing her long yellow hair over one shoulder. "Of course. I need to practice. I've done so many press-ups. Isn't it time I actually did something?"

He scanned her quickly. Nothing wrong stuck out. What made her look so ill? And blood? Red, hot, human blood.

An icy needle of fear slowly punctured his heart. Did her body finally decide to reject the runing? Some kind of delayed reaction? His eyes went to the patents in her hand. She claimed a witness at the fleece fair said a Runer left it. If she believed that, then she also believed another Runer lurked in Hatal. Understanding dawned, calming him somewhat. She wanted to come to Hatal to find that other Runer. Someone who would know what was wrong with her who was not him. He clenched his fist.

"We'll go first thing in the morning," he said and almost smiled.

⁂

"A QAREEN?" Sybal repeated, writing down every word the young lord said on a piece of parchment she'd dug out of her bag.

Tzarik watched her closely as she interacted with the young, handsome, tall man. Until he met Sybal, he had never seen a human being that tall. Now here stood a man who looked down on her. She had the Northica blood from her mother that made her tower over most. What excuse did this man have? His eyes glittered an uncommon green from his dark, smooth—almost gold—skin. Clearly, he had never spent much time outside in the leathering sun. He donned a silken turban that matched the sky, and golden prayer beads dangled from his long, strong fingers.

"There is no other explanation," the young man said, simpering. He pushed himself off his throne and came down the golden steps to take Sybal's hand in his.

Tzarik imagined what his skeleton would look like if his flesh melted off.

"My father has always been a good, fair man," he went on. "But now he punishes the servants, drives our riggers into dismay, and spoils the funds on discord beyond our borders."

"Qareen have distinct patterns, signs," Tzarik cut in, stepping so close the man had to drop Sybal's hand. "Have you seen animals behaving in a way they normally wouldn't? Seen ectoplasm?"

The young man, Hakim, looked back and forth between the two of them. "The cattle do not milk. And...well, let me show you."

Hakim led them down to the cellar where barrels of oil lined the walls. In the center of the refinery, a huge burst of black shot out from a central point on the stone floor.

"A blast?" Sybal said, tapping her chin. "I recognize it. My family owns a mine. Tzarik?" She turned to him.

He circled the charred ground, scanning it easily. A qareen often never proved to be a hostel enemy. They were more gray than black or white. He had only run into a hostile qareen once and dispatched it fairly easily. Like most spirits, they fell to orichalcum and simple spells. This would be a good job for Sybal to test her abilities. Learning about the monsters they hunted came with experience and time.

"Qareen are sulfurous," he explained. "Like a lot of spiritual beings. Either intentionally or by accident, it ignited a barrel of refined oil. Their ectoplasm is more vaporous than solid. It must have touched the barrel." He looked up at the low ceiling then pointed. "Ectoplasm."

Along the ceiling, like a slug's trail, a black ooze in spidery outlines, dotted the ceiling here and there as if the monster tried every now and then to emerge through the ceiling.

"Do we fight it?" Sybal asked, clearly not understanding how their orichalcum could touch a spiritual monster.

"In a way," Tzarik answered. "We force it to materialize in our realm through a runic circle. Then banish it or fight it. Depends on if it's hostile."

Hakim moaned sadly. "Why my father?"

Tzarik flexed his lips to stop the smirk that sprang to his face. "They attach themselves to those who seem weak. Either to take over, possess that individual, or to eventually move to a permanent host." He raised his brows at the young man.

"Me?" Hakim gasped, pressing his gilded hand into his silken chest.

Tzarik tilted his head, raising one brow. "I don't understand the thought process of spirits either."

THAT NIGHT, they used Hakim as bait. Tzarik had him stand in the center of his throne room and call out to the qareen.

"Won't it know this is a trap?" Sybal asked, crossing her arms.

"Doubt it," Tzarik said simply, sitting on the steps, his sword in one hand and runes in the other. "They tend to attach themselves to hosts of their intellectual level."

"Stop," she barked suddenly. "I don't care for your classist remarks."

He was about to bite back when she took a shuddering breath and flexed her hand.

"Runers!" Hakim shouted from his post in the center of the room, interrupting them. "I see it!"

Sybal stood up, teetered but regained her footing. "I don't see it!"

"Use atan," Tzarik instructed, staying back to let her practice. "It illuminates for us but also reveals hidden creatures."

Slowly, Sybal began to trace the rune before her, clutching it in her hand. Her arm shook and her left leg stumbled, looking like she lost all feeling in it.

With a silent shout of pain, her left side went limp entirely. Her head tilted, slumping onto her chest. With one last shriek, her spine bent her backwards so her brown eyes locked onto Tzarik behind her.

Hakim screamed and covered his eyes in terror. "What's happening?"

Springing into action, Tzarik caught Sybal and laid her down, drawing atan with his other hand. Once he set her safely on the ground, though convulsing, he ran to Hakim's side. When the aura of light from his hand reached the qareen, they saw it together.

"Father?" Hakim gasped at the terrifying specter.

"It's not!" Tzarik grunted, swinging at the ghostly monster. The qareen hissed, opening its abominable maw and roaring. The thing resembled a human, but its fiery, drooping flesh and balding head showed otherwise. When it roared, the entire bottom half of its face opened up to spit hellish slime.

Tzarik pushed Hakim out of the way and held up atan again. The qareen screamed and backed away. With a quick flick of his wrist, Tzarik drew halat and tossed it behind the creature. As it tried to flee, it ran into the quickly dissipating protective shield, dazing it. Charging after it, Tzarik drew buhkar, slid behind it as mist, then arched his scimitar through the exposed spirit. It shrieked as he severed it in half and exploded in a black fire, scorching his exposed flesh.

Hakim panted, almost weeping on the floor, praying to his gods in thanks. Tzarik ignored him and ran to Sybal, scooping her up in his arms.

"Wait! Is it gone?" the young lord cried. "That last Runer said—"

"What Runer?" Tzarik strode back to Hakim and gripped the front of his silken robes hard, shaking him. "What was his name? Where did he go?"

The young man didn't chance angering him this time after just witnessing the demise of an untouchable, spiritual monster. "I don't know where he went. He didn't kill the thing!"

"Give me a name!" He reached for his dagger.

"Korvoth! His name was Korvoth. One of those pale Runers from Caerwren. Could hardly understand his accent."

With Sybal unconscious and unable to intervene, Tzarik cocked his fist back and punched Hakim hard on the bridge of his straight nose. The young man rolled away, clutching his bleeding face.

"Have your man deliver the payment to the Eastern Star Inn," he spat back, taking Sybal and leaving the lavish manor.

⁂

WHEN HE RETURNED to the inn, he instructed the maid to inform him if a man named Korvoth showed up. To his surprise, she knew who he meant and promised to fetch him right away.

"I'm so sorry," Sybal sighed, wiping her face down. She pressed her palms into the vanity, hunched over the basin back in their room.

"Why didn't you tell me?" Tzarik asked, arms crossed, standing behind her, trying to get a look at her face in the mirror in front of her.

"Could I?" She dried her face and turned to face him, arms limp. She shrugged helplessly. "Would you keep me if I was broken?"

Tzarik glared, dropping his arms. "What does that mean?" he snapped.

She bit her bottom lip, nervously tapping her palm with her fingers. She cast her gaze around, looking for something to hide behind, distract her tension with. Finding nothing, she shrugged, her eyes shining with sudden tears.

"I just thought that if I wasn't working out, you'd..." Her voice caught and she cleared her throat. "I thought you'd leave me again. Abandoned. And sick."

He hated what she said. It almost hurt. She was right, of course. During her trial, she asked for the trial of two. By law, he had to accept if he performed the runing and train her until she chose to be on her own or died in the process. When she hadn't died, he hoped she'd be grateful to be alive and stay. Be a reason.

When he didn't respond, her shoulders dropped and she looked away. He crossed his arms again and turned away from her. Through his peripheral vision, he caught her waiting on him. She wanted him to say something. The guilt that had tried to arise in him earlier now filled him.

"Sira?" a soft, female voice said from the other side of the door. "That man is back."

"Man?" Sybal asked, putting aside the emotions from before.

"You were right," he said, relief quelling the flooding remorse. "There was another Runer in Hatal. I thought if I found him, he might know something I didn't. Runers may be guilty men but each has led different and experienced lives."

A genuine, bright smile cracked Sybal's worried brow. "And I thought Runers were rare!"

Tzarik scoffed lightly through his nose. "They are. I'm honestly just as surprised as you."

Heading down the stairs together, she asked, "How many have you met in your life?"

After a disheartened grunt, he replied, "One and a half."

She giggled as they entered the common room with the front door. "A half?"

"Yes," Tzarik replied, scanning the great room before them. "My mentor, Azar, only counts as half."

Before Sybal could ask why, Tzarik nodded towards the massive hearth at the back of the room. Seated in a soft, wingback chair near the fire with his massive, booted feet up on the table, pipe hanging from his lips, sat Korvoth. The man had to be as tall as Sybal if not taller. His arms and legs were thick as trees and his pale skin almost hid the white veins beneath. His stubble and hair differed from theirs. Where Tzarik had streaks of the bright white appear over time, this man's entire head and long ponytail glowed pure white in the firelight. His eyes, which he opened and closed now and then to watch the traveling performers on stage, were the same icy, glowing blue. They didn't distract as much when not in a dark face.

"Korvoth?" Tzarik asked politely, approaching the lounging Runer.

"Runer?" the Northica man greeted in reply, puffing a perfect smoke ring up into the rafters. "And who might you be?" With a light slam, he tipped the wingback chair back onto all fours and offered his calloused hand to Sybal.

Tzarik looked away to roll his eyes and Sybal proffered her hand in response.

"Sybal. This is Tzarik, my mentor."

Korvoth squinted at Sybal and motioned for them to join him. "A woman Runer." His accent made the words of Al'Myrah strange and elongated on his tongue but he spoke it well. "You've made it past the worst; you survived." He smiled.

His orichalcum sword sat on the table before him, out of its sheath, shining like a rainbow badge of honor for all to see. The strange straightness of it caught Tzarik's eye. Apparently, where this man came from, Runers were more respected. He never displayed his sword like that and hid it in his black cloak.

"I'm not sure," Sybal replied, sighing heavily, unable to catch her breath. "I keep having fits. Everything hurts."

Tzarik reached up and gently pulled her hood down motioning for her to look towards the firelight. When she did, the blood red veins in her eyes shone bright.

Korvoth gently put his pipe down on the table and leaned in. "Your veins are weak." He gently touched her chin to move the light across her face.

"Have you seen this before?" Tzarik asked quickly.

"Do you go numb?" the Northica Runer asked.

"Yes," Sybal said, excitedly.

Korvoth nodded, his face darkening. "I've seen it. My mentor..." He folded his hands on the table and looked down. "I call it the Runer's death."

The ominous name had its due effect on the two sitting across from him. Tzarik and Sybal exchanged glances.

"It's fatal?" Tzarik asked.

"I had a theory," Korvoth went on. "He stopped, you see. Stopped working. Stopped using the runes. He was finished. He wanted to go, he said. I've been a Runer for twelve years—changed at eighteen—and as far as I know, I'm the oldest in the business. I've seen this a few times. Some men were not cut out to be monster hunters. But a woman..." He smiled kindly.

Sybal smiled and winked at Tzarik. He fought to not return the grin.

"Ha, how old are you?" Korvoth chuckled, seeing the interaction.

"Thirty-five." Tzarik almost boasted. "Runed for twenty years."

"Wow," Sybal and Korvoth said together.

"You didn't know?" Korvoth asked Sybal, smiling and calling for a pint. "This is cause for a drink."

"But I've been alone," Tzarik said, getting back on track. "I don't know what's happening to her."

The maid brought them three huge mugs of mead and he toasted them before going on.

"The sulfates—our blood—are not science. They are magic. If you stop utilizing it, it will turn against you. Go bad, as it were. I imagine if you start to practice again, it will reverse." He eyed Sybal. "You using runes? Keeping in contact with that magic blade of yours?"

Tzarik did not miss her eyes darting to him and back to the strange Runer. "Not as much as I should, perhaps?"

The foreign Runer narrowed his eyes over his hovering mug. He slowly scanned Tzarik then said to Sybal, "Use them. Every day. You're new. Your body took to the runing so that's good. Means you're strong and can handle the life we lead. But you can't stop. You've been saved from whatever crime you committed and you have to pay for it now. You have to fight monsters. Kill. Protect the innocent. Most people have never in their lives hunted so much as a jackalope."

"A what?" Sybal and Tzarik chimed together.

Korvoth laughed heartily, pounded the table, and took a long drink. "One day, come to Caerwren. I'll make you such a jacka-lope stew!"

He downed what remained in his mug and tossed a few coins onto the table. "I have to be on," he said. When he stood up and stretched, he almost touched the low ceiling. Those on Al'Myrah were genetically shorter than those from the north and their archi-tecture could hardly contain the taller, white man. "Lady Runer, you were found guilty of crimes against Al'Myrah. Serve her now by protecting the innocent. Save a life. Do good."

"It's been an honor," Sybal said, taking his hand and shaking it. "And thank you. But do you have to go? We've not run into another Runer before."

"Ah," Korvoth grunted, taking up his sword and shaking his head. "Pleased to help, but my homeland calls. I give freely when I can save a life. And such a special life as yours is worth my knowl-edge. Runers are few and far between here in the south for some reason. And I've never seen a woman in our profession. You'll be famous. But I cannot stand another blistering day in this blinding sand."

He motioned to their dark skin and blue eyes.

"I suppose it's harder to hide. And is more foreign. But I don't mean to judge your people." He clasped his black cloak around his shoulders. "Stay safe, lady Runer."

Tzarik watched Korvoth languidly pass through the patrons, smiling at the pretty girl carrying a tray of mead. He was bold, fearless, and spoke the truth: Sybal was special.

Chapter 22
Eye for an Eye

THE NEXT CLOSEST CITY WAS ALA'NAR. TZARIK DIDN'T WANT to take Sybal back to her home city, afraid she would try once again to stay with her family. With the information Korvoth gave them, he hoped she would not leave. She had to learn to use the runes, practice fighting techniques, and become accustomed to the ways of the Runer life. She could do it on her own. Maybe she didn't need him.

Frustrated at the foreign feelings and thoughts Sybal put into his head, he kicked her awake just as the sun rose.

She shouted curses at him. "Why?" she groaned, rolling up her bed.

He didn't waste any time. "We're going to Ala'Nar. But you cannot see your family. You cannot go back to them. They won't accept you as you are and you need to keep practicing with the runes. We are going to find you a job, something easy, so you can work on listening to your instincts."

He turned away from her to pack the horses but heard her scoff angrily and felt her mood shift.

"I wouldn't go back to stay," she started. "But what's the harm in visiting them?"

"No!" Tzarik snapped.

She froze, glaring at the back of his head. "I heard Korvoth, all right? I'm not going to stop using the Runes. I've done days of training with them now. I haven't had a fit in almost a week. I understand."

She had gotten better, her eyes changed one night. One day, something inside her clicked, releasing the magic she held back. She drew runes all day as they traveled, only stopping when a caravan passed them and they pulled their black hoods up to hide their faces. She made the rest of her runes, colored them to her own liking, and wore them around her neck underneath her chemise and leather armor. She disciplined herself to stretch out before lying down to sleep and usually trained with her sword before breaking camp. She had come a long way after the meeting with the northern Runer. He thought her progress would please him. Or that he would be glad she neared the time in her training that he could leave her again.

"It's carnival, you know," she mentioned like a warning as they made the last couple miles journey towards the city. "The streets will be full with merchants, visitors, performers—so many people. You sure you want to go in?"

On the one hand, maybe they could blend in. On the other, some creatures were drawn to crowds and revelry. It might take a day or two of carnival for one to make enough of an issue that someone sought out a Runer, but such gatherings often proved lucrative.

He also hoped the necromancer would be drawn out. If Tarkan hunted them after their desecration, he'd start in the city closest to Porsh. He had to put Ala'Nar in danger to find his mark.

"I don't have an account!" Tzarik shouted, pounding his fist on the golden desk of the bank. "Someone left me coin."

The old lady on the other side of the gilded bars looked up at him over gold-ringed spectacles. She blinked once, not put off at all by the monster hunter's barbaric behavior.

"We can open an account for you then," she droned in a high, but at the same time guttural, monotone. She felt safe behind the bars in her crisp black and gold uniform. "I will need the address of your permanent home—"

"I don't want any of that," Tzarik snapped. "A man, a scholar, named Abigor Sharar has an account and he left word and coin here for me."

At the mention of the scholar, the woman's left eye twitched in recognition. She pressed her purple-painted lips together so hard they almost touched the bottom of her hooked nose. "There has been communication of a Runer coming. But how do I know you are that Runer?"

"What Runer is going to come into a bank? Has one ever come in?"

"Mmm," she mused. "No."

Turning away, she went behind a wall and he heard the plethora of keys on her hip jingle and one slip into an old lock. A few moments later, she came out with a black velvet bag and a letter.

"This is not written in the scholar's own hand, but one taken down by a messenger," she explained, writing something in a ledger before slowly pushing the items underneath the bars towards him.

"He didn't leave word?" Tzarik asked, annoyed.

"As you see," she pointed to the little scroll, sealed with the bank's emblem, "he said he would be in town for carnival. You may be able to find him if you can navigate the caravan guests. Always glutted during carnival."

"Great." He snatched up the purse, disappointingly light, and broke the seal. The parchment was written in a sloping, elegant hand but he could not make out any meaning. Angry, he stuffed it in his pocket. He'd have to ask Sybal to read it.

Outside, he found her watching a juggler in the streets. Ala'-Nar's air vibrated and pulsed with the sound of drums and the ululations of dancers in colorful, revealing costumes—men and women alike. A peculiar Masakh, part woman part snake and draped in scarves, coiled herself up and down a pole. Every performer had a hat, bucket, or wooden box set out before them for coin.

"We could always do that," Sybal joked. She pointed out an act of contortionists with a high wire, a strange wheel the size of a man, and other dare-devil equipment he couldn't name.

He almost smiled at her joke but caught himself. "We just need to wait, keep an ear to the ground, ask a few people, and a job will arise."

He caught Sybal's eyes quickly snap to the velvet bag and up again. What was the point now in keeping it from her?

"I need you to read something for me," he sighed, speaking so softly she leaned in to catch what he said.

"Buy me hot food and I will," she bargained, smiling down at him.

Fair enough. They snaked their way through the crowds to a vendor selling meat soaked in sauce then cooked over an open fire while the cook continuously mopped the savory mixture over it. The vendor set up a table out the back of his vardo and served a few people sitting on colorful rugs with cushions. He sold a mead he called The First Apple. Light, golden, sweet, and tart, Sybal ordered two mugs of it before their dripping meat was ready.

The man handed them brass bowls of rice with the savory meat generously laid on top. He offered them flatbread and refilled Sybal's tankard before leaving. Tzarik waited to see how Sybal would eat the dish. Unsure what stayed his hand, he watched her tear a piece of the round bread off and used all five of her fingers to pinch a healthy amount of rice and meat into it. She opened her mouth impossibly wide, shoved the entire fist full into her mouth, and chewed ravenously. Seeing a trickle of brown sauce gracefully slide between her lips and down her chin almost pulled a grin from his tired face. She looked up, noticing his gaze and he stopped himself.

Sybal motioned to a dancer who coyly had been sneaking closer to them while they waited. She reached over and took a coin from the velvet bag Tzarik laid next to his boots as they sat down and flashed it towards the dancer. The woman's keen brown eyes caught the glint of gold and shimmied her way over, winking at them both in turn. She offered her bejeweled hip to Sybal where a beaded bag hung with a few coins inside. Sybal reached to drop the coin in but the dancer playfully bounced her hip away. She grinned, touching her finger to her red lips and smiling at Sybal, once again offering her hip. This time, she allowed Sybal to drop the coin into her beaded bag. With an ululation of thanks, the dancer whipped her long, golden-clasped hair around, and practically slithered to the next table with fluid movements.

Sybal faced Tzarik. "I'm amazed," she said, picking up her food again.

"Why?" Tzarik asked. "She wants to eat just like the rest of us."

"No, you pebble in my sandal." She smiled playfully at him. "I'm amazed you didn't stop me from taking your money."

He shifted uncomfortably and looked away, pretending to be interested in a sword dancer at the next table over. "You're my charge now. *Most* of what's mine is yours."

He felt her warm eyes boring into the side of his head, demanding he turn and say that to her face. He hardened his resolve and didn't look back.

After a few moments of silence, Sybal reached over and took the parchment Tzarik had been holding on to and unrolled it, reading it quickly once then a second time. He could tell from how her eyes flicked back and forth all the way to the bottom, then started again at the top. She opened her mouth to speak but Tzarik leapt to his feet.

"What?" she asked.

"Smell," he barked at her, raising his head like a hound. "Brimstone. But not hot, fiery brimstone. Almost stale."

It was nearly impossible to smell one distinct scent amidst the potpourri of meat, alcohol, sweat, and incense but she caught it. Sybal's face paled. "Oh, no."

Not waiting for her to stand up, Tzarik tossed her his long, black bow and quiver. "Follow me out, find a place high up, hidden. Shoot when you have a clear shot. Don't worry about hitting me."

He heard her try to argue but ignored her. He was coming and Tzarik knew in his heart of hearts that Tarkan had death and destruction on his mind. He must have gone to his home—for whatever reason—seen what had happened and come to exact revenge. Just as he planned.

"Run!" he screamed as she galloped towards the eastern wall of the city. By now, the pulsating wings of the risen dragon could be heard, and already the carnival patrons screamed, running for cover.

A blast cracked across the sky, not aimed down at the city, but shot as a warning. Vaulting up some barrels and eves, Tzarik landed on the rampart overlooking the outside desert. High above, Tarkan made circles on his dragon. Tzarik's eyes were drawn to the desert sand below him. He couldn't say what pricked his instincts, but he felt something wrong. Something else waited out there.

"Come out, Runers!" Tarkan shouted, diving low over the city. He maneuvered his risen beast to the minaret where it landed hard, shattering many of the statues and symbols as it clung to the side, wrapping its tail around for support.

A city guard watching near Tzarik turned to look at him. He laid his hand on the shaft of his scimitar.

Not waiting, Tzarik leapt over the wall and ran to confront the necromancer. "Here I am, fiend!" he shouted up at him. To his right, he saw Sybal rushing stealthily out from a sewer tunnel to hide behind piles of rocks and discarded city wall from years past.

"Why, Tarkan?" Tzarik shouted instead.

The necromancer and his dragon leapt off the minaret, landing in a sandy cloud several yards in front of the Runer.

"You know what you did," Tarkan hissed. "I should ask you why."

"I have a reason," Tzarik replied, relaxing his stance and lowering his blade. "You took innocent lives before we even crossed paths."

"I had no choice!" Tarkan shouted back. Holding his hand out, fingers flexed, he forced the undead dragon to shoot a blast of dark energy at Tzarik.

The Runer jumped to the side, but the sand slipped from the force and he didn't get very far. The explosion shot sand at him and he felt it sting his neck. "I had no choice either!" he panted, realizing what Tarkan spoke of. He tried to push himself up.

Sybal stopped her aim when she heard this and relaxed the black bow.

"The Runer who made me left me. And the crime I stood trial for was not mine. But I had to accept the hand that fate dealt me. I am what I am by my hand alone."

The necromancer shrieked in laughter. With a strained wave of his pale hand, Tarkan forced the dragon to bring its leathery claw down over Tzarik. Sybal gasped and almost ran from her cover. Tzarik grunted in pain as the huge talons pressed him into the sand. The necromancer could kill him now!

"You are just as fooled as the rest, Runer," Tarkan gloated down at his captive. "I thought since we are cousins in the magic you might know that. But you don't! You were given a gift. This power you hold makes you better than the mortals you serve. Whatever your crime, it can be avoided. You should join me in laying waste to those who would spit upon us! Those who deign to take what we love."

Tzarik raised his scimitar again, wiggling to try to slide out.

"Or let me take you." Tarkan's voice turned gentle, almost soothing. "I see your soul, Runer. You don't want to go on with this life you pretend to defend."

"That's not true."

"Anymore," Tarkan added. "Was it the girl? Did she give you a reason for living? Are you using her to quell the loneliness that comes with being a guilt-ridden criminal and blood-coin lover?"

The necromancer seemed to have the ability to read people like a Runer. Maybe it came with the dark magics they used. Maybe it just came from being abused by the majority of living beings. Tarkan hit his mark, though. Tzarik's guilt rose up, ready to consume him. He fought to keep the shadow from his eyes, but the necromancer saw it.

Tarkan smiled, gleeful at his discovery. "So it is the girl. Does she know she's just a tool to you? Does she know she can't love you? Oh, that's it isn't it! She loves you and you know it." He shook his head disapprovingly. "That's a terrible way to use a woman's heart."

"You don't know!" Tzarik shot back. With a powerful roar, he pushed himself out from under the dragon's paw, moving now to get a better angle on the dragon, its white eyes tracking him.

Sneering, the necromancer shook his head. "Oh, I know, Runer. I know."

A thick, black shafted arrow hissed out from where Sybal hid, striking the dragon right in its filmy, dead eye. To their surprise, it lurched, screaming. Thrown from its back, Tarkan's black robes billowed as he fell. Leaping at the chance, Tzarik charged past the beast, slicing a thick, bloodless wound along its long neck as he passed. He saw the necromancer struggling to get up, clearly winded from his fall.

Whatever he had sensed underneath the sand before now started to move. He wanted to charge onward, sever the necromancer's head from his body but his better judgment stopped him. The sand shifted, fell away, and with moans and bone-chilling cries, dozens of risen bodies burst up from the sand. In varying stages of decay, some were full flesh with no bones showing. Others were merely more than armored skeletons, muscles and a few organs swinging from the exposed bones.

Taking a step back, Tzarik scanned the city wall he could see. Not dozens of risen corpses. Hundreds. Thousands surrounding the city.

"Get inside the walls!" he screamed to Sybal, fleeing from the undead army that stood between him and his mark.

Chapter 23
White Bloods

RARELY DID HE SLIP ON SAND IN A PANIC. BORN AND RAISED on Al'Myrah, Tzarik knew how to navigate the slippery, ever-shifting sands of his home. Even before his life turned to hunting monsters and specters he could keep his feet under him. Too much recently had he been taken off guard. As the risen slowly blossomed out of the sand, this was one of those times. Torn between wanting to slice Tarkan's throat right there and fear of the unknown made him push off the golden sand too hard and slip. In the seconds he fell and got back up again, the dragon raked at its wounded eye, not pursuing him.

He made sure to sprint several paces before turning to take in the dusty, screeching hoard that moved in on Ala'Nar. They couldn't all have fit into that small black box he had seen Tarkan traveling with before. The necromancer must have known that deep beneath the sand a millennium of dead soldiers lurked. Maybe he had been casting his spells while he distracted Tzarik with banter. Not knowing the details of his prey distilled doubt as well. He had entered unknown trials and didn't like being out of his depth.

Rushing past a few stragglers, he made it behind the walls. Quickly, he scanned the immediate area hoping to find Sybal. He spotted her black cloak billowing, her blond hair gleaming in the sun as the wind and sand began to swirl around them. She ran to a few travelers from the caravan outside the walls, hurrying them in. She clutched the black bow in her hand, her sword not drawn.

"Sybal!" he shouted over the terror. "Get inside the walls!"

She stood to her full height, over most people's heads, and shouted back, "We have to get them inside!" When he didn't budge, she added, "More dead means more risen!"

The slight way in which her inflection dropped right at the end told him she didn't mean it like that. She just said it in a way that would convince him to help. But the turrets around the city were armed. They had ballistas, archers with huge bows, and a good vantage point. If he could just get up to a captain of the guard and explain the undead. He froze, unable to decide between helping Sybal and rallying a defense. Never having experienced indecision like this, he roared in frustration.

"Leave it!" she screamed at a monkey-type Masakh as he struggled to haul his donkey and wagon towards the city. Glancing over her shoulder, she spotted Tarkan as a dot on a distant dune. So he had backed off? In the chaos, she remembered a bit in the book about focus. The necromancer had to focus to cast his spells.

Finally getting the last from the caravan closer to the city, she glanced up through the swirling sands to the wall where Tzarik stood. He hadn't moved. Assessing the situation as best she could, she caught his head whipping back and forth between her and the nearest turret. He shouted angrily at nothing.

"Tzarik!" she called again. "Get the guard to the towers. They need to be rallied and focused. I've got this."

As though cut free from a binding leash, he bolted across the battlement to the first turret. Smiling, she hastily congratulated herself on being able to read her mentor just once.

Drawing buhkar, she turned to black mist and slipped

between the horde clogging the city gates. She was delighted to find that the wind did not push her about in her vaporous form. The magic must have changed her shape is all, not her density. A few guards tried to close the gate but when she appeared before them, they staggered back in surprise.

"Don't shut the gates yet. Leave two men here and the rest of you with me. We need to evacuate those tall apartments." She pointed to the higher parts of the city built on the ascending hill. "That dragon will go for them. One blast will devastate most of it. We have little time."

A few of the younger guards nodded and took up their spears but a couple older ones with salt and pepper beards scoffed. "And who are you?"

Throwing her hood off with a grunt of annoyance, she showed her white veins and startlingly blue eyes. She raised her hand, flexing her fingers to show the runes draped around them. "I'm a Runer. That's a monster. Do as I say."

With a gaggle of worried guards following her, she dashed through the center of the city on her horse and up the hill to the residencies above the rest of the city. She almost faltered as she passed her gate, seeing the reconstruction on her burned home. The last estate before the rise of the hill. She forced herself to look ahead, unable to help them now. The entire city needed her aid.

Keeping her head cool, she kicked down door after door of homes, pulling families out and creating a chain of information as she went: head to the lower areas, get inside a cellar, don't get distracted, hold hands. The higher up she went, the more she could see the rural homesteads. The well where she committed her crime was a black dot in the distance. Staring for too long, she almost envisioned Xiaoh crawling out as a risen corpse. The sulfates in her froze the longer she thought about it. No, she had to focus!

"This entire district is empty," one of the older guards reported to her.

"Good, now get—" She screamed.

A blast rocked the upper levels. Shards of exploding rocks, colored glass from the few windows that had it, and other debris ripped past her. A few pieces of shrapnel would have cut her face and hands, but her instincts finally spoke to her. She felt the blast before she heard it and heard it before it shoved her against a sandy wall. That time she had between knowing the danger came for her and feeling it granted her a moment to lift halat above her head. The quick motion only let the protection last a split second—too fast for the guard to see—but long enough to save her and him from the deadly shards. When she lowered her hand, she caught the city guard panting, eyes wide. She smiled.

"As I was saying," she smirked, pride swelling her chest, "let's get out of here."

THE RISEN DRAGON SWOOPED DOWN, claws reaching and scratching for any stragglers but coming up empty after it blasted part of the city atop the hill. Tzarik watched it carefully from the turret where he loaded the ballista. When he got there, he ordered a runner in each direction around the wall to pass orders on to the next turret and so on. But now he had a chance. The temple's minaret blocked half of his view so he didn't want to take the shot.

"Tell the northernmost tower to fire!" he roared to one of the helpless guards next to him, helping him load a bolt onto the giant war machine.

"There are people in those homes!" the guard gasped, wiping sweat and sand from his brow. "That's a residence section."

Tzarik scanned what he could see from there. The beast finally landed, sliding down a golden dome and stopped when it grasped a glimmering spire. No one ran out screaming. Sybal went that way. Did she evacuate everyone?

"If we hit the structure just right, it could collapse. That's what these are for," the guard pleaded.

He trusted her. She would have known getting the people out of the highest point was a good idea. With a grunt, he swirled the ballista around and looked through the brass crosshairs.

"No!" the guarded shouted.

He flipped the lever. The rope let out a puff of dust as the bolt hissed through the air. The guard threw himself onto Tzarik, crushing him under the bulk of his heavy armor. Seeing he had Tzarik pinned, the guard tried to grasp his wrists to keep him from harming the people of the city more. Tzarik drew the rune buhkar to slide out in the form of black mist but nothing happened. Gasping, he opened his hand to see the buhkar rune cracked. Not broken, but the carved rune upon the rock splintered down the center.

Enraged, Tzarik drew jiun. The fury boiled the white blood in his veins but gave him the inhuman strength for just a moment to shove the bigger man off. He drew his sword, the fury taking over and forcing him to act more on his emotions than his sense. He raised it to slice the man.

"I don't know what that is!" Sybal's voice cut through just long enough for the seconds of fury to dissipate.

Blinking and coming back to himself, he turned to see her sweating and pointing down into the city.

"What?" he asked running out of the tower. Looking up to where he shot, he saw he had hit the beast. It's black, fell blood spattered the aureate domes but the thing was nowhere to be seen.

Sybal grabbed him by his cloak, pulled him out onto the wall, and pointed down into the breached city. Tzarik couldn't keep the surprise off his face when he saw a man in cruel looking armor marching down the main street of the city...sideways on the walls.

As though the walls of the shops, homes, and other buildings were the cobbled streets, the man marched horizontal down the main way, his blood red cloak hanging down his back rather than reaching to the earth. He carried a straight, western blade, red with the blood of the people. The risen seemed to follow him deeper into the city.

"There are too many firsts today," Tzarik mused as he rushed past Sybal to lead her down to it.

"We're going to fight it?" she gasped, following despite her fear.

"I don't know what it is so I don't want it getting away!" he called.

Together, they vaulted over walls, wagons, and barrels, and slipped through the throngs. They dispatched a few risen as they went. Sybal didn't see one fire an arrow at her and Tzarik blocked it with a quick drawing of halat. She heard the shot break on the barrier and smiled a thanks at him.

He didn't have to tell her what to do this time. She read his mind and moved before he could instruct her. This was what he had hoped for: her instincts to kick in and know how to battle off each other's strengths. Since she was taller, she stood behind him and slowly drew the barrier around both of them as they approached the monster. It leapt from the wall now and clawed a man's face with its bare hands.

Together, they ran and Tzarik swung. The thing spotted the attack, bent backwards so its head almost touched the ground behind it, and met their eyes. Sybal squealed in disgust at the things flexibility. When it snapped back up, it instantly lunged. Thinking she could get the jump on it, Sybal pivoted out to the side and lunged with her scimitar. It blocked Tzarik with its straight sword and caught hers in its gray hand. Fresh, red blood splattered out from the thing's palm before it spun away.

"It's living," Sybal gasped. "It's got red blood!"

Not convinced, Tzarik drew jiun again. The fury boiled his veins further, the pain more excoriating with how slow he drew the rune. But the speed it granted him allowed him to clip the monster on his shoulder, rib, and neck. With Tzarik cleaving the creature into a corner, Sybal took a breath and shot her arrow. The black shot ripped through the thing's throat. It lurched, screaming in a deep, guttural voice.

Curious, they let it stumble backwards. With the speed of a viper, the strange man snapped up an oncoming city guard. Its jaw ripped open too far and he buried his teeth deep into the man's neck. Tzarik saw its thin neck moving as it swallowed deeply.

"Sybal, it's an edimmu," he shouted, gripping halat in his hand. "A body possessed, drinks red blood to live."

She reached for the same one.

"No, use atan," he corrected her with no malice in his voice. "Light to us, reveals creatures to be what they are."

Together they charged at the feeding edimmu.

"I thought you just said what it was," Sybal asked.

"Edimmu are specters. This one is in a body."

Tzarik went low and Sybal went high. The edimmu fought back with only a few deft movements. Either from weakness due to loss of blood or because it didn't care about being caught in Tzarik's magical barrier, it sloppily aimed a stab at him and missed. Once within the faint, glowing golden circle of halat, the edimmu dropped its sword. More man than monster now, it scanned the carnage around it.

"What are you doing here, monster?" Tzarik commanded, slowly drawing the rune again to keep it up. Sybal did the same with atan behind it.

The man closed his black eyes and slowly took a deep, lustful breath. "I want the blood of the virgin." Its smile cracked its blood-soaked lips, showing gleaming fangs. It eyed Sybal.

Tzarik's eyes quickly flitted to Sybal and back. Finally, halat revealed the creature. A ghostly outline of a much longer dead man than the body the spirit inhabited showed like moonlight inside the host. The garments and facial structure told them it had been a man from Xia. Tzarik started, unable to handle any more shocking firsts, and halat wavered. In the split second the barrier flickered, the edimmu launch itself onto Tzarik, taking his throat in a death grip. The creature leaned in to bite him.

"Buhkar!" Sybal shouted, unsure what to do now with the creature so close to Tzarik.

But he couldn't; his rune was cracked!

"Slash it!" he shouted, drawing another protection and fighting to shove the thing off all at once.

Despite her better judgment, she arched her scimitar around, lopping the edimmu's head clean off. As she finished the mighty stroke, the last of atan showed the ghostly inner spirit flee towards the temple graveyard. The Xian spirit that possessed the corpse vanished into the holy grounds, trapping itself.

Kicking the corpse off, Tzarik turned and ran back the way they had come.

"What are you doing now?" she called, chasing after him.

The risen had overrun the city. Dead, chewed on citizens littered the streets. They couldn't see the extent of the damage in the huge city but the headless, limbless walkers told them that no amount of lopping limbs would stop the risen ones. They had to get to Tarkan.

"You have to get him," she panted when they reached a turret with a ballista.

"I figured," he gasped, heaving a bolt onto it.

Together they cranked it back. Closing one eye, he aimed out.

"He was far off to the south," Sybal supplied. "He was on a dune. But there's so much sand blowing, I don't know how you'll see him."

"Here?" Tzarik asked, aiming to where she pointed.

She waited just one breath, remembering, using her instincts, and then nodded. "Don't aim too high."

He released the lever. They held their breath for four agonizing seconds. One moment later, the risen on the walls that they could see, collapsed like scarecrows. A few more steadying breaths and the cries began to rise into the sudden silence. Some kicked the heads of the fallen risen. Others stabbed them mercilessly. They met each other's blue eyes over the war machine. He sensed she did not expect praise.

"You...did very well," he panted. The shock on her face almost forced him to grin but he stifled it.

Sybal beamed, pressing her lips together tightly and looked down, kicking a wall fragment. "All that training actually paid off. And it felt good, but..."

His heart sank unexpectedly. But? Anger roiled underneath the shock of whatever she wanted to say.

"I have to see my family now." She sheathed her sword.

"Why? No," he corrected quickly. He glared at her. His white blood boiled in rage as though he had drawn jiun for a day. The edge of madness came into view. "We made a great team today, you've made massive strides. Your instincts are good."

She giggled. "Don't worry, I'm not leaving you. I just..." she motioned to everything around them: the destruction, the dead, the cursed bodies, "I have to see them. Make sure they're all right. They left me—I'm in no hurry to stay."

Begging did not suit him so he let her go. The weakness that made him praise her—let her leave— built up. He clenched his fist tightly. This was why he didn't want a companion. They made him weak.

Chapter 24
Red Bloods

Tzarik was hot and cold like a frying pan lost on the dunes at night. Sybal shook her head, exhausted from the battle and her mentor's ever-changing attitude. He should have been happy—he said he was proud of her! Why not untether her for just a night to check that her kin lived. Make sure they had not been eaten by an edimmu, blasted by a dragon, or flayed by a risen dead.

She got distracted on her way, helping here and there with lifting or carrying an injured person to safety, holding a wound, or comforting a wailing child while a father stitched his mother's arm. By the time she reached her family's gates, the sun set long ago. Gladness filled her lungs as she gasped: the torches were lit. Last time she saw her home, almost half of it had been engulfed in flames. They rebuilt some of it, but large parts of the upper rooms were still boarded over, scaffolding framing the areas they were fixing. Not only that, but she could see the miners, under her father's instruction, helping people with nowhere else to go for shelter for the night. She spotted the kitchen staff handing out bowls of stew, her mother directed a gaggle of women washing linens, cutting them into bandages. A man she didn't recognize ran through a broken side of the fence, carrying a large and wounded man.

"Mother, this man first. His head has been cracked deep."

Sybal's jaw fell open. The tall, bearded man—strong enough to lift a miner—was Abdul her brother. This could not be the boy she left behind. The one who would not so much as confront their workers and left her to carry the sword.

She was not the same either. Raising her hands, she touched her leather armor and ran her hands down her muscle-hardened body to her belt laden with Runer items. Her crossbow lay over her backside with a near empty quiver, her sword stained with blood. No doubt her hair stuck up, frizzy and matted with sweat at the same time. She wondered if she had blood on her face.

"Sybal?" a woman's voice gasped, choking on the name.

Freja stood up from where she knelt over the man with the head wound. Jarred back to the scene before her, Sybal swallowed hard but couldn't speak. At least her mother recognized her. When Freja spoke, most everyone near her stopped and spun to look at the warrior woman at the gate. Even her father took three quick, but doubtful, steps in her direction.

When they didn't rush to her, take her in their arms, and pull her inside the gate, the gladness inside her leaked out in a shaky sigh. Would she always only be a criminal—a murderer—in their eyes now? Had that judgment tainted her forever? The idea of runing was to atone for her crime. She had not lived the life Tzarik had, did not have his scars. But she had fought and earned her gold.

Maybe the pardon required a lifetime?

"It is I," she whispered apologetically. "I didn't mean to disturb you. I wanted to make sure you were alive."

Freja cantered to the gate but stopped just short of opening it. "Was that you? Did you defeat the beast?"

Now pride swelled up. Not to match the pride she felt when Tzarik praised her, but a good kind nonetheless. "I did. It was quite a battle. We worked together to defeat the beast. It was amazing!" She checked her excitement in the presence of the hurt and wounded.

"We?" Riyadh asked cautiously. He joined Freja behind the gate, putting one hand on her shoulder to hold her back.

Sybal caught his body language instantly. The arm at his side did not hang but went rigid, his fist clenched. But he did not show anger in his face. His brows subtly pinched up and his brown eyes betrayed his worry for her. Freja leaned forward. If her husband had not been holding her back, Sybal knew she'd have thrown the gates wide and brought her in. Seeing their hidden intent made her smile and relax. No wonder Tzarik always seemed so aloof; he knew what people were thinking all the time.

"Yes, the man who the Qadi brought to rune me. Remember, I requested the trial of two. That is an old myth in these magical professions that says he had to take me and train me until I am ready to stand on my own. It was the only way I could think to guarantee my safety if I survived the runing."

Freja pressed her hand to her chest but forced her face to remain calm. Sybal saw her lips twitch. Such a strong woman.

"And he takes care of you?" her mother asked softly to hide her trembling voice.

Sybal took too long to answer. Before she took a breath to reply, a deep, manly voice called to them, "Stop standing in the gate and let my sister in!"

Abdul waved for them to do as he said and Freja leapt at the opportunity. Grasping the now rickety gates in her delicate hands, the tall woman used her entire body to heave them open. When she did, a few of the miners looked up and saluted her.

"You look starved," Freja cooed, wrapping one slender arm around her daughter's waist and taking her hand in her other as she led her towards the main house. "Does he not feed you?"

"Mother." Sybal allowed herself a chuckle. "We live under the stars. We eat what we can. And money was so scarce to start. When I found him—"

"Found him?" Riyadh cut in, his fatherly tone coming back as though it had never gone. "He left you?"

Sybal sighed and nodded. "It's a long story."

"One we will hear over dinner!" Abdul encouraged her with a wink and a smile.

"And I want to know what happened to my brother!" she gasped, pinching his rock-hard arm between her fingers. "Who is this man before me?"

They all shared a modest smile. Before they could settle in, they set up as many wounded as they could. Sybal helped hand out blankets to those who could fit in the safe areas of the mines and the barns. She made sure each group of people had a skin of water before she joined her family in their home.

"We could fit more people in the foyer," she offered once they entered the main house.

At this, Sheikh Riyadh glared at his daughter as though she suggested they sell their home and take up the lives of gypsies.

"That is not the way of Al'Myrah," Abdul put in, kindlier than his father would. "You know that, Syb. They would take and steal. We must protect ourselves as well." He shook his head. "You are forgetting the ways of civility, sister."

She'd forgotten. The family motto: Protect what is yours.

"Would you like time to wash up before you sit at the table?" Freja asked kindly. Sybal saw her brace herself. She didn't know for what.

"I'm fine," she answered simply, shrugging. "I'm used to fishing grass or rocks out of my food anyway."

That's what Freja braced for. When she finished speaking, her mother raised her head high as she did when trying to cope, and nodded stiffly. "Then let's sit and eat."

"COME ON, BE A MAN!" Sybal cried, sweat beading on her forehead and in her palm where she clutched her brother's with such ferocity, she thought she might break his arm.

"Do you have to arm wrestle at the table?" Freja pleaded, picking up her wine glass as Sybal screamed and sprawled across the dining area.

"You've bested me!" she crowed. "I fully intended to come home, strong as I am, and beat you in a wrestling match." She looked him over once more. "I cannot believe this. How long has it been?"

Riyadh said carefully, "Six months. Since the fire."

This took Sybal by surprise. The days did not seem to fly that fast. A few days travel here and there. Sometimes it took more than a week to get from one proper civilization to the next. They had done odd jobs. They trained. Six months?

And the fire. Her doing.

Her mother patted her arm gently. "We missed you. I was so worried after...everything. We wanted to come after you, chase you down."

"Freja!" her father snapped, shaking his head over his golden goblet.

"We did," Abdul said sternly, not looking at his father. "But it would look bad. Our family is a staple in this city. We had to maintain that appearance. You understand. And your absence inspired me. I had to step up."

"I thought I did understand." Her voice came as a whisper. The idea seemed so distant, almost foreign. "But you don't hate me?"

"Sybal," Freja cooed again, a tear falling down her pale cheek, "you are my daughter. Of course I love you. You know things aren't that easy."

"Easy?" She didn't check her tone and all three of them started. "I-I—" she took a breath to steady herself. "I lost everything. I walked out of here, blood down my thighs, thinking you didn't love me. Rahul." Her voice caught. "I went to him and he died. I loved him. I really loved him!"

This was her family; she could weep before them, right? Some new guard went up around her heart, blocking the tears. Instead of weeping, she took a deep breath, a long drink, and said steadily, "Nothing has been easy. The training is grueling. The hunting is terrible and terrifying. There are monsters I had never imagined and sometimes they hunt us. I have Tzarik but I'm also alone. He's closed off, hard."

Someone hurt him. Or maybe just living this life for twenty years made one that way. Remembering how she used to be and seeing the reactions to what she became made her understand, if she lived that long, that might be her one day, too.

"And I can't even leave this life," she went on, looking up into their worried faces. "If I don't use the runes, touch the orichalcum —the sulfates reject me. I was so sick. I thought I'd die. I wanted to come back, I did everything in my power to fight this new life."

To fight her atonement. Had that been the wrong thing to do?

She noticed Abdul incline his head towards her as she glared down at his father. Freja bit her lip.

"What?" she quipped. When none of them offered information quickly enough, she snapped, "Tell me what all these glances are about!"

"There is a warlock in one of the settlements outside the city," Freja spit, scared, as though Sybal had cracked a whip over her head.

"A man of science?" she shrugged. "A tea mixer. Someone who makes their living selling love potions to those too afraid to unbottle a djinn?"

Her father made a holy sign over his heart at the mention of a demon.

"Witches and warlocks are good people," Abdul put in. "They

know things about plants, crystals, medicines that we don't. They are not magic users but they are wise."

She didn't know where they were going with this. "Are you ill? Why have you been to see a warlock?"

"No," Freja assured her. "This warlock is from Alika but he studied on Caerwren under a master who used to be a healer in the Northern army. They know different things there."

Sybal still did not follow. That Runer they met came from Caerwren. They seemed to have very different learning over there. And Runers were more common.

"Abayomi, the warlock, thinks that a transfusion might reverse the runing."

Her breath left her like an opened window on a summer's day. Her hand went limp, the flatbread she had been chewing on dropped to the colorful cushion she sat on. A runing, after all, was just a glorified transfusion. She remembered her red blood seeping down her naked body and the jars and vials of the white sulfates pumping into her. The pain had nearly killed her.

"If this is true, why hasn't every Runer done it?" she asked. Her voice came from deep within her, weak and afraid.

"We don't know if it's true," Riyadh cut in. "He's never done it. No one has. He mentioned it when your mother spoke too much while getting tea." He was about to say one last word but stopped himself, shaking his head.

For the first time in six months, hope flared up in her useless stomach. "I want to see him."

THE NEXT MORNING, while the cold air rose up rapidly from the dunes, Sybal and Freja walked slowly through the desolated city out through the west gates to the smaller settlements speckling the golden sands beyond the walls. Most of the farmers this far out were saved from the attack. The risen had clawed their way out of the sand closer to the city. A few thatched roofs burned and some in the community wore wrappings and limped. Mostly, the outcropping homes were untouched.

They went up the rocky path into the red cliffs where more plant life bloomed. Sybal spotted the warlock's home instantly. A western style house with gables and a white picket fence blossomed into view, surrounded by more colorful plants than she could name. A brick chimney stuck out near the back puffing a strange, purple smoke.

"I always wondered who lived here." She smiled at the quaintness of the home. A golden dirt path led up from the white wooden gate to the rectangular door painted a deep, electrifying purple. "What a funny door!" she mused out loud.

"They say they are sturdier," a smooth, staccato voice said behind them.

Turning around they beheld a tall, black-skinned man coming towards them with a crate overflowing with fruits, flowers, and green leaves. He wore a loose, brightly colored tunic with no sleeves, trimmed in gold. His pants hung full and flowing off his narrow hips. His hair had been divided into thin braids and entirely wrapped in vibrant strips of cotton. His eyes glowed like golden suns out of his dark face as he smiled at them.

"Abayomi?" Sybal asked.

"Runer," he replied kindly. "What can I do for you today?"

His accent came in a mix of the staccato accent of his Alika people but also elegant and pronounced like the people of the west.

"We are here to ask about your experiments," Freja said quickly, unable to hold back anymore. "With the un-runing."

Abayomi's step did not falter but his brow furrowed gently. "Come inside for tea. I have a wonderful new mix with honey and lavender to try."

The inside of the square cottage was just as strange as the outside. Cobbled together from round river stones, the fireplace puffed a delightful purple smoke where a black cauldron boiled in strange, high, musical notes. Herbs hung from the angled ceiling and shelves of jars and fabrics colored every inch of the wall.

He ushered them to a small rectangular table and handed them delicate cups with floral designs dancing around the rim. He dipped a matching, round pot into the cauldron and placed a lid on it before pouring a generous helping of the lavender-colored tea into their cups.

"More honey than I usually put in, but that's the secret." He smiled generously at them then settled into a chair himself.

Sybal had sat in a chair maybe three times in her life at a table. The sensation of being so high off the ground made her smile. "I am sorry to get to the point quickly, but can you tell me about the process a little bit? What made you think this is possible?"

"No harm," Abayomi offered, sniffing the tea and closing his eyes. "I see you are new. Your veins are not as pronounced as other Runers. Your eyes are clear, though."

"Actually..." She shifted, tapping the rim of the teacup. "I'm not. I didn't train or use Runes until recently."

The man looked up, interested. "What happened then?"

She swallowed the sweet tea. When it hit her stomach, a calming sensation immediately washed over her. "I seized. My body froze. My mind just got snuffed out. Another Runer said he called it the Runer's death. He was from Caerwren. Korvoth?" she added, wondering if he knew him. "I heard you studied on Caerwren."

"I did. Met a lot of Runers. Learned a lot." He leaned back in the chair and surveyed the women before him. His eyes roamed up and down Sybal's frame but did not pry or make her squeamish. He looked with the eye of a healer: inquisitive, searching for harm, a desire to help.

"The process you are interested in is something I have never done before," he said honestly, offering a flat, yellow sweet biscuit. "I wrote about the theory while observing a runing in Hovandel. To my untrained eye, it seemed like a simple transfusion. I could be very wrong, sabi." He offered her the address of her people. "Runing is not a science like my herbs and crystals. Witches and warlocks know measurements, setting a bone, when to not amputate an arm, how to stop flesh rot. Runes are...magic. Do you understand?"

Sybal couldn't stop the way her face fell. "Forgive me, but I don't," she admitted.

Abayomi steepled his fingers and leaned onto the table, nodding and frowning in thought. "Science can be seen. We know the sun rises and sets. The stars move the same each rotation. I know this plant," he picked up a leaf that somehow smelled like lemon, "will burn in my eyes, yet soothe my stomach. It is the same every time. I can measure how much venom it takes to kill a man. Then I can calculate how much it takes to kill a larger or smaller man. I know this," he shook a vial of clear liquid she thought was water, "will clean a wound and save a life. Every time."

He reached up to her collar bone and lifted the leather string laden with the five runes. "These are not the same every time. I have no cure for a ghost. There is no scientific reason the edimmu drinks blood. It is all based on faith. Trial and error where each trial produces a different error."

"But you're educated!" she pleaded, taking his hand that held her runes. "You can make an intelligent guess!"

Now his face fell. He pulled his hand away. "There is also the law. You were judged and this was your choice. You saved your life by taking up the runes. If anyone were to find out, the law could be brought against you. Say it works, and the sulfates are gone. You bleed red again. You have discarded the sentence handed down to you. You could be tried again. Executed."

Freja whispered an oath in her native northern tongue and closed her eyes.

"I can risk it." Sybal stood up. She had never felt so sure in her life. Used to taking risks, what was the worst that could happen? She had to leave Ala'Nar? Visit her family in secret? At least she'd be alive, safe, and have the life back she deserved.

The warlock stood up as well, taking her hand and shaking it lightly. "Let me read my notes. Prepare. I will find you when I am ready."

"What can I pay you?" she asked.

Abayomi shook his head, looking away. "I will not take gold for this."

TZARIK STOOD in the open window on the tiny balcony of the public house. His eyes scanned the city, snapping to every black-clad motion. She did not return the night before. The day wore on into the late afternoon. Still, he watched over the city, waiting for her. A man with a stringed instrument he thought he recognized passed beneath him into the tavern.

He rubbed his temple. His eyes stung from the sand that slashed them the day before. With Sybal gone, he took the time to look over himself. His armor needed to be repaired; he took it to a leatherworker and dropped his weapons off to be mended and sharpened as well. In just a tunic and pants, he felt naked standing there. Also foolish. Closing his eyes, he reflected on his meditation from the night before. Tried to ground himself back into his reality. Being alone, dirty. These were things he could do. Sybal—with her unfathomable power—reduced him to base emotion in just a few months. Maybe it would be best if she left. He could go back to hunting something that would put him out of his misery.

Thinking about ending his life came back to him like a familiar, dark tunnel. A comfortable place. He knew that place. It was easier than being with Sybal. He could go back if he had to...

"Tzarik!" her high voice rang up the stairs.

Steeling himself, he didn't turn to face her as she burst through the door. She came to his side, her smile visibly lighting up the room.

"There is a warlock, a man of science, who might be able to reverse the runing. He said he's not sure, but he studied it on Caerwren and has a theory." She stood in front of him, beaming, taking his shoulders in her hands. "He might be able to save me. *Us.*"

His worst nightmares all came rushing in at once, drowning him in a sea of horror. "That's not how it works." He didn't check his tone and let the venom spit from his lips. "It's not a science. It will kill you! The Runer's death, remember?"

She stepped away from him, disgust twisting her face. "This warlock is educated. He has traveled, seen things. He can read."

He saw her instant regret but the blade that stabbed him quickly blotted out any forgiveness her sad eyes warranted. "I knew you'd change your mind if you went back to see your family," he hissed. "That's why I didn't want you to go."

Her jaw dropped. "You lied! You said they wouldn't love me like this."

"They want to change you!" Now he argued like a child, shouting. Being out of control enraged him further.

"They love me; that's what blood does." She stamped her foot and marched away from him towards the door.

His heart pounded as the words burst from his lips. "We are blood, Sybal!" Using her name made it real. Dizziness made him sway on the spot as he let the words out. "Not them. You are not their blood anymore."

She stopped, her cloak swaying from the force of her motion. "You are obsessed with being the other." Her voice drifted across the room, low and dangerous. She faced him over her shoulder.

"You want to take me down with you, don't you? Rejects together. I thought you weren't lonely, just angry and hateful. But I see it now. You're a lonely killer. Or no?" She turned slowly to face him squarely. "My crime was justified, Tzarik. What was yours? I observe too, now, just like you taught me. You don't kill people. You don't sleep with anyone. You do nothing a holy man might consider a sin. What was your crime? *How many crimes?*"

He caught his breath and his mind stopped reeling. Slowly, he took a deep breath. He became hyperaware of his hands, his unlaced tunic. Like a fool, he believed she might stay. Might save him. Only a weak idiot believed in such things. He was right before; there was no point to life, living, or trying to change. It would be better if he had never met her.

She turned and slammed the door behind her.

Chapter 25
With the Jongleur

Tzarik slammed the brass tankard onto the table three times fast and hard to signal the server to come over and pour him another stream of red, liquid comfort. The room around him tipped and blurred slightly but he didn't care. His throat screamed for water but he tossed the wine down quickly to quiet the roar. He was overdue to leave word for the scholar but what could he do without Sybal? Tell the banker everything he knew, have them read the letters, and make a guess about necromancers?

The rage felt childish and stupid.

"My old friend!"

A tall, lithe young man with long hair swept up into a high ponytail planted himself across from Tzarik, slapping his shoulder jovially. Wincing into the dim lamplight of the tavern, Tzarik saw the young man from before he thought he recognized: Vicdan with a new, glossy wheel fiddle on his shoulder.

"I am not your friend," he slurred as dangerously as he could. Keeping his eyes peeled around the common room since he knew Sharar was somewhere in town, he made a quick sweep of the place until his eyes came back to Vicdan.

He noticed the disinherited man scrutinizing him with compassion. He should have felt shame at his appearance, but right now he didn't care about anything. If he guessed right, Vicdan had probably seen many a drunk man in his life. Most likely sprawled over his family's estate. Rich men often drank away their empty lives. Curious, he asked, "Why were you disinherited again?"

The man pressed his lips together and feigned shock by comically pressing his hand to his chest. "Me? Disinherited?" He grinned and held his arms out to the entire tavern. "The sky is my roof and the road is my coin. The world is my home!"

The change from the man before—confused, lost, desperate for anything—gave Tzarik pause.

"What happened to you?" Tzarik asked, choking on a swallow he took too fast.

"Glad you asked!" Vicdan uncrossed his legs and tilted onto one knee, coming close to the edge of the cushion he sat on. Leaning over the round table, he whispered. "I need some...protection."

Now that the young man mentioned it, Tzarik squinted and focused on his face. A black eye caved around his temple down to his cheek. A few other bruises and cuts contoured his face. A barely visible hand-shaped bruise wrapped around his slight neck. He double-checked the way he leaned on the cushion on the seat. The slightest bit of remorse trickled into his soul.

"I have a job," he quipped, taking a shot of the clear bottle the server just brought over. "Besides, with luck I won't be around much longer."

Vicdan's brows twitched up quickly in amazed concern. "Oh, no," he whispered. "I know that tone. I do, really. Not again, Runer."

Tzarik's left brow matched his in an ironic twitch. "Do you, now? What could possibly make you want to just take one more step off that precipice?"

"I know." He smiled charmingly. "Son of a great sheik. What do I know of struggle? Not much till a few months ago. It's not been a khafla, Runer. I just need you to stick around. I'll go where you go."

If he believed in a god, he would have sworn an oath at the suggestion. "Sybal's left," he said dryly, taking another shot. This time, it rebelled. The alcohol rose in his gut the moment after he drank it. Breaking into a sweat, he kept it down and didn't shoot the poisonous contents of his stomach all over the jongleur.

"What willpower," Vicdan praised simply, watching him swallow the bile. "I'm sorry she's left you. But I can be of help."

"How?"

Apparently, the rich young man thought his offer of aid would be enough and when confronted with exactly what he planned to do, he just blew a long breath out, puffing his cheeks and looking away. "I can read," he offered offhand.

"Can you?" Tzarik perked his aching head up.

Vicdan smiled and leaned across the table again. "Yes. And write. And," he quickly checked the corners of the room as though a spy lurked in the smoky shadows, "I can forge a few things. I know what documents look like. And I can sing for room and board." He lovingly tapped the wheel fiddle.

"I don't care about that," the Runer interrupted, sloppily waving his hand. "I need you to read a book and some script in a crypt. Can you do that?"

The jongleur narrowed his eyes and bit his lower lip pretending to think. "Can you make sure no more men pull me down dark alleys?"

Tzarik winced. "While you're with me, no one will lay a hand on you."

The first genuine smile—one that didn't expect anything in return—spread across Vicdan's handsome face and Tzarik didn't want to punch him.

"Where are we going?" he asked.

"Porsh," the Runer replied.

AFTER THAT, Tzarik couldn't quite remember what happened. He remembered Vicdan helping him up to the room and forcing a trough-full of water down his throat. Maybe he did the right thing because the morning sunrise didn't bother Tzarik as much as he thought it should when they set out. They had to buy a horse for Vicdan since he didn't have one and the man promised to pay Tzarik back when they stopped at a city on the way. Porsh lurked farther south than Vicdan had probably ever been and Tzarik braced himself for the chatter that would ensue. With the amount of time Vicdan spent talking, the Runer realized that the younger man might just have been born to be a storyteller.

"I don't know much about Porsh," Vicdan confessed the first night they sat around a fire out in the open desert. "At least not any more than we were taught in school, which wasn't much if I'm being honest. The island defected from the eastern treaties during the reign of Sultan Kahli because they disagreed with his Bahratt heritage. But all that ancestry did was bring our two continents closer together. Furthermore, he was responsible for the caravan roads we travel so often. He also oversaw the building of the ocean road the riverboats take. If it weren't for the religions—no offense to Bahratt, but why so many arms and tongues on the gods—then really our two societies might be interchangeable to an outsider looking in. But that's, obviously, very untrue to anyone who lives there. Now, I'm not sure when Porsh discovered the evil tome that would eventually turn their ruling government to necromancers, but—"

"Good." Tzarik handed him the book he carried, desperate to cut him off. "Read this and tell me what it says."

Clearing his throat, Vicdan opened the tome and began, "Chapter the first, a minor introduction on the temple's laws and black pacts."

"No," Tzarik cut in. "Find the interesting parts. Read them, then tell me."

"Sounds like twice the work on my part," Vicdan sulked. "And I'm tired. I've been on the horse all day. I had no idea I could sweat so much between my legs."

"Really?" Tzarik groaned, taking out a smooth runeless stone to replace the one that broke. "I thought all you rich men did was sleep with beautiful women."

The younger man cocked a wicked grin. "And I thought all you Runers did was sleep with sirens and banshees."

The Runer dropped the smooth stone but quickly snatched it up. "I've never heard of such a thing. Sounds dangerous."

Vicdan smiled but turned his face down to the book. "Oh, yes. Monster hunters sleeping with snake women, sirens, even spectral ghosts. And those—I can't think of the name—the women who seduce men and take their soul or some such nonsense."

"Duwais," Tzarik supplied, amused at the boy's thoughts.

"That's the one! Most people say if a Runer's crime is not rape, sleeping with another man's wife, or what have you, he sleeps with anything that will have him—even if he kills it in the morning. I suppose as a man of your profession, most normal women won't want to have you in their bed, no offense of course. I have no hate for a man who has committed a crime if he does his time, as you are. And maybe you do engage in other crimes to excess because you cannot do the one that damned you, but so what? Many monster hunters engage in couplings with the attractive creatures to stem that tide of loneliness."

"Do they?" Tzarik grimaced, keeping his eyes down.

Vicdan looked up. "Don't they?"

Tzarik had never heard of such a thing, let alone engaged in such activity. Unless a certain magi counted as a monster...

"Do you like women, Runer?"

"My name is Tzarik. And I don't like anyone. Perhaps you should just read instead of talking. You'll live longer."

"Oh, of course you don't like anyone." Sighing and shrugging, he turned his face back to the book. "Not much scares me anymore, Tzarik." He sat quietly reading for perhaps a minute before he said, "I do apologize. That's the story, though, you know. Runers sleep with monsters. Sleep with anything and anyone who might have them, actually."

"Hmm."

Vicdan rubbed the side of his nose before he said, "I am glad to find out it's not true. Don't know why."

"Read!" Tzarik brandished his carving knife at the boy.

The stars came out and a few wild dogs ran amok in the sands around them as a few moments of silence finally passed.

"I can teach you to read," Vicdan said, breaking the silence again.

Tzarik literally bit his tongue when Vicdan's voice cut the silence again. "I don't care to read."

"Well, if you could, you wouldn't need me. Or anyone. If you can read, you can learn anything. Complete independence and the ability to take over the world. That's what knowledge gets you, you know. And you are so clever. You could teach yourself anything."

Tzarik stopped chipping away at the stone and finally gave in to listening to the young man. Vicdan noticed and looked up to meet his blue eyes over the fire. Somehow, the man put him into a sense of calm. Made him feel like he could tell him anything. His warm brown eyes invited his darker secrets out over the embers. The way he looked up through his brows with a genuine smile that showed his white teeth. Behind the empathic mask, a new chapter of hurt and trial lurked but the boy didn't let it blacken his innocence. The storm raging in his head subsided a little. Enough to tempt him into conversation.

The change must have come across his unguarded visage because Vicdan asked softly, "What is it, Tzarik?"

"You are not the same as the last time I saw you," he offered in a stilted, guarded voice. His hands buzzed with numbness and he couldn't work the stone anymore.

"A lot has happened to me in the days since I've seen you." He smiled warmly. "And to you. You talk the same but there is less..." He wrinkled his nose and looked to the stars, searching for the right word. "There is less rage inside you. But it's not been replaced by a candle of kindness or hope in a dark window. It's just...gone."

He hit the mark like a trained archer. Where once Tzarik felt anger, frustration, and fear now echoed black and empty. Numb. He'd moved the rage out to make room for Sybal. But now that was gone. He didn't know how to say it. No doubt the wordy younger man would know how to put it.

Realizing he sat too long looking hopeless and desperate, he shook his head and went back to his work. He couldn't bring himself to shout at him again to read.

"I see," Vicdan said soothingly. "That's all right, you know? It just means something is missing from your life. Something you can find!" he interrupted when Tzarik tried to cut in. "You don't have to stop life to cure the emptiness you feel. I read about a man who was a healer of the mind and he said—"

"That you should read or a Runer might put a blade between your ribs," Tzarik barked. He stood up and walked to where the horses were tethered. "We leave before sunrise. Go to sleep."

"God of the sun," Vicdan exhaled into the stale wind as the floating islands and structures of Porsh came into view through the eldritch fog. He wrapped a scarf around the bottom half of his face, afraid the blighted, glass sand might infect him somehow. "They say even the sand withered when the first lich raised his army."

Tzarik walked slowly over the blasted, black sand for Vicdan's benefit. Sybal could not see well in the dark mist so Vicdan had to be practically blind. "Lich?"

Vicdan slipped and grabbed Tzarik's arm tightly to not fall onto the sharp crags. "Think of it as an ascended necromancer. The book said he is one who has read the Mahit'onomicon and has achieved unlife. Necromancers raise the dead, among other things, and liches do not die in essence. But there can only be one."

"In the whole world?" This interested Tzarik.

"So it seems."

He steered them through the frightening city back to Tarkan's family's crypt. It took a little convincing to get Vicdan to go underground but once there, the man's eyes went wide.

"Necrotic scriptures!" Vicdan gasped. "I read horror stories about this as a boy. I had a tutor who loved all things dark and frightening. She told me about djinn and goblins."

"Fascinating no doubt," Tzarik cut in, carefully making his way over to Ishmael's stone coffin. "I want you to find a reason in here."

"Reason?" Vicdan squinted at the vials and jars lining the walls.

"Why would a necromancer attack Ala'Nar? What does he want?" He stopped. The lid to the coffin lay tilted a fraction of an inch. Someone moved it after he and Sybal set the man to flame. "Does fire kill a lich?" he asked.

Vicdan quickly caught a beaker he tipped over and replaced it on the shelf. "Doesn't sound like it would. A lich gains his power from death, so he kills his heart. That's what the book said anyway, but it might have been a metaphor." He stopped in front of the family tapestry. "Necromancers are infertile, both male and female. How is this line so long?"

Tzarik looked up at this. At last, someone worse off than himself. "Runers aren't."

"Must be where the myth of your bestiality comes from," Vicdan smiled.

"We don't make children though." He stopped himself. Why open up to this idiot boy?

Sensing the change, Vicdan didn't press on. Tzarik saw his brow furrow though, confused by the statement as if something didn't add up.

"How did Ishmael have children then?" Tzarik asked, joining him at the tapestry.

"You can become a necromancer at any time in life, just like Runers." Vicdan traced the line from Ishmael to Tarkan and the destroyed name. "This one didn't." He touched the hole gently then ran his finger over the name beside it. "Tarkan did. Ishmael must have had children then chose to follow the cult. This one did not take the necrotic scriptures to his skin. Tarkan did."

Tzarik listened enraptured. His foe became more and more fleshed out the more the boy went on. He held his tongue to encourage Vicdan to continue.

"Zeva?" he asked, pointing to the hand-written name.

"So they are like us? Like me?" Tzarik finally asked when Vicdan did not go on.

"From what Sybal told me about her runing, yes." The other man stepped away and began to inspect the rest of the crypt. "But they are far more hated. Whereas you are tolerated, the Porshains do not aid the remaining innocent creatures. They are not near as abundant. Only one lich to rule them all. They used to travel in tribes. I assume this is why one might come out: to find an apprentice. Someone to pass the teachings on to in the hopes of becoming a lich. Or..." he turned back to the tapestry again, tapping his lips. "Who is Zeva?"

"Maybe he hates being the other as well," Tzarik said, starting to piece together his own theory. "There are times I want to kill a bystander. Maybe Tarkan is the same way. Raising a bigger and bigger army to show the rest of the world that he will not stand for their hate."

Vicdan made a high humming sound and tilted his head, unsure. "Warranted hate."

"What has a necromancer ever done to you?" Tzarik quipped.

"Directly? Nothing. But when the first lich found the Mahit'o-nomicon, he killed many people. Took over a city. Not every Porshain followed him and he killed those who opposed him, turning them into his army. If not for the rise against Porsh, we all might be undead servants to a few students of the necrotic scriptures. I think this Zeva is the key."

"Why?"

"One sibling is missing." He pointed to the hole next to Tarkan's name. "This Ishmael must have tried to change his children, but one refused. He might have killed him before Tarkan's eyes, forcing Tarkan to take up the scriptures. They tattoo them onto their skin—they have to—showing their flesh no longer belongs to them but to the dead. If this happened when the children were not old enough to flee or defend themselves, there is no way Tarkan has a child. Zeva must have been given to him."

"What?" Tzarik started at this. "Or he took her from a loving family to become a disciple."

Again, Vicdan squinted, not sure. "What if she died? An innocent child killed because she traveled with a Porshain? What if Tarkan did love her, just desiring that which he cannot have?"

Tzarik swore and turned away, going back to the suspicious coffin. "Monsters don't love, Vicdan. You ought to know that."

"Don't they?" He didn't join Tzarik by the coffin. "Don't they throw fits when their apprentices decide to leave them? Don't they become more compassionate when someone they can care for enters there life? Ah!"

Vicdan gripped his arm where a short, black crossbow bolt tore through the top of his shoulder's flesh. Tzarik put the bow back onto his belt.

"Do not ever assume to know me, boy. And never assume I feel anything for anyone."

Knowing that Vicdan would not go near him now, with blood dribbling down his arm, he pushed the coffin lid on his own, grunting with the effort. He almost lost his footing when the taller man did join him and helped push the lid off.

The boy made a holy sign over his heart when they saw what lay inside.

"How?" Tzarik gasped.

Inside, Ishmael lay just as he had. Perfect skin, hair glossy and shining. Except now a huge gaping hole in his chest yawned up at them showing mutilated lungs and nothing where his heart should have been. His head also lay on his hips now, decapitated and placed there with a scroll in its mouth.

"We burned him," Tzarik explained as Vicdan dry retched away from him. "He came alive and we closed him inside. I thought he'd be dead."

Taking a few calming breaths, the boy explained, "Must be the lich then. Someone killed him though. See how his heart, which would have been crystal, is missing?" He peeked over the side again. "And the head removed for good measure. Someone knew what they were doing. Ew, don't!"

The Runer reached in and pried the scroll out of the dead lich's mouth. It made a hissing, scraping sound as it slid over his teeth. He unrolled it but could not read it. He'd have to hand it to Vicdan who still clutched his bleeding arm.

"I'm..." The Runer cleared his throat. "I'm sorry I shot you."

"Don't hurt yourself apologizing, I'll read it." The jongleur took the scroll with a resigned sigh.

Tzarik watched his eyes scroll right to left rapidly across and down the parchment.

"He knew you would come," Vicdan said, eyes still trained on the paper. "He's like you, he says. He can read your intentions before you even know them. He says he knew you tried to destroy his family. 'The difference between us, Runer, is that I don't care about my blood. An eye for an eye, shall it be? I will attack Ala'Nar where your pet so desires to return to. You will return here to see what else you can learn about me because I am a monster and I must be stopped, is that right? While you read this over my father's dead body, I am raising the freshly dead in Ala'Nar to once and for all lay waste to the city. Desecrate me and my family and I will desecrate yours with their own dead. It didn't have to be this way, but you had to hunt me down. You put yourself in the equation. I will suffer for this but I am used to making sacrifices. Are you?'"

Vicdan's head shot up. "He killed people in Ala'Nar. He'll raise them up as they are being buried. Tzarik, the city is in danger from within!"

And Sybal was more vulnerable than any of them right now.

Tzarik dashed up the steps so quickly, pieces of withered sand broke up underneath his boots.

"We'll never make it in time!" Vicdan cried.

"He'll make sure I'm there."

This realization chilled the Runer's white blood.

Chapter 26
The Razing of Ala'Nar

THE RED BLOOD DRIPPED SLOWLY DOWN THE STRANGE TUBE, past the wax seal, and through the final corridor of the large needle before entering her veins. Her other arm lay in a basin of hot water, the white blood blossoming out into the water like spilled oil. She watched it gently swirl. As it caught the midday sun, parts of it glinted like broken glass. The area in her other arm pulsed hot where the new, living blood filled the veins. She rubbed her fingers together, feeling the electrifying white sulfates.

When Tzarik had been wounded, lost so much blood that he needed an emergency addition of the sulfates, he talked her through a very similar procedure. Remembering the fright, her own blood leaking out, made her almost reconsider. She feared he'd die, leaving her alone again. That fear of loneliness drove her every action and discussion. Not this time. After this, she'd go back to her life. Her family. People who loved her.

"Do you have Runers in Alika?" she asked, to keep her brain alert.

"Oh, yes," Abayomi replied measuredly. He had been going about his warlock tasks in his strange house but stopped to press two fingers to the vein on her neck and count steadily, furrowing his brow. "Very few. Some are Masakh even. I have never seen so

many Runers as on Caerwren, though. Must have a lot of crime."
He smiled.

"Does it bother you that I am a murderer?" Unsure of her own
convictions, she hoped he'd give some wise answer and put her at
ease.

Abayomi went back to the shelves near his hearth and began
dividing plants up into piles, some to be stowed in leather satchels,
others in glass jars. "You have told me your story and I understand.
Was it the right thing to do? No. But we make decisions based in
the moment. An outsider looking in, me, can condemn you from
where I sit. But it does not mean I am wrong to condemn you. You
broke the law, committed one of the worst crimes a living being
can. It doesn't matter that the man from Xia was evil. It was not
your place. You were lucky—and wise—to choose trial by runing.
It gives you another chance at life."

Sybal's guilt mounted. "Do you think I am cheating the system
by asking you to do this?" She squeezed her hand in the basin
where her white blood flowed out.

"Yes." The warlock smiled kindly despite his words. "And I
think your body will reject the red blood."

Scoffing, she leaned back in the chair. "Then why let me?
Won't this kill me?"

"I don't know. It may just make this Runer's death worse.
Maybe put you into a long sleep where you don't wake up...I
suppose as a man of science I am curious."

The hard chair put her backside to sleep. How could people in
Caerwren sit on such furniture? She squirmed and tried to adjust
while the glass of red blood finally showed some progress.

An earsplitting shriek rended the silence from the direction of
the inner city. Sybal's heart immediately began to beat, pumping
the white blood. She listened, trying to pick up clues and felt her
heart flutter. The sensation concerned her, but she had to push it

aside. The clanging of steel and the cries of dozens of terrified people rose up over the city walls to reach her ears.

"Ala'Nar is under attack again!" She ripped the needle out of her vein, wrapped a waiting cloth around her other incision, and took up her runes and sword.

"Sybal, you'll bleed if you fight in this state," Abayomi called after her.

"I made the wrong choice. I can't leave him! I know he's out there, waiting to fight." She stopped, glaring down at the stunned warlock. "Thank you for trying."

She cursed, screaming to herself. How could she leave him like that? Did he guilt her into staying with his sad looks, lies to keep her?

She galloped back towards the city on her horse, tossing the leather necklace of runes around her neck. Before she reached the walls, her instincts told her what she would find. Near the temple, where all the fresh dead had been buried, the earth crumbled away as Ala'Nar's recently deceased rose up. Others, in memorial rest inside family homes, attacked their loved ones. Untouched corpses in alleys shambled towards beggars and the homeless.

Leaping from her horse, she drew buhkar, slipping between malicious swords and biting teeth of the risen. As the effect from the rune wore off, she gasped as her heart pounded desperately. A blackness encroached on her peripheral vision and she stumbled. She couldn't seem to get air into her lungs. Forcing herself onward, she ignored everyone else crying out for help and weaved her way towards her home. They had taken in some wounded and she knew a few had died. They'd rise inside the gates.

As she clambered over the ascending city's roads, vaulting over buildings and dashing through the streets, she kept her eyes peeled for the dragon and the small black figure of Tarkan. This began to feel personal. Did he destroy her home because of what she and

Tzarik did to his? They should have left him alone. Why did he agree to this job?

The fighting grew thicker the closer she got to her block where wealthier families had their own graveyards, crypts, and memorials. A few city guards aided the sheikhs but most of the people in her realm of the city were not warriors. They had training but the lack of wars in the past years made the people of Ala'Nar soft. There was no way to prepare for such a battle.

When she crested over the last hill, gasping, sweating, her heart palpitating unnaturally, she froze. Freja and Abdul lay strewn across the marble steps leading up to her home, blood spattered around them. A black robed figure stood over their dead bodies.

"Tarkan!" Sybal screamed, unsheathing her sword, tears burning down her cheeks and sweat stinging her eyes.

The necromancer turned to face her. He raised both hands, dripping in blood, and with two fingers, wiped the blood of her family over his eyes and down his pale, tattooed cheeks. She caught a shake of his hands and a glimmer of emotion in his icy blue eyes. She ignored the strange regret and charged at the evil man.

He skirted away from her approach, holding out his hands, fingers flexed. Two dogs—dead with gashes in their skulls— charged her, followed by a ravenous undead horse. Quickly, she drew halat and shoved it towards the charging animals. The two dogs hit the smoky ring and stopped, dazed by the impact. The horse leapt over them and snapped at her with its teeth. She ducked, gripped its mane, and vaulted over it while drawing artiah to mend her cut arms enough to fight.

When she landed on the other side of the risen horse, it fell, dead once again. Confused, Sybal spun around and glared at the necromancer. Her blood froze. Flanking him, Freja and Abdul stood slouched, gripping spears in their hands. Their white eyes locked onto her.

"Don't do this," she wept. She didn't care that her enemy saw her tears right now.

"This didn't have to happen," Tarkan replied, one hand reaching out to each of her dead family.

"What do you want?" she screamed, staying her blade from crossing weapons with her brother and mother. "Leave Ala'Nar and be on your way. We didn't do anything to you."

"You did." Tarkan began to step away. "I hated my father but dishonored me by what you did to him."

She noticed his eyes quickly look her up and down.

"Don't change back, Sybal. It will kill you." He simpered mockingly then smirked. "Then I'll have your corpse. Tzarik would fall to your undead blade without a fight."

She fought to keep her position, she would not attack her family, even if they were dead. "This isn't the life I wanted. I chose wrong."

"I didn't get a choice!" Tarkan shrieked back. Thrusting his hands forward the risen bodies of her mother and brother lurched forward, death in their eyes.

Driven to the defensive, she drew jiun quickly to give herself the power to override her feelings and attack the risen bodies that came at her. They were not her family anymore. She had to push past that. She parried a blow from Abdul and used buhkar to drift between them and get at Tarkan.

He said he did not get a choice. Tzarik said as much one day. Could that be why he hated her so much? He had not been allowed to choose the Runer's life and she did. Did he hate her for willingly taking on a punishment he was forced into?

Finally, she had no choice but to stop Freja and Abdul. Tarkan had too much control over them and she could not get past them to kill him, make him bleed, see what color the splatter of his blood would be. With a roar of anger, she went on the attack, nicking her family here and there until finally she made an opening and severed her mother's head with a scream, tears flying from her own eyes.

Seeing this, the necromancer's eyes went wide in fear—disbelief? He spun sharply and fled down the path.

"Don't run from me, coward!" She charged after him. A series of blasts from the lower parts of the city rocked the ground, followed by an explosion of an oil mine. The heat from the sudden fire reached her sweating flesh before she saw the flames rapidly crawl over the city. Looking up, she saw the damned dragon laying waste to the remains of Ala'Nar with blasts from its decaying maw. With that one glance, she lost the black figure in the onslaught of death, destruction, and terror.

A strange calm washed over her as exhaustion from using the runes and the battle settled into her bones. Behind her, the temple erupted into a blaze and the minaret tilted, ready to collapse. She held up both her arms. Underneath her dark skin in one arm, the red blood could hardly be seen. In the other, her stark, white veins popped like a ghostly branch of a tree.

"I have to accept my choice," she whispered as the minaret gave way, falling on itself into a cloud of debris and sand. She could not save the city, but she could save one man. Abayomi deserved to live. He tried to warn her but bowed to her wish.

Sprinting back the way she came, she ignored everyone and everything around her: The screams, the dead, the slippery patches of the street drenched in blood. She had to avoid the fire that spread like a flooded river. Knowing she could not save Ala'Nar somehow freed her, allowing her to move easily and quickly. Sooner than she expected, she leapt over a remnant of a wall. Landing, she caught sight of two black figures in still confrontation. Tzarik, his orichalcum blade glittering like a savage rainbow cut off Tarkan's escape. The necromancer spoke.

"I'm finished with you, Runer! Leave me be."

Tzarik bounced his sword in his hand, ready to pounce. "You're a monster now, mancer. Runers hunt monsters. And there is a good price on your head."

"Ala'Nar cannot pay you," Tarkan retorted, his arms hanging at his sides signaling the end to their exchange. "Look at my power, Runer. Even now you cannot strike me down. Today I let you live. If you come for my blood again, you will not be as lucky. You will not have the death you seek; you will be a soldier."

Tarkan spotted Sybal as she subtly removed her bow from her back. Seeing the long-range danger, he motioned some of his risen towards him, and the shadow of the dragon passed over them. With only a tiny window to fire, she let the shaft fly. The necromancer leaned just quick enough to dodge the arrow. Tzarik charged while he was distracted and slashed at his prey. He caught his calf as he dodged the close blow. Black blood smattered out over the sand and Tarkan moaned loudly, pulling back to where his dragon would land.

"Don't come after me, Runer," he pleaded almost earnestly. "You don't understand. We are not that different."

Sybal saw Tzarik stall. He took in Tarkan's words, staying his hand.

"He killed my family!" she shrieked, charging past her mentor. But too late. The dragon blasted the two Runers back, breaking up the ground in front of them. Tarkan leapt up onto its proffered foreclaw. She fired another sloppy shot but missed the dragon and its rider.

Behind them, the risen fell when Tarkan departed. The fires spread over Ala'Nar, and buildings toppled from the dragon's blast. She didn't turn to look at it. Instead, she glared down Tzarik.

"I have to tell you something."

Chapter 27
Separate Ways

THE RUNERS DID NOT SPEAK OR MOVE FOR SOME TIME. Tzarik's eyes stayed on Tarkan as he disappeared into the horizon to the east. Rarely had a monster he hunted escaped him. One who had done it several times presented a challenge he had never encountered. It fascinated and angered him. The old thoughts of ending his futile and violent existence came less in the time since tracking down Tarkan. The necromancer gave him purpose. Gave him life.

"Did you let him escape?" Sybal finally said, the snapping and roaring of the fire filling the air as the risen fell and the wind died. "Is this what you wanted?" She threw her hand towards what remained of Ala'Nar when he didn't answer. "You wanted my family out of the way. You lied to me to get me to stay with you. You let him go to continue the wild hunt?"

He'd had enough of the woman. Spinning around so fast, his cloak and tools of the trade swirling around his hips, his eyes snapped onto Sybal.

"I wanted to spare you any rejection. Others don't accept Runers, Sybal. They hate us. Whether from jealousy, fear, or misunderstanding, they hate us. You've seen this! How can you think they would take you back with open arms?"

"Because they did!" She stepped towards him now, ash drifting around her face.

He imagined that's what snow looked like based on what he'd

heard. This also reminded him that she towered over him, even more so as he sunk into the sand.

"They love me and would take me back no matter if I was the girl from nearly eight months ago or if I was a hunchback with one leg and an extra arm!"

How did she know? He stayed the words, knowing she would have an answer.

"No one loves like that," he said instead. "They remember you as you were. They tried to change you back. It would have killed you if you went through with it. They would be glad to be rid of you."

Sybal shouted, rolling her eyes and finally turning away from him. When she caught sight of Ala'Nar, her body went stiff then relaxed as she accepted she could not save her home.

"He did this because you desecrated his family," she said calmly.

"He hated his father, he said as much," Tzarik argued back.

"Doesn't matter." She took a long breath in, holding it, then breathed out loudly. "I hope this was worth the coin you are being paid to hunt him down."

"You don't have to come with me anymore." He hoped this would reassure her, maybe start to steer towards recompense. He couldn't apologize, he just didn't want her to hate him.

She scoffed humorlessly and inclined her head gently towards him. "Finding him, killing him—or stripping him of his powers is the right thing to do. I will find him, and I will kill him."

"How? He's shown his powers. He is stronger than us."

She lightly touched the scar on her arm from where Abayomi had stabbed the needle into her soft flesh. "I have an idea. And when we bring this necromancer to justice, somewhere everyone can see, they will thank us." Her voice cracked and grew thick with emotion. "For my family. And if not them, for everyone else. His power is so impossibly beyond what we can handle." She gasped now, tears no doubt trickling down her dirty face.

"How will you take him down? With runes?"

"Yes." She sniffed, getting herself back under control. "I will use this curse for good."

"For revenge," he corrected casually. "Don't do that, Sybal. That's a long, spiraling, black road. It leaves a permanent mark on you. Makes you into someone you can't come back from being."

She smirked. "You sound like you know that road well. Did you write the map?" Taking another breath, she marched towards the destroyed city, clicking and whistling for her horse. She didn't look back once.

He had only called to someone once in his life and the urge to do it now nearly overpowered him. Steeling his desire, he let her go. She would have to learn on her own that no one would accept a Runer. A murderer. Someone who turned to magic as their last resort. Maybe she had never been taught about the mark of magic.

She disappeared.

"Runer!" a deep voice shouted from the east where the smaller homesteads lay.

Tzarik turned and saw a tall, black skinned man sprinting towards him, long hair clasped in gold ornaments waving with every step. He recognized his clothing as Alikan but his accent leaned more towards the enunciated vowels of the west. The items on his belt showed him to be a warlock.

"Who are you?" he asked, squinting up at the man when he slowed down, gasping for breath.

"My name is Abayomi, I was the warlock that woman came to. Are you her mentor?"

He used to be. His eyes drifted to the horizon where Sybal vanished, not sure how to answer. Abayomi guessed the situation and shook his head sadly.

"She is confused and driven by a fiery rage," he began. "She did not mention a Porshain hunted her."

"He's not," Tzarik corrected him. "I am hunting him. I might have made a bad decision to try to draw him out."

Abayomi's eyes lighted on Ala'Nar's remains. "I would say yes, you did. This is...inexcusable. The suffering. Ala'Nar was a great city. Word of this will reach the sultana for sure. Fear and terror at the thought of what one necromancer can do will shroud our continent in evil and hate once again. They will hunt him down. I cannot say what this might amount to."

Realizing he had miscalculated the impact of the mark he took, Tzarik fought to keep the guilt at bay. He had not felt these things —regret, guilt, fear, hope—in so long. He perfected the art of numbness. Apathy. Ever since he saw Sybal shackled in the hall of justice, things started to change. That damn woman.

"I can't change what's going to happen," he said stiffly.

"But you can." Abayomi fixed his black eyes on Tzarik's blue ones. "A man with your knowledge and skill could perhaps stop this before our continent is thrust into a frenzy it will not soon come back from."

"I've already tried!" Tzarik fought back, turning away from the warlock and whistling for his horse now. The smoke and ash filled his lungs and he coughed.

"I have a lead for you if you will take it." The warlock easily strode up beside him with his longer legs, keeping pace, unwilling to let the Runer give up and leave so easily.

"Why didn't you tell Sybal while you were killing her?"

"I don't know what would have happened if the transfusion finished," the warlock defended easily.

"She would have died. Trust me."

"And I did not know a Porshain, one so powerful and vindictive, walked among us. No doubt an acolyte in line to be a lich."

From out of the quivering horizon and fire came his black

horse, Vicdan clutching the saddle, his face black with ash. Clean tracks ran from his eyes. Whether the tears were brought on by the smoke or the fear, Tzarik couldn't tell anymore.

"I tried to catch up with Sybal," he coughed. "Then you called and this damn horse wouldn't heed my orders. I lost her."

"That's fine," Tzarik took the reins and helped Vicdan down. "Go on, warlock. What do you think will help me stop him?"

Abayomi's face lit up. "You will follow my lead?"

"I'm not promising anything."

"He's very dark and brooding, you see," Vicdan added, wiping the tears off his cheeks the smoke drew out.

The warlock's face darkened seriously. "There is a seaside city to the north-west called Moshav. Small but wealthy. There was an uproar nearly twelve years ago when a pious man—a religious man who the entire city looked up to—made a deal with a necromancer to take complete control of the city."

Vicdan gave a soft curse at this. Tzarik didn't understand.

"A deal?"

Abayomi nodded. "Perhaps you do not understand the faith of your people, Runer. It is a deadly sin to make blood oaths. Especially with one who spits in the face of the gods like the Porshains do, denying eternal life in the next world."

"What happened?" Vicdan asked softly, clearly enraptured by the tale.

"The man destroyed the city. I don't know the details and most of the stories are hearsay. But they all have a few traits in common: the man desecrated the temple, lost his home, and made a blood oath with a necromancer." He waited for Tzarik to speak but he didn't. "I advise that you go to Moshav, speak to the people."

"Is this blasphemer still alive?" Tzarik asked, guessing the cryptic answer.

"I do not know," Abayomi replied. "But it is not ancient history. Most on Al'Myrah do not associate with Moshav because of their western sympathies. They answered the call when Caerwren begged for aid in their civil war. Their holy war as some called it."

"No doubt protecting their coast," Tzarik said in defense.

He noticed Vicdan watching him.

"Fine," he said, pulling his hood over his head. "I can't do anything here. Ala'Nar will kill me if I stay. What was this man's name?"

Abayomi looked to the heavens, asking for forgiveness for uttering such a sinful man's name. "Ziyad. He had a son who may still be living there. Even if he is no longer living, someone in Moshav will be able to tell you what happened and perhaps shed some light on how to track and stop the necromancer."

Vicdan tilted his head. "If there was necrotic movement only twelve years ago, why was there no outrage then? No fear?"

"As I said, there is little love for Moshav on Al'Myrah," Abayomi replied. "They are a small city compared to most others on the continent as well. Word probably has not reached far outside of..." his eyes lighted on Tzarik briefly, "our kinds of circles. If you find a holy man of any variety, they might know as well. Blasphemers are rare."

Flipping the reins over his horse, Tzarik prepared to mount. "Thank you, warlock." He reached down and helped Vicdan up behind him. "I know there are few Runers on our continent, but please, do not ever try that witchcraft again. It will kill a Runer. It's not science."

Abayomi shook his head and held out his hands. "As a man of science, I have to help those who ask me for it. It is my oath."

Turning his horse north, he countered, "Trust this uneducated Runer, warlock." Clicking his tongue, he kicked his horse, starting a gallop towards the coast.

Chapter 28
Son of the
Blasphemer

To cut down on any talking Vicdan might want to do, Tzarik eventually merged with a caravan moving across the sand towards the rockier and clay earth of the western coast. Splitting the younger man's attention between more listeners spared him from the ramblings.

Abayomi spoke truth: most on Al'Myrah did not travel out of the larger provinces of Ala'Nar, Bagdula, or Hatal. Porsh, though close to Al'Myrah, was its own principality—they did not acknowledge the sultanas, the royal bloodline, or their government. He had all but forgotten Moshav existed. Considered traitors to the other provinces for their siding with the west during Caerwren's civil war seventeen years ago.

The closer the caravan got to Moshav, the fewer creatures traveled with them until only some care-worn Xians and a few Masakh trundled along in wagons so well-traveled Tzarik kept expecting to see them collapse after every rut or rock they ran over. Once they had traveled for days, the sun at their backs, a wonderful, crisp smell hit deep into their nostrils.

As the sun set before them, Tzarik led his horse, giving it a rest from carrying two, when Vicdan perked up and squinted in the direction they walked.

"What a wonderful, glittering field!" he exclaimed. Standing up in the stirrups, he covered his eyes with one long-fingered hand and squinted towards their destination. "The sea was a silken blanket, over the golden shore. The sun like a living god, setting to be no more," he composed out loud.

"This makes you a living?" Tzarik prodded, almost smiling. "I'd pay you to stop singing."

"Sometimes they do. But my voice is wonderful, Runer. You just have no taste." Taking a deep breath, he repeated the phrase in a wavering, melancholy melody.

Nodding and shrugging slightly so Vicdan could not see, he agreed silently. The boy had a strong, alluring voice. In a few more years, and if he could live through some hardships, he'd make a fine man perhaps.

"A ship, a tall ship!" Vicdan cried out, pointing again.

Finally, Moshav came into view. Tzarik had been distracted, looking to the left towards a spine of green mountains so covered in trees and ferns they waved like prairie grass he had only ever heard about. Above the crags and peaks, a thick, black blanket of storm clouds flashed with lightning, pouring torrents of rain onto them. He'd heard of mysterious monsoons like that but thought they were myths. Beside him, Vicdan composed another verse about the ships.

The last remnants of the caravan drifted away from them to go around Moshav and find the coast. The city, that they could see had once been grand and golden, lay dismal before them. A few finer walls and buildings reached to the sky and a minaret spiked up from the very center of the city. One estate, with great marble domes and spires of gold, stood in better repair than the rest. From where they walked towards it, only a few bodies could be seen milling about on the shore.

"Be quiet," Tzarik snapped. The darkening clouds overhead and the undead look of the city pricked his instincts' caution.

Beyond the city pulsated the ocean. That's where most of the movement came from so Tzarik weaved his way underneath the arching sabats to the rickety docks. The group there, boarding a long, thin boat with triangular sails, wore robes of yellow and green. Their bald heads reflected the gray light back to the sun. The man directing them had one long braid coming from the center of his head down to his knees. Before Tzarik and Vicdan were close enough for him to hear them over the roar of the ocean, he turned to face them.

With the elegant features of a Xian, Tzarik guessed they were monks of some kind. The man stood calmly, his hands inside the wide, sweeping sleeves of his monastic robe. When their eyes met, he smiled sadly at them, then turned back to his ship.

"I don't like the way he glanced over here," Vicdan said softly, staying the horse. "Almost as if he was sorry for our fate."

Thinking fast, Tzarik evaluated everything Abayomi told him about Moshav. They were outcasts of the continent. Shouldn't they be more worried about their own fate? Why would an entire ship of Xian monks be disembarking?

"We need to find this son of a blasphemer or find shelter," Tzarik said cautiously, leading the horse back into the quiet city.

"The weather is so strange." Vicdan said out loud what Tzarik thought. "The dark sky—and during the day! Do you suppose it rains here often? It makes me uneasy. So unfamiliar."

Glad someone could put his scrambled thoughts into words, Tzarik didn't argue. The sound and air from the living ocean and the storm clouds were foreign. He had only experienced pieces of ocean storms and didn't like even those small parts.

Distracted by the eerie, quiet city, Tzarik missed the guards closing in around them silently until one man, wearing armor emblazoned with a family crest, stepped out and thrust a spear into his face.

"Halt!" the older guard growled. "Keep your hands where I

can see them, Runer. No drawing for you. Don't move!" he warned Vicdan when the other man clenched his fists in fright.

"We're just travelers," Tzarik said calmly. "We are here to see someone for information." Scanning the guard, he quickly assessed he was not a city guard. The crest on his armor belonged to a private family. He could tell from the detail and the specific imagery like the ship and two peacock feathers on either side. This man also bore scars and held himself too well to be just a city recruit. This man had seen battle.

"Take them," he ordered.

A pair of armor-clad men rushed the horse, making it whinny and toss its head as they pulled Vicdan off and threw him to the ground. When he fell, they began to beat him into submission to bind his arms without a fight. Tzarik took an instinctive step forward to stop them, but the older guard's spear touched his cheek threateningly when he did.

"No, hands up," the guard ordered when Tzarik began to lower one arm. "I know how you Runers operate."

"Stop hurting him!" Tzarik snarled.

The older guard quickly glanced at the other two and flicked his head, telling them they had done enough. They stopped and hauled Vicdan to his feet, blood running down his pale face.

"Shall we take them in, Malil?" one of them asked.

"No, not a prison!" Vicdan burst suddenly.

Tzarik snapped, "Why, what have we done?"

His words were cut short as a few more henchmen charged him, painfully yanking his arms behind him, holding so tight he felt bruises blossom under his skin. They held him so he could not move without dislocating his arms. The man called Malil approached him now. Reaching just under Tzarik's tunic, he tore away his string of runes and ordered others to remove his belt and weapons.

"To the tower of justice," Malil snapped.

Roughly, obviously not caring if their prisoners tripped, straining their aching arms, the posse forced them into the heart of the city to a large square, stone fortress. Tzarik didn't fight until they were across the bridge into the fortress that he saw now had been built in the water—no doubt to deter escapees. They led the prisoners down several steps to a block of damp, cold cells.

"It's a matter of intercontinental safety," Tzarik tried as they were shackled to gray stone walls the likes of which he had never seen before. The guards didn't speak, locking the Runer's ankle to a short chain attached to a wall. They did the same to Vicdan in the cell next to him.

The other guards stood just outside the cellblock doors but the one called Malil faced them. Vicdan made himself as small as possible in a dark corner, foolishly showing his fear.

"We need to see the man they call the blasphemer," Tzarik said when Malil only scrutinized them with dark eyes.

"Of course you do," Malil replied. "Everyone of your ilk does."

"What does that mean?" Suddenly the cold made its way past his skin and into his white blood. Almost instantly, a painful stiffness set in.

"Runers are evil men and evil men are drawn here," the guard replied simply.

"I'm a jongleur!" Vicdan tried but Malil didn't pay him any heed.

"I came to peacefully get information," Tzarik said, his voice beginning to shake from the cold. Unlike red blood, the white poison in his veins did not keep his body warm. He had not been parted from his runes in over fifteen years and felt their absence quickly.

Malil laughed dryly. "The last Runer that came to Moshav was drawn and quartered. Stretched out on a slab outside the temple. White, cursed blood splashing onto the street. It rained that day too."

In his weakened state, Tzarik could not stop his hands from subconsciously wrapping around his middle in disgust.

"How?" Vicdan whispered, still cowering in the corner. "Why?"

"I bet you thought your friend here was invincible," Malil offered, pointing to Tzarik. "Runers do pose themselves that way, don't they? They are protected by foul magic and outdated laws. No one should be able to beg for trial by runing."

While the guard spoke, a surge of pain shot up Tzarik's arms, seized his shoulders, then trickled down his spine, cramping his lungs. An involuntary moan of pain escaped his lips.

"Listen to me," he growled through the pain. "Ala'Nar has been razed to the ground. By a necromancer. He has brought armies back to life and I don't know where he'll strike next. He's done things I've never seen before. He raised a dragon! I was told Moshav has seen something like this before."

At the mention of a necromancer, Malil's face darkened into slack hatred. "Is this true?" he whispered to no one in particular.

Vicdan gathered his courage and replied, "I didn't believe it until I saw it with my own eyes. It's horrifying."

"Are you sure it was a Porshain?" the guard asked.

Eager to pounce on this sudden opening, Tzarik nodded and described the necromancer. "Pale, blue eyes, a black script on his skin. He stands back, away from his risen armies, to command them. He carries them in a black box."

Malil's eyes widened and glassed over, remembering something dark and horrible. "Once a necromancer came to Moshav. He made a blood oath with my lord Ziyad. His name was Tarkan."

"That's him!" Vicdan shouted, finally allowing himself to come out of the corner.

Malil nodded soberly. "I will tell the master of the city what you have said and we will see."

Swallowing the pain of being separated from the runes, Tzarik grunted, "Time is not a luxury we have!"

The captain didn't stop, his back vanishing behind the thick, dark, prison door as it slammed shut with a clinking of keys.

BOTH MEN HAD their arms tightly bound behind them and then escorted to the largest, least decayed mansion in the city. Like most eastern wealth, a gate and guards protected the place. Tzarik couldn't guess what this rich man feared in his dying city, but he kept those kinds of comments to himself. Playing nice to get information was not something he did often and he had to focus to keep his comments behind his lips. The entryway to the home opened onto a beautiful fountain that must have been stunning before the destruction and dryness turned it into something that resembled a risen fountain. The marble pillars and floor chipped and to the left, a set of stairs crumbled away. He could make out a garden behind one wall through the windows. The garden spread over several yards, organized, elegant, and maintained.

Malil shoved them through a broken doorway to the most habitable room. Rugs covered the destroyed floor in patching colors and swirling circles. An oil chandelier hung blackened above them, illuminating the bookshelves and a table covered in tomes and maps in a faded, brown light. The two were ushered in and placed against a far wall while they waited for the master of the house to arrive.

Without ceremony, not even flanked by more guards, in marched a young man with a defined but weary step. The rhythm and strength of his footfalls reminded Tzarik of soldiers he saw once walking home. The light from the oil chandelier hit the young man when he drew closer. At first, he looked to be clad in the silken robes of a sheikh but Tzarik caught a glance of light armor beneath. The way the man stepped onto his right foot told him a knife concealed just below the lip of the boot waited to be unsheathed. His scimitar hung, almost hidden by the silks, at his side, tied down to his thigh.

"I hear you've run into Tarkan," the younger man offered in a dignified, deep voice. He didn't motion to have them unbound.

"Who are you?" Vicdan cut over Tzarik. "Why do you live in this ghost city?"

The man smirked in a way that pitied the ignorant traveler. "My family fought hard to keep this city. Sacrificed a lot."

"Blood oath?" Tzarik asked, narrowing his eyes to gauge the man's reaction.

"Yes." His face went slack, premature lines resting into place near his eyes. "If you did not know Tarkan, I would have had you killed. But I see you are here on business." Sighing heavily, the man glanced at Malil then back, hooking his hands into his belt. "If you swear to leave so I don't have to kill you in the public square, I will tell you whatever you want to know. But you have to leave Moshav. And if I find out you mean any dark intent, I will kill you on this very floor. Both of you."

"Why?" Vicdan moaned as the guards forced them to a lower table and sat them down.

The man did not join them on the floor and instead stood, his hand on the hilt of his sword. "Any magic is evil, my bardic friend," he said in the lightest tone they had heard yet. "All of it. And Runers worst of all."

"Of course." Tzarik kept his sigh as light as he could.

"Yes," the man snapped back. He took a step back and controlled himself. "My name is Sahir. I am the only son of the man who used to protect and govern Moshav. Magic destroyed our city. Runers flocked to us when they heard of the necromancer. As a boy—stupid and foolish—I thought Runers could not kill because of their oath."

"Only if murder is their crime," Tzarik corrected him.

"Exactly," Sahir began to pace with a slight hitch in his steps as he recounted the tale. "You might not know this about living creatures, jongleur, but when there is only one crime you cannot commit they will throw themselves into the others with voracious passion."

Vicdan glanced over at Tzarik. The Runer met his eyes, for the first time unable to read what he looked for.

Sahir went on, pausing in the arched window to look over his abandoned city. "If a man is charged with murder, for example, he may rape and never suffer a consequence. Most principalities on Al'Myrah will not charge the same man twice. This was believed to be because a runing was bad enough. The punishment had been fulfilled. And they did good: killing the monster we cannot."

Again, Vicdan looked to Tzarik, wondering if he could see the proof of this on a man. Tzarik adjusted under the scrutinizing and judgmental gaze and fixed his eyes on the back of Sahir's head.

"It kills most," Tzarik added, more defensive than he meant to sound. "A slow, painful death. The sulfates are not kind to your body. And being drained of blood is not instant death. You feel every drop leaving your veins. And the sulfates give you waking nightmares, burning the very marrow of your bones as you transform or die."

Sahir scoffed lightly. "Pity. Poor rapist. Sad murderer, having to suffer." He took a deep breath and turned to face them again. "So they glory in the crimes they can commit. Stealing, lying, cheating, or killing. A man who stole someone's wife, requesting trial by runing, will have a body count higher than any man who has led a holy war. And there is nothing the law can do about it. So the people take justice into their own hands." He motioned to Tzarik. "This is the kind of man you are traveling with, my friend."

Vicdan's face, rapt in attention, snapped into disbelief and he shook his head fiercely. "Tzarik is not like that at all. The worst thing I have seen him do is drink himself to death. Have you met any Runers like that?" he asked his companion.

Tzarik was taken aback by the kind, supportive words of the disinherited boy beside him and it took him several seconds to process that warm feeling in his gut before he replied somberly. "I never got to know many Runers. I met one from Caerwren not long ago. He did not seem like the type to throw himself into other crimes. But I can't say it's not possible."

Sahir smirked again. "Just not you, right? You are the exception to all the other Runers. You don't do that."

Clenching his jaw, glaring at the man who dared threaten his life, Tzarik growled, "I commit no crimes."

Fascinated, Sahir quickly looked Tzarik over like an exotic animal laying bound before him. "You are not so different from your necrotic prey. Tell me, how did you trace Tarkan back to Moshav?"

Finally on topic, Tzarik let the threats and attitude slide. Just for now. "I ran into him by chance. But I know little about necromancers. As you seem to know, Runers don't kill man or Masakh. I need a way to stop him. And capturing him would financially benefit me as well."

Genuinely curious, Sahir furrowed his brow and took a few steps towards them absentmindedly. He touched a ring on his finger that bore the same crest as the one on the guard's armor.

"What has he done?"

"Razed Ala'Nar to the sand," Vicdan cut in, impatient with how casual and calm Sahir behaved when asking about the necromancer. "Murdered the entire city and then raised them to fight and kill any who remained."

Seeing the disbelief darken Sahir's eyes, Tzarik added, "It's true. We witnessed his attacks again and again. Each time more vindictive." He lowered his head, adjusting his aching shoulders, a cold sweat beginning again. "The second time was my fault."

"Go on," Sahir waved his hand, rubbing his sharp jaw with the other in thought.

"I was tasked to study the necromancer—"

"His name is Tarkan," Sahir cut in.

The way the younger man kept talking about the necromancer gave Tzarik pause. Why did he lecture so vehemently against Runers but seemed to want to beg pardon for the necromancer? Wondering if he could get Sahir to explain of his own accord—without force, lured in by equal discussion—he went on.

"An eager scholar asked me to track him. Bring him in. I tried and it enraged him. He attacked the home of my...of my apprentice's betrothed."

Sahir's eyes shined and he smirked darkly. "I would have never guessed that this Runer before me took on the trial of two."

Vicdan glared meanly at Sahir in defense of Tzarik.

The Runer ignored the jibe. He needed to offer his story to get Sahir's in return. "To try to learn about him, I went to Porsh."

"Brave," Sahir mused.

"I found his home and desecrated his father."

"The lich." Sahir dropped his hand and cast his eyes to the ground. "Foolish choice."

"So it would seem." Tzarik read every tilt of Sahir's head, every eye twitch. Yes, this man knew everything—protected it behind his tight-lipped replies—and he needed to squeeze that knowledge out. "In a rage, he attacked Ala'Nar. Once to kill the people and have a fresh army inside, I am sure. Then again when he knew I would track him down and allow him time to enter the city undetected."

Sahir smiled in admiration. "He is very clever. Not unlike you."

"You've seen this firsthand?"

It worked. The younger man nodded, clasping his hands

behind his back and beginning to pace with pent up agitation. "He is not evil, Runer."

"Ha!" Vicdan cawed, unable to stop the sounds coming out of his mouth as usual.

This did not deter Sahir. "He's not. See, my father—Ziyad the blasphemer as they call him—went to the west. You might detest me then as I know answering the west's civil war call was not a popular decision. But politics aside, he came back after many years. I tried to step into his place, but my mother, never able to be alone, took up with another man. We received word that every man who went west perished in that stupid war. So I bore the burden of accepting another man who would sleep in my mother's bed and sit on my father's throne. Moshav is small and my father built this city up. The people saw him as their king.

"When he returned, this other man challenged his authority. But you see, like most on Al'Myrah, Moshav followed the government of the temple. Very religious. My father was the most pious man I know and insisted on faith and practice of that faith. This other man, Inaam, knew Moshav would never disobey the temple and so he weaponized it, using all my father's gold to buy their loyalty. When my father returned, he could not take his seat again. To overthrow Inaam, he made a blood oath with Tarkan. Gave him an army to take back Moshav and Tarkan could have whatever came from his home as payment."

Tzarik nodded. "An ancient law. Runers used to practice it as well, to acquire apprentices, but with no crime to hold them back they were uncontrollable and the magic blighted."

Sahir nodded, raising his brows. "Even you agree Runers are an unruled lot."

"What happened?" Tzarik growled.

"Tarkan did his part. Took out the temple army, my father killed Inaam, and he got his payment."

Now Tzarik glanced at Vicdan, wondering if he missed something in the story. "This tells me nothing."

Sahir cast his eyes to the dirty floor and turned away, tensing his shoulders as if waiting for a blow to fall. With his face hidden from them, he asked, "Did he have a woman with him? She would be just seventeen at most. A child."

"Zeva!" Vicdan cawed suddenly. He turned his eyes, huge and horrified, on Tzarik.

Understanding hit the Runer like a knife between the ribs, cutting off his breath for just a moment. And they called Runers evil. "He gave her up? Your father gave your sister to a necromancer? Did she come to him from the house?"

"Contrived by my mother." Sahir's voice lowered to just a rumbling mumble as he recounted the evil of his family. "What my father did was wrong. Killing his own people, making a blood pact with evil magic. But when Inaam entered my mother's life, she thought he would not take her if she had a young child of Ziyad's. I was a grown man, he couldn't stop me, but I didn't try. She knew that. So she hid my sister away, telling me she died from the wet fever—something a child can catch during the monsoon season. She hid Zeva with another family to ensure Inaam would not leave her."

"Bitch," Vicdan spat in defense of a girl he had never met. "When she knew Inaam failed, she brought Zeva back, didn't she? A revenge. She must have loved Inaam."

"Doubtful," Tzarik scoffed, flexing his arms and hiding a groan of pain.

At this, Sahir smiled sadly. "I don't doubt it. Runer, living beings will do dark, evil, incredibly wicked things for those they love. Even raise the dead. Kill a city they built with their own hands. This is what comforts me in your story."

"How?" A faintness began to take Tzarik's mind. He blinked,

breathing slowly to keep his mind aware. He needed the runes back. This is what Sybal must have felt.

"Knowing that Tarkan is willing to wreak such devastation for my sister brings me joy. I loved her for the few years she was in my life. I miss her. I don't want that life for her. Now I have hope that she might not have taken the oath of a necromancer."

"If Tarkan took her twelve years ago, he has no doubt turned her to his ways."

"Think, Runer. Don't your kind deduce at miraculous speeds?" Sahir waited, his hands at his sides.

The fog in Tzarik's head grew thicker, expanding against his skull. Did Sybal feel this as well? Could this be a small taste of the Runer's death?

"He needs the runes back," Vicdan said quickly after looking Tzarik over. "He can't use them if you keep his hands tied. Please?"

The younger man narrowed his eyes, evaluating the situation. "How do I know you are telling the truth and he won't rend me to ribbons the moment I put these back around his neck." He reached out to Malil and took the runes he stowed in his satchel.

"Runers have to hold them, then draw the held rune," Vicdan supplied, helpfully.

Tzarik didn't try to stop him. It wasn't exactly a trade secret, but it did give this man and his hidden motives power over him. But the pain began to mount to unbearable heights. Groaning, collapsing onto his knees, he said through gritted teeth, "Vicdan's right." A bolt of pain down his spine forced him prone, sweat beading on his brow. "And I need the rest of your story."

Sahir watched the Runer with cruel interest as he writhed on the floor. After what felt like an eternity, he soundlessly motioned Malil to drop the leather string of runes around the Runer's head.

The moment the magic circle dropped around his neck, Tzarik moaned in relief. The sulfates calmed under his skin, his head cleared. Like drinking a cold spring in an endless desert. Embarrassed, he shakily pushed himself up onto his feet.

"Do you want to save Al'Myrah?" Sahir asked genially as if he had not just forced a man to endure hours of torture in a dark dungeon.

"It's not my job." Tzarik stood up to his full height even though he didn't reach Sahir's shoulders. "I am being paid to capture Tarkan."

At long last, a different light passed behind Sahir's eyes. His face softened and his eyes dropped in a sadness he fought to hide. "Tarkan is not an evil man. I have found you do not believe in love, Runer, but most do. Even necromancers. Porshains value their tribe. You said Tarkan was alone. He would not have abandoned Zeva, my sister. Neither would someone as persecuted as a Porshain decide one day to raze a city. You know this," he said suddenly, seeing understanding behind the Runer's eyes.

Weak, Tzarik could not hide his reasoning like he usually did. He realized Sahir spoke truth. "He might have taken your sister and disappeared into the sands like Porshains tend to do. But Zeva was taken from him. She may still be alive. Why would he care for her so much to reap revenge like this?"

Sahir shook his head and moved behind Vicdan. The jongleur flinched but relaxed when the other man untied his arms.

"When the necrotic scriptures are inked into one's flesh, you lose that which gives life," Sahir explained. "Every necromancer can raise the dead. Not a one can create life. They are sterile. All of them. For a tribal people, this is a curse."

"Perhaps," Tzarik said too quickly. He caught Vicdan rapidly looking away from him.

"I have no doubt that Tarkan took good care of Zeva, waiting until she wanted to take the scriptures to her own flesh. The anger Tarkan is showing tells me she has not yet done so: she is an innocent. A good thing he wants to protect. Someone took her from him. Asked him to do their dirty work. Tarkan is a pawn in a larger scheme."

When Sahir did not move to also untie Tzarik, the Runer forced himself to remain genial. He wanted to hear what Sahir said. He tried to understand. He had done things he'd never dreamed of since meeting Sybal. It wasn't love, it couldn't be. Something about companionship turned him into a weaker man, forcing him to take his emotions into account. He didn't like it. She gave him a reason, though. For months, the thought of death and ending his own life left him. The feelings frightened him.

What had this woman done to him?

"Can a necromancer enter a blood oath as well?" he asked finally. "One could enter an oath with a necromancer, but does the magic work against them as well? If he made an oath with someone else—who you think might have Zeva—he would have to do as they say or perish."

He stopped. Someone who didn't want to die. Someone who wanted to live for the sake of someone else. Amazing.

"Yes," Vicdan said when Sahir did not answer. "I read it in that book you made me read. A blood oath can go either way but there have been very few recordings of necromancers entering into one. They work hard for their immortality, I suppose. It'd be a shame to snuff it because some bastard wanted a boon from you."

Sahir shuddered. "I am afraid to think of the power someone who could enslave a necromancer would wield."

"They might not have to have great magic or power," Tzarik said, realizing what any man would do if someone he loved and protected was taken. He began to realize what he might do—what he should do—to keep Sybal. "They just needed Zeva. They wouldn't kill her."

Now he saw Tarkan in a light like his own. Maybe he was not pure evil. He made dark and malicious choices to keep himself and Zeva safe. Whoever took Zeva wouldn't harm her, thus giving them a chance to reach Tarkan and perhaps come to an agreement. Together, they could save Zeva and stop whoever held the blood oath over Tarkan.

"Unless..." His white blood froze and he unconsciously pulled against his restraints to instinctively lay his hand on his sword. "Unless Tarkan disobeyed orders. He attacked Ala'Nar out of spite. He said he would suffer for what he did. The second attack, the killing of Sybal's mother and brother, was an act of revenge. Whoever has Zeva might hurt her to rein Tarkan back in."

"Why? What happened?" Sahir barked, laying his own hand on the hilt of his sword and striding up to Tzarik.

"We desecrated his family crypt. I wanted to draw him out. But I didn't know."

Sahir, with the speed and a striking viper, seized Tzarik's entire throat in one hand. Tzarik immediately choked, unable to move his arms to defend himself.

"Don't move!" Sahir shouted when Vicdan valiantly dashed to the rescue. "Listen, Runer, I was hardly comfortable with knowing my sister would one day raise the dead and perhaps come back and slaughter me for letting her go. I had to force myself to accept that she would be protected and cared for. I stayed, praying she'd be better off than coming back to Moshav. She'd be an outcast. Hated. Despised and probably tortured to death. But if a creature like you has put her in harm's way—"

"We can save her!" Vicdan pleaded behind the guards who moved to hold him back.

With a grunt, Sahir shoved Tzarik to the ground. Scrambling away, the Runer gasped for breath. Vicdan ran to him, awkwardly trying to help him up and not infringe on his dignity at the same time.

"I was just doing my job," Tzarik gasped.

"Always about the coin with Runers," Sahir spat. "So here is another job for you, Runer. Find whoever holds the reins over

Tarkan. You and the necromancer are not that different. I'm sure you can come to an agreement. Then find Zeva and bring her to me."

"You said Moshav would kill her," Tzarik reminded him.

Sahir nodded casually, lightly raising his brows. "If she has taken the oath of the necrotic scriptures she will need to be laid to rest. That is my duty."

Vicdan scrambled behind Tzarik and began to untie him. "You're a sick, rich man. Your own sister!"

The young man threw his arms open wide, not stopping him from releasing Tzarik. "No black magic can be permitted to walk free. See what it does? You've told me yourself."

Once Vicdan had Tzarik free, the Runer marched at Malil. The guard handed him the rest of his effects without a fight, stepping away quickly once he was free of them.

"Hypocrite," Tzarik snapped, slinging his belt and weapons over his shoulder.

Sahir smiled maniacally, shaking his head. "I am the son of the blasphemer!"

"You preach about how love can drive a man and yet you would kill any who are different than you."

"Dark, twisted magic is a little more than different, Runer." Sahir snapped his fingers and a posse of guards opened the door to escort them out. "I'm surprised you think someone like you would ever be accepted in civilized society."

"We came to you for help," Vicdan added, following Tzarik out.

"I've said far more than I should." Sahir's face fell. "I just hope you use the knowledge I gave you to make a wise and merciful decision."

Chapter 29
Burn the dead

"Father?" Sybal shouted over the soft mourning, deafening rumbling of moved rubble, and shouts from workers moving debris.

Ala'Nar's walls may have been destroyed, her streets broken, and her homes devastated, but her people marched on. A hard desert people, the eastern citizens of the city knew they had to clear the destruction before the image set in. While war had not exploded into the city, let alone the continent, for over a decade, the people knew to remove that which could tarnish their memories forever. Sybal made her way through this desperate parade but caught sight of something worse than the death.

As she weaved through, a whisper followed her. She ignored it at first, thinking someone must have been weeping. But then she caught the words Runer and mark. Unconsciously, she pulled her cloak over her head to hide her eyes and white veins.

"That's one of them," a few wounded passersby said.

Despite the hot sun, her blood ran cold. One child threw a large, sharp shard of building at her as she passed only to be quickly swept away by an older sister and told that Runers were evil and powerful. As she wound her way up the city back to her parents' home, she imagined the crumbled walls closing in on her. They hated her...just like Tzarik said they would. One lady—whom she thought she recognized—glared at her until she rounded a corner. Her heart stopped when she heard her name. They knew her name. Suddenly, what Tzarik said about never coming back to her place of birth started to make sense. She thought he was just a grumpy, sullen man but his philosophy played out.

"Father?" she gasped when she came over the hill to her deserted home, the gates twisted and broken. The bodies of her mother and brother lie in a line of many covered corpses.

Riyadh slowly stumbled through the front garden. He didn't look up at her, his eyes trained on the earth, looking for something. His head shined bear in the sun. Sybal couldn't remember the last time she saw his head uncovered.

"We..." She choked, moving to her mother and brother. "We have to burn them. Or he might come back. We can't let him use our people this way. We have a duty. We can send a messenger to the sultana."

"A war for one man?" Riyadh mumbled, still not looking at her. "We are one city on a great continent. The sultana will not turn her eyes our way for this. Burn them? So they may not have their bodies in the afterlife?"

Parched, she couldn't swallow and had no words for her poor, destroyed father. "I'm so sorry," she wept. "I was so scared, alone. I had to come and see you."

"Was it worth it?" Riyadh suddenly shouted, rounding on her. Sweat, tears, and spit flecked his white beard. "Freja! My snow queen!" he bellowed to the sky. "My only son! I have nothing left."

Sybal clutched her chest. "I'm here, father. I'll never leave you. Not again. I won't even seek revenge."

"No one." He collapsed, his face in his hands. Quicker than she could register, he pulled a long, straight dagger and plunged it into his own chest.

"Father!" she screamed. She fell to his side and gently laid him next to her mother. She gripped his robe, hoping to pull him back from the edge of death. How many more people did she have to lose?

"Runer?"

Her ears pricked up at the title but she didn't move. A man behind her called her. She didn't need to turn to hear him approach her. His steps were cautious at first then quickened. She heard a change in his weight—going for a weapon?

With a scream of defense, she drew her scimitar and slashed at the approaching man. She saw him leap back in a flurry of scholastic robes, clutch his spectacles to his nose, and run away. She didn't want to speak to anyone. Taking up her father's dagger, she marched back down the hill.

"Sabi?" a miner she hardly recognized asked as she flew past him. "Sybal?"

"Gather the bodies," she shouted back. "We have to burn them before he comes back."

She shouted at everyone on her way down to gather them. Burn them. This started an uproar she didn't expect to walk away from. The Runer, the one they hated, the one responsible for this, telling them to burn the bodies? Any minute now the city would revolt and attack her.

"You!" a woman further down the road shouted. "You, murderer! Harbinger of death!"

Now Sybal caught her eye and knew her. The woman from the trial. The one who begged for her execution.

"Leave Ala'Nar," the woman shouted, eyes trained on Sybal as she approached. "We will do whatever we must to see to it that the gods bring justice to you and your evilness. You will pay. You will die! What should have been brought upon you will come to pass!" She followed Sybal, shouting.

Nothing would have given Sybal more pleasure now than to sever the lady's head, stopping her guilt-inducing words. The weight of the dead sat heavy on her shoulders. With her entire family—and lover—gone, she had nothing left to do but find Tarkan and kill him. Even if it meant the Runer curse taking her with it.

Closer to the borders of the city, leading her horse, she contemplated where to start. She didn't know much about tracking; that was one of Tzarik's skills. She had an idea of where to start. Probably somewhere with dead things. The temple and the graveyard shared a city wall near the southern entrance. Remembering the edimmu, she hoped his spirit hadn't gone far. Tzarik said those things liked to latch on to decay and death. The aura of Ala'Nar had to be powerful enough to keep it there. She wasn't sure; just a guess, but she could make an educated guess now.

A new confidence rushed through her veins as she set up camp in the graveyard. She found a spot between two mausoleums and the wall. The sun passed below the sandy horizon by the time she had a small fire, had eaten, filled her waterskin at the decorative fountain near the front, and thought her plan through.

The night bugs sang and somewhere in the dunes, a wild dog cried as she slowly drew halat and atan, one in each hand, to reveal the spirits and protect herself. The moment she finished, in the light of atan, a ghostly woman gasped soundlessly and ran away. Cringing from the sudden apparition, Sybal steeled her nerves and took one step forward.

Whispers, cries, soft voices begging for answers reached her ears when she made it into the first lane. The domed mausoleums, triangular monuments, and other marks suddenly loomed foreboding and ominous in the flickering light. Remembering that she was a Runer, she stepped out into the graves. The spirits only came into view when the light from her hand where she clutched atan touched them. Sometimes she only saw a foot dash around a corner, or a weeping woman turn and cover her face, confused and scared. Most spirits cowered in her light. These ones must be new to the afterlife, unburied, forgotten. Those were the ones that would come back as vengeful.

She couldn't quite remember what the edimmu looked like out of his possessed flesh but knew him the moment she spotted him standing near the cliff edge of the graveyard; the only spirit unafraid. He appeared in his spirit form, more like a man than last time. She recognized the emblem on his ghostly cape as a Xian dynasty symbol from centuries ago.

"You! Edimmu!" she hissed past all the wailing ghosts in her ears. She raised her hand to spread more light onto him. As she did, the dynasty symbol changed like wax melting off to reveal a new image: a serpent and a long, wingless dragon with a lion's main intertwined. She froze mid step. She knew that symbol. "Whoang Xiaoh?" she gasped, stepping back and drawing her sword.

"Ah, Sybal," the man sighed, his far eastern accent dropping his Ls hard. "I can't be angry at what you have done. I admire you, in fact. You are stronger than most of my generals. Than the men who left me behind in death. You can't hurt me, stupid girl." He turned to face her as she passed her blade through his ghostly middle.

As she gazed upon the man who once threatened her and her family, she did not fear him. His eyes now looked wider, sadder. His face, once twisted in rage and lust, now smoothed over in a youthful desolation. She could see where she had stabbed him. Through him, she saw the cliff drop off and the white sands beyond the city.

Before she spoke, she drew halat around him but he did not fight, disappear, or charge to possess her.

"I can only take a dead body," he smiled, meeting her eyes. "And I'm not sure, but I think those sulfates protect you from possession."

"What's wrong with you?" she snapped, still holding her sword out as if to cut him in two for a second time.

"I am a jiangshi now, Sybal. Edimmu as you call them. An angry spirit that possesses a dead body, drinking blood to live. But

I have not found a body I like. Too...Al'Myrahn. Your eyes are too wide. Your bodies, too big."

"Did Tarkan find you?" she cut in, still on edge.

Behind her, a woman gasped, cried, and vanished in a snap of fire and black smoke. She held her breath from fright.

"They are burning some of the bodies," Xiaoh offered. "Helps them move on to the next life."

Sybal almost smirked. "They'll never find your body."

"Tarkan did," Xiaoh said simply. "But it was quite uninhabitable. He gave me the body I had. You ruined it. Like my last one."

Confused, Sybal lowered her sword but drew halat again to keep the spirit trapped. "Why are you being so cordial to me?"

"Death changes a man, sabi. Most never get to experience that." The Xian smiled. "Why not? I can't do anything to you. I have to be given a body. You can't do anything to me. I'm already dead. By your hand. I cannot move on. You can. I have no reason to stop you, Sybal. I won't. I want to see Tian. The eternal city. The afterlife."

She eyed him in the moonlight. "You want me to burn your body?"

He lowered his head, his black hair covering half his face. "I wish you would. But if you don't, I won't tell you where he is. That's what you want, isn't it?" He pointed with a transparent hand at her runes. "You have paid dearly for my death. You cannot kill him, you know."

She smirked darkly. "You're wrong there. I will kill him. And go down with him."

Xiaoh joined her in the dark grin. "I admire you so, Sybal. So strong. Fearless. If only my son were half the man you are."

"Where is the necromancer, Xiaoh!" she barked over his lamentation.

His eyes snapped to an oil lamp on the side of the mausoleum and back to her. He assessed the ring around him. She noted his every move. And the lamp on the wall.

"Tarkan wanted me to help him stop something so terrible, so evil that he promised me one thousand bodies if I did."

"I've had enough of the cryptic talk." Sybal reached up to the wall and plucked the oil lamp off. "Tell me what he said, Xiaoh. I will kill you again."

What she read in that book suggested that a trapped spirit might perish if burned with light and oil from a graveyard. Some legends even suggested that those holy lights kept the spirits at bay. Or trapped in the graveyard, it would seem. From the way Xiaoh flinched when she grabbed it, he believed it.

"He is bound by oath to someone," the spirit said quickly. "Sybal, wait."

"I have no mercy for you, warlord," she interrupted, grinding her teeth.

"Burn my body?" he asked, holding up his hands in surrender. "Let me move on. Release me. I've done my time trapped in this world."

"You put children on spikes, alive, outside their homes, Xiaoh." The flame twitched as her hand shook, poised over her shoulder, ready to throw. "You enslaved your own people, skinning men alive who dared stand up to you."

The Xian warlord held his head high. "And died at the hands of a woman while I took a piss. She then dumped my body down a well, poisoning the water of a lowly outcropping settlement in her own city where her family lived atop a diamond mine. Then she killed an old woman, to cover up the murder of an evil warlord."

She relaxed the hand poised to throw the oil lamp and looked away from him. "Fine. I will destroy your body and let you move into the afterlife. To..." She swallowed. "To be at peace."

The specter dropped his hands and nodded in thanks. "The necromancer spoke of a djinn. I don't know if he possessed a djinn or not, he wasn't very clear. He was...afraid. You will find him in the old mines beyond Ala'Nar. He uses them to move undetected with his fell beast and transport his crate of bodies."

Xiaoh had been awfully helpful. Told her everything she wanted to know. Djinns were extremely dangerous. She couldn't remember now what it meant when a mortal being got their hands on one, but demons were no light matter. Sighing, she realized she needed Tzarik. He'd know.

"Thank you, warlord," she smiled deviously. "You won't be rewarded in Jannah."

With a scream, she smashed the clay lamp into the circle where the spirit stood trapped. Her theory turned out to be right. Combined with the border of the rune, the graveyard light engulfed Xiaoh. He screamed but his voice crackled and burned, vanishing with his ghostly form. She didn't know where dead souls went, but it would not be paradise—Jannah. She gasped, calming herself, knowing that the warlord was more gone now than she would ever be.

࠰

"I won't serve a Runer!" the blacksmith gasped as she slammed his head onto his anvil. "Not you! Not after what you let happen. I'd rather die."

"You will," she growled into his ear. She slammed her father's bloody dagger onto the anvil close to his eyes. "Remove this blade. I want an orichalcum blade. Straight, like the ones in the west. Good for stabbing."

She reached around to her belt, pulled off her entire sack of rupees and coin and bludgeoned him with it before pushing off him to stand up.

"Take everything in there." She leaned against the opposite wall and motioned for him to start. "I'll be gone if you make it.

And so will the man who did this to our city." She crossed her arms and raised her brows when he didn't move. "Don't make me torture you. You know I can't kill. But I can make you forge this blade."

Shaking, the young smith quickly snatched up her black leather bag of coin. He took two quick steps back to put space between him and the Runer. "Fine, but the moment it's finished, you have to leave."

Sybal scoffed. "Nothing can keep me here."

She left the smith, knowing it would take him a few days to craft the weapon she desired. In the meantime, she found a burned out, abandoned shack to lie low in. She trained, pushing her body harder than she had before. Watching the people pass by the boarded up windows, she spotted the man who sneaked up behind her while she wept over her father's body. She recognized him as the man who offered Tzarik the job after Rahul's death. Crouching by the window, she watched him comfort a woman who dropped a sack of oranges that rolled down the street. The simple act condemned her. Guilt about who she had become welled up in her gut, making her sick. Tzarik could not comfort her, but she wished he was with her.

Chapter 30
The Hunt

"WE'VE TRAVELED TOGETHER FOR DAYS; THINGS ARE GETTING interesting!" Vicdan pleaded when the remnants of Ala'Nar came into view. The horse dragged its hooves and both men were worn, tired, and hungry.

"I won't tell you again, boy," Tzarik growled. "This 'interesting' you speak of can kill you. You'll be in the way. You should leave the principality. Maybe even the continent. I don't know what we're dealing with. I can't protect you. And I don't want to cut your risen body down."

"Good, then don't tell me again," Vicdan chirped, resituating his hands around the Runer's middle. He sighed heavily. "It's devastated. Almost leveled."

A new mass grave rose up on the eastern side of the city. Smoke and the smell of burning flesh hit them in the face when the wind picked up. To Tzarik's surprise, Vicdan didn't cover his face. His brown eyes glimmered with tears in the sun.

"Do you think she's still here?" Vicdan rubbed his eyes.

Tzarik nodded, scanning the people and the parts of the moat and city he could make out through the rubble. "She wouldn't leave yet. She'll want revenge."

A tingle ran down Tzarik's spine the closer they got to the smoldering mess. He felt eyes on him, even though he heard a few curses. Shutters slammed shut when he passed, citizens hurried away when they caught sight of him. If he'd had hackles, they'd have been raised. He tightened his core and pricked his ears up.

"What's wrong?" Vicdan whispered, feeling the Runer's body tense in front of him.

He didn't reply. Fight or flight took over, his lips pressed closed, his eye sharpening. Sunset always put him on edge—the time the monsters came out—but this time he sensed he was the prey. In the corner of his eye, a white figure in a hood and long robes moved into a glaring beam of setting sun. When he snapped his head to catch the figure, it vanished like sand on the wind.

"Did you see that?" he asked Vicdan, keeping his voice low.

The jongleur shook his head, but he shivered. "I thought someone's eyes were on me though. Like it wanted to eat me."

The feeling of being hunted.

"Tzarik!"

The voice he'd been waiting to hear hissed at him from behind a boarded up door. He whirled his horse around and saw Sybal's striking blue eyes glowing out from between broken shutters of an abandoned home.

"You're alive!" Vicdan crowed only to have Tzarik backhand him gently for making too much noise.

The two slid off the horse and slunk through the bottom half of the door that Sybal sawed for quick, sneaky entry. A small home for a four-person family; a firepit sat in the middle of the room designated as the kitchen, dining room, and lounge area by the furniture shoved into the corners. Tzarik observed her pack and bedroll near the fire. From the way her metal plate had been caked in dry reserved food, he guessed she'd been bunking here for over a week. A unique smell hit him deep in his nostrils: smoke, body odor that can only come from a woman, death, the tangy smell of used runes. She had been training. He almost felt pride for her.

"I was hoping you'd come back," she said softly. She picked up her cloak to make room for them around the small fire. "I tried to get them to burn the bodies. That seems to cut down on angry, lingering spirits." She handed them mint tea in stolen glasses. "Are you going to help me?"

Taken a little by surprise by her boldness, Tzarik gave in to her eagerness. "What did you have in mind?"

Sybal leaned over the fire and handed Vicdan tea as well. When she did, her tunic, loose from not being bound in the leather armor anymore, fell open and the jongleur looked at the little of her cleavage that came into view. He quickly glanced away and met Tzarik's thunderous eyes. Stammering, he said, "I'll help with what I can."

Sybal smiled at him kindly. "That man who paid you to follow the necromancer is here, Tzarik. I want to finish what he paid us to do. I want to capture him."

She stopped speaking but he felt the words she didn't say.

"You want to capture him? Make him pay for taking your mother and brother?" he asked. "You know what will happen if you kill another sentient being, Sybal?"

When he said her name, her eyes shot up to meet his. Her lips parted in controlled shock. She quickly shook her head.

"I want to find him but not to harm him," he said steadily, knowing this would shock her even more.

She focused on the fire before her. "I've felt like my own life is out of my control. Like events are just pulling me along and I have no purpose in it. I won't do that anymore. I will take action."

"We've learned new information." Tzarik guarded his tone, keeping it even.

She held her tongue, but her eyes flared with the reflected firelight. She sucked her cheeks in and distracted herself by oiling her scimitar.

He went on. "Remember Zeva?" He waited patiently while she fished in her pack for more oil and a fresher rag. "She is Tarkan's adopted daughter. She was taken from him. Whoever stole her is forcing him into this hellish escapade against his will. I spoke to a man who knows him." He stopped when her eyes flashed, daring him to go on.

"I don't care. Especially not with a djinn involved, I'm assuming?" She wanted to know if a demon like a djinn should be something to fear.

"A djinn?" Tzarik asked measuredly.

"I caught the edimmu," she explained, inspecting her sword. "Made him tell me about Tarkan. I know where he is, how he travels, and I have a plan to stop him."

Tzarik adjusted his legs where he knelt by the fire. As cautiously as he could, he made eye contact with Vicdan. He hated asking for help, but the young man had a way with words. And women.

Vicdan poured himself more tea after waiting for a group of people to pass by outside the boarded-up door. "Sybal," he said softly with a boyish desperation that became him well. "Zeva is innocent. She has not yet taken the necrotic oath. She needs to be saved. From her captors and from the life of a necromancer."

Delicately, Vicdan took a strand of Sybal's yellow hair between his finger and thumb and ever so gently tucked it behind her ear. When he dropped his hand, he let it slide through her locks slowly. He sighed, touching her elbow and resting his hand there.

"She deserves the life...the life that none of us will ever have." His eyes passed sadly over Tzarik and back to Sybal.

The Runer could not believe what he witnessed. The jongleur could have had anyone in bed in a matter of minutes, no doubt. But he didn't lie. His words were honest and sincere. He must have been able to read people like a Runer. The flirtation was so genuine that a wave of relaxation washed over Tzarik in the glowing, warm light.

Sybal, more gently, nudged Tzarik with her boot. "And you

care all of a sudden? About someone innocent who doesn't deserve to be part of this life?"

The Runer's tongue stuck to the top of his mouth, which went dry as the desert. He had an answer to that question, but he could not say it with Vicdan here. He'd rather not say it to her either. When he listened to the voice in his head a moment longer, it told him he was ashamed. Ashamed of what?

"We cannot fight him with that beast," he finally said when the other two shifted back to their respective awkward tasks. "We track him, kill that beast before he knows we're coming. Then we'll have access to him."

"The crate?" Vicdan reminded him.

"Burn it," Sybal quipped.

Tzarik nodded. "He needs time to cast his spell. We can have them destroyed before he raises them."

"How?" the jongleur asked.

"Oil," the Runers said together.

ONCE SYBAL TOLD Tzarik that Tarkan used the old mines to get close to his marks, tracking the necromancer was easy. Unlike Runers, the necromancer didn't care about leaving tracks. No one ever tracked a necromancer. They rode out to the mine entrance and left the horses since stealth was most important. As they skirted down the dark, sandstone halls, Tzarik tapped Sybal's arm and pointed up. Along the earthen ceiling, stalactites broke here and there, and scrapes along the sides showed where the dragon moved underneath the earth.

Vicdan gasped, quickly muffling himself by pressing his hands to his mouth and nose. They smelled it too. Death. Corpses. Tarkan must have thought neither the Runers nor the citizens of Ala'Nar would chase him if he hadn't gone deeper into the caves.

The Runers could see better in the dark so Sybal took Vicdan's hand to lead him. They could not risk light. They wound down several yards into the cave, cautiously peeking around bends before moving on. Tzarik put his hand up to stop Sybal and her follower when he heard it. Crackling. Tarkan must have lit a fire. If he was awake, they had to be quick.

Tzarik led them down slippery steps into almost complete darkness, following the smell. Unable to see in this new space, he quickly drew atan, covering it with his other hand. He almost gasped, stepping back and instinctively putting his hand up protectively to stop Sybal and Vicdan from coming forward. Before them, outlined in black, lay the undead dragon, the black wagon, and crate of corpses just beside it.

Once they all three relaxed, Tzarik pulled them close, just inches from his face. "Douse the crate," he hissed. "Thoroughly. Vicdan, do not light it until Sybal tells you, do you understand?" His hand shook, all of his motives scrambling his nerves. He didn't want to kill Tarkan. He needed Sybal. "Sybal, sever that head in one stroke. It's all you'll get."

"Where are you going?" A tinge of worry inflected her words.

"To him. I'll have just seconds of distraction to capture him and bind his hands."

Her hand on his wrist told him she didn't want him to be the one to capture Tarkan. She wanted to. Could he allow it? A risk.

"All right." He exhaled slowly. "I'll sever the head. You take him. Sybal." He gripped her upper arm. "Do not kill him."

She threw his grasp off, pulled her hood over her head, crouched, and vanished perfectly into the shadows. Vicdan swallowed loudly in the cave's silence.

"Hurry," Tzarik ordered. He navigated around the crate of bodies to the dragon, placing the glowing atan orb closer to Vicdan so he could see. The dragon didn't breathe, sigh, dream, or twitch. It lay really and truly dead, waiting for its master to raise it once again. The way it lay made it look like the beast went to sleep, neck stretched out, wings folded gently by its side.

Taking the jars of oil they carried down on their backs, Vicdan poured carefully, liberally soaking the creature's insides through the cracks. Tzarik climbed up on the dead dragon, almost slipping as he slathered the oil over the large, leathery corpse. This was going to stink.

"On three," Tzarik whispered, handing the man flint and steel. Taking his orichalcum scimitar in hand, he raised it up, counted up, and with all his might, severed the head in one fell swoop. The long dead, sun ripened flesh and muscles crunched and slipped under his curved blade.

Behind him, the crate blazed, pushing his long hair in a heated wave of sudden wind. Dropping his sword, he grabbed the other flint and struck the decapitated dragon's corpse. The light blazed so suddenly that his eyes burned and he went blind in a white flash. He stumbled backwards, covering his, face and fell into Vicdan's arms, saving him from the blazing crate.

"Go!" he ordered, tears streaming down his face from the pain. "She'll kill him!"

Chapter 31
Making of a Necromancer

TRIPPING OVER ROCKS HE COULD HARDLY SEE IN THE blinding white light, Tzarik clutched to Vicdan as they leapt over boulders and crags to where Sybal slinked off to. Fortunately, Tarkan ran around the circular tunnel away from Sybal, towards the blazing bodies. He came face to face with the two, skidding to a stop. His eyes adjusting, Tzarik saw Sybal leap out like a falcon in dive, her cloak billowing around her. A shining, straight dagger arched over her head.

It all happened too fast. Tarkan's blue eyes went wide when he caught sight of Tzarik, slipping and falling. Sybal landed on the necromancer not one second later, plunging the dagger into his chest. But she didn't stop there. Like a viper, she struck again and again, the necromancer's black blood smattering her face and the sandstone around them. Tzarik had never seen her move so fast before.

"Stop!" he cried, scrambling up to pull her off. He expected her to turn on him, attack him with the same ferocity but she didn't. She screamed, arms and legs flailing like a despondent child —all elegance and strength gone.

"Here!" With one hand, Tzarik pulled his belt off and tossed Vicdan his hip satchel. "Inside is a vial of black sulfates and some bandages." With a grunt, he held Sybal's arms down.

She collapsed back into him, her screams turning to wails of sorrow. She threw the knife from her like it burned and clutched the front of his leather armor as if she might drown into the sand if she let go. He felt her shaking, the weight of every death, loss, and trial coming out all at once. He wanted to chastise her, tell her to be silent. Straining, he held back, cradling her instead as he caught his own breath. He had to allow her to weep. To feel.

Tarkan coughed, a black fountain bubbling up in his mouth as his hands flailed at his lacerated chest. A moan of panic bubbled out of his throat. His breath gurgled and shuddered. The powers of the necromancer might have been strong and terrifying, but without his army of undead, he was just a man. Once he feared him. Now the sight of his prey bleeding out, a wounded animal, softened the predator inside.

"Tell him he's fine," Tzarik hissed over Sybal's head to Vicdan.

"It's true," Vicdan panted, a knowledgeable frown turning his once boyish face into calm concentration. He dabbed quickly but gently at Tarkan's wounds with the black sulfates. "My brother was a medical man before father decided he'd be better suited to running the family estate. Human organs—not even disturbed by this dark stuff— are very slippery, sira," he said to Tarkan. "They squish out of the way when a small blade like that pierces your flesh. You've been hurt, but won't die if we can stitch you up. No cauterizing need be applied."

The necromancer's face drained of what little color remained in his veins, the black script on his flesh standing out like black, spidery trees over snow. "Save her," he gasped. Vicdan's soothing touch calmed him enough to allow words out from his strained throat. "If I don't..."

"You'll be fine, I promise." He stopped, making sure Tarkan looked into his eyes as he spoke. "Tzarik is here to help you. You will see her, we will save her. All of us." Vicdan pressed hard onto the wound with one hand, firmly gripping his shoulder with the other.

Tzarik watched with respect once again, almost at a loss for words. "You might have made a good healer."

After several more tense minutes of pressure, applying the dark medicine, and finally cleaning up the wound enough, Vicdan unlaced Tarkan's robes, exposing his chest and the stab wounds. The necromancer didn't fight. He lay still, his eyes danced over the cave ceiling, wincing and unfocused. With his delicate fingers, the jongleur took extra care to press the wounds together. Larger necrotic scripts arched over Tarkan's chest and stomach. He made sure to line them up well then began to gently stitch him up.

"There is not much to work with, I apologize," Vicdan said softly. "I'll do the best I can and wrap the bandages tight."

Curious if their magics were similar, Tzarik laid Sybal down, handing her the wineskin from their packs, and knelt by Tarkan. Vicdan halted, the needle pulling at the necromancer's white flesh, and looked up at the intrusion like a man who had been interrupted during a good book.

Tzarik, not speaking, reached into his black tunic and pulled out the runes. Clutching artiah in his palm, he hovered his hand over the necromancer's chest. "I don't understand your magic or the death you wield," he warned. "I hope this works."

Tarkan closed his eyes, raising his chin. "I cannot fight you, Runer, even if I knew it'd kill me. Not now. You see me as I am: a desperate man."

Taking a cloth in his other hand, he dabbed away at the necrotic blood. When he hit a particularly deep wound, Tarkan winced and squeezed his eyes tighter.

"We are all desperate," Tzarik mumbled, half hoping the necromancer didn't hear him. "It's best not to tempt such a man. But I have to know something."

With a shuddering breath, Tarkan cut in, "Why didn't I kill

you when I had you under the dragon's claws? Or when I faced you after?"

So he knew? He decided in those moments—with the man hunting him at his mercy—to not take his life. Even after what he'd done to his family's sacred burial grounds. Confusion washed over him. He searched for an answer in Tarkan's face, but like him, the necromancer perfected the emotionless mask that looked back up at him, desperate to hide his truth. Deciding to save Tarkan from having to confess, he went back to work. He knew Tarkan spared him and that had to be good enough.

"I want to help you," Tzarik slowly began to draw artiah over Tarkan's chest again.

The wounded man's eyes glimpsed Sybal behind him. "It's terrible what they do to you, isn't it?" he whispered. He gasped, clenching his eyes tightly as his flesh knit just enough to hold together without the careful stitches Vicdan administered.

"Sorry," Tzarik sighed, sitting back on his knees when all the wounds turned to white scars. "I wasn't sure how our magics would mix."

He motioned Vicdan to go to Sybal, then put Tarkan's arm around his own neck and helped him over to the fire. The chaos that had been the last ten minutes slowly released the tension. He noticed the necromancer's eyes flit to the tunnel where the burning piles of flesh no doubt smoldered by now.

"They're gone," he whispered so only Tarkan could hear him. "We burned them."

Tarkan didn't reply. He gazed down the tunnel, hope in his eyes watched to see if Tzarik lied and at any moment, several rotting bodies would walk up and show him they were fine. When the truth settled in, he closed his eyes where he sat and turned his face away.

To his surprise, something like guilt or regret rose in Tzarik's chest. It had been easier than expected to break the necromancer.

Drawing on his own strength, he reminded himself that relationships did this to sentient beings—weakened them.

The Runer wanted to question Tarkan now but no one besides him was in any state to have a discussion. Giving Sybal a drink from a wineskin, he fed the fire Tarkan already had going and laid out their bedrolls. Several moments later, Sybal sat with her eyes glassy and focused on the fire; Tarkan was bandaged and Vicdan began to make tea.

No one spoke.

Vicdan handed everyone a glass from his own pack. As he poured, he said, "We went to Moshav, necromancer. Met a man named Sahir."

To their surprise, Tarkan almost smiled despite the pain and tense company. "He was a boy last I saw him. Not a bad man."

"He said the same about you," Tzarik said quickly, interested to know how a necromancer could be so highly spoken of. "Mentioned a blood oath. And Zeva."

A sudden change passed like a shadow over the necromancer's eerie façade. The Runer thought he saw him take a quick, fearful breath. Tarkan glanced around as if hoping she might come out of the shadows. Or was he on alert for someone else?

"Who are you bound to?" Tzarik pressed.

"Why'd you kill my family?" Sybal cut in softly, her voice raw from weeping. She didn't move from where she sat, leaning against Vicdan. Her bloodshot eyes glared over the fire, reminding Tzarik of a hunting jaguar.

Tarkan bravely met her eyes. "They were dead when I arrived that second time. I think he killed them. He's coming after me now." He said it as a warning.

"Who?" Tzarik guarded his tone, not wanting to snap. "I don't need to remind you how quickly I could kill you, Tarkan. I'm giving you a chance to go on living. I'm offering to help you find her."

"Very rare," Vicdan smiled.

"I don't want to fight you." Slowly, the necromancer took a long drink of the mint tea, lubricating his throat for the long story ahead. "I didn't want any of this."

Tzarik almost apologized when Tarkan stopped there but held his tongue. He needed to hear what came next without interruption or tainting what Tarkan would say.

"My father took up the necrotic oath after I was born. I had an elder brother too. Once the oath is taken, we cannot create life. At all."

Sybal looked up through her swollen eyes. "What?"

"Our vocation is death. Most necromancers do not take the oath until they have produced a child. We are a tribal people, after all. I can't explain to those who do not understand. Tribe is vital. Porsh destroyed that when the first lich rose up. Damning us all. But I didn't get that choice. I had no choice at all."

Tzarik shifted, a memory prying its way into his mind. They grew more alike the more he hunted him. He focused on the necromancer.

"My father told me and my brother that we had to take the oath or he would kill us. I would have rather died than take the oath. So he killed my brother before my eyes. Eviscerated him with his own hands. I wanted to leave him. But after that..."

Glancing over at Sybal, Tzarik saw her face soften. Her eyes shone like tears might once again flow, but this time for someone else. She understood. He tried to feel what she did but nothing came. Wishing he understood her made a hollowness in his chest ache.

"Wanting to belong," she whispered. "Forced to leave. Alone."

"It wasn't until almost one hundred years later that I found my chance." Tarkan lightly touched the perfectly wrapped bandages around his chest.

"One hundred?" Vicdan gasped, his loud exclamation echoing

down the cave. "You look great for a man who has lived in the desert for a hundred years." He pressed his lips together and looked away.

Tarkan's lips weakly turned up in a dead smile at the young man's shock. "I took a chance with a man named Ziyad. He wanted to use my undead army; I wanted an apprentice. Thinking it would be his son Sahir who came first from his gates, I made a blood oath with him. 'I will drive this man from your land if you give me the first thing that comes from your house,' I told him. He agreed. Probably thought I'd end up with a goat."

Here the necromancer stopped and grinned. Tzarik almost smiled back; the necromancer had an infectious way about his joy. The more he spoke, the more genuine it felt.

"But his wife—who had hidden away a daughter from her new husband—brought out Zeva." Tarkan's eyes dilated, watching his past. Now a true smile did lighten his face. "She was so small. So sweet. Scared. Beautiful."

"You took a little girl from her home?" Sybal's tone dropped to accusatory disgust.

Unafraid, Tarkan locked eyes with her over the fire. "Yes. And I loved her. She is a young woman now. She wants to come with me and take the oath, but I will not let her. She is innocent, could love, could bear children. But she wants to give it up to stay with me. I am afraid I have made her believe I will not be happy without her."

"Will you?" Tzarik surprised himself with the sudden question.

Sighing, Tarkan leaned against the cave wall, closing his eyes. "I doubt it. Whether I like it or not, she has changed who I am as a living being. The aspirations I had before have dissipated into the past. I would trade my lifetime to relive the last twelve years I have had with her."

Vicdan refilled Tarkan's cup with more tea. "Where is she now?"

"A scholar came to me," the necromancer went on. "Offered me gold to raise beasts, monsters, even ghosts. I did for a time but Zeva didn't trust him. So he took her, forcing me to do his bidding alone. When I saw what you had done to my family—even though I despised my father—I took revenge on Ala'Nar. He was furious at me for straying from his plans. I was supposed to go unnoticed. Not draw attention to him. He...He tortured Zeva and me. Rage took over and I went back to Ala'Nar knowing he had been following me. Sabi," he said to Sybal, "I swear to you, on my scriptures, your family was dead when I got there. I have been trying to evade this man's capture ever since."

Sybal glared in disgust over the fire, leaning harder into Vicdan. She had still crossed blades with their corpses. Tarkan had taunted her. He had done wicked things.

Tzarik let a few moments of silence go before he said, "He didn't trust you from the start. A scholar?" he asked for clarification. "Spectacles, talks fast. Makes you feel ignorant."

"Abigor Sharar," Tarkan supplied, curious.

Tzarik nodded. "He asked me to follow you. Track you down. Capture you."

Sybal sat up straighter now, gasping, her brows furrowed. "Xiaoh mentioned a djinn." She looked to Tzarik. "Could he...?"

The Runer and the necromancer shared a meaningful glance as well.

"Could he have made a wish?" Tzarik asked.

"Djinn?" Vicdan asked. "Like a demon?"

Slowly, Tarkan nodded. "Throughout recorded history, there have been two sorcerers that I know of."

"Sorcerers?" Sybal asked.

Tzarik adjusted to face the other three. "A djinn is a powerful demon. Evil. They are bound to ossuaries—some kind of container. If a creature finds one and releases it, they are granted three wishes and powerful magics. This can create a sorcerer. An almost unstoppable being. Given that absolute power so quickly drives them to madness and destruction."

"Wouldn't we know if a sorcerer had risen?" Vicdan asked. "If the power was so corrosive?"

Tzarik saw Tarkan come to the same conclusion as him. "Not if he's smart," he offered. "He'd plan slowly. Taking his time. Which might mean his plans are designed for a long, intricate devastation."

Vicdan's shoulders sank and fear wrinkled his brow. "What does he want with such power?"

"Always the question," Tzarik mused. Before he spoke again, he contemplated what he'd say. He was no hero but he also didn't want to stir the hornets' nest. "He hasn't done anything yet. There is a chance we can calm the storm and leave."

"What do you mean?" Tarkan asked. "I'll not let him rest until I have Zeva back by my side."

"I wouldn't ask you to." The Runer tented his fingers, choosing his words carefully. "I will meet with him. Say we have caught you and make a swap. You for Zeva."

Sybal spoke surprisingly softly when she asked, "Will he believe you?"

In the warm light of the fire, Sybal's yellow hair glowed like a setting sun. Her smooth skin gently covered her vivid white veins. Looking into her blue eyes, he lost all his courage and his voice quaked as he said, "I need to speak with you. Follow me out."

Chapter 32
Coming Together

SYBAL FOLLOWED TZARIK OUT THE WAY THEY CAME IN. Outside, the sun had set and a huge, white moon moved its light lambently over the sparkling sand. Taking a deep breath of the cool desert air cleared her head. Her face was stiff from tears and her brow ached from tension. The familiar pain came from weeping so earnestly. She hadn't meant to let everything out so suddenly, but a dam in her heart had broken, releasing the floodwaters of months of pain, loneliness, and despair. Realizing she lied to herself about what she believed when Tarkan said he had not killed her family, she believed him. Still, she never intended to live this life. As they exited the mouth of the mines, she suddenly thought about the gold slippers she wore when Tzarik runed her. Too small, uncomfortable and bejeweled, she found them stupid now. She smiled and shook her head.

Once they were a few feet away from the entrance, in case their voices carried, Tzarik turned to face her. Looking down at him, she read his body quickly: his knees were locked, he clenched and unclenched his fingers, and she saw his jaw muscles flex as he bit down hard. The strange behavior put her on edge.

"What's wrong?" she asked, opening her hand to place it on the hilt of her sword if the need arose.

"You could have died!" he hissed suddenly.

She took a step back. "What?"

"Your crime is real. That magic is real." His blue eyes shone in the darkness, livid. "There are a lot of things I do not know or understand and I'm sorry I fail you with my ignorance. But the runes are binding, Sybal. I have seen them take their vengeance when an oath is broken. If you killed Tarkan, you would have died and sentenced an innocent girl to death. You have to think beyond yourself before you act!"

The injustice of his accusations stung like a hot blade. Tears filled her eyes again, this time in rage. "You never think of anyone but yourself. You left me, remember? And why do you care about Zeva?"

He licked his lips but didn't waver in his gaze. She saw his throat tighten as he tried to speak. Should she dare make him say it? Did she make him this way? She didn't want to flatter herself. Especially now. After what she tried to do, guilt condemned her.

A tear fell down her cheek. "I've failed you."

He relaxed, confused.

She calmed herself with a breath. "I used to want to help. When I asked for trial by runing, I thought I could atone for my crime. I didn't think I would get drunk on this power. You showed me that I could be better, train, turn myself into a weapon to defend the weak. I had a vision in my mind and I took that beautiful dream and corroded it. After you sacrificed to keep me."

"Sybal, stop."

Her heart fluttered when he said her name again.

"This is hard for me to say." His gravelly voice came in shamed whispers. "I don't want to make excuses for myself but the truth is, I didn't have a choice about my runing."

Nothing burned harder or longer inside than the desire to hear her mentor's story. Knowing where he came from would explain why he defended himself the way he did. But did it matter now?

"You don't have to explain yourself to me," she said kindly. "You never should." *I like you the way you are,* she thought.

"For me then," he pleaded, his hands facing palm up, begging her to let him speak. "The one who runed me—Azar—left me, just as I left you. But unlike you, I only tried once." He pulled his tunic out from the top of his pants and lifted the hem, revealing a particularly dark, large scar. "He attacked me to get me to leave. I've been on my own ever since."

She heard the untold parts of the story. Not wanting to press him, she nodded, lost for words. Not only had he been changed, hurt, tortured, and left, but the one who should have been there for him tried to take his life.

"I had it easy by comparison," she mused.

"Don't ever compare your suffering to someone else's," he said quickly. "I did not suffer as you did."

Her hand went to her stomach: empty, useless. "I know how he feels," she whispered, the emotion making her words ragged again. "Wanting a family. A child. I can't imagine having found one, especially if she loves him, and then having them taken from me."

She sobbed again, gripping her face in her hands, embarrassed at weeping in front of Tzarik again. "I'm useless!" she gasped.

Tzarik took two steps, bringing himself close to her. He gently placed his hands on either side of her face, pulling her hands away. Tilting her head down, he rested his forehead against hers, pulling her closer.

"That's a lie, Sybal. You..."

She opened her eyes when his voice caught. She couldn't see him but felt his head against hers. His hands were so strong on her face, afraid she'd be pulled away.

"You saved me. Do you understand?" He pushed away and met her eyes. His glittered like a blue sky full of stars. He went on. "I wanted to die. I was ready to die. I tried to find a monster that would best me, take me down. Guilt-free suicide. Twenty years of pain, hate, agony, exile—just gone. Then *you* happened. When they asked me to come to the trial of a woman wanting to be runed, I came with the hope that you'd want to pursue a hunter's life with me. I had never met someone so brave before. I realized I was unworthy. So I left.

"When I saw what runing did to you, I thought you'd come to resent me. But I did that on my own. I did want to use you. I wanted you to stay with me. I lied to keep you with me, a sad man desperate for companionship. I hope you see. I know what I did was wrong, but I cannot let you go without a fight. And I'm sorry I made you this way."

Love and affection like she had never felt for anyone before washed over her. A new respect for her mentor lit up inside her. His vulnerability opened her heart to his apology. He meant what he said. She held him out at arm's length and beamed down at him.

"I suppose if I saved your life then I'm not that useless."

He gripped her forearms. "Stay with me, train, and you will see your value."

Unable to help herself any longer, she pulled him to her chest, hugging him around his neck tightly. Praying he didn't pull away, she held on while the shock of her action set in to him. When she didn't let go, he wrapped his arms around her middle, leaning into the embrace. The tension in his body eased.

They stood in this manner long enough for her to learn the scent of him coming off the top of his head. She pressed her cheek to his hair, committing his fragrance to memory. Sighing with satisfaction, they pulled apart and faced the moon over the mountains. Above them, a shooting star jetted across the sky.

"I'm fearful of meeting with Sharar tomorrow night," he confessed more easily then she guessed he would have just moments ago.

"Why?" she questioned gently.

"Any other man with a djinn would be terrifying. But Sharar is intelligent. What he's done to Tarkan and I alone is enough to give me pause. And now I have something I've never had before...I have something to lose."

She smiled knowingly, allowing him the privacy of not looking over at him. "We are not alone, though," she offered.

He nodded. "We can't let Sharar know that we have learned he has a djinn. That might be the catalyst to him moving faster, more ruthlessly."

"I agree." She nodded.

A few more moments of silence passed while he contemplated. She wanted to help him plan, but her mind went back to the day of the trial. The angry woman she ran into again in Ala'Nar floated to the front of her mind. She laughed out loud suddenly.

Tzarik looked at her questioningly, annoyed at her interruption.

"When I was on trial," she smiled, "this angry woman asked why I should be given the chance to be runed. I was dangerous and had killed a woman. And I replied, 'So I can banish her vengeful ghost ass when she comes back to haunt you.'" She laughed out loud at her own wit.

Tzarik smiled and a deep chuckle escaped his lips.

She froze, her eyes popped in shock and she held her breath. Tzarik's face fell when he caught sight of her shock.

"What?" he said, itching his left brow.

She spat, stumbling over her words. Suddenly realizing she might offend him after such a wonderful night of openness, she shrugged and shook her head. "You have a really nice smile. And a good laugh."

He crossed his arms. "I think I know what to do." He steeled himself. "I'll meet him tomorrow night. I'll send word from the bank since Tarkan thinks he's here."

"He is. I saw him."

"I'll tell him we have Tarkan and want to swap for Zeva. He'll believe me when I mention you, but that's a risk."

"We can take that risk. I'm willing."

"We'll meet near here to do the swap. But we'll have a trap. While I meet with Sharar, you and Vicdan gather bodies and plant them here."

She winced. "Why?"

"Have Tarkan prepare his spell as far into the casting as he can. We will meet here. Once we have Zeva, they rise, we attack. That should give Tarkan time to flee with Zeva. You and I will have to fight the risen though, to keep Sharar from understanding what is going on. With any luck, he will offer to have us capture him again. And we don't. We leave."

A bolt of sorrow struck through her heart as his meaning sunk in. "You mean leave Al'Myrah. Get off the continent. My home. Our home."

"We'll have to. This is bigger than I can handle. Even us together. I know when I've been beat."

His breath shuddered as he drew it in. Sensing he still feared meeting the sorcerer, she slipped her hand into his, gripping his shoulder with her other hand. Maybe her ignorance kept her calm. She didn't understand her mentor's fear but his trust in showing her this vulnerability overshadowed any fear she might have learned. This was the partnership she had imagined: when one fell, the other would stand. Now she knew he'd do the same for her.

"Not alone," she promised.

Chapter 33
The Sorcerer

THE BANKER, BEHIND A HAPHAZARD BARRICADE OF RUBBLE and golden bars that might fall if one leaned on it too hard, glared at Tzarik.

"I said we are closed for business right now." She motioned at the nearly collapsed walls of the domed building. Her old, wrinkled face was made worse by a scowl and bandage around her head.

"I don't need to withdraw," he growled for the second time. "There might be a letter for me. Addressed to Tzarik or Runer."

When he mentioned his title, the woman's white brows twitched together and her lips pursed together so hard they disappeared into her wrinkles. "Runer, hmm?"

She abruptly turned and walked back towards the desolated vault. She stuck her head behind a gilded wall, whispering to someone behind it. Tzarik strained to hear but her old voice lilted so softly he couldn't catch any actual words. Whoever she spoke too quickly took off, the back-door slamming shut.

"I do have a letter." She came out clutching a crumpled scrap of parchment. "A man of high repute dropped it off last night." She smiled, showing her white teeth. Tzarik thought she had too many and half expected a snake tongue to lash out and back in.

He snatched it from her and unrolled it, pretending to read it. The letters were sloped, thin, elegant, and swooping: Sharar's writing. He examined the parchment for anything else that Sybal would not be able to read. Not a single stain gave away if he had been drinking while he wrote it, no crumbs, no blood, not even the hard to detect smear of oils from flesh. He understood who he was working with.

"Where are you staying in town, Runer?" the banker asked calmly. "Or are you leaving town?"

Immediately the hairs on the back of his neck stood up. A threat from this old lady? He frowned at her over the top of the parchment he still held up.

"Business?" she motioned to the parchment when he didn't reply.

"None of yours." He crumpled the letter in his hand and left, cautiously watching over his shoulder as he did so. The banker watched him, eyes trained on the back of his head.

As he passed through a crowd just outside the bank's double doors, he once again caught sight of something clad in white. He swore he looked directly at the stalker but lost them immediately in the clump of citizens. Not one of them donned white. They parted the longer he stared, allowing him to pass out of fear. He didn't have time to track the white ghost. The letter in his hand might state a meeting time or have information. It had been some time since he left word for Sharar and the scholar no doubt wanted to meet since he had been in the city when Tarkan attacked.

Tzarik tried to wrap his head around all the moving parts. He fought to be calm. To understand that this time, for the first time in his life, he had backup.

Arms crossed, Tzarik tapped his upper arm impatiently as Sybal read the elegant hand.

"He was here," she said, sweat dripping down her chin from moving bodies with great stealth all day. Behind her, Vicdan and

Tarkan kicked around the sand to smooth over the makeshift grave-yard. "He writes as if he doesn't know that you are aware he pitted you and Tarkan against each other."

"Good," he sighed. "Why was he here in town?"

"He followed Tarkan. He says, 'I don't know why the vindication of the necromancer has risen, but you may be in danger. After what he has done to Ala'Nar I can only guess what his next move will be. This may be beyond you. Meet me at the public house called The Sultana's Room at sunset. I have a new proposition for you.'" Sybal folded the parchment and looked up at Tzarik, worry wrinkling her face. "Can't we just leave now? What if he hurts you?"

Tzarik looked over her shoulder at Tarkan where he now stood still, hands raised in front of him explaining something to Vicdan. "He might not deserve to have her. He's...evil as well. But she deserves to be saved. She still has a chance to walk away from his life. We cannot leave her imprisoned to be tortured again."

Sybal sighed in melancholy resignation. "I'll see you soon. Watch your back. Something isn't right in town."

His hood pulled far over his face, the front clasped shut, not one of his Runer traits showed in the moonlight. Since the destruction, the city lamps had not been lit. Ala'Nar looked like a grave-yard: stones standing erect against the sky, a low moan of chants coming from the temple and minaret. Anyone out moved slowly or ran from one place of safety to the next.

The tavern Sharar mentioned loomed half destroyed near the edge of town where the homeless and poorer lived. A single oil lamp sat above the gently waving wooden sign. The ground floor windows were boarded up, but soft, warm light came through the tiny gaps in the wood. Touching his runes, he pushed open the door and strode in.

Sharar sat right in the center of the common room near the large brazier in the floor. He lounged against several cushions, smoking a colorful pipe as though not one care in the world loomed over him. He blew a smoke ring into the air and watched it hit the ceiling above him. Tzarik quickly tried to look him over. A djinn had an ossuary: an object it was bound to, inside. Sharar wore so many silks and layers, Tzarik could hardly tell if he even carried a weapon let alone some unassuming object that might house a djinn.

"Runer!" Sharar called, waving him over.

At the exclamation of the title, a brief hush fell over the crowd. Several eyes turned on him and not one shined with kindness.

"Now, now, my good people," Sharar called, waving his hands at them, "I will have a word with him."

"What are you doing?" Tzarik hissed, hand on his hilt. "These people want to draw and quarter me."

"I know." The scholar smiled, pouring some golden mead into another glass. "I have spoken to some of the most influential families in the city, expressing my intent to discourse with you. They trust an educated man." He gently pushed his spectacles further up his perfectly straight nose. "But no matter what agreement we come to, I'd still leave town if I were you."

Confused, on edge, and close to rage, Tzarik sat down when Sharar pushed hard on his shoulder. He didn't take the drink. Shrugging, Sharar smiled.

"I am so impressed with you, Runer. I didn't think you could do it, but you have brought the necromancer out of hiding. This is bold for one man. I am fascinated by the power he showed, raising that dragon. So resourceful too. I have so much good information for my books and it's all thanks to you."

Deftly, he reached between his robes and pulled out a sack of rupees and gold. When Tzarik didn't take it, he took the Runer's hand in his own and plopped the bag into his palm. The gems inside clinked seductively.

"Cheer up, Runer. Take the gold. Leave town. But I do want to make you another proposition seeing as you are so resilient, resourceful, and—how should I say it—can take a beating?"

Sudden courage flooded Tzarik's veins. He dropped the bag onto the round table between them. "We caught Tarkan."

Sharar sat up, the glee dimming behind his eyes. "You have him in hand? How?"

Tzarik's left brow twitched and tilted his head. "Not easily. We desecrated his family's crypt. That, apparently, was not the right thing to do. Though he hated his father, the tribe mentality runs deep."

"His father!" Sharar leaned over the table, putting his hand on Tzarik's wrist. "Tell me what you found!"

Taking a deep, covert breath, Tzarik said, "No."

Sharar pulled back.

"We...interrogated him for information. He told us someone kidnapped his daughter Zeva. That villain did this to force him to test his necrotic abilities out on monsters, creatures, even spirits." He shook his head. "The things we seek to kill, this man wanted risen again. Tarkan is hardly innocent, but Zeva is."

As he spoke, he gauged Sharar's reactions. The scholar guarded himself but not in a way that said he smelled ulterior motives. He kept his head raised high, frowning in thought. He wanted to play innocent as well. Now came the scary part.

"We know you took her, scholar," the Runer said flatly, softly so the onlookers could not hear. "We have no love for Tarkan after what he did to Sybal's family." He stopped.

The corner of Sharar's lips ticked ever so slightly. The skin under his eyes tightened.

It took all of Tzarik's strength to not choke him, cut his guts open, right there. He had to hide the discovery and horror by taking a drink of the sweet alcohol or else the game would be up. Why? Just to pit the Runers and the necromancer against each other even more?

"I've been watching you, Runer. Following you as you hunt my necromancer." Sharar set down the hose to the pipe he had been about to inhale from. "Tarkan no doubt thought I was following him. Don't be angry, just as I am not angry that you know I paid both you and the necromancer. Why is not relevant right now." He eyed the Runer.

Tzarik forced himself to sit still. "All we want is the girl. The woman who I travel with wants to save an innocent girl who need not take up the necrotic life. We can place her with a temple of magi. She will be safe. You are a man of education, Sharar, not a warden."

"Oh, no, don't pretend to know me, Runer." He rested the smoking pipe on his lips, the water bubbling as he closed his eyes and took a long taste of the smoke. "I believe in balance. I cannot get my hands on Tarkan but you have. I want to study him, learn the ways of the necromancer without marking my own flesh. Let us come to an agreement. I will release Zeva to you if you bring me Tarkan. I should have bound him when first we met but he seemed so compliant with Zeva's fate in the mix. When he attacked Ala'Nar out of revenge, I knew I had lost my control over him. I had to rein him back in, but he would not meet. So I sent him a warning."

A chill emanated from those last words. Tzarik could only guess at his meaning.

"But it wasn't enough. He attacked again. You and that necromancer have a vitality and an endurance I will never understand!" He smiled, expecting Tzarik to take the compliment. "He is too emotional, not like you. I fear I must deal with him myself."

"What do you have in mind, scholar," Tzarik pressed. Had he done enough to lure Sharar into the deal?

"A swap," he said simply.

Relief flooded Tzarik, cooling the anxiety flowing in his sulfates. "Sounds reasonable," he said. Just as the words left his mouth, he regretted agreeing too quickly.

The scholar narrowed his eyes just a little. "I don't know how you caught the necromancer, but there are precautions you need to take." He sat up, reaching to a silken traveling pack at his side. He opened it and handed Tzarik a large, heavy wrapped piece of equipment from inside. He motioned for him to open it.

Carefully, equal parts cautious and curious, Tzarik unwrapped a part of the bundle. His heart skipped a beat when he saw what the metal instrument was: a scold's bridle.

"Necromancers need to speak their spells," Sharar supplied, smiling at the horror on Tzarik's face. "This doesn't allow it. I am sure once you convince him that Zeva will be safe, he will let you place it on him. But he is not that strong either. Without his army of undead soldiers, he is but a weak man. Bind his hands behind his back so he cannot use them for his spells.

"And, Runer," he added putting his pack to the side again. "I am interested in what compelled you to suggest saving this girl." He looked at him knowingly.

Seeing no harm in the truth, Tzarik replied, "Sybal's heart is set on saving people. Even ones that might not deserve it."

"Ha!" The scholar clapped his hands together in delight. "So a woman has melted the stone heart of a Runer. How fascinating. But you are still the same inside, yes?"

Tzarik frowned, ready to leave and be away from the scholar. Never had he met a man so interested in his organs.

"Hasn't it been fantastic?" Sharar took a drink. "Hunting another sentient being? Brought you back to life, didn't it? Gave you purpose." He smiled when Tzarik didn't answer. "Wonderful.

Even after this little rift in our working relationship, I hope to see you again, Runer. You fascinate me. And don't forget: you owe me your body when you die."

Unable to stomach any more from the scholar, Tzarik grabbed the scold's bridle and stood. "The mouth of the caves at sunrise."

Chapter 34
Swap

NONE OF THEM SLEPT THE REST OF THE NIGHT AFTER TZARIK returned to the old mines. He came back in to find Tarkan standing before the burned out crate and the smoldering remains of the dragon they had killed...twice. He stopped, the torture device swinging from his hand.

"They were from Porsh," the necromancer sighed, weakly indicating the crate. "My people. I knew three of them well, fellow necromancers."

Tzarik snapped his head to face the necromancer. He had never suspected that bodies so violently dealt with would be the corpses of someone Tarkan knew, maybe even cared for. He couldn't imagine carrying Sybal—even Vicdan—with him for years, forcing them to fight for him, stitching them back together after a battle. He should have felt compelled to apologize, but the life of the necromancer turned his stomach.

"I had one tribe mate, Ashkan, who would have made a promising lich. The trouble was he knew that." Tarkan ran his hand through his hair, pushing his hood off for the first time. "He had a wife called Elahel. She was devoted to him beyond sense, often putting herself in danger."

"There used to be more of you?" Tzarik asked, the horror coming out liberally in his tone.

Tarkan heard it and smiled. "Yes. Four, including my apprentice Shiva who took the necrotic oath before I even found her. We were the ones who took Moshav." He sighed and smiled as if remembering a fond memory. "We were unstoppable, and yet we never harmed anyone unless asked."

Knowing they had precious little time to prepare themselves, the Runer interjected, "What are you trying to say, Tarkan?"

The necromancer turned to face him, his blue eyes also glowing in the darkness. "We are not that different, Runer. And yet we are. There is not a lot of magic in this world and those who wield it often deal in death. Therefore, the greater the power the greater the fear of that power. Someone could change that perception if they saw value in that harbinger of death."

Now he saw the necromancer was delusional. "No one can change, in a single lifetime, the way Runers are seen by the masses. A single man could say we are not to be persecuted, but a city will call for my head every time. Those with power must also live in fear, Tarkan." He held up the scold's bridle. "Sharar is taking precautions and we need to be prepared for his discretion."

Tarkan stepped away from the charred bodies and took the device into his hands. He ran his tattooed fingers over the edges, the lock, and the metal bar inside the mouth. "Stop me from speaking. Unlike you, Runer, I need my eyes, hands, and tongue to cast my spells."

"I should warn you." Tzarik took the bridle back and quickly unhooked the lock, placing it back to try again, faster this time. "If he takes you, I am not coming after you. Our mission is Zeva and getting her to safety."

The necromancer met Tzarik's eyes and he keenly became aware that Tarkan stood just as tall as him.

"I'd gladly be taken for her, but I'd rather not if you can help it." He scanned Tzarik carefully, looking for a trick, a lie.

"I will do my utmost. But I never promise anything."

"Where will you take her if I do not make it out?"

Realizing he needed Sybal's long, lithe fingers to unclasp the bridle quickly after failing for a third time, he led the way back to the camp where the other two waited. "There is a palace of magi where a woman I know is mother to many girls. She's...not my favorite person in the world, but she takes good care of the women, training them to read the stars and oceans. They learn to read, are taught science and politics, and often become diplomats to sultans and even to a Grand Niaz. It is a good life for a woman. They hold power and often lead their own lives."

Tarkan nodded. "Sounds like a good life."

Tzarik heard the anguish in the necromancer's voice. Of course he wanted what was best for Zeva, but perhaps—like him—he just wanted her to stay with him.

He knew this to be the truth when he came around the bend in the cave and found Sybal leaning back to back with Vicdan near the fire, the jongleur singing a ridiculous song about a monk who feigned muteness to sleep with women. Sybal's blue eyes glittered as she laughed at his forced rhymes. Just one moment of merriment for her amidst a year of tragedy. She deserved better but this was what she chose, even if she didn't realize it at the time.

He smiled.

Beside him, Tarkan whispered, "See? You understand."

THE SUN ROSE and stabbed through a few eroded holes in the cave walls beside them before any of them realized how much time passed around the fire. Vicdan seemed the saddest to see his time with the wild company he kept go. Still, he nodded seriously when Tzarik told him to create the distraction just two minutes after they met with Sharar.

Sybal had been flipping the clasp on the scold's bridle all night, practicing to quickly and discreetly undo the lock so Tarkan could finish the chant to raise the bodies they buried just inches below the sand. She mentioned being grateful runes did not take too much time to cast depending on the strength one wanted to put behind it.

Tzarik led them all close to the mouth of the cave then approached Tarkan. Wordlessly asking for the necromancer's trust, he slipped the bridle over his head, the metal bar pinning his tongue to the top of his mouth, stopping all speech. Then he pulled Tarkan's arms behind him and tied them tight enough to look immovable. He slipped once before mindfully calming himself. Sybal came up beside him, her hand on her sword hilt.

"We can do this," she said with no doubt on her face, her shoulders square, and her eyes glaring in determination.

Tzarik restrained himself from telling Sybal that Sharar confessed to killing her mother and brother, afraid she would fly into a murderous rage again. Today, as he looked up into her face, he saw more of a calculating Runer and less of a vengeful woman.

The two of them marched out, Tarkan between them. Vicdan doubled back through the tunnels, leaving out a back way closer to the city so he could give the impression of coming from the city to create a diversion, hopefully giving Sybal the two seconds she needed to unhook the straps, allowing Tarkan to mumble through the last parts of his spell. Above them, a mysterious amount of clouds rolled over the mountains and dunes. Tzarik noted the thick, dark storm heralds with fearful animosity. Rain was not common this time of year. The suddenness of the gray skies warned him of the power of a sorcerer, whether Sharar meant it to or not.

The three of them were not two hundred feet out from the cave when they spotted the scholar, his robes gently waving in the cool breeze that came over the mountains towards them. His spectacles were missing from his face, drawing attention to his angled brows and narrow, malevolent eyes. He was alone.

"Where is Zeva?" Sybal said sternly, standing behind Tarkan.

Tzarik stood abreast with the necromancer.

Sharar smiled in amazement and scoffed in surprise "I thought you were lying, Runer. I really did. But here he is. You really are amazing." His eyes scanned Tarkan. "And wounded too. You were worth every penny."

"Zeva, Sharar," Tzarik snapped. He adjusted his foot in the sand to get a better grip in case he needed to spring into action. "Where is she?"

The scholar smiled, looking more like a sorcerer as he held his hands out, allowing his sleeves to billow in the climbing wind. "I have been keeping her in various locations in Porsh, actually." He gasped, putting on hand onto his angled cheek. "I do hope she is all right. Didn't you two light a fire beneath the lich's manor?"

Beside him, Tzarik felt Tarkan pull against his restraints and moan a threat into the bridle. He glanced at the necromancer and saw Sybal gently touch his palm behind him, calming him.

"How do we know she's alive or even in Porsh?" Tzarik asked.

"I have no reason to lie to you about her," Sharar reasoned. "I am just a humble scholar. You have brought me the greatest specimen of my research so far. Trapped, thanks to you. I have ways of making a helpless necromancer do what I want."

"Runers!"

Vicdan's high, melodious voice screamed over the cold wind to them. Looking over Sharar's shoulder, they all saw him sprinting towards them.

"Assassins!" he cried, panting, slipping on the sand. "Coming to kill you."

Grinning maniacally, Sharar turned back to face the Runers. "I suggest you hurry. Could be Reavers."

"Reavers?" Sybal asked, genuinely confused. "What are those?"

The white shadow that Tzarik had been seeing out of the corner of his eyes came back to him in a flash of realization. Most citizens spoke of them in hushed tones to put fear into Runer's, but he had never heard of one actually existing. The Grand Niaz in Rhostrana threatened him with a Reaver when he demanded pay.

"The old wives' tale of Runer Reavers," he said quickly. "An assassin who kills Runers. They say only a Runer can kill a Runer but most are murderers. So Reavers were created to do what a Runer could not."

Spurred by a new fear, Tzarik signaled Sybal to free Tarkan. The plan unfolded just as he hoped. Sharar latched onto the ruse, allowing Sybal one second to unlatch the bridle. Tarkan murmured the last sentence and when she had his hands free, he raised his arms with a final cry.

Beneath the Runers, the ground shifted. Sybal screamed and Tzarik lost his footing as the risen clawed their way out of the sand. Vicdan stopped in his mad dash towards them, cowering as the bone and flesh creatures brandished a plethora of weapons, moaning their war cries.

"Runer?" Sharar gasped, shrinking away from the cutting sand and howling winds.

"Get back, scholar!" Tzarik cried, moving to defend Sharar from the onslaught of corpses. "Sybal, get away!" he commanded.

It may have been part of their plan, but the risen were still dangerous. Under Tarkan's control, they didn't have too much to fear, but the necromancer could only tell them to attack, not how kindly. He threw off the unhinged bridle and pulled back, instructing a half dozen of risen soldiers to protect him. He couldn't watch them all at once.

Sybal misted between the risen, reappearing by his side, her scimitar in hand. "Vicdan, get away," she screamed back to him. Then she looked to Tzarik for orders.

Sharar coward between them, demanding to know what had gone wrong. Tzarik chose to ignore him and leapt into battle with the twelve or so risen who advanced on them. Sybal had his back, spinning into combat, covering him with a quick shield from halat. As she slashed at two approaching risen, Tzarik blinded one with atan before misting around Sybal to cover her right side.

"Behind you!" she cried.

Tzarik knew he wouldn't have time to draw, move around her, and sever the risen's head before two others made it to Sharar. "Take my hand!" he cried.

She read his intent. Grabbing his hand as he drew halat, he leapt and she pulled. Fluidly, he arched over her head. When he landed, halat burst, flinging back the three risen trying to engage them.

"Wonderful!" Sharar cried, watching the perfect tandem movements of the Runers.

Stopping to look at Tzarik, Sybal grinned widely. The next moment, taken in her by her grin and not seeing it, a corpse slashed her across her shoulder where her leather armor did not cover. She cried out, falling into Tzarik's arms from the blow.

"He's getting away!" Sharar screamed, his hand going to his belt as he took a few quick steps after Tarkan.

Behind them, while they fought to defend their employer, Tarkan rose a decaying horse from the sands and charged away towards the mountains. The moment he crested a dune, the risen fell, crumbling into the sand. The Runers collapsed together into the sand, Sybal's white blood soaking through her black tunic.

The scholar watched the necromancer vanish, the winds and sand dissipating. Panting, the veins on his neck pulsed and he clenched his fists. Gripping his hair, he screamed into the desert. Above, lightning ripped across the sky and thunder rolled in to meet it. Tzarik held his hand to Sybal's shoulder. A surface wound, she might not even need stitches.

"You'll be fine," he whispered to Sybal between calming breaths. He leaned down even closer to keep what he said next between them. "And that was amazing. Well done."

She smiled, handing him a bandage from her belt satchel. "You're so short, it was easy."

He shook his head, poking her wound, making her hiss. "Don't insult me with your blood on my hands."

Sharar marched back to the Runers. "You are in a dire situation, you two." A threat laced his voice. "The city is enraged against you. Reavers? *And* you let Tarkan get away."

"Let him?" Sybal cried, rolling her shoulder to relax the muscles. She took Tzarik's hand, helping her up. "Are you blind, scholar? Something went wrong."

"It did," Sharar snapped back. "Pity. I thought we could work well together. But if Ala'Nar has called for your assassination, I will not stand in the way of Reavers."

"We don't know it's Reavers," Tzarik cut in. Vicdan could have chosen to shout Reavers thinking it the best way to cause a panic. Or he could be sincere. There was only one way to know.

"I'd leave, Runer," Sharar said simply, smoothing his robes. "I am livid, but I know an asset when I see one. I don't want to push you away, but I cannot wait around for you to uphold your end of the deal again. And I dare not be associated with you with these rumors. Ala'Nar will have my head." He clenched his jaw and looked to the horizon, visibly angry about the turn of events. "Yes, I must go. I cannot stay."

Sybal followed him for a few steps, holding her hands out, crying, "What are we supposed to do? How do we get in contact with you?"

"You don't, Runer woman," the scholar shot back. "Tarkan has ruined any working relationship we could have by razing Ala'Nar and turning one of the greatest cities on Al'Myrah against you. I should have killed him when I had the chance."

"What do we do?" Sybal called out after him.

"Run, Runer. Save yourself."

Overhead, the gray clouds darkened to almost black,

completely hiding the sun. Lightning struck not far, charging the air. Tzarik jumped at the strike and whistled for the horses. Sharar marched away, his robes billowing. He didn't say anything as he passed Vicdan. The jongleur caught up just as the horses trotted to a stop.

Taking the reins, Tzarik swung up onto his huge, black steed. "Don't follow us, Vicdan," he ordered. "Leave Ala'Nar if you can. Go north."

"Leave you two?" Vicdan gasped, his eyes turning sadly up to them. "But—"

"Leave!" Tzarik shouted, kicking his horse. He wheeled it around, leaving Vicdan in the dust, Sybal just behind him.

Chapter 35
Sojourn

THE DAYS IT TOOK TO TRAVEL TO PORSH WERE THE QUIETEST the two Runers let pass between them in some time. As they rode during the day, they didn't speak. At night, Tzarik hunted and Sybal made fire and tea. She didn't know the reason for her mentor's silence but let it go on the entire journey. Desperate to know what Reavers were, she tried to find them in the book he made her read. There was one instance where the author mentioned the word in reference to myths. During one of the rises in Runer rebellion, where a group partook in excess crime, it mentioned offhandedly that a sect of Reavers quelled the uprising. That's it. Not who they were or how they overtook an organized group of one of the only magic-wielders in the world. The only worthwhile information it gave was that civilians called them White Death.

When Porsh rose into view, they galloped in to find Tarkan's horse outside his home. Together, they crept down to the crypt, not wanting to alert the necromancer that they followed him. They misted down to almost the last step but he wasn't there. Sybal frowned, shrugging when Tzarik looked back at her. Before they moved, they heard a cry above them.

"The family rooms," Tzarik whispered.

They sprinted back up and dashed up the crumbling stairs to the upper levels of the mansion. Sybal made to continue up when Tzarik threw his arm out to stop her. Pointing down the dark hallway, she followed his finger. A door stood open, decaying white veils wafted in a gentle, stale breeze. Two forms knelt on the ground of the old bedroom. One was Tarkan, cradling the body of a beautiful woman.

"Is she...?" Sybal gasped, taking two steps forward.

"Wait." Tzarik didn't let her pass. "Let him."

Tarkan shook Zeva gently, calling her name. When she didn't stir, he reached to a crystal vial on his belt and tipped the contents into her mouth. He held her head while the tincture trickled down her throat.

"Zeva?" he whispered, checking her body for any wounds. When he did so, Sybal caught sight of infected lacerations, bruises, and other marks of torture Sharar inflicted on her for Tarkan's disobedience.

Just when the two Runers thought she might not stir, she gasped and cowered in Tarkan's arms. "Don't, please!" she wept.

"Zeva, it's me," Tarkan said soothingly, taking her hands away from her face gently in his own, holding them to his chest.

"Tarkan?" the young woman gasped, tears freely flowing down her face. "I thought you were him. He kept coming back. He wouldn't let me leave! Made me drink that poison. And I saw them..."

She threw her arms around the necromancer's neck and buried her face into his shoulder. She regripped him several times before crying in joy and relief. "Don't leave me again, please don't leave me. Let me take the oath, let me take it!"

Tarkan protested softly and Sybal watched with rapt attention, gripping Tzarik's shoulder. She wanted to stay and behold the beautiful scene forever, but her mentor stood up from where he had been kneeling.

"Let's go," he whispered, taking her up and forcing her to quietly leave. She tried to protest but he motioned for her to be quiet and not give their presence away.

Together, the two Runers trotted through the city towards the salty river they had to cross to get back to the mainland. The black architecture and floating landmasses seemed far less threatening than before. The winding streets still muffled the hooves of their steeds and the eerie atmosphere lingered, but it did not threaten or frighten them anymore. Sybal smiled weakly.

"We did a good thing, I think. At least, I hope we have." Her shoulders slumped from the proud way she had just held them. "He's done so much wrong though. He's..."

"We are not judges," Tzarik cut in. "As Runers, we cannot cast a sentence onto him. We can only do what we can do."

"That sounds like something a holy man would say," Sybal mused. "The ones who go out into the world to convert others, bringing them peace and purpose to life."

Tzarik's left brow flicked in amusement but he didn't smile. "Hardly holy." He adjusted in his saddle. "We have to be careful now. We should probably—"

A zipping sound cut the air, interrupting Tzarik. It zoomed past Sybal as she leaned down to pat her horse's thick neck and hit him between his shoulder blade and spine. He cried out, gripping the foreign object.

Sybal went into immediate alert, crouching over in the saddle and sweeping the walls, buildings, and streets with her eagle-like vision. The sun glinted white off the withered city, blinding her too much to see into the darker shadows of the alleys. She took up her smaller crossbow just in case something came into sight.

While Tzarik moaned in pain, she clicked her tongue to make the horses move.

"It came from behind," Tzarik called through clenched teeth. "Run!"

Screaming a command to her horse, Sybal skidded into a

gallop. She followed Tzarik down a narrow street that wound around with many pathways branching off it to throw off the tracker. Out of the corner of her eye, she saw a rippling, white shadow.

Coming to the same defensive idea, Tzarik and Sybal reached into their black garb and pulled out buhkar, drawing it as slowly as they dared. Turning to black vapors, they slid off their horses and back around a separate alleyway. Just before rematerializing, a metal hissing sound zipped past her ear, cutting through the black mist that was Tzarik. Groaning again, he immediately fell out of the mist. He quickly snatched up the small bolt that fell from his shoulder, clutching the other one. Sybal saw that whatever had whizzed through the air this time had cut his other shoulder while he was shrouded in the rune. How? Why didn't the unseen blade pass through the black mist?

Grabbing him and running faster than his shorter stride could keep up, she called for the horses. The two came galloping around the corner, eyes bulging as they snorted in fearful madness. She leapt up into the saddle, following Tzarik down the main road.

Spinning around, standing up on her stirrups to see farther, Sybal looked behind. She spotted the assailant, unafraid, standing tall on the short remains of a minaret tower. A man—she could tell from his height and broadness of his shoulders—clad in white that rippled and moved in the slight breeze making it almost impossible to focus on him. His robes covered him from the deep hood over his head and mask over the bottom half of his face to the white boots covering his feet. As she watched him, he squatted down, one hand on the wall to steady himself. She could see no weapons on his person but knew beneath the clean fabric lurked a deadly crossbow at least.

"He's not coming after us," she panted, kicking her horse into a gallop. She glanced at Tzarik as they broke through the borders of Porsh and onto the shores of Ala'Nar.

Tzarik pulled the reins of his horse, turning circles, glaring back the way they came. The dense, suffocating fog made it impossible to see across the river. He clutched the removed arrow from his back in his bloody hand. The arrow shaft gleamed white, the tip silver, narrow and barbless.

"I've never seen an arrow like that," Sybal said, glaring at the evil instrument. "It almost looks like it's meant to be pulled out. Most arrows have tips that make it too risky to pull them out."

Her mentor nodded. "It's a warning. Anyone who follows us into Porsh is more daring than any I've met. But he didn't come to kill us or he would have. He must have been following us for days, could have killed us while we slept."

Sybal caught her breath, covering her mouth in shock, scanning the dunes around them. "What's he want?"

"To kill us." Tzarik stowed the bolt into his saddlebag. "But not yet. It's an old war tactic; I'm not sure where it originated from. They call it the stages of submission. The first stage consists of the hunter frightening the pray, making them uneasy. Driving them to paranoia. Then they move in closer for the second stage, usually disrupting things we do for survival like spoiling food, poisoning water, making it hard to sleep at night. This leads to a kind of hysterical obsession where the victim can hardly function. Then... submission. They move in. He's just trying to scare us right now. Attacking us in Porsh was part of that. We thought we were safe, away from any sane person so our guard was down."

Thinking back to what Vicdan had cried out, and the one passage she read in the book, she braced herself for Tzarik's backlash of criticism and the verbal lashing she'd receive for believing in old wives' tales.

"A Reaver," she whispered, hoping it didn't sound weak.

She watched Tzarik closely when he didn't immediately laugh at her. His blue eyes dimmed a little and she noticed his back weaken. He didn't meet her gaze, focusing on the horizon.

"Maybe," he sighed, touching the slash wound on his shoulder. "We have to leave," he repeated, this time with far more conviction. "I think Sharar put the idea in Ala'Nar's head to hunt us down. They probably didn't need much convincing. They knew we were the ones hunting Tarkan. I'm surprised they didn't come after us sooner, knowing you cannot kill another sentient creature."

Sybal handed him some bandages from his saddlebag, keeping her eyes on the horizons. "I hate that they know that."

"That's why you never tell another soul your crime. And that's why you leave," Tzarik mumbled, wrapping his bolt wound.

At that very moment, she wanted to ask him. What had he done? Why had he committed the crime that damned him to the life of a Runer? If she knew, she would be a weakness for him. Someone could rip his most protective secret from her lips, putting him in more danger than ever before.

No, she would not ask. She did not want to know. *I could never put him in so much danger,* she thought. Where he came from would also have to remain a mystery. As far as she knew, he'd been everywhere. Did he not fear any place? One day, she'd be just as fearless.

"We'll head to Moshav," he said, cutting into her reverie. "It's the closest port."

"Hatal is much closer?" she questioned.

Tzarik winced. "I'd rather not cross paths with our sultana after what has happened..."

"Will you see that man—in Moshav—who told you about Tarkan?" she asked.

Tzarik scoffed. "No. I think he'd like to kill me. We'll take a boat from there to Bagdula to hide our trail. Then cross the Caravan Sea."

"The far east?" Sybal gasped, tears immediately filling her

eyes. "Tzarik, this is my home. I've never left the continent. The first time was when we went to Bahratt. But I had solace there…"

What did she have now? Once, almost a year ago, she had everything. A home, a family, money, status, safety, a man to marry who loved her. Hardly any woman her age had prospects and most women—no matter the age—never married a man who loved them. She had been blessed with Rahul. But he was gone. They were all gone. Her entire city, gone.

Looking to her right, Tzarik stood strong, unwavering. He took a chance on her, thinking he could escape her but she ran after him again and again. The trial of two bound them. She wanted to be with him. He was her solace now. All she had was this man, the clothes on her back, and a mission to rid the world of monsters; monsters far more powerful and evil than any she had ever imagined.

"To Moshav then," she smiled. "And the far east. To Xia."

He turned his head and met her eager face, their blue eyes locked on each other. He smiled.

To be

continued…

Tzarik and Sybal will return in *Season of the Runer Book II: Sojourn*

The Runes

Artiah: The rune of healing. Drawing artiah will mend minor abrasions and heal larger wounds enough to allow escape. Artiah will also take away a small amount of pain.

Atan: The rune of light. Drawing atan will create an orb of light for all eyes to see by. Atan also reveals hidden spirits and can show disguised monsters in their true form.

Buhkar: The rune of mist. When buhkar is drawn, the Runer
dissolves into a black, smokey mist able to slip between tight
spaces, evade a grip, and blend into shadows easily to be
undetected.

Halat: The rune of protection. When halat is drawn, the caster is
safe inside a circle of protection. Anything that wishes the caster
harm cannot pass the boundaries of the protective circle.

Jiun: The fury rune. Jiun—the most dangerous of the runes—turns the Runer into a berserker. Cutting off all feeling to wounds and ailments, the rune pushes the caster beyond their inhibitions. Jiun also lends temporary strength and heightened senses.

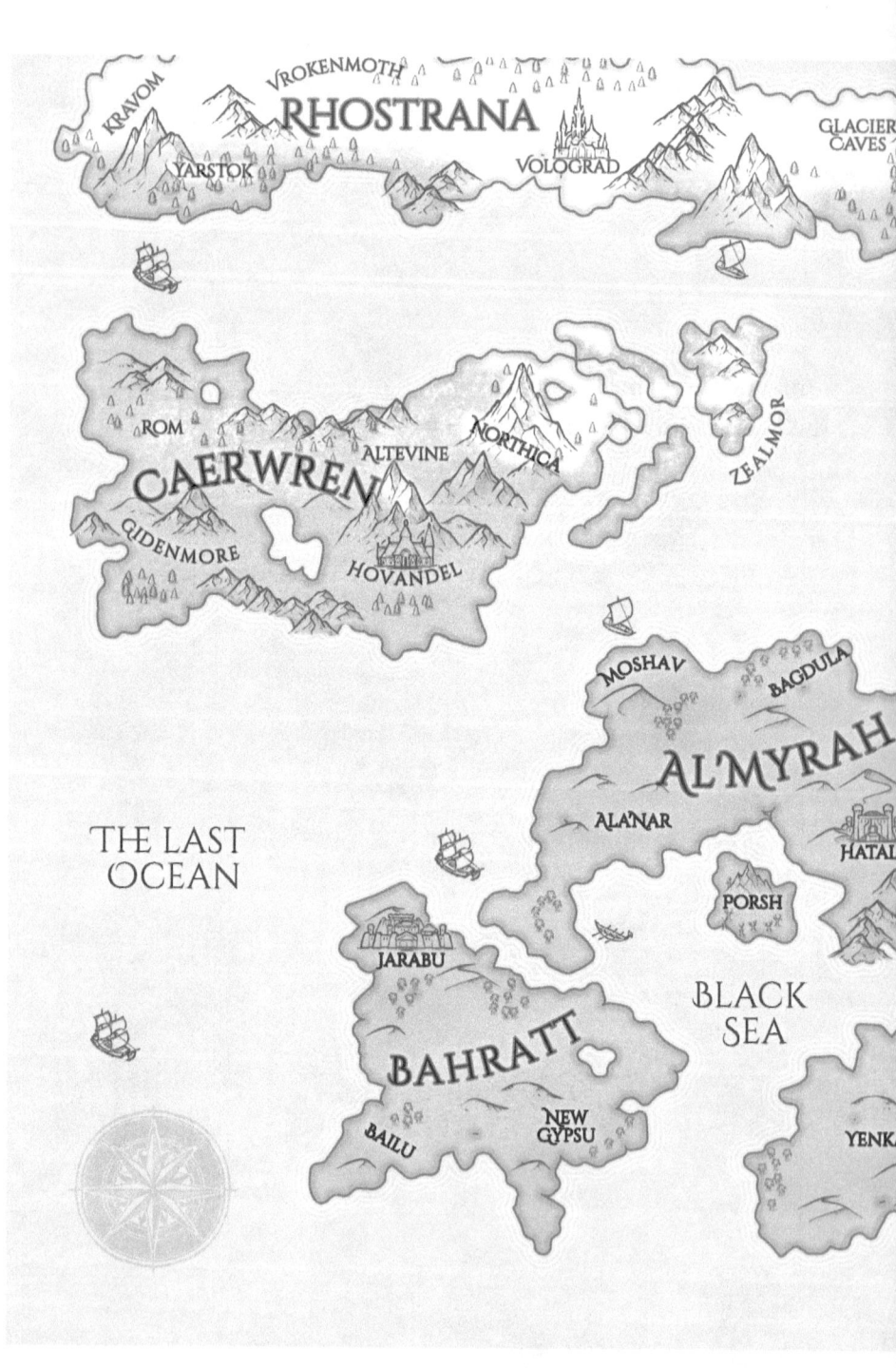

THE FROZEN NATION

SHEZAI OCEAN

HIKOMI

SHIUKI

MUENGO
YAI

SINGAD

WU-TANG

XIA

ZE'OUL

THE CARAVAN
SEA

OCEAN SKY

GYPSU

ALIKA

MYSIR

LONG TILL

ZHIGO

LYBRIA

OCEANYA